CELOS AUN DEL AIRE MATAN

PEDRO CALDERÓN
DE LA BARCA

CELOS AUN DEL
AIRE MATAN

An Edition with Introduction,
Translation, and Notes by
MATTHEW D. STROUD

Foreword by Jack Sage

Trinity University Press

San Antonio

*Trinity University Press gratefully acknowledges
the assistance of the Ewing Halsell Foundation
in making this publication possible.*

*Endsheets: Engraving by J. Romano, The death of Pocris.
Courtesy of the Biblioteca Nacional, Madrid.*

*Signature of Calderón de la Barca, 1662 on page 57
courtesy of the Biblioteca Nacional, Madrid.*

For Louise, Lowell, and Judy

Qui grate beneficium accipit,
primam eius pensionem solvit.
Seneca, *De Beneficiis,* 2.22

ACKNOWLEDGMENTS

As is the case with any rather complicated work, many people and institutions have provided valuable assistance in the preparation of this edition. Of primary importance is the support, both monetary and moral, granted by the Ewing Halsell Foundation of San Antonio. Mr. Gilbert Denman, Miss Helen Campbell, and Mr. Robert Washington made the entire project possible and offered useful advice throughout the production of the present work. In addition to the publication of the text, the Halsell Foundation donated major funding for the modern world premiere of *Celos aun del aire matan* in February of 1981. Also indispensable was the help offered by libraries and research societies. The Biblioteca Pública in Evora, Portugal, helped me not only in locating the manuscript but in obtaining the illustrative photographs of the music that are contained in this volume. The Director, António Leandro Sequeira Alves, and his assistants, Inácia Maria Fernandes Sardinha Paias, Cecília Joaquina Mourinha de Carvalho, and José Marques Rosado Chitas, were more than cordial and patient with my less than fluent Portuguese, and they offered me every assistance. Likewise, the staffs of both the Hispanic Society of America in New York and the Biblioteca Nacional in Madrid were more than accommodating in researching both information and engravings for use in this edition.

Trinity University itself made a commitment to this project above and beyond its normal support of faculty research. Thanks to a special summer grant, I was able to do research in Spain and Portugal in June and July of 1980 and have this text ready for publication in early 1981. The administration of Trinity University has at all times been encouraging, and thanks are due to Jean S. Chittenden, Chairperson of the Department of Foreign Languages; George N. Boyd, Dean of Humanities and the Arts; J. Norman Parmer, Vice-

President for Academic Affairs; and Ronald Calgaard, President of Trinity University. In addition, a number of Trinity people were both individually and collectively instrumental in obtaining grant funding for the project, and for their interest and support I thank Peggy Birkeland, Director of the Office of Sponsored Projects; Donald Corben-Smith, Associate Director of Development; Leon M. Taylor, Vice-President for University Affairs; and Rudolph M. Gaedke, Dean of Records. In the Trinity University Library, Craig Likness, Humanities Reference Librarian, Mary Clarkson, Education Reference Librarian, and Katherine Pettit, Special Collections Librarian, supported the project with enthusiasm and an endless supply of arcane data. Mrs. Patricia Cárdenas deserves my appreciative thanks for her continued optimism and help. Gerald R. Benjamin, Associate Professor of Music, who is preparing a companion edition of the music of *Celos aun del aire matan* also based on the Evora manuscript, proved himself to be not only a learned scholar in the area of Spanish Baroque music, but a good friend and an enthusiastic colleague as well.

Apart from institutional aid and support, special thanks must go to Ms. Mary Ann Bruni, whose vigor and imagination helped to formulate the concept of this project in the autumn of 1978; to Professor Jack Sage of King's College, London, who not only wrote the splendid foreword to this edition but who also extended to me every courtesy and assistance in a manner consistent with the fine gentleman that he is; and to John T. Davis of St. Philip's College in San Antonio, without whose encouragement this project could not have been carried out.

Finally, I would like to express not only my appreciation but also my admiration for the staff of Trinity University Press. Director Joe Nicholson, Editor Lois Boyd, and Officer Manager Virginia Cabello demonstrated their patience, knowledge, enthusiasm, and commitment to this project, one that turned out to be much more complex that I would ever have imagined. In particular, Lois Boyd deserves a commendation as editor, confidante, therapist, and friend.

CONTENTS

FOREWORD

For over a century now Calderón has been acclaimed as one of Spain's great dramatists. Indeed, some hispanists, beginning with the German Romantics and the researchers Keil and Schack and confirmed in our day by scholars such as E. M. Wilson and A. A. Parker, have seen him as Spain's greatest playwright. On that score alone, then, a new edition of a Calderón drama is to be welcomed without the need for any accolade from me. There are, however, other reasons why this edition deserves a specially warm and wide welcome.

One of these is important as regards Spanish literary and musical history. For the fact is that *Celos aun del aire matan* is an opera with a libretto drawn from classical mythology and music based on recitative, aria, and chorus along the exact lines established by seventeenth-century Italian operas by such librettists as Rospigliosi or Busenello and composers as Cavalli or Monteverdi. Like Calderón's *La púrpura de la rosa, Fortunas de Andrómeda y Perseo*, and many other musical dramas of the time, *Celos aun del aire matan* provides significant evidence that Spanish culture during the Golden Age forged closer links with its European counterparts than has been generally supposed.

Another is that the text throws light upon the standard history-book notion of Calderón as the creator of the Spanish *zarzuela*. A study of the play in conjunction with earlier texts like *El laurel de Apolo* will show that Calderón, along with his composer Juan Hidalgo, far from trying to create a peculiarly Spanish form of musical play, set out to foster *opera seria*.

Perhaps the most important, however, is that *Celos aun del aire matan* is the product of Calderón's maturity. While I do not take it for granted that a writer writes better as he grows older, I do maintain that literary history – not to say commonsense – shows it to be generally true. Who could say that Shakespeare's early *Comedy of Errors* or *Titus Andronicus* holds more for posterity than *King Lear* or *Macbeth*? Did not Verdi declare his personal preference for *Falstaff,* written when he was nearly eighty? Now, Calderón went on writing until near the end of his eighty-one years; and the surprising fact is that the plays which have so far caught the fancy of literati were written before he was forty or so. For instance, *El príncipe constante* was finished when he was about 26, *La vida es sueño* when he was about 33, *El alcalde de Zalamea* when he was about 40; whereas *Celos aun del aire matan* did not appear until he was sixty or thereabouts. There is, to be sure, a complicating factor which may help to explain this relative lack of interest in his mature works. After 1651, when he took holy orders, Calderón seems to have written no more secular plays for the popular stage but concentrated instead upon providing the court with spectacular shows heightened by breathtaking scenery, dancing, and music. Something like one third of Calderón's total dramatic output consists of palace *fiestas* of this kind; and these were nearly all written, let me repeat, in the latter half of his long life. Could it be that literary historians have been put off by a semi-conscious judgment about the nature of the court to which our dramatist played? May it not be that they have simply transferred from the pages of Spanish imperial history to the cultural activity of the Spanish court a judgment about "decadence" which ought to be challenged? I doubt if a court which drew to itself creative artists of the calibre of Velázquez, Hidalgo, Bocángel, Antonio de Mendoza, Quevedo, or Calderón should be readily labelled "decadent." After all, by 1651 Calderón was indisputably Spain's leading writer of religious drama; he had from the first pointed assiduously to the moral dangers of vanity; and he was a priest. That he should now start purveying facile entertainment for a supposedly frivolous and foppish court is simply an untenable assumption. I believe that a close study of Calderón's mature court plays, such as *Fortunas de Andrómeda y Perseo* or *La estatua de Prometeo,* will reveal a broader view of faith, reason, justice, fate and freewill, weal and woe than is to be found in his more celebrated plays. Of this kind of play, *Celos aun del aire matan* is a good example.

JACK SAGE

King's College
University of London

CELOS AUN DEL
AIRE MATAN

Pedro Calderón de la Barca, 1684 engraving from Gaspar Agustín de Lara's *Obelisco fúnebre*. Courtesy of the Hispanic Society of America.

moral responsibility and in his charge as King. Unfortunately, he was too weak to live up to the demands of his nation, in which the economy was suffering badly and in which the common people were being severely taxed for high-minded but ill-conceived "religious" wars in the Netherlands and in Germany, and to resist the overtures of the Conde-Duque de Olivares. When Philip married Isabel de Borbón, the Conde-Duque was only too happy to encourage their mutual love of the theater. Not only were state occasions and holidays reason enough for a grand dramatic spectacle, but there were also many *particulares* performed in the Alcázar during the first years of Philip's reign. From October 5, 1622 until February 8, 1623, no fewer than forty-five *particulares* were performed in the quarters of the Queen.[9] During the same period there were, in addition, several *fiestas palaciegas* performed by the *meninas*. The first of these *fiestas palaciegas* to be noted in history was that of *La gloria de Niquea*, by the Conde de Villamediana, performed on May 15, 1622.[10]

As with the *comedia* in general, the Spanish Baroque lyric drama and opera derived much of its form and technique from Italian models. The idea of an opera, that is, a work in which the dialogue, as well as the chorus and dances and songs, were sung, was just beginning to take shape in Italy.[11] Orazio Vecchi created early attempts at lyric theater toward the end of the sixteenth century. While Vecchi's works were more on the order of vocalized symphonic concerts, a second generation, mostly of Florentines, created a recitative style. Monteverdi was the first to give importance and stature to monody in his operas around 1607, and soon his brand of opera had made its home in the palace of the Barberini in Rome, acquiring a rather conventional character. After the height of Barberini influence, more spontaneous forms of opera developed, such as the musical comedy variety performed in the Teatro della Pergola in Florence, the historic operas performed with great machinery in Venice, and the melodramatic operas in Naples. As a result, there were three basic Italian branches of opera to influence the development of Spanish musical drama: the Florentine, with its beginnings under the patronage of Conde Bardi; the Roman, with its aesthetic refinement under the patronage of the Barberini; and the Venetian, with its public character accessible to all. There is evidence that Spanish touring companies travelled in France and Italy during the first half of the seventeenth century, and it is not unreasonable to imagine that they could have been affected by these new artistic currents, especially those relative to stage design and music.[12]

The first drama indicated as having been completely sung was *La selva sin amor*, by Lope de Vega (1562-1635), performed in 1629 on the occasion of Philip's recovery from an illness. The production of *La selva sin amor*, however, also introduced into Spain Italianate staging, brought by the highly acclaimed Cosme Lotti, an engineer of widespread fame for his design and execution of stage machinery, had previously been in the employ of the Duke of Tuscany when Philip had brought him to Madrid in 1626. While the *transforma-*

IV that the idea of specially commissioned works to be put on by professional actors for the King and his court (and often for the public as well) came into practice.

Philip IV (1605-1665) was an eccentric man whom the light of historical consideration has not favored.[8] He was a devout Catholic and a great believer in

Philip IV, 1666 engraving. Courtesy of the Hispanic Society of America.

mances to various hospitals. The performers of the *corrales* were members of professional acting companies. Each company included a musician who played the *vihuela*, the guitar, or the harp, and who even sang when the need arose. Every fourth woman in the company was designated a "singer." Large productions would necessitate calling upon the resources of more than one company. In 1622, the basic instruments of the accompaniment were trumpets, *chirimías*, viols, lutes, flutes, *bajoncillos*, and guitars. The music was intended in some way to echo or mirror the sentiment of the poetry,[4] and in some instances text painting is quite obvious. Because of the strophic nature of the dance and popular song rhythms, it was not unusual for both the poetry and the music to make use of *estribillos*, early *ritornelli*, to unify the action within scenes. Some early *estribillos* acquired a popularity of their own and were incorporated in more than one play.

A *comedia* production was quite a complicated affair, both in the *corrales* and in the court. The presentation would open with a *loa*, either a monologue or brief skit that introduced the play, with the three acts following. During the intermissions, however, other one-act plays were performed. These plays were of several different types, *entremeses*, *bailes*, *jácaras*, and *mojigangas*, all of which had simple forms at the beginning of the seventeenth century and developed over the course of the century with respect to the number of characters and the complexity of the plot. *Jácaras*, for example, which initially were the simple telling of the events surrounding the punishment of some wrongdoer (to the delight, no doubt, of the crowd), sung by one of the sopranos in the first intermission, later developed into several styles, including a *jácara a lo divino* and a *jácara entremesada*, the latter employing several characters and eventually giving rise to the *tonadilla*.[5] *Mojigangas* were mummeries and often associated with the masque tradition.[6] After the conclusion of Act Three, the performers would begin a dance in which, at court performances, the courtiers and the King would participate. Even in presentations of plays without music, there would be music in the event as a whole because of the *jácaras*, *bailes*, and *entremeses cantados*. These auxiliary pieces were probably changed for each production, as dedications and circumstances warranted.[7]

The practice of presenting plays at court did not flourish until the reign of Philip III. Charles V and Philip II had not been very interested in drama, considering it probably immoral. The Duque de Lerma (the favorite of Philip III) and the Conde-Duque de Olivares (the first favorite of Philip IV), however, looked upon the dramatic spectacle as not only good public relations for the court in the eyes of people both at home and abroad, but also as an excellent diversion for the King to give the favorite more freedom in carrying out his policies. Initially, there were two major varieties of court presentations besides outdoor pageants. The first was simply a private performance of a *corral* production using the same actors. These were called *particulares*. *Fiestas palaciegas* were written for and performed by the ladies in waiting and members of the royal household, principally the women. It was only later in the reign of Philip

INTRODUCTION

Calderón and the
Development of the Spanish Baroque Lyric Drama

Music and dance were part of Golden Age Spanish drama from the earliest sixteenth-century works of Juan del Encina.[1] Music in the theater had three primary sources: the plain song and other religious music, the tunes and madrigals of the early *vihuelistas* such as Luis de Narváez,[2] and the *romance*, both *viejo* and *nuevo*. As music became part of the early drama, its form primarily took that of incidental dances and popular songs only loosely or not at all connected to the plot. Little by little, more substantial parts of the dramas were sung. In general, this musical participation was in the form of strophic variations repeated many times, perhaps twenty or thirty. Very often dancing accompanied the music, either instrumental or vocal, and *bailes* were practically inseparable from the *comedia* performance. It seemed that everyone danced, from the King on down. Unfortunately, very little is known of these dances, except that many were considered quite scandalous. The most shocking dance was the *zarabanda*, but the *chacona*, the *escarraman*, and other more specialized dances caused the arbiters of public morality to speak out on more than one occasion against the drama in general and its dances in particular.[3]

That playwrights throughout the sixteenth century indicated musical portions of their plays is evidence of the extent to which music and dancing were part of the *comedia*. Lucas Fernández, Gil Vicente, Torres Naharro, Sánchez de Bada-joz, and Cervantes all included music in their works, and there are even some occasional *villancicos* in the *pasos* of Lope de Rueda.

Plays were performed publicly in the *corrales*. *Cofradías*, or religious service organizations, ran these theaters and would donate proceeds from the perfor-

ción, or rapid scene change (to astonish the spectator), had been used before in
Spanish stagecraft, Lotti perfected its usage. He also introduced such remarkable effects as triumphal cars, artificial lighting (so that for the first time productions could be done at night), and portable machine stages (for greater
variety of production), and combined them with the special effects of the *comedia* already existing in the *corrales,* such as trap doors, machines representing
clouds that moved up and down, an upper gallery (both for performance and for
access to some of the machines), and the device for discovery, in which a
character can be made to appear suddenly on stage. He finished the scene with
Italianate perspective stage scenery, rather than the flat, rather sparse affairs
of earlier Spanish sets. The set design now became one of wing and shutter.
The theatrical relationship between Spain and Italy was mutual, and, in
exchange, the Spanish stage exported to Italy the *bastidor del foro.*

Two professional theatrical companies existed in 1629, that of Roque de
Figueroa and that of Juan de Morales Medrano, and very likely one or both of
these companies performed *La selva sin amor.* In the dedication of his *égloga
pastoril,* Lope provides some interesting details of the production, including the
fact that the musicians were to remain out of sight.[13] Lope calls the play "cosa
nueva en España," although there has been some dispute about exactly what
the novelty of *La selva* was.[14] Pedrell and Cotarelo maintain that the novelty
was the use of stage machinery, while Stevenson insists that its being entirely
sung was what was new.[15] Because the *comedia* in the *corrales* had for quite
some time used trap doors, transformations, and some machinery, one is

View of the Prado with the Buen Retiro to the left. Engraving by Isidro González
Velázquez (1765-1840). Courtesy of the Hispanic Society of America.

inclined to agree with Stevenson's more modern assessment of Lope's statement.

Performances continued to be produced in the Alcázar and at the Royal Palace in Aranjuez,[16] but the Conde-Duque de Olivares had the idea for a pleasure palace to be built in the gardens of the Buen Retiro on the eastern edge of Madrid. The Palacio del Buen Retiro, as it was called, was finished in October 1632, although its inaugural festivities did not take place until late the following year. Meanwhile, performances continued in the Alcázar, often accompanied by the musicians of the Royal Chapel. In 1633, this orchestra contained two *bajones,* one *bajoncillo,* three harps (one of which was played by Juan Hidalgo, later to be named director of the chapel musicians), two *vihuelas,* two viols, *chirimías* and cornets. Two years later, seven violins were added. The completion of the Buen Retiro palace offered even more opportunities for staging dramas with musical accompaniment.

After the death of Lope de Vega in 1635, Lotti began to work on a new play by a younger dramatist, Pedro Calderón de la Barca. Calderón had been born on January 17, 1600, to parents of noble lineage.[17] At one point, Calderón's father was the Secretario del Consejo de la Hacienda under Philip II, and his mother was a descendant of the Flemish family of Mons de Hainaut. Although little is known of the early years of Calderón's life, it has been determined that he attended the Jesuit Colegio Imperial in Madrid from about 1608 to 1613. After his studies at the Colegio, he attended both the University of Alcalá (1614-1615) and the University of Salamanca (1615-1620), from which he obtained a degree in canonical law.[18] The literary career of the young poet was launched by the competitions from 1620 to 1622 in honor of the patron saint of Madrid, San Isidro, and he was praised by the eminent figure of Lope de Vega.

In 1621, Pedro, with his two brothers, was involved in a murder case, but all three of them were let off with a moderate sentence. He saw the first performance in Madrid of one of his plays, *Amor, honor y poder,* in 1623. Between 1623 and 1635 the details of his life once again are sketchy, although in 1628 he was implicated in another scandal in which one of his brothers was wounded. The years 1630-1650 mark the high point of Calderón's literary output, especially for the public *corrales,* and, after the death of Lope, he was appointed court dramatist by Philip IV.

Calderón's art, coming as it did at the culmination of the high Baroque in Spain, represents the fusion of medieval scholasticism, Renaissance humanism, and Baroque tension.[19] In the drama, it is clear that he learned his stagecraft from Lope de Vega, and he rarely departed from the standard traditions of the *comedia.*[20] Calderón's principal contribution to the *comedia* was the philosophical and religious treatment of plot and character and the great artistry of his poetry.[21] According to Cossío, Calderón was able to take the currents of *cultismo* and *conceptismo* and elevate the style beyond mere poetic elegance.[22] In a way, his poetry is the extreme example of a literary movement that began in the last decades of the sixteenth century. Otis Green has described what happened by the phrase, "Se acicalaron los auditorios."[23] In effect, the audience grew impatient with mere plot, character, and good taste. They demanded more paradoxes, more spectacle, and more complication as wit replaced formal beauty as the goal of literature. For Calderón, it was no longer enough to present a theatrical event on its own terms; it had to convey some statement on the human condition and do so in a way consistent with Baroque ideals of *admiratio*.[24]

It was this consummate Baroque *poeta faber,* then, who had an interesting argument with Cosme Lotti over the staging of a play in 1635. Lotti, it seems, designed the play without taking into account Calderón's text, and a row ensued in which appeal was made directly to the King.[25] A compromise was worked out in which Calderón would adapt some of Lotti's ideas into his play, but Lotti would have to work with Calderón's text. The play, *El mayor encanto amor,* was performed on June 23 utilizing the pond of the Retiro.[26] *El mayor encanto amor* was so remarkably successful that it was performed four times between June 23 and July 5, and four more times between July 29 and August 3. With the music and the dances, each performance lasted six hours, ending at one in the morning.

To increase the possibilities for dramatic spectacle at the Palacio del Buen

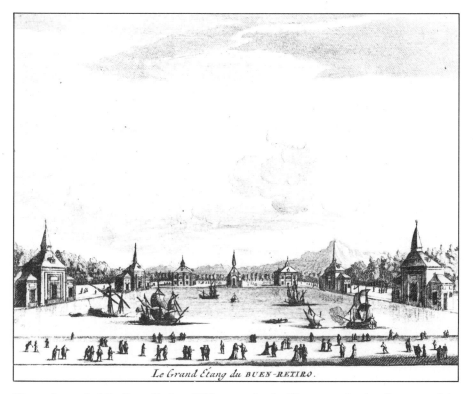

Le Grand Étang du BUEN-RETIRO.

The main pond of the Buen Retiro, 1730 engraving by Pieter van der Aa. Courtesy of the Hispanic Society of America.

Philip IV hunting with a canvas trap, 1634 engraving by Pieter Perret. Courtesy of the Hispanic Society of America.

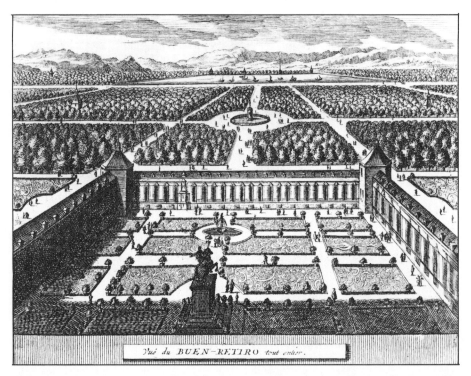

The gardens and pond of the Buen Retiro, engraving by Juan Alvarez de Colmenar. Courtesy of the Hispanic Society of America.

Retiro, a true theater was added in 1640. Called the Coliseo, the theater opened on February 4, 1640 with a production of *La gran comedia de los bandos de Verona,* written by Rojas Zorrilla and staged by Lotti. Lotti had helped design the Coliseo; as a result, the theater could accommodate not only *particulares* but *comedias de tramoyas,* or machine spectacles, as well. In the Coliseo, the King, the court, and the people saw plays together, with the same contributions donated to the hospitals as by the public playhouses. The plans of the Coliseo show that there were three rows of four boxes on either side, a *cazuela,* or ladies' area facing the stage, and over the *cazuela,* a royal balcony. There is an indication of a fixed proscenium, but, unlike the *corrales,* the stage did not project into the auditorium. The staging for each play, including the proscenium, was new and unique but appropriate to the machine-play genre. Later plans of the Coliseo show eleven *bastidores,* or wings, on each side of the stage with a shutter, or backcloth, in the rear, all of which would produce the Italianate perspective staging.[27] The King allotted boxes on each side to grandees, in turn. The public theater atmosphere was imitated in the Coliseo to such an extent that Pellicer y Tobar related that the Queen liked to hear the audience jeer whether the play was good or not.[28] This desire by the Queen to see common people as they might have been in the *corrales* prompted staged quarrels in the *cazuela,* including hair-pulling and shouting matches, and boxes of mice were even reported to have been released to cause more chaos among the rabble.[29]

On February 20, 1640, a fire occurred in the Palace itself, but it did not harm the Coliseo. The play scheduled for that night, however, was postponed until the following night, Shrove Tuesday. The *comedia de tramoyas* of February 21, 1640 was indeed a grand affair. All the Councils were ordered to attend. The King arrived at four in the afternoon; the play began at five and lasted until midnight. Despite its success as a theater, the Coliseo was used only a short time because of the Catalan Revolt in June of 1640, in which Calderón served his King as a soldier, and the Portuguese Revolution in December of the same year. Palace performances on a limited basis, however, did continue in the Alcázar.

Because of a remarkable incident on February 14, 1662, a little about the earlier workings of the Coliseo is known. On that day there was discovered a plot to burn the sets, theater, and Palace of the Buen Retiro being prepared for a production of Calderón's *El Faetonte (El hijo del Sol, Faetón).* Arrested was the Marqués de Heliche, producer of royal court theatrical presentations since 1655, and his testimony revealed the interesting workings of the machinery.[30] The famous "discovery," according to the Marqués, was carried out by means of a large canvas curtain called the *bastidor del foro* or *cortina de los foros.* There was as well, unseen by the audience, an upper gallery necessary to get the actors and actresses up into the machines. Heliche, found guilty, admitted that he had not wanted someone else to receive credit for machinery he had helped to build. The stage machinery of 1662 was the result of twenty-five years of stagecraft experience. The rapid development of the *comedia de tramoya,* the use of professional actors rather than amateurs (such as the *meninas),* and the adoption of Italianate conventions of transformation and perspective scenery all took place between 1635 and 1645. Outdoor pageants, popular before 1640, were replaced by indoor spectacles in the Coliseo, the Alcázar, and in other royal sites such as Valladolid and Aranjuez.

Philip IV, eighteenth-century engraving by Cosimo Mogalli. Courtesy of the Hispanic Society of America.

In 1644 and 1646, Philip IV suffered two great emotional setbacks. The first was the death of his adored wife Isabel; the second was the untimely death of his only male heir, the handsome and dashing Prince Baltasar Carlos. On both occasions a ban was imposed on dramatic productions, and, coming as they did so close to each other, many dramatic companies were forced to disband. In the same year, 1646, a new papal Nuncio was sent to Madrid in the person of Giulio Rospigliosi (1600-1669). At the time of his appointment to Madrid, Rospigliosi already had written the librettos to several operas and provided a valuable source of Italian influence in Madrid. During his stay in Madrid from 1646 to 1653, he undeniably knew Pedro Calderón and Juan Hidalgo. When he returned to Italy, later to become Pope Clement IX, he had in his repertoire of operas several based on Spanish plots. He liked very much the mix of tragic and comic elements typical of the *comedia,* and it is supposed that *Dal mal il bene* (1653) was based on plots taken from the *comedia.*[31]

With the lifting of the ban on theatrical productions, court festivities began with a production of *La piedra cándida,* by Gabriel Arcángel y Unzueta. This production, in honor of the birthday of Mariana of Austria, who was to become

Queen Mariana of Austria, 1660 engraving by
Bernardino de Rebolledo. Courtesy of the
Hispanic Society of America.

Philip's second wife, took place on December 21, 1647, in the *salón dorado* of
the Alcázar. On Mariana's birthday the following year, the Royal Chapel Choir
performed together for the first time as a whole. The Choir sang from two
raised platforms invisible to the audience, and *chirimías* sounded during the
scene changes. Also in 1648, in celebration of the upcoming marriage of Philip
to Mariana, there was a production of *El jardín de Falerina,* with text by
Calderón and music by José Peyró. Stevenson comments that Peyró's music
was not merely an adornment of the text but that it made a musical statement
concerning the text while unifying the structure of the play at the same time.[32]
In 1651, the year in which Calderón was ordained a priest, he ceased to write
for the *corrales,* concentrating instead on the *fiestas cantadas* of the court and
two *autos sacramentales* per year.[33]

As has been mentioned, the Coliseo itself fell into disuse after 1640. For Car-
nival of 1650, however, a special play presented in honor of the new Queen led
to the theater's being totally refurbished. By 1651, the Coliseo was again open
to the public, with the lessee of the *corrales* administering the finances of the
Coliseo. The rejuvenation of the Coliseo prompted a new surge in the development of the *comedia de tramoya,* and from 1652 until the death of Philip IV in
1665, plays were regularly performed in the Coliseo and in the Alcázar. With
each production the plays became more complicated. Shergold speaks of an
unnamed play produced on May 15, 1653 that called for sixty-six actors and
actresses and included a *loa*-masque danced by twelve persons carrying
torches.[34] These productions were exorbitantly expensive. Shergold mentions
that a machine play in 1655 would have cost approximately 50,000 ducats, with
some, such as the extravagant burlesque *La restauración de España,* costing
some 100,00 ducats.[35] The more and more complicated machinery (it was said
that one machine could carry twenty-four women) inevitably created delays
and hardships on the acting companies.

The strong ties between the court performances and the public performances
were great, not only in the general format of the productions, but also in the
personnel. When the King ordered a play, the actors and actresses necessary
for its production left the *corrales,* even though it meant that the public performances already planned had to be cancelled, sometimes as the audience was
arriving. The actors received remuneration but the lessee of the theater lost his
revenue from tickets and had to appeal through bureaucratic channels for reim-
bursement. This paperwork, dating from as far back as 1635, enables the study
of precise information about many performances, including personnel and
expenses.

After Cosme Lotti died in 1643, the King employed another Italian, Baccio
del Bianco. Bianco died in 1657. The first performance known to have been
staged by Bianco was Calderón's *La fiera, el rayo y la piedra,* in 1652. This production had seven scene changes and lasted seven hours. In an unprecedented
run it was presented on forty successive days, once for the King and Queen,
once for the Councils, once for the officials of the City of Madrid, and thirty-

Scenic designs from the 1690 production of Calderón's *La fiera, el rayo y la piedra*. (This page and the following two pages.) Courtesy of the Biblioteca Nacional, Madrid.

seven times for the public. Historically, *La fiera, el rayo y la piedra* is of immense importance, because it is one of a very few plays before 1700 for which there are complete sets of drawings of the stage scenery.[36] These drawings, many of which are reproduced in this edition, clearly demonstrate the Italianate perspective staging techniques, although it will be noted that the *bastidores,* or wings, had flat faces only, without decorated perspective sides.[37] It is also somewhat curious that the special effects are shown without any indication of machinery.

In 1653, Calderón was named Chaplain of the Fundación de los Nuevos Reyes in Toledo. Although he spent the next ten years in Toledo with his sister Dorotea, who was a nun, he is known to have made trips to court from time to time. During these ten years some of the most important of Calderón's *comedias de música* were produced: *El golfo de las sirenas* (1657), *El laurel de Apolo* (1658), *La púrpura de la rosa* (1660), *Celos aun del aire matan* (1660), *El Faetonte* (or, *El hijo del sol, Faetón*) (1661), *Eco y Narciso* (1661), and *Siquis y Cupido, o Ni amor se libra de amor* (1662).

On January 17, 1657, all the machinery necessary to present a *comedia de tramoya* was carted from the Coliseo to the Palacio de la Zarzuela. This small hunting lodge had been built originally for the King's brother, the Infante Don Fernando, but when Don Fernando left Spain to govern the Low Countries in 1634, Philip had the palace enlarged. On days when inclement weather made hunting impossible, the King instructed actors to put on plays to entertain him. As a result, the first "fiesta de la Zarzuela" appears in the exaggerated documentation provided by Barrionuevo of a huge feast for thousands of guests, highlighted by the theatrical production of a play generally believed to be *El golfo de las sirenas.* Produced by the Marqués de Heliche, the same man who would be responsible for the 1662 Coliseo fire and the son of the King's new favorite, Don Luis de Haro, and performed by the companies of Diego Osorio and Pedro de la Rosa, including the famous *gracioso* Juan Rana, the production of this *égloga piscatoria* cost 16,000 ducats. Calderón himself was paid 200 doubloons for his efforts and made a grandee three days after the event. The spectacle, a huge success, was repeated on the twelfth of February in the Retiro. Because this play was the first one to carry the designation "fiesta de la Zarzuela," and because it is considered to be the archetype of the Baroque zarzuela (one or two acts, mythological theme, music, and dialogue,[38] or music and recitative), Calderón is often given credit for being the creator of the modern zarzuela as a genre.

In the same year, Baccio del Bianco was succeeded, upon the recommendation of Rospigliosi, by yet another Italian, Antonio María Antonozzi. The change in scenic director, however, did not delay the production of more grand spectacles. Indeed, the years 1657-1662 marked the height of royal interest in the *comedias de tramoyas.* In the autumn of 1657, Calderón again was commissioned to write a machine play for the Zarzuela. This play was to be one of many to commemorate the birth of a new heir-apparent, Philip Prosper, born

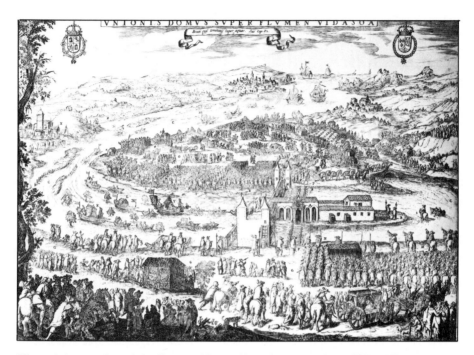

View of the meeting of the Courts of Philip IV of Spain and Louis XIV of France on the Isle of Pheasants, 1659. Courtesy of the Biblioteca Nacional, Madrid.

on November 27, 1657. Due to various changes and complications, the play was finally produced, not in the Zarzuela, but in the Coliseo on March 4, 1658. The *loa* to *El laurel de Apolo* contains Calderón's own definition of the zarzuela genre:

> No es comedia, sino solo
> una fabula pequeña,
> en que a imitación de Italia
> se canta, y se representa.[39]

Music accompanied the text, and the characters began to assume more of the musical responsibility from the chorus. There are no musical interludes that are purely ornamental; all in one way or another contribute to the development of the plot. The play was repeated many years later to celebrate a birthday of Charles II.[40]

By the time of the production of *El laurel* in 1658, Calderón already had accomplished the union of mythology, drama, music, and dance in his zarzuela genre.[41] The conception of Greco-Roman mythology that Calderón expressed is one that resulted from centuries of scholastic discussions about the propriety of pagan myths in Christian doctrine. There were many manuals on the interpretation of myths that were approved by the Church and that actually became material for an academic study of their meaning to Christianity.[42] In Spain, this medieval, moralistic tradition continued throughout the Counterreformation,[43] and it is almost a certainty that Calderón was exposed to two of them: *La philosophia secreta* (1585), by Juan Pérez de Moya, and *Del teatro de los dioses de la gentilidad* (1620-23), by Baltasar de Vitoria.[44] Pérez de Moya presented the myths and then gave a triple "declaración" about each, relating the historic (the gods as real Greek and Roman people), physical (the gods in astrology), and moral (the gods as allegorical examples) traditions common to the interpretations of the myths.[45] Calderón chose the moral interpretation for his gods, often making their actions seem quite guilty due to their all-too-human failings.[46] The myths were "fingimientos" on the part of the poets for formal use in ethics and morals and not to be interpreted as history.[47] As a result, Calderón's mythical plays are rich in allegory and moral purpose in keeping with the strictly Catholic world view seen in other works by Calderón in particular and in the Spanish Golden Age in general.[48]

Likewise, one can observe Calderón's moralistic use of the literary medium when the music is added to the text. In general, Calderón saw no great difference among any of the fine arts in terms of their ability to affect human beings.[49] For him, all the arts shared a common art theory based on the theocentric and scholastic ideals of the Spanish Counterreformation.[50] Because Calderón believed that the arts are able to influence greatly the actions of human beings, he was careful that the music that was added to his text would ennoble and enrich.[51] Calderón must have known music, at least theoretically,[52] and he was exposed to theatrical music not only in the *corrales* of Madrid, but also in the Italian tradition of the *sacra rappresentazione*.[53] Jack Sage has identified certain types of music that are consistently employed in such a fashion as to suggest a certain moral quality associated with them. In *La estatua de Prometeo,* for example, Sage correlates dialogue with human beings, *tonos humanos,* or secular songs, with falseness, both of gods and of people, and recitative with classical gods.[54] A folklore song implies nearly always a deplorable attitude of *carpe diem,* and sensorial music is associated with the devil. In a sense, "bad" music is beautiful and aesthetic and causes one to become distracted from God's will.[55] Stock devices in the *comedia,* such as refrains and echoes, take on new allegorical functions, and there is a direct functional correlation between the repetitions and refrains of the music and the analogies and *plurimembraciones* in the poetry.[56] Because the music is never sensual but is almost always evocative, Subirá terms some of this music "Iberian musical expressivism."[57] Perhaps one of the reasons there are so many four-part sections in the accompaniments to these works is the belief of Calderón himself that four-part harmony was the closest to perfection, "la armonía del cielo," in that it reflected the perfect combination of the four elements of nature.[58]

As one might expect from the fusion of two media, these *fiestas* are difficult to define generically. Subject matter alone does not determine the genre of a play, for many of the same myths are found in Calderón's *autos* as well as in his *comedias de música: Psiquis y Cupido (= Ni amor se libra de amor), El Divino Jasón (= Los tres mayores prodigios), Andrómeda y Perseo (= Fortunas de Andrómeda y Perseo)*, etc.[59] Yet, if these plays are not *autos*, neither are they *comedias*. Aubrun lists several differences between these *fiestas* and the generic Golden Age *comedia*. For example, in the court spectacles, the outcome of the plot was known beforehand due to general acquaintance with the myth; plot changes tended to be in the nature of character transformation; narrative elements often took precedence over theatrical ones in the telling of the mythological background; and even the theater itself was compromised by the spectacular elements (music, dance, sets, etc.) of the performances.[60]

Neumeister claims that the generic whole in these plays is greater than the sum of its component parts.[61] Calderón brought together these disparate elements to create an entirely new genre of musical drama, neither *auto* nor *comedia*, neither *entremés* nor *jácara*.[62] Moreover, even though these plays were presented at court and were meant to flatter the King and his realm, they are not masques in a Jonsonian sense.[63] Northrup Frye places the genre of masque between those of comedy and *auto*, but these plays are not exactly masques either.[64] While they are not so different from masques in appearance (drama, music, spectacle, etc.), their concern with moral righteousness and their failure to compromise completely mimetic drama for the sake of court revelry keep them from being generic masques. They are masque-like operas, a genre apart.

Two important productions took place in 1660. One was performed on January 17 in honor of the marriage of the Infanta María Teresa to Louis XIV of France, the other on December 5 to celebrate the third birthday of Crown Prince Philip Prosper. Because the eyewitness accounts from 1660 mention no name in connection with either play, confusion has arisen as to which plays they were. Cotarelo, who had originally believed that *El jardín de Falerina* was produced on January 17 and *La púrpura de la rosa* on December 5, later came to believe, as have many authorities, that in fact *La púrpura de la rosa* was produced on January 17 and *Celos aun del aire matan* was presented on December 5. The date previously given for *Celos* was 1662.[65]

The production of *La púrpura de la rosa*, on January 17, 1660, was presented by the companies of Pedro de la Rosa and Juana de Cisneros.[66] The *loa* of the play indicates that the work was entirely sung "a la italiana," that is, with recitative rather than spoken dialogue. The purpose, according to the *loa*, was so that other nations might see "competidos sus primores."[67] One of the characters, Tristeza, says, however, that the Spanish public might not support such a novelty. *La púrpura* was performed again on January 18, 1680, and it is supposed that the composer for both productions was Juan Hidalgo, although none of his music for this play exists. In the restaging of the play, there was only one man in the cast, according to Stevenson, who presents the music for *La púrpura* from a production done in Lima in 1701 with music by Torrejón y Velasco.[68]

Cristóbal Pérez Pastor first printed an account of the events leading up to the theatrical production for the King on December 5, 1660.[69] This account begins on November 23, when the writer, Matías de Santos, Escribano de Teatros, noticed the absence of posters announcing productions by the company of Diego Osorio. Osorio explained that the King had requested a play for Sunday, November 28, in honor of the third birthday of Philip Prosper. The accounts of November 24 through 27 mention continuous rehearsals in a house rented by the Marqués de Heliche and guarded by *alguaciles*. On November 28, the date originally set for the production, the author indicated that the companies were still in rehearsal and that the production had been delayed due to the great amount of work necessary to mount the production of this "fiesta grande cantada." November 29 saw further rehearsals, and on November 30 the author had an interview with Diego Osorio in which the latter said that the players were rehearsing every morning and afternoon. Also on that day, the author saw Calderón and Hidalgo attending the rehearsals. The rehearsals continued from December first through the fourth and on December 5, a Sunday, the author went at noon to the rehearsal house and saw the actors still rehearsing. At three-thirty on the same afternoon, the author saw the companies entering the palace to give the long-awaited performance.

We now assume that the play in question was *Celos aun del aire matan,* performed by the companies of Diego Osorio and Juana de Cisneros. An edition of the play published in 1663[70] lists the cast, except for the character of Aura, as being composed of the following personnel:

Diana	Josefa Pavía
Pocris	Bernarda Manuela
Floreta	Bernarda Ramírez
Mejera	María de Anaya
Alecto	María de los Santos
Tesífone	María de Salinas
Zéfalo	Luisa Romero
Eróstrato	Mariana de Borja
Clarín	Manuela de Escamilla
Rústico	Antonio de Escamilla
Chorus of Nymphs	10 women
Chorus of Men	6 men

All of the principals were quite famous.[71] As in the Lima production of *La púrpura*, all but one of the principals were women,[72] perhaps because of the origins of court drama presented by the *meninas,* perhaps because of aesthetic reasons for which the court liked the very high tessitura of the soprano voices (even the man was a tenor), or perhaps because of a pedestrian reason, such as that the best singers were women. Many of these same singers had performed in *La púrpura de la rosa* and were to be seen again in *Hado y divisa* (1680).

Whether because of the demands of three acts of sung text, or because of the tastes of the court, Calderón never again wrote a play to be sung completely. In fact, there is some speculation to the effect that the play was not terribly successful because it was never again produced in Spain, and only twice more in any of the records of the Spanish empire (Lima, 1708, and Mexico City, 1728).[73] Nevertheless, Calderón and Hidalgo continued to collaborate on court productions, including *El Faetonte (El hijo del sol, Faetón),* produced in the Buen Retiro on March 1, 1661 and repeated twice more in 1675 and 1679 at the request of Queen Mariana; *Siquis y Cupido, o Ni amor se libra de amor,* presented on January 19, 1662 and repeated in 1669;[74] *La estatua de Prometeo,* probably in 1669; and *Hado y divisa de Leonido y Marfisa,* the last collaboration between Calderón and Hidalgo, presented on March 3, 1680, in honor of the marriage of King Charles II to his first wife, María Luisa d'Orléans, niece of the French King Louis XIV.[75]

Calderón's play production in the last twenty years of his life continued, and he worked with many famous, contemporary composers, most notably with Gregorio de la Rosa (ten *autos* between 1662 and 1679) and Juan de Serqueira (nine *autos* between 1677 and 1681).[76] In 1663 Calderón was made the Royal Chaplain and moved to Madrid permanently. Soon after, however, the theaters were closed in mourning of the death on September 17, 1665 of Calderón's

Philip IV, 1657 engraving by Pedro de Villafranca y Malagón. Courtesy of the Hispanic Society of America.

great patron, Philip IV. Calderón suffered not a little from the loss of royal
patronage; Charles II simply was not the benefactor of the theater that his
father had been. The theaters were closed until November of the following
year, at which time the owners petitioned the Queen Regent for permission to
reopen. Play production began again on November 30, 1666.

The genre that Calderón had helped to formulate soon proliferated in the
hands of other playwrights and musicians. Juan Bautista Diamante was an
early contributor to the genre with his *Triunfo de la paz y el tiempo,* presented in
the Zarzuela in 1659. Another of Diamante's plays, *Alfeo y Aretusa,* was the
first to be called the "fiesta de zarzuela" in a generic sense with a small "z" to
mean no more than two acts, mythological theme and setting, and a great use
of machinery.[77] Other distinguished playwrights to create *fiestas cantadas* were
Juan Matos Fragoso (1608-1689), Antonio de Solís (1610-1686), Juan Vélez de
Guevara (1611-1675), Francisco Antonio de Bances Candamo (1662-1704), and
Antonio de Zamora (1664-1728). One play by Juan Vélez de Guevara, *Los celos
hacen estrellas,* has particular significance today because it represents a complete document of a production, consisting of the libretto text, the music, and
drawings of the scenery used in the production.[78] These various playwrights
worked with several composers, such as Cristóbal Galán, Miguel Ferrer, and
Sebastián Durón, the last one being the director of the Royal Chapel under
Charles II and under Philip V until 1705.

Calderón de la Barca died in Madrid on May 25, 1681. On July 14 of the
following year, the theaters were again closed, this time because of the plague,
but the tradition of opera and zarzuela continued in the fatigued and decaying
court of Spain under Charles II. The final two years of the seventeenth century
saw the resurgence of opera, the first completely sung productions since *Celos*
in 1660 and the first to be called "operas."[79] *Celos vencidos de amor y de amor el
mayor triunfo,* with text by Marcos de Lanuza, the Conde de Clavijo, was performed in 1698, and *Júpiter e Io,* also written by the Conde de Clavijo, was
presented in 1699. Both of these productions indicate the use of orchestras with
strings (including guitars and *vihuelas),* woodwinds, and percussions. As the
operatic tradition continued to develop under the Bourbons, not only in
Madrid, but also in Barcelona, Valencia, Lima, Mexico City, Puebla, and
Havana,[80] the sung recitative became a part of the zarzuela genre in the early
eighteenth century, although it was never to replace the spoken dialogue completely. In the end, the spoken dialogue prevailed, and the zarzuela became the
musical dramas and comedies familiar today.

In 1689, Father Ignacio de Camargo in his *Discurso theologico sobre los theatros
y comedias de este siglo,* spoke against the licentiousness of the music in the
theaters, but ironically paid a great compliment to the state of the art:

> The music of the Spanish theater today is in every
> regard so advanced and so highly developed that it
> seems that it can achieve nothing more. I say this

because the sweet harmony of the instruments, the talent and fineness of the voices, the conceptual sharpness of the notes, the sound and repetition of the refrains, the charm of the affectations, the interest of the drumrolls and the counterpoints make the harmony so smooth that it keeps its listeners entranced and bewitched.[81]

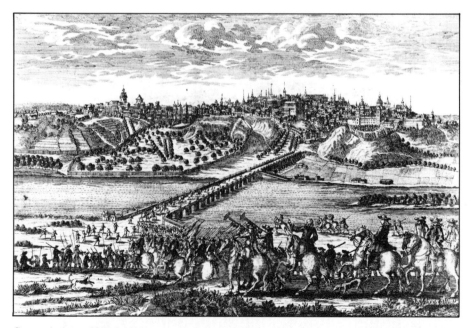

General view of Madrid, seventeenth-century engraving by the Aveline family. Courtesy of the Hispanic Society of America.

Celos aun del aire matan, *1660*

Plot

Aura, a nymph of Diana, has fallen in love with Eróstrato. Pocris, another nymph and Aura's best friend, discovers the love and tells Diana. Diana, who considers love a blasphemy to the principles that she holds dear, orders Aura to be put to death by arrows. Aura cries in lament and condemns Pocris to fall in love herself. Her shout is heard by Céfalo, a noble hunter, who happens to be nearby. Céfalo comes to the aid of Aura and, in so doing, incurs the ire of Diana who threatens Céfalo with her fabled spear that never misses its mark. Venus, never seen, intercedes to resolve the immediate dangers by turning Aura into air and by causing the spear of Diana to fall from Diana's hand. Céfalo retrieves the spear and Diana exits. Pocris, attempting to recover the spear for her mistress, wounds herself with its blade. The scene changes and we see Eróstrato talking to the gardener Rústico. Rústico relates the details of Aura's discovery and transformation, and Eróstrato rushes off into the forest swearing revenge on Diana. Rústico, hearing the approach of his sweetheart Floreta, the servant nymph, hides in order to find out why Diana is questioning Floreta. From Floreta, Diana learns that Rústico admitted Eróstrato to Diana's garden. As a result, she places a spell on Rústico so that each one who sees him will see a different animal. Diana leaves and Rústico approaches Floreta who, upon seeing him as a beast, shouts. Pocris enters to find out why Floreta is shouting and shouts herself. Céfalo and Clarín, his servant, hear the shouts and come to the aid of the women. The act closes with the double love duets of Céfalo-Pocris and Clarín-Floreta, with Pocris clearly rejecting Céfalo's overtures.

Act Two opens with the residents of Lydia bringing offerings to Diana. Eróstrato and Céfalo have both entered the temple with the crowd, Eróstrato to take his revenge and Céfalo to see Pocris again. Clarín does not carry an offering, and Céfalo orders him to pick some fruit from a nearby orchard. In the orchard is Rústico, whom Clarín perceives as a dog. Since the dog is nice to Clarín, he decides to take him as an offering instead of some fruit. The three men present their gifts—Eróstrato a bow and arrow, Céfalo an iris for Pocris, and Clarín a dog for Floreta. Rústico, not able to be understood by the rest, despises the thought that he is a gift for his own sweetheart. In the midst of the celebration, however, Aura appears overhead and expresses her praise of love. Diana cannot tolerate such treason and orders the gifts to be abandoned. She leaves to take her complaint against Venus to Jupiter. Céfalo renews his courtship of Pocris. With Aura's help, Pocris begins to succumb to Céfalo's words of love. Clarín also tries to woo Floreta but Rústico is barking too loudly. They chase him away, and he returns as a wild boar and attacks Clarín. Céfalo enters and hears the explanation of what has happened when he is interrupted by shouts of "Fire!" Eróstrato enters to say that his vengeance, the fire, has been successful. Céfalo says he will go into the inferno to retrieve whom he can. In a final scene of great confusion, Céfalo rescues Pocris as Aura repeats her wish for a vengeance of love against Pocris.

As the curtain rises on Act Three, Pocris and Céfalo are now married, and Diana, incensed by all the treason around her, sends the Furies abroad to cause Eróstrato to flee from people into the hills, to confuse Céfalo's senses, and to make Pocris jealous. To prove that she is not vengeful, Diana has Rústico return to his original form. Pocris does, in fact, wonder why so much of Céfalo's time is spent in hunting, and she asks Clarín what happens on their hunting outings. Clarín says that Céfalo isolates himself from the rest and, lying under a tree, invokes the name of "Laura." Alecto, the Fury, enters and causes Pocris'

The death of Procris, 1695 engraving in Adrien Schoonebeeck's *Pictura loquens.* Courtesy of the Hispanic Society of America.

suspicions to turn to jealousy, correcting the mistake in Clarín's story by repeating the name, "Aura." Pocris, sure that this is part of Aura's revenge on her, determines to disguise herself and follow Céfalo. Eróstrato, now turned into a wild man, has his senses confused by Mejera. He encounters Rústico, back in human form, but Rústico does not recognize Eróstrato in his current state. Céfalo and Clarín enter, hunting, as do Pocris and Floreta, in disguise. Céfalo tells Clarín to wait in the clearing, and Pocris tells Floreta the same thing. Clarín, Floreta, and Rústico then have a conversation to try to clear up some of the misunderstandings, but their talk is interrupted with the shouts of people warning of a fierce beast on the loose. In another part of the forest, Céfalo, hot and tired from the hunt, invokes a breeze to come cool him, using the words "Come, Aura, come," which Pocris understands to be an admission of his love for Aura. Eróstrato comes in, and Tesífone makes sure Céfalo will perceive him as a fierce beast. Eróstrato flees into the forest, and Céfalo begins to pursue. Pocris, not wanting Céfalo to follow such a horrible monster, stands in Céfalo's way, still out of his sight. Céfalo hurls the spear of Diana, and it hits Pocris. He discovers the terrible mistake and learns from Pocris, just before she dies, that she was jealous of Aura. Diana and her nymphs enter, congratulating their victory over love, but Aura appears to undo the tragedy by turning Pocris into a star and Céfalo into a breeze. The play ends as Céfalo and Pocris ascend to heaven in the company of Aura.

Characters

The characters in *Celos* represent several of those common to the *comedia* in general: the *galanes*, Céfalo and Eróstrato; the *damas*, Pocris and Aura; the *graciosos*, Clarín and Rústico; and their female counterpart, Floreta.[82] Seen from another point of view, the characters represent four of Aubrun's categories of characters in the mythological plays: a goddess, two heroes and two nymphs (plus a chorus of nymphs), three servants, and a chorus of shepherds and shepherdesses.[83] The only one of Aubrun's divisions not consistently presented is that of the monster, but we might consider Rústico as such for half the play.

All the women in the play are extraordinarily beautiful. Diana is the goddess, supercilious, vengeful, *pundonorosa*, petty. She knows her power and how to use it. She is a strict authoritarian, a role frequently played by the *padre* in the *comedia*. Pocris is a pale reflection of Diana. She too has a sense of honor and of her obligations as a nymph of Diana, but she is not strong and succumbs to the combined forces of Céfalo, Aura, and Venus. She never really seems comfortable in the love scenes. She spends two full acts rejecting Céfalo and in the last act is querulous and jealous. Love for her clearly is an act of revenge, not a positive state of human existence. Aura, also a nymph of Diana, has the strength of her convictions. She seems to embrace love willingly and to accept the consequences of her acts. She is effective in love, in revenge against Pocris, and in resolution of the plot at the close of the play. She is a clear symbol of the higher state of love. After her transformation, she appears on high and in regal trappings. Floreta is a stock comic figure of the *comedia,* the woman of the subplot for the *graciosos.* She is stupid, flirtatious, naive. The three Furies are standard representations of the classical idea of the Furies—dark, sinister, powerful, scary beings who go about the world wreaking havoc.

The male characters are evenly divided into two nobles and two *graciosos.* The two nobles are alike in their sense of honor and their willingness to pursue love through all kinds of obstacles. Eróstrato is more impulsive, deciding to take vengeance on Diana. He becomes a wild man, a familiar feature of the pastoral tradition. Céfalo is even-tempered; a hunter, a gentleman, a swashbuckler. He is naive and shallow. He abides by the rules and is unable to understand any complication in life. The *graciosos* are comic figures, although Rústico is more comical than Clarín. In a sense, Rústico is the cause of the entire play, because as Diana's gardener he let Eróstrato enter against Diana's wishes. Furthermore, because of his appearance as an animal, he is in a special position to cast light on the comic actions of Floreta and Clarín. He is nevertheless loyal, steadfast in his love for Floreta, and rather courageous, considering his disobedience of Diana. Clarín is a coward and a fool, interested only in the creature comforts of his life, the perfect opposite of the noble values. He is prone to run away from problems, and he is not a very good servant, doing his master's bidding under protest.

There is a chorus of men and a chorus of women. The chorus of women is either one of nymphs or one of shepherdesses; the chorus of men is always one of shepherds. Not only do the choruses in the play serve as background for the actions of the principals, but they provide commentary on the plot, take an

Anonymous engraving of Cephalus and Procris with the dog Laelaps and the infallible spear. Courtesy of the Biblioteca Nacional, Madrid.

active role in the processionals, and serve a vital musical function by reinforc-
ing the strophic variations.

Of all the characters, only Aura, Pocris, and Céfalo are touched by this play,
that is, receive rewards or punishments after the final curtain. The rest, we
may assume, continue their lives as before, Diana with her nymphs and Rústico
with Floreta. What happens to Clarín without his master is a mystery, perhaps
intentionally drawn to show that one who puts nothing into life gets nothing out
of it. The only character to show any lasting personality change through the
action is Pocris. She starts out as a love-hater, succumbs unwillingly to a love
for Céfalo, then is transformed by love at the close. Even this, though, is not
really her doing; it is Aura's. Aura and Céfalo achieve their blessedness
because of the nature of their love. Pocris achieves hers almost as a consolation
for having been killed as a result of the combined vengeance of Diana and
Aura.

Source

The Cephalus and Procris myth comes from Ovid's *Metamorphoses,* Book
VII, lines 661-862, from the *Ars Amatoria,* Book III, lines 685-746, and from
Hyginus, *Fabulae,* 189.[84] When asked about the provenance of his remarkable
spear, Cephalus responds with his story. His wife was Procris, daughter of
Erechtheus and sister of Orithyia. One morning while hunting, Aurora, goddess of the dawn, spied Cephalus and stole him away. Because Cephalus kept
Procris in his heart above Aurora, the latter sent him away with the oath that
he would wish he had never known her. Not satisfied with returning to his
beloved wife, Cephalus decided to disguise himself (with Aurora's help) and to
test her faithfulness. Procris resisted Cephalus' wiles until he promised her
great gifts, upon which she hesitated. At this he chastised her for her
faithlessness. Ashamed, she wandered about the mountains, having dedicated
herself to Diana and chastity. Finally, she returned to Cephalus, giving him as a
gift a dog faster that all the others. In addition, she gave him a spear.

Soon a monster began to plague Thebes, and Cephalus went with the other
youths to capture the beast. The beast, however, was too swift, so the hunters
called upon Cephalus' dog, Laelaps. Both the beast and the dog were so
magnificent in their races that a god turned them both into statues so that
neither would be vanquished. As for the spear, it served Cephalus infallibly,
and, when he had hunted all he wanted on a certain day, he would retire under a
tree and ask the breeze (Aura) to cool him. "Come, Aura, come," he would call,
and he would be refreshed by the cool wind. Someone told Procris of these
occurrences, but misunderstood their meaning. Procris was led to believe that
"Aura" was the name of a nymph, yet she wanted to see for herself. The next
morning Procris followed Cephalus in his pursuits. When once again he called,
"Come, Aura, come," he heard a cry and, thinking it was some beast, hurled his
spear at it, striking Procris. Just before drawing her last breath, she told him
the reason for her death—her suspicion of his relationship with Aura. She died

in his arms with a content expression on her face.

A second, classical source for the play is historical. In 356 B.C. a certain Herostratus, in order to obtain fame, confessed having put to the torch the temple of Diana in Ephesus, then considered as one of the seven wonders of the world. Because this event occurred the same night as the birth of Alexander the Great, Hegesias of Magnesia, a Greek historian, said that Diana could not stop the fire because she was away attending the festivities of the King's birth. Herostratus was condemned to death by the inhabitants of Ephesus, and, under penalty of a similar demise, no one was allowed ever again to pronounce his name.[85]

Of the Cephalus and Procris myth there were several other treatments before and during the Golden Age, including one burlesque play entitled *Céfalo y Pocris* and attributed by some to Calderón himself. In addition, Subirá gives a list of subsequent operatic adaptations of this myth from 1694 to 1792. Whether or not they in any way reflect the effort by Calderón and Hidalgo is unknown.[86]

Myth as Literature

In the Calderonian play, the unfolding of the mythical action between Céfalo and Pocris is not only parallel to, but also dependent upon, the actions of other characters, namely, the lovers Eróstrato and Aura, the two *graciosos* Clarín and Rústico, and the nymph Floreta with whom both the *graciosos* are in love. In addition, the play presents the personification on stage of Diana, now an avenging goddess who acts with all-too-human motives to disrupt the workings of Neo-Platonic and courtly love among the others. All of these characters, both human and divine, have as motivations the traditional *comedia* themes of love, honor, and jealousy. The Baroque elaboration of these themes into a parallel yet interactive structure depends, in part, upon the fact that what remained abstract or nonexistent in the myth, i.e., Aura (Aurora), the beastly target of Céfalo's spear, and the angered gods, are put in love and honor situations of their own that are typical of intrigues one finds in the *comedia*. Aura, the sole object of Pocris' jealousy, is neither a goddess (Aurora) nor an inanimate object (the wind). Instead, she is another nymph of Diana, set to be punished for being in love with Eróstrato. Although she is changed at the last minute into a breeze by Venus, her cries nevertheless call Céfalo to the scene, and he, because of his sense of duty to help a lady in distress, comes into his first ill-fated contact with Diana. Later, when Pocris overhears Céfalo's praise of the breeze, which he calls "Aura," she thinks not of the breeze comforting the hunter but the nymph whom he saved on that earlier occasion. Pocris' jealousy of the air has more substance because of the dramatic realization of the metaphor (Aura-air) and the subsequent connection between the general (air) and the specific (Aura).

The target of the infallible spear (not given to him, but taken by him from Diana with the help of Venus) is not a supposed wild beast in the woods, but

Eróstrato, who has become a wild man, forced to live in the wilderness and bring ruin to others, all because the loss of his loved one, Aura, made him insane. The wild man is a standard person in the *comedia*,[87] but the use of this stock figure again makes concrete and specific the target of Céfalo's spear. Moreover, the plot develops along the lines of its internal logic based on Golden Age themes with the characters not quite so victimized by chance.[88]

The antagonist here is Diana in the role of the avenging authority figure. She is motivated by jealousy and honor, and she takes concrete steps through characters on stage in order to effect her revenge. At various times, she takes revenge on Aura, Pocris, Eróstrato, Céfalo, and Rústico, but she does not win. Her power is not equal to that of Venus. Venus is the only force left in the abstract, but we do have concrete examples of her presence and power: she turns Aura into air, she causes Diana to lose her spear, and she resurrects Pocris and turns her and Céfalo into natural phenomena. This last abstraction is made concrete as we see Céfalo and Pocris ascend to the heavens as the final curtain falls.

As abstract or mythological elements are realized on stage, so too are metaphors and images common to the traditions of the *comedia*.[89]

Love is associated with a great many of the images and metaphors of the courtly and Neo-Platonic love traditions.[90] Love enters through the eyes because the beauty that they behold attracts the soul. As is customary in the *comedia,* all the women in this play are extraordinarily beautiful. It is not surprising that Céfalo should fall in love with Pocris at first sight.

Traditionally, once one has fallen in love, that person may expect all sorts of suffering. Among the negative attributes of love mentioned by name in the course of the dialogue are "yerros," "tristeza," "tragedia," "pena," "dolor," "lágrimas," "suspiro," "pesar," "penar," "sufrir," "lástima," and "infeliz." The *estribillo* of the opening section of the play, "Ay, infeliz de aquella/que hizo verdad haber quien de amor muera," sets the tone for the first part of the play and implies the danger of love's resulting in at least figurative and emotional, if not literal, death. The play opens with the real threat of death for Aura because she has fallen in love. But if love is not necessarily death, it can be a wound to the soul. Pocris and Céfalo act out the wounding when Pocris tries to recover Diana's spear from Céfalo. The spear becomes a symbol of love when Venus causes Diana to drop it in order to prevent her from killing Céfalo. Therefore, the spear, as love, is able to draw real blood when Pocris and Céfalo engage in a lovers' struggle. It is small wonder, then, that Eróstrato warns of the danger of love, especially considering his own situation.

Eróstrato, who is the cause of Aura's love-suffering, leaves civilization and becomes a wild man. This wild-man image is the theatrical realization of love as madness, another standard idea associated with love. Eróstrato's madness leads him to start a fire in Diana's temple to avenge his lover's loss. Earlier in the play, Pocris and Céfalo had mentioned poetically that love was like a fire that could inflame the soul. This real fire, which closes Act Two, is the dramatization of fires of love felt by those characters who oppose Diana.[91]

Yet another dehumanizing effect of love is couched in comic terms. Rústico, servant of Eróstrato, is discovered (through Floreta's indiscretion) in Diana's garden, and Diana has him change, in rapid succession, into a lion, a bear, a wolf, a tiger, and, finally, a whippet. Moreover, he is dressed in skins, adding the uncivilized aspect to the dehumanization of animal masks. As a dog, he becomes Clarín's pet as Clarín courts Rústico's sweetheart, Floreta. In addition to the obvious irony of the love-pursuit situation and the realization of the dehumanizing quality of love, Rústico's plight points out that one in love is not aware of the ill effects of love or how others may perceive those effects.

Naturally, a great deal of the unpleasantness of love is the direct result of jealousy, without which no love in the *comedia* could exist for long. If we include Diana's protection of the chastity of her nymphs as a form of jealousy *(celos de honor),* then clearly that jealousy is the cause of all the plot complications. Diana, jealous of the love between Eróstrato and Aura, causes Aura's removal from the early realm of the stage action. It is the separation that causes Eróstrato's insanity. Moreover, because Diana attacked Céfalo, again to protect her inner sanctum, Céfalo was able to obtain possession of the magical spear. Then, in Act Three, Diana sends forth the Furies to create in the dramatic action a specific cause of Pocris' jealousy with a specific result, from which we derive the title of the play. Diana orders the Furies to make Pocris suspicious of Céfalo's actions and interests, to confuse Céfalo's good hunting skills, and to cause Eróstrato to flee into the forest where Céfalo is. Her motives are clearly on a human level, typical of other love-honor situations in the *comedia.*[92] Céfalo mistakes Eróstrato for a beast, and Pocris for Eróstrato, and kills her. While it is true that this is an example of *engaño a los ojos,* because of the nature of this play in which all the ideas of love are made to have anthropomorphic origins, we can see that this *engaño* is again the direct result of Diana's actions. Naturally, to a purely mortal victim, these inner workings would remain mysterious.

As mentioned earlier, love can very easily lead to death. Céfalo, because of love and jealousy, kills his own wife. What keeps this play from being a tragedy is the added Neo-Platonic idea of love as redeemer. Aura was to be killed by Diana in Act One. Venus intervened and changed her into air. Venus again intervened to cause Diana to drop her spear. The apotheosis of love comes at the close of Act Three when Venus changes Pocris into a star and Céfalo, now Céfiro, into a breeze. Venus clearly wins over Diana.

Although the play is unequivocally based on the ideas of love and its consequences, there are nevertheless two other themes, honor and fate, which are developed. Diana considers the loves of Aura and Pocris as affronts to her honor. We can see in the traditions of honor in the *comedia* a reason for Diana's desire for the death of those whom she perceives to be traitors. On still another level, Céfalo gains his motivation for involvement from honor. Although Clarín warns him against becoming involved from the very beginning, Céfalo responds that it is impossible for him to allow a helpless woman to remain in despair without attempting to rescue her. His sense of honor leads to his love for Pocris.

Fate is a curious force in this play. While the characters often use expressions that should refer to a Christian God, clearly they are not acting within Christian parameters. Because the play is mythological in nature, we are able to see the machinations of the gods, and what might be considered Fate to a real person who cannot know the reasons for some accident here are the actions of anthropomorphic gods who have very human emotions and very human motivations. The frequent use of *deus ex machina* is a manifestation of Fate of a sort, but without the mystery. It is as though the gods as well are functioning on a level *de tejas abajo.*[93]

Moreover, because the actions here are dramatic and not real, they respond to yet another kind of "fate" – literary, dramatic convention. The plot of the Cephalus and Procris myth was set centuries before Calderón.[94] The additions to the plot on the part of Calderón respond in one way or another to conventions of the *comedia.* The use of the two *graciosos* augments and comments on the actions of the heroes. As discussed, the various conceptions and consequences of love in the play were standard fare for the Baroque, and the honor motive was anything but original. But while art in the Baroque was basically imitative and produced its own imperatives, it nevertheless continually tried to achieve the marvelous. *Celos,* because of its elaboration of the original myth, its wide use of many concepts of courtly and Neo-Platonic love, and its dramatic realization of mythological and poetic metaphors, can certainly be said to reflect the desire for *admiratio.*

Literature as Myth

Because *Celos,* as well as other court spectacles, were based on Greco-Roman myths, it might be assumed that such plays would be excellent subjects for interpretive criticism based on mythic, archetypal, and ritualistic considerations. There are a number of reasons why this group of plays offers substantial problems to such an analysis. For example, inherent in the archetypal approach is the belief that a literary work communicates its content to the audience, that the author chose the plot of the work, consciously or not, in such a way as to provide an adequate medium for the theme or idea that he or she was trying to communicate, and that the theme communicated is of such overt or covert depth that it can speak to any audience about those concerns that affect all human beings in a collective way.[95] These court spectacles, however, are first and foremost pageants, spectacles in which the event itself takes precedence over considerations of the plot, character, or theme. A play such as *Celos* was not the result of an author trying to communicate a sense of the human condition to people as a whole; rather it was a work commissioned by one man, viewed by only a few people whose attention was probably more focused on the King and the court than on the play, and subordinated, at least in its effect on its audience, to matters of music, dance, and spectacle.[96] The plot in *Celos* has become a vehicle for extraliterary purposes, but that fact does not keep us from appreciating the play as literature nor from determining its archetypal structure. We should merely be aware that these plays pose special problems in our search for literary "truth" because they are, in fact, excellent examples of compromised poetry.

Having dispensed with the necessary *caveat,* we can now begin to perceive in *Celos* some rather unexpected archetypal associations. Clearly, the play is the rebirth after adversity of the two lovers. Céfalo and Pocris, who have been fighting not only outside forces but each other as well in their search for common bonds of love, finally find peace and a unity of spirit in the heavens. What is somewhat troubling about their apotheosis is that something so simple as an honorable love between a man and a woman should not be allowed to occur without dire consequences while they are still earthbound mortals. The nature of the preconditions to the plot provide the reasons for their lack of worldly success. Pocris (as well as Aura) has already made a pledge to the goddess Diana to uphold her ideals of chastity and to reject Venus totally. As a result, the two nymphs have already made a religious vow; to break that vow, to deceive the (or a) divinity, is naturally bad *mana* and sure to result in destruction. Pocris' rejections of Céfalo throughout all of Act One and much of Act Two are manifestations of her devotion to Diana; her jealousy in Act Three is a result of the revenge of the goddess.

The organization of the cosmos as seen in this play has Jupiter as a rather remote god who serves in an appellate capacity in cases of altercations between lesser gods. In this case, these two lesser goddesses are Venus and Diana. While the two of them do not actually represent opposite poles of the human condition (good and evil, for example), they do indeed have antithetical attributes. Diana, in *Celos,* is seen only in terms of fierceness, rage, and revenge. Her very ideals of chastity are unnatural in this world where male-female bonding is necessary for the preservation of the species. Yet she also represents work, the hunt, "paradise lost," as it were. The peasants, who labor to bring forth the crops, return a portion of those crops to her in sacrifice. She represents the necessary but unpleasant aspects of human existence: the need to eat and, therefore, to work, the predisposition to violence necessary to survive in a violent world, the world apart from considerations of love and sex.

Venus, on the other hand, is love, respite, and redemption. It is of some interest that Venus never appears in the course of the play. We come to know Diana as a goddess with human attributes, perhaps because she is the deification of the baser aspects of existence. Venus, however, has ultimate control over the plot without ever appearing on stage. It is precisely her nonappearance that gives Venus a much more symbolic role in the plot, for we cannot accuse her of human failings: she never appears in human form.[97] In the cosmography of this play, Venus has superiority over Diana, and, it may be assumed, the backing of Jupiter in the dispute over the fate of Céfalo and Pocris. Diana goes to appeal her defeat to Jupiter, but there will be no change in the outcome. As a result, one may deduce that the love principle takes precedence over the violence principle.

That the lovers die anyway is not so easily understood in terms of the mythic structure as discussed thus far. Of the various pairs of lovers in the play (Céfalo-Pocris, Eróstrato-Aura, Rústico-Floreta, and Clarín-Floreta), the only one with any possible chance of success in this life is that of Rústico and Floreta, and even with them we are not sure how they end the play. Eróstrato is forced to abandon a community of men and live a life of animalistic despera-tion. His situation is different from that of Céfalo in that his beloved is no longer within his reach. In the terms of the play, with the love-element having been taken from him, he can only resort to its alternative, violence. His violence leads to destruction when he burns the temple of Diana, and he cannot possibly hope to win in a contest with the goddess on her own vengeful terms. She causes his lovesick madness to become true insanity and then animalism. It is love that ennobled man and separated him from the beasts; the deprivation of that love takes his civilization and humanity from him. He is, of course, not an animal, because he still has the capacity for noble love, but in appearance he cannot be distinguished from lower forms. Likewise, Rústico is kept apart from love because of his animal appearance. Having been changed into a beast through Diana's anger, he cannot pursue his love for Floreta. Only when, again through the actions of the goddess, he regains his human appearance is he able to assert his love and preempt Clarín's overtures to his beloved.

To return to the question of the satisfactory reunification of the principals after death, however, one must enter yet another series of mythic associations. The redemption of life's suffering through divine grace after death is one of the most important myths to the Christian faith, especially to the Catholic doctrine to which Calderón adhered. Metaphors and images typically associated with Christian literature throughout Europe in the Middle Ages, and in Spain through the Counterreformation, speak of the acceptance of this myth as the true condition of man in both life and death. Life as a vale of tears, death as the great reward, the *topoi* of *memento mori* and *desengaño* among others are all themes that illustrate the redemptive quality of Christian death. Love for Calderón is paradoxical in that the human spirit can accept only a spiritual love while the body demands a sensual, and therefore imperfect, love. These two contradictory facets of love keep secular love from achieving total satisfaction in this life.[98] Even though *Celos* is based on pagan plot elements, its morality is Christian and orthodox: love (Christ/Venus) will prevail over hate and destruc-tion (Satan/Diana) for true disciples (Christians/Aura, Céfalo, and Pocris). Such belief may in fact lead to great hardship while on earth, even to ostracism by an unfriendly society (Eróstrato), but the rewards are great in the end. This cou-pling of pagan and Christian myths is one of the great master-strokes of

Calderón and the Baroque.[99] The commonality of those myths with collective myths found in human societies on the whole (for example, the struggle between creation and destruction, life after death, redemption through religious faith) keeps the mythological plays intelligible to any human society in any age.

In conclusion, we find that the moral of *Celos aun del aire matan* is not so different from that of any number of other Golden Age plays, namely, that life is a struggle subject to the whims of fate and divine providence, that in the final analysis love and faith will win out over distrust and destruction, and that, in the meantime, a human being must continue to strive towards goals of honor, justice, and dignity as though there were no higher forces exerting pressure on human lives and actions. The moral, the theme, the plot structure, the presentation, and the poetry are all conventional;[100] the play may be appreciated for the artistry of Calderón in combining all these component elements with music, dance, and machine spectacle in a single work consistent with Christian interpretation of pagan myths. *Celos* is, above all else, a work of the Spanish Baroque in its ability to focus diffuse and disparate elements into a unified and satisfying whole.

Metric and Stylistic Considerations

Versification

Act One
1-356	Silva en asonancia (e-a)
357-386	Silva de consonantes
387-430	Seguidillas
431-562	Cuartetas (8-8-12-12) semilibres
563-699	Romance (ó) con estribillo

Act Two
700-710	Romance dodecasílabo (u-e) con estribillo
711-726	Romance (u-e)
727-733	Romance dodecasílabo (u-e) con estribillo
734-833	Romance (u-e)
834-840	Romance dodecasílabo (u-e) con estribillo
841-876	Romance (u-e)
877-884	Romance dodecasílabo (u-e)

885-899	Estancias de 7 y 11 (abbaA)
900-903	Cuarteta de 8 y 10 (abBA)
904-908	Estancias de 7 y 11 (abbaA)
909-920	Villancico (abba:*ac*:*c*dde:ED)
921-930	Estancias de 7 y 11 (abbaA)
931-978	Villancico (abba:*ac*:*c*dde:ED)
979-994	Romance (é)
995-998	Romancillo (é)
999-1010	Romance (é)
1011-1014	Romancillo (é)
1015-1102	Romance (é)
1103-1106	Romancillo (é)
1107-1165	Romance (é)
1166-1168	Romance endecasílabo (é)
1169-1188	Estancias (8-8-8-11-11)
1189-1200	Romance (é)
1201-1213	Romancillo (é)
1214-1283	Romance (é)
1284-1309	Silva de consonantes
1310-1393	Romance (e-o)
1394-1396	Octosílabos monorrimos
1397-1424	Romance (e-o)
1425-1428	Octosílabos monorrimos
1429-1432	Romance (e-o)

Act Three

1433-1508	Endechas reales
1509-1560	Romance semilibre de arte mayor (10, 11 y 12) (í)
1561-1608	Sextetos-liras de 7 y 11 (aBaBcC)
1609-1742	Romance (a-a)
1743-1838	Redondillas (abba)
1839-1886	Romancillo (i-o)
1887-1896	Quintillas
1897-1934	Romancillo (i-o)
1935-1949	Quintillas
1950-1969	Romancillo (i-o)
1970-1974	Quintilla
1975-2104	Seguidillas
2105-2167	Villancicos (abba:ac*c*)
2168-2319	Romance (a-a)
2320-2329	Estancias de 7 y 11 (aBabA)
2330-2346	Romance (o-e)
2347-2350bis	Romancillo (o-e)
2351-2410	Romance (o-e) con estribillo (11-12)

Analysis: The figures in this chart represent the number of lines and the corresponding percentages of each metric type in each act and in the play as a whole.

	Act One	Act Two	Act Three	Total
Romance	137 (19.6)	525 (71.6)	363 (37.1)	1025 (42.5)
Romancillo	0	25 (3.4)	110 (11.3)	135 (5.6)
Romance de arte mayor	0	36 (4.9)	52 (5.3)	88 (3.7)
Silva	356 (50.9)	0	0	356 (14.8)
Silva de consonantes	30 (4.3)	26 (3.6)	0	56 (2.3)
Seguidillas	44 (6.3)	0	130 (13.3)	174 (7.2)
Redondillas	0	0	96 (9.8)	96 (4.0)
Endechas reales	0	0	76 (7.8)	76 (3.2)
Cuartetas	132 (18.9)	4 (0.5)	0	136 (5.6)
Quintillas	0	0	30 (3.1)	30 (1.2)
Estancias de 7 y 11	0	30 (4.1)	10 (1.0)	40 (1.7)
Estancias de 8 y 11	0	20 (2.7)	0	20 (0.8)
Sexteto-lira	0	0	48 (4.9)	48 (2.0)
Villancicos	0	60 (8.2)	63 (6.4)	123 (5.1)
Octosílabos monorrimos	0	7 (1.0)	0	7 (0.3)

The analysis of the versification scheme reveals a number of interesting facts.[101] First, Act One is considerably less polymetric than either of the later two acts. Second, despite the fact that *romances* of various lengths make up half of the total number of verses, there is a surprising variety in the versification of the others. *Seguidillas* account for more than seven per cent of the total verses, and *silvas* for almost fifteen per cent. The true interest in the versification in this play, however, is in the number of atypical verses. One hundred thirty-six lines can only be classified as *cuartetas* since they have varying meters and rhyme schemes; some of them are only *semilibres* at best, showing remarkable irregularity within a general pattern. Moreover, there are two kinds of *estancia,* the first being almost a *lira* except that it rhymes aBabA instead of aBabB, the second being a totally new combination of three lines of 8 plus two of 11. The *villancicos* are not what might be considered traditional *villancicos* in that they do not necessarily state the refrain at the beginning, and the *mudanza* part of both is rather more elaborate than that usually associated with the popular verse form.[102] Nevertheless, instead of referring to them as slightly irregular *estancias,* I prefer to consider them as slightly irregular *villancicos* because of their use of the refrains.

In addition to the variety of metric forms, there are other stylistic features of *Celos* that can be attributed to the interaction between the text and the music. The most outstanding of these phenomena is the use of nine different refrains.

These *estribillos* are the poetic equivalents of musical *ritornelli,* and the action of the play can be said to develop around these refrains. As some of the refrains change over the course of the play, they reflect some of the transformational aspects of the characters, especially those due to Venus. The following is a list of the refrains (and their variations) and the line numbers corresponding to their usage.

1. a. "¡Ay, infeliz de aquella
      que hizo verdad haber quien de amor muera!"
                         (13-14, 27-28, 41-42, 97-98, 207-8)
   b. "¡No ya infeliz de aquella
      que hizo verdad haber quien de amor muera!"
                         (227-28, 249-50)

2.   "Inspire suave el aura de amor."
                         (623, 652, 661, 666, 699)

3.   "Venid, moradores de Lidia, venid,
      venid, que hoy de marzo la luna se cumple . . ."
                         (700, 708, 731, 838, 877)

4. a. "¡Muera el amor y viva el olvido,
      viva el olvido y muera el amor!"
                         (902-3, 919-20, 941-42, 953-54, 965-66)
   b. "¡Viva el amor y muera el olvido,
      muera el olvido y viva el amor!"
                         (977-78)

5.   "no enmienda al amar
      el aborrecer."
                         (997-98, 1013-14, 1105-6, 1129-30, 1203-4,
                         1212-13)

6.   "si el aire diere celos,
      celos aun del aire matan."
                         (1735-36, 1739-40, 1741-42, 1769-70, 1781-82
                         1837-38, 2318-19)

7.   "Pocris por quien muero,
      Aura por quien vivo."
                         (1923-24, 1925-26, 1933-34, 1968-69)

8.   "Ven, Aura, ven."
                         (2111, 2112, 2118, 2125, 2126, 2132, 2139, 2140,
                         2146, 2153, 2154, 2156, 2160, 2167)

9.   "que aunque son nobles tal vez las venganzas,
      tal vez blasonadas desdicen de nobles."
                         (2353-54, 2367-68, 2389-90, 2399-2400, 2409-10)

Existing Versions of *Celos aun del aire matan* used in this edition

Manuscripts

L   Until 1927, there was no tangible evidence that Spain had ever produced a fully sung opera in the Golden Age. José Subirá had the good fortune to
find a manuscript of Act One of *Celos* in the library of the Palacio de Liria in
Madrid. Located in Caja 174, no. 21, the cover of the manuscript bears the title:
Musica de la Comedia Zelos aun de del Ayre matan. | Primera jornada |
Del | M.° Juan Hidalgo. Subirá announced his discovery in *La música en la
casa de Alba* (1927) and later he published the *voz y bajo* parts in *Celos aun del
aire matan: Opera del siglo XVII,* using Hartzenbusch's *BAE* edition for correc-
tions. His discovery was further heralded by Otto Ursprung and Charles van
den Borren who, along with other musicologists, mentioned the historical
importance of the document even if they did not agree on its musical
excellence.[103]

E   In 1942, Luis Freitas Branco, while working in the Public Library in
Evora, Portugal, discovered yet another manuscript of the text with musical
voz y bajo accompaniment for *Celos aun del aire matan.* The manuscript is in
three paste-and-parchment bound volumes, catalogued together under the
number CL 1/2-1.

Volume One, which contains Act One, has 40 folios of music with 4 additional

Folio 26^r of Act One of the Evora Manuscript of *Celos aun del aire matan,* corresponding
to lines 491-97 of the text. Courtesy of the Biblioteca Pública, Evora.

folios as flysheets. The title on the cover reads: No. 3 | Zelos aun del Ayre matan | Comedia de D. Pedro Calderon | Muzica de Juan Hidalgo | voz |1ª Jornada. The recto of the first flysheet bears the catalogue number. The recto of the second flysheet repeats the title: Musica de la Comedia | Zelos aun del ayre matan | (Rubric) | 1ª Jornada | Musica de Juan Hidalgo. The final two flysheets are blank. The cover dimensions are 290mm x 215mm; the pages are 282mm x 211mm, irregularly cut. Pages are numbered twice, one set occurring regularly in pen every four folios (indicating pagination prior to the cutting and binding of the folded pages), another set occurs regularly in pencil on the recto of each folio that contains music and text. It is evident from the sequence of pages of music that it was written with binding in mind and not on long sheets folded later.

Volume Two, which contains Act Two, has 50 folios plus four flysheet folios. On the cover is written: No. 4 | Zelos aun del Ayre Matan | Muzica de | voz | 2ª Jornada. On the recto of the first flysheet appears the catalogue number. On the recto of the second flysheet is the title: Musica de la Comedia | Zelos aun del ayre matan | (Rubric) | 2ª Jornada. Folio 50 has musical staffs drawn in but neither music nor text. The final two flysheets are blank. The cover dimensions are 292mm x 212mm. The pages are 280mm x 208mm, irregularly cut. Pages are numbered only on the recto of each folio. The handwriting is different from that of Act One.

Folio 27ʳ of Act Two of the Evora Manuscript of *Celos aun del aire matan,* corresponding to lines 1122-33 of the text. Courtesy of the Biblioteca Pública, Evora.

Volume Three, which contains Act Three, has 59 folios plus four flysheet folios. On the cover is the title: No. 5 | Zelos aun del Ayre Matan | voz | 3ª Jornada. Flysheet one bears the catalogue number. Flysheet two repeats the title: Muzica de la Comedia | Zelos aun del ayre matan | (Rubric) | 3ª Jornada. Folio 59ᵛ has musical staffs drawn in but neither music nor text. The final two flysheets are blank. The cover dimensions are 298mm x 213mm; the pages are 286mm x 210mm, irregularly cut. Pages are numbered twice as in Act One. The handwriting is different from those of Acts One and Two.

In general, pages each have four to five double lines of music (*voz y bajo*) with text between the lines. There are numerous errors in copying and several omissions of text. There are instances in which text or character notations have been cut off because of the binding, thus indicating that, even though the pages were written to be bound, they were written before the binding took place. The binding, paper, and handwriting are typical of manuscripts of the late seventeenth and early eighteenth centuries. Some abrasions in the paper cover reveal underneath printed matter of the era used as binding material.

The manuscript most probably made its way to Evora through the acquisitions of Don Fr. Manuel do Cenáculo Vilas-Boas, the archbishop of Evora who began the library in 1805 and who was particularly interested in acquiring manuscripts and music.[104] Many musicologists have expressed opinions on the value of the music.[105] Although such musical evaluation is beyond the scope of this edition, it is worth noting that in general the music reflects the text with respect to both syllabification and emotional effect, implying that Calderón and Hidalgo must have been in agreement about the music and its textual underlay.[106] The music does, however, reflect a very strong Spanish musical heritage with its use of syncopation (hemiola) and refrains which are possibly an artistic reworking of sixteenth-century popular *villancicos*.[107] In addition, certain Italian elements are evident in the "Pocris bella" lament in Act Three, and we know that the opening song of Act Three became popular and was included in published collections of songs.[108]

Published versions

Celos aun del aire matan was curiously omitted from any of the authorized *Partes* collected and published by Calderón's brother José.[109] The play has never been published in a paleographic edition although Subirá made initial attempts at comparing previous versions in "Calderón de la Barca, libretista de ópera: Consideraciones literario-musicales." In that article he made reference to his version of the text and music based on the Evora manuscript. Since that time (1966), however, no such work has been forthcoming. In comparing the following editions, one finds many insignificant variations and several major ones. The choice of text that appears in this edition does not always depend upon the antiquity of the version. As E. M. Wilson indicated, the fact that a text is earlier does not mean it is better.[110]

C   "La gran comedia, Zelos avn del ayre matan. Fiesta que se representó á
sus Magestades en el Buen Retiro. Cantada. De don Pedro Calderón." In vol.
XIX of *Comedias nuevas escogidas de los mejores ingenios de España.* Por Domingo García y Morras. Madrid: Imprenta Real (Melchor Sánchez), 1663.
According to Valbuena Briones, this is to be considered the *editio princeps* of
the published versions.[111]

P   "La gran comedia, Zelos avn del aire matan. Fiesta que se representó á
sus Magestades en el Buen Retiro. Cantada. De don Pedro Calderón." In *Parte
qvarenta y vna, de famosas comedias de diversos avtores.* Pamplona: Ioseph del
Espíritu Santo, n.d.[112]

V   "No. 307. La gran comedia, Zelos aun del ayre matan. Fiesta cantada,
que se hizo á sus Magestades en el Coliseo de Buen Retiro. De don Pedro
Calderón." In vol. VII of *Comedias verdaderas del célebre poeta español don Pedro
Calderón de la Barca . . . Nueuamente corr., publicó don Juan de Vera Tassis y
Villarroel.* Madrid: Viuda de Blas de Villanueva, 1683.[113]

J   "No. 307. La gran comedia, Zelos avn del ayre matan. Fiesta que se
representó á sus Magestades en el Buen Retiro. Cantada. De don Pedro
Calderón de la Barca." In Parte XXVI of *Jardín ameno, de varias y hermosas
flores, cuyos matices, son doze Comedias, escogidas de los mejores Ingenios de
España. Y las ofrece a los curiosos, vn aficionado.* Madrid: n.p., 1704.

M   La gran comedia, Zelos avn del ayre matan. Fiesta cantada que se hizo
á sus Magestades en el Coliseo del Buen-Retiro. De don Pedro Calderón de la
Barca." In *Septima parte de Comedias del celebre poeta español, D. Pedro Calderón
de la Barca . . . Que nvevamente corregidas, publicó Don Jvan de Vera Tassis y
Villarroel su mayor amigo.* Madrid: Juan Sanz, 1715.

T   "La gran comedia. Zelos aun del ayre matan. Fiesta cantada, que se hizo
á sus Magestades en el Coliseo del Buen-Retiro. De don Pedro Calderón de la
Barca." In vol. X of *Comedias del célebre poeta español don Pedro Calderón de la
Barca, que saca a luz don Juan Fernández de Apontes, y las dedica al mismo don
Pedro Calderón de la Barca.* Madrid: Viuda de M. Fernández, 1763.

B   "Num. 78. Comedia famosa. Zelos aun del ayre matan. Fiesta cantada
que se hizo á SS. MM. en el Coliseo de Buen-Retiro. De don Pedro Calderón de
la Barca." Barcelona: Francisco Suria y Burgada, n.d. Published "A costas de la
Compañía."[114]

H   "Celos aun del aire matan, Fiesta cantada." In vol. III of *Comedias de don*

Pedro Calderón de la Barca. In vol. XII of Biblioteca de Autores Españoles. Ed. Juan Eugenio Hartzenbusch. Madrid: Atlas, 1945, pp. 473-88.

S   *Celos aun del aire matan: Opera del siglo XVII. Texto de Calderón y música de Juan Hidalgo.* Ed. José Subirá. Barcelona: Institut d'Estudis Catalans, Biblioteca de Catalunya, 1933. Edition of L manuscript.

A   "Celos aun del aire matan." In vol. I of *Obras completas.* By Pedro Calderón de la Barca. Ed. Angel Valbuena Briones. Madrid: Aguilar, 1959, pp. 1785-1814.

R   Pitts, Ruth E. L. "Don Juan Hidalgo, Seventeenth-Century Spanish Composer." Diss. George Peabody College for Teachers 1968, pp. 152-81. Pitts presents a study of the music but does not present the full text or the full partitura. Moreover, she made several textual changes without explanation.

G   García Valdecasas, José Guillermo, and Andrada Vanderwilde, trans. and adapt. "Celos, aun del aire, matan: (Céfalo y Pocris) de Pedro Calderón de la Barca." Madrid: José Guillermo García Valdecasas, 1977. Unpublished, unbound typescript of version of Evora manuscript with changes made by the editors. Superficial introductory notes, no explanations of changes. Consulted after this current elaboration was completed. Found in the Biblioteca Nacional (Madrid), catalogue number M 32[13].

This Edition

This edition is the result of an interdisciplinary project at Trinity University to bring to the public the first modern production of *Celos aun del aire matan.* As such, the work on the edition was done in collaboration with Gerald R. Benjamin, Associate Professor of Music, Trinity University, whose critical edition of the music by Juan Hidalgo is to be published separately. The purposes of the project are several: 1) to commemorate the three-hundredth anniversary of the death of Calderón de la Barca in 1981; 2) to publish the first critical edition of one of Calderón's lesser-known mythological plays; 3) to bring to the non-Spanish-speaking public a translation of *Celos.* In large part, this project was made possible by a grant from the Ewing Halsell Foundation of San Antonio, Texas, and by internal funding by Trinity University.

The Spanish text as it appears is based on the Evora manuscript. As such, it does not necessarily represent the "best" edition of the play but the one that most nearly adheres to the only complete handwritten version in existence. It has been necessary to make certain textual changes, of course, and those changes are indicated in the text in the following manner:

–Punctuation, capitalization, and accentuation have been modernized without notation or explanation.

—Asides and parenthetical remarks are set off by dashes rather than parentheses.

—All changes and additions to the text are indicated by the use of brackets in the Spanish text. Spelling has been changed only when the change is morphemic (as in the change from *ves* to *vez*). Missing words or letters have been supplied from other sources as have been alterations in the Evora text. Such alterations occur only in the event of obvious miscopying or unintelligibility in the manuscript, or in those cases in which the syllables of a line do not fit the music and alternate versions provide a better textual underlay for the music. All stage directions have been added and the Hartzenbusch (H) version found in *BAE* is the source for the additions. All the changes and additions listed here are mentioned in the footnotes and, when more information is necessary, in the endnotes, with one exception. Only when the Hartzenbusch stage directions have been altered for use in this edition is there any indication of the stage directions in the footnotes.

—All words or letters deleted from the Evora version remain in the Spanish text between parentheses. Such deletions are indicated in the footnotes as well.

—Contractions and abbreviations found in the Evora text are noted here by italics in the text and by underscoring in the character notations in the left margin. No further notation of such changes appears.

In addition, markings to indicate choral participation have been left as "A4" and "A8" when they appear as such in the manuscript. Due to the great number of lines that contain metrical irregularities, no attempt has been made to indicate all the instances of dieresis in the Spanish text. Line numbers are continuous throughout, but exact textual and musical repetitions (such as the duet between Tesífone and Pocris in Act Three) are considered one line of text but two lines of music. As a general rule, music repetitions that are not part of the plot are not considered in this edition.

The footnotes are by line number. The marking "Ac." after a line number refers to the stage direction following the line number indicated with the exception of those directions at the opening of the play, which are noted as "1 Ac." Versions are noted by a letter corresponding to a particular version. The letter designations are those listed in "Versions" above. Within the footnotes, different variations of the same textual entry are separated by a semi-colon; different entries found on the same line are separated by a virgule. In addition to the textual alterations, the few musical notations (such as "despacio") that occur in the manuscript are also indicated in the footnotes.

The endnotes provide explanations of archaisms found in the Spanish text and more detailed information concerning alterations made in the Spanish text, problems in translation, and factual documentation to aid in reading the text. The endnotes are not those of a teaching edition, but neither do they suppose a profound knowledge of Golden Age theater.

The translation that accompanies the text is not to be considered an artistic work in itself. No attempt has been made to adjust the English syllabification to fit the Spanish, but the translation does follow the Spanish line for line as much as possible. The English version provides a working translation of the Spanish for basic comprehension and does not pretend to compete with the artistic creations of poetic translations.[115]

Notes

1. The factual information in this history represents a concordance among the following sources: Emilio Cotarelo y Mori, "Actores famosos del siglo XVII: Sebastián de Prado y su mujer Bernarda Ramírez," *BRAE,* 2 (1915), 251-93, 425-57, 583-621, and 3 (1916), 3-38, 151-85; Cotarelo, *Historia de la zarzuela* (Madrid: Tipografía de Archivos, 1934); Cotarelo, *Orígenes y establecimiento de la ópera en España hasta 1800* (Madrid: Tipografía de la *RABM,* 1917); Hugo A. Rennert, *The Spanish Stage in the Time of Lope de Vega* (New York: Hispanic Society of America, 1909); N. D. Shergold, *A History of the Spanish Stage* (Oxford: Clarendon Press, 1967); and Robert Stevenson, ed., Introduction to *La púrpura de la rosa,* by Pedro Calderón de la Barca (Lima: Instituto Nacional de Cultura, 1976), pp. 15-68.

2. For a discussion of early *vihuelistas* and their music, see José Subirá, "Le style dans la musique théâtrale espagnole," *Acta Musicologica,* fasc. 2 (1932), 69.

3. Rennert, *The Spanish Stage,* pp. 69-71, offers quotes from contemporary critics. For an encyclopedic treatment of the subject of the moral licitude of the theater in the Golden Age, see Emilio Cotarelo y Mori, *Bibliografía de las controversias sobre la licitud del teatro en España* (Madrid: Tipografía de la *RABM,* 1904).

4. Cf. Lope's dedication of *La selva sin amor:* ". . . Cantaban las figuras los versos, haciendo en la misma composición de la música las admiraciones, las quejas, los amores, las iras y los demas efectos," in *Obras escogidas,* ed. Federico Sainz de Robles, 3d ed. (Madrid: Aguilar, 1967), III, 531-32.

5. For a study of the *tonadilla,* see José Subirá, *La tonadilla escénica,* 3 vols. (Madrid: Tipografía de Archivos, 1928-1930).

6. Jacobean masques were considerably more complex and elaborate than the *mojigangas,* but different in scope from the Spanish court spectacles. See Enid Welsford, *The Court Masque: A Study in the Relationship between Poetry and the Revels* (New York: Russell and Russell, 1962); Stephen Orgel, *The Jonsonian Masque* (Cambridge: Harvard Univ. Press, 1965); Stephen Orgel and Roy Strong, *Iñigo Jones: The Theatre of the Stuart Court,* 2 vols. (Berkeley: Univ. of Calif. Press, 1973); and Percy Simpson and C. F. Bell, *Designs by Iñigo Jones for Masques and Plays at Court* (New York: Russell and Russell, 1924; rpt. 1966). The latter two sources are well illustrated.

7. Gerald E. Wade, "A Note on a Seventeenth-Century *Comedia* Perfor-

mance," *BCom,* 10 (1958), 10-12, provides a prejudiced but interesting account of a *comedia* performance offered by a visiting Englishman.

8. The biographical information on King Philip IV is from Martin Hume, *The Court of Philip IV* (London: Eveleigh Nash, 1907).

9. Rennert, *The Spanish Stage,* pp. 234-36, provides a complete list of these *particulares.*

10. A discussion of the presentation of *La gloria de Niquea* and other early lyric dramas can be found in Charles V. Aubrun, "Les débuts du drame lyrique en Espagne," in *Le Lieu théâtral à la Renaissance,* ed. Jean Jacquot (Paris: Editions du Centre National de la Recherche Scientifique, 1964), pp. 423-44.

11. For an overview of the origins of Italian opera, see Donald J. Grout, *A Short History of Opera* (New York: Columbia Univ. Press, 1947), pp. 27-47.

12. Sebastian Neumeister, *Mythos und Repräsentation: Die mythologischen Festspiele Calderóns* (Munich: Fink, 1978), p. 48; Subirá, "Le style," p. 69.

13. Lope de Vega, p. 531.

14. Felipe Pedrell, "L'Eclogue *La Forêt sans amour,"* *Sammelbände der International Musik-Gesellschaft,* 11 (1909), 55-104, and "La Musique indigène dans le théâtre espagnol du XVIIe siècle," also in *Sammelbände,* 5 (1903), 46-90; Cotarelo, *Historia,* p. 37.

15. José Subirá, "La ópera 'castellana' en los siglos XVII y XVIII," *Segismundo,* 1 (1965), 26; Stevenson, *La púrpura,* p. 16.

16. For a list of performances in the Alcázar from 1623-37 and 1653-54, see N. D. Shergold and J. E. Varey, "Some Palace Performances of Seventeenth-Century Plays," *BHS,* 40 (1963), 212-44; and, by the same authors, *Representaciones palaciegas: 1630-99* (London: Tamesis, 1977).

17. The biographical data on Calderón represents, unless otherwise indicated, a concordance among the following sources: Cristóbal Pérez Pastor, *Documentos para la biografía de D. Pedro Calderón de la Barca* (Madrid: Fortanet, 1905); "Pedro Calderón de la Barca," in *Enciclopedia universal ilustrada europeo-americana* (Madrid: Espasa-Calpe, 1908-1933), X, 655-63; Emilio Cotarelo y Mori, *Ensayo sobre la vida y obras de Calderón* (Madrid: Tipografía de la *RABM,* 1924); Everett W. Hesse, *Calderón de la Barca* (New York: Twayne, 1967); and Jack Sage, "Calderón," in *Die Musik in Geschichte und Gegenwart,* ed. F. Blume, vol. XV (Kassel: Bärenreiter, 1973), 1248-1251.

18. Cotarelo, *Ensayo,* pp. 62 and 71, mentions only that Calderón went to the University of Alcalá in 1614 and that he spent five years studying at the Colegio Imperial. Hesse, *Calderón,* p. 11, takes that to mean that he was in the Colegio from 1608 to 1613. Sage, "Calderón," p. 1248, places the dates at from 1609 to 1614. The *Enciclopedia universal* article says that Calderón was still in the Colegio in 1615, and only spent two years in Salamanca (1617-1619).

19. Ernst Robert Curtius, *European Literature and the Latin Middle Ages,* trans. Willard R. Trask (New York: Pantheon, 1953), p. 568; Neumeister, *Mythos,* p. 107.

20. "Calderón," *Enciclopedia universal,* X, 657.

21. Angel Valbuena Prat, *Calderón: Su personalidad, su arte dramático, su estilo y sus obras* (Barcelona: Juventud, 1941), p. 19.

22. José María Cossío, *Fábulas mitológicas en España* (Madrid: Espasa-Calpe, 1952), pp. 610-11.

23. "Se Acicalaron Los Auditorios," in *The Literary Mind of Medieval and Renaissance Spain* (Lexington: Univ. of Kentucky Press, 1970), p. 125.

24. Helmut Hatzfeld, *Estudios sobre el barroco*, 3d ed. (Madrid: Gredos, 1972), pp. 224-51, gives an excellent overview of Baroque and Manneristic elements in Golden Age literature.

25. Léo Rouanet, "Un autographe inédit de Calderón," *RH*, 6 (1899), 197-98.

26. N. D. Shergold, "The First Performance of Calderón's *El mayor encanto amor*," *BHS*, 35 (1958), 24-27.

27. Shergold, *A History*, illustrations 3, 29, and 30, show grounds plans of the Buen Retiro including the Coliseo.

28. Juan Antonio Pellicer y Tobar, *Avisos históricos*, in *Semanario erudito*, ed. A. Valladares (Madrid: Don Blas Román, 1788), XXXI, 139, cited in Shergold, *A History*, p. 299.

29. Cotarelo, "Actores," p. 596, cites Barrionuevo's *Aviso* of 27 February 1656 (ed. A Paz y Melia [Madrid: M. Tello, 1892-94]), in which he relates a similar event. Cotarelo casts doubt upon the reliability of the information, however.

30. Gaspar de Sobremonte, "Información por decreto de Felipe IV referente al intento de incendio del Coliseo del Buen Retiro," in "Papeles del Buen Retiro," 1662, Biblioteca Nacional (Madrid), MS. 2280; cited in Shergold, *A History*, pp. 325-27.

31. José Subirá, *Celos aun del aire matan: Opera del siglo XVII. Texto de Calderón y música de Juan Hidalgo* (Barcelona: Institut d'Estudis Catalans, 1933), p. x.

32. *La púrpura*, p. 19.

33. W. G. Chapman, "Las comedias mitológicas de Calderón," *Revista de Literatura*, 5 (1954), 35.

34. *A History*, p. 311.

35. *Ibid.*, p. 312. Based on Rennert, *The Spanish Stage*, pp. 108-9n., we know the following particulars concerning Spanish money in the seventeenth century: 1 ducado = 11 reales; 1 real plata = 34 maravedís; 5 reales plata = 12 reales vellón; 74 reales vellón = 4 pieces of eight = 1 doblón. The value of the coins is hard to determine, but Rennert cites statistics to the effect that room and board for a man and his servant in 1596 cost 4 ducats (or 44 reales). For comparison, Rennert also cites (p. 107) the fact that a satin skirt cost 330 reales in 1602.

36. Pedro Calderón de la Barca, *La fiera, el rayo y la piedra*, with *loa* by Francisco Figueroa, 1690, Biblioteca Nacional (Madrid), MS. 14614, with 25 illustrations first published by Angel Valbuena Prat, "La escenografía de una comedia de Calderón," *AEAA*, 6 (1930), 1-16.

37.   Cf. Orgel and Strong, and Simpson and Bell, for English seventeenth-century perspective stage plans. Barnard Hewitt, ed., *The Renaissance Stage: Documents of Serlio, Sabbattini, and Furttenbach,* trans. Allardyce Nicoll, John H. McDowell, and George R. Kernodle (Coral Gables: Univ. of Miami Press, 1958), provides an interesting contemporary account of Italian and German techniques of stagecraft and the manner in which the machines worked.

38.   Jack Sage, "La música de Juan Hidalgo," in *Los celos hacen estrellas,* by Juan Vélez de Guevara, ed. J. E. Varey and N. D. Shergold (London: Tamesis, 1970), pp. 169-70, says that the zarzuela was not more than half music as Cotarelo, *Historia,* p. 42, had asserted but more on the order of 20-25%.

39.   *BAE,* IX, 656c-57a; cited in Neumeister, *Mythos,* p. 73.

40.   Everett W. Hesse, "The Two Versions of Calderón's 'El laurel de Apolo,'" *HR,* 14 (1946), 213-34.

41.   Cf. Neumeister, *Mythos,* p. 71.

42.   Chapman, pp. 46-51.

43.   For a history of Spanish treatments of Ovidian myths in the Middle Ages and the Renaissance, see Rudolf Schevill, *Ovid and the Renascence in Spain,* Univ. of California Publications in Modern Philology, No. 4 (Berkeley: Univ. of California Press, 1913), pp. 1-268. Arnold Reichenberger, "Klassische Mythen im spanischen Goldenen Zeitalter," in *Studia iberica. Festschrift für Hans Flasche,* ed. Karl-Hermann Körner and Klaus Rühl (Bern: Francke, 1973), pp. 495-510, provides an overview of literary use of myths from the Marqués de Santillana to Calderón.

44.   Juan Pérez de Moya, *La philosophia secreta* (Madrid: Imprenta Real, 1585), and Baltasar de Vitoria, *Del teatro de los dioses de la gentilidad,* 3 vols. (Madrid: Imprenta Real, 1620-1623). Their authority and influence is cited by Valbuena Prat, *Calderón,* pp. 171-72, by Neumeister, *Mythos,* p. 103, and by Chapman, p. 50.

45.   Jean Seznec, *The Survival of the Pagan Gods,* trans. Barbara F. Sessions (Princeton: Princeton Univ. Press, 1953; rpt. 1972), provides an extensive background on the historical, physical, and moral interpretations of classical myths.

46.   Jack Sage, "Texto y realización de *La estatua de Prometeo* y otros dramas musicales de Calderón," in *Hacia Calderón. Coloquio anglogermano,* ed. Hans Flasche (Berlin: Walter de Gruyter, 1970), p. 52.

47.   Otis Green, *"Fingen Los Poetas*—Notes on the Spanish Attitude toward Pagan Mythology," in *The Literary Mind of Medieval and Renaissance Spain* (Lexington: Univ. of Kentucky Press, 1970), p. 119; Valbuena Prat, *Calderón,* p. 175; Chapman, p. 35.

48.   Curtius, p. 558; Chapman, p. 42; Neumeister, *Mythos,* p. 107.

49.   Valbuena Prat, *Calderón,* p. 21.

50.   Cf. Calderón's own "Deposición en favor de los profesores de la pintura . . . ." in *Caxón de sastre,* by Francisco Mariano Nipho (Madrid: Gabriel Ramírez, 1781), p. 33; cited in Curtius, pp. 559-70.

51. Curtius, pp. 558, 561, and 568. Jack Sage, "The Function of Music in the Theatre of Calderón," in *Critical Studies of Calderón Comedias*, ed. J. E. Varey (London: Gregg, 1973), pp. 218-19, discusses Calderón's philosophy of music as part of a Platonic-Augustinian heritage.

52. José Subirá, *La participación musical en el antiguo teatro español*. Publicaciones del Instituto del Teatro Nacional, No. 6 (Barcelona: Instituto del Teatro Nacional, 1930), p. 29.

53. Alice Pollin, "Calderón de la Barca and Music: Theory and Examples in the *Autos* (1675-1680)," *HR*, 41 (1963), 362-70.

54. Sage, "Texto," p. 52.

55. Sage, "The Function," pp. 221-22, and "La música," p. 200.

56. *Ibid.*, p. 225. For more on poetic *plurimembraciones,* see Dámaso Alonso and Carlos Bousoño, *Seis calas en la expresión literaria española,* 3d ed. (Madrid: Gredos, 1963), pp. 111-75.

57. Subirá, *Celos,* p. xiii.

58. Pedro Calderón de la Barca, *Obras Completas,* ed. Angel Valbuena Briones (Madrid: Aguilar, 1959), III, 1503; cited in Stevenson, *La púrpura,* p. 32; Jack Sage, "Function," pp. 217-18; E. M. Wilson, "The Four Elements in the Imagery of Calderón," *MLR,* 31 (1936), 34-47.

59. *Mythos,* p. 104.

60. Charles Aubrun, "Estructura y significación de las comedias mitológicas de Calderón," in *Hacia Calderón. Tercer coloquio anglogermano,* ed. Hans Flasche (Berlin: Walter de Gruyter, 1976), p. 149.

61. Neumeister, *Mythos,* p. 49.

62. *Ibid.,* pp. 12, 72; Valbuena Prat, *Calderón,* p. 21.

63. Neumeister, *Mythos,* p. 24.

64. *Anatomy of Criticism: Four Essays* (Princeton: Princeton Univ. Press, 1957; rpt. 1973), pp. 289-93.

65. Those sources that give incorrect dates for the performances of *La púrpura* and *Celos* are: José Subirá, *La música en la casa de Alba* (Madrid: Sucesores de Rivadeneyra, 1927); Juan Eugenio Hartzenbusch, "Catálogo cronológico de las comedias de don Pedro Calderón de la Barca," *BAE,* XIV, 679; Subirá, "Le style," p. 73; and Cotarelo, *Ensayo,* p. 312. All other sources agree with Cotarelo, *Historia,* p. 15, who provides the correct date given here.

66. Subirá, *Celos,* p. xv.

67. Cited in Calderón, *Obras Completas,* I, 1765.

68. Stevenson, *La púrpura,* based on MS. C1469 in the Biblioteca Nacional (Lima). Stevenson provides more information on Torrejón in "The First New World Opera," *Americas,* 16 (1964), 33-35, including the interesting detail that Torrejón grew up in the Court of Philip IV and might well have witnessed the 1660 operatic productions.

69. Pérez Pastor, pp. 277-79, reproduced in Subirá, *Celos,* pp. xvi-xvii, and Ruth E. L. Pitts, "Don Juan Hidalgo, Seventeenth Century Spanish Composer" (Diss. George Peabody College for Teachers 1968), pp. 103-105.

70. In vol. XIX of *Comedias nuevas escogidas de los mejores ingenios de España* (Madrid: Imprenta Real, 1663), reproduced in Subirá, *Celos,* p. xvi. Of some interest is the fact that the name "Aura" is missing in the list of *dramatis personae* in this version and in all other versions published before 1800 except in the B version (Barcelona: Francisco Suria y Burgada, n.d.).

71. For biographical data concerning these performers, see Cotarelo, "Actors"; Hugo A. Rennert, "Spanish Actors and Actresses between 1560 and 1680," *RH,* 16 (1907), 334-538; and Varey and Shergold, *Los celos,* pp. lxxxix-xcii.

72. José Subirá, "Calderón de la Barca, libretista de ópera: Consideraciones literario-musicales," *Anuario Musical,* 20 (1965), 61, indicates that the practice was not unheard of and continued into the next century.

73. The two New World performances are documented by Everett W. Hesse, "Calderón's Popularity in the Spanish Indies," *HR,* 23 (1955), 12-27. For possible reasons why *Celos* was not performed again in Spain, see Subirá, "Calderón," p. 72, and Varey and Shergold, *Los celos,* p. lxxiv.

74. Hidalgo's existing music for *Ni amor se libra de amor* is most likely from a 1679 revival of the play. See Sage, "La música," p. 69n. For more on Hidalgo's life and works, see José Subirá, "El operista español D. Juan Hidalgo: Nuevas noticias biográficas," *Revista de la Ciencias,* 1-2 (1934), 1-9.

75. For documentation on these Calderón-Hidalgo collaborations, see Gilbert Chase, *The Music of Spain,* 2d ed. (New York: Dover, 1959), p. 101; Stevenson, *La púrpura,* pp. 25-33; Sage, "La música," pp. 201, 205-207.

76. In addition to contemporaries, José Subirá, "Músicos al servicio de Calderón y de Comella," *Anuario Musical,* 22 (1967), 197-208, lists subsequent composers who set Calderonian texts to music.

77. The definition of zarzuela that accompanies *Alfeo y Aretusa* is cited in Varey and Shergold, *Los celos,* p. lxxiii.

78. Varey and Shergold, ed., *Los celos,* based on MS. Cod. Vindob. 13.217 in the Oesterreichische Nationalbibliothek (Vienna).

79. Subirá, "La ópera," p. 26.

80. Stevenson, *La púrpura,* pp. 33-36; Hesse, "Calderón's Popularity."

81. (Salamanca: Lucas Pérez, 1689), pp. 55-56. Translation mine.

82. A good study of standard character types in the comedia is that of Juana de José Prades, *Teoría sobre los personajes de la comedia nueva* (Madrid: C.S.I.C., 1963)

83. Aubrun, "Estructura," pp. 149-51.

84. Ovid, *Metamorphoses,* trans. Frank Justus Miller (Cambridge: Harvard Univ. Press, 1951), pp. 388-403, and *The Art of Love,* trans. J. H. Mozley (Cambridge: Harvard Univ. Press, 1962), pp. 166-71; Hyginus, *Fabulae,* 189, cited in Henry M. Martin, "Notes on the Cephalus and Procris Myth as Dramatized by Lope de Vega and Calderón," *MLN,* 66 (1951), 239.

85. "Eróstrato," *Enciclopedia universal ilustrada,* XX, 537, cites Theopompus as the historical source.

86. Cossío gives indications of versions by Arboreda, Arnal de Bolea, Lomas Cantoral, Montemayor, Porras, Rejón de Silva, and Rodríguez. Subirá, "Calderón," p. 62, gives the list of subsequent operas. An edition of Calderón's *Céfalo y Pocris* has been published by Alberto Navarro González (Salamanca: Almar, 1979). In addition, Martin gives a cursory comparison of *Celos* and Lope's *La bella Aurora.*

87. For a treatise on the "wild man" as a *comedia* figure, see Oleh Mazur, "The Wild Man in Spanish Golden Age Drama" (Diss. Univ. of Pennsylvania 1966).

88. Alexander A. Parker, "The Spanish Drama of the Golden Age: A Method of Analysis and Interpretation," in *The Great Playwrights,* ed. Eric Bentley (Garden City, N.Y.: Doubleday, 1970), I, 683.

89. For a discussion of the importance of metaphor and symbol in the works of Calderón in general with applications to *El hijo del sol, Faetón,* and other plays, see A. A. Parker, "Metáfora y símbolo en la interpretación de Calderón," in *Actas del Primer Congreso Internacional de Hispanistas,* ed. Frank Pierce and Cyril A. Jones (Oxford: Dolphin Book Co., 1964), pp. 141-60.

90. For a background in the tenets of Neo-Platonic and Courtly forms of love, see Otis Green, *Spain and the Western Tradition* (Madison: Univ. of Wisconsin Press, 1968), I, 207-63.

91. Sebastian Neumeister, "La fiesta mitológica de Calderón en su contexto histórico (*Fieras afemina amor*)," in *Hacia Calderón. Tercer coloquio anglogermano,* ed. Hans Flasche (Berlin: Walter de Gruyter, 1976), p. 164.

92. Albert S. Gerard, "The Loving Killers: The Rationale of Righteousness in Baroque Tragedy," *CLS,* 2 (1965), 209-32, discusses the concepts of love, jealousy, frustration, punishment, and revenge with respect to two *comedias,* Lope's *El castigo sin venganza* and Calderón's *El médico de su honra.*

93. Fate and fortune are discussed at length by Otis Green, *Spain,* II, 279-337.

94. Cf. Aubrun, "Estructura," pp. 148-149.

95. Cf. Northrup Frye's discussion of archetypes in *Anatomy,* pp. 131-239; and Harold H. Watts, "Myth and Drama," in *Myth and Literature: Contemporary Theory and Practice,* ed. John B. Vickery (Lincoln: Univ. of Nebraska Press, 1966), pp. 75-85.

96. Neumeister, "La fiesta," p. 157. Everett W. Hesse, "Courtly Allusions in the Plays of Calderón," *PMLA,* 65 (1950), 548-49, suggests that Calderón seriously compromised his art by pandering to royal tastes.

97. L. C. Knights, "King Lear as Metaphor," in *Myth and Symbol: Critical Approaches and Applications,* ed. Bernice Slote (Lincoln: Univ. of Nebraska Press, 1963), p. 29, makes a similar point with respect to Shakespearean character presentation.

98. Parker, "Metáfora," pp. 157-58.

99. Neumeister, "La fiesta," p. 168, makes the point that *Fieras afemina amor* concerns the triumph of Chrisitan love, not sensual love.

100.   M. Menéndez y Pelayo, *Calderón y su teatro* (Madrid: Tipografía de la Revista de Archivos, 1910), p. 313.

101.   Analysis of versification is based on Rudolf Baehr, *Manual de versificación española,* trans. K. Wagner and F. López Estrada (Madrid: Gredos, 1973); Pedro Henríquez Ureña, *Estudios de versificación española* (Buenos Aires: Univ. of Buenos Aires, 1961); Tomás Navarro Tomás, *Arte del verso,* 4th ed. (México: Colección Málaga, 1968); and also by Navarro Tomás, *Métrica española: Reseña histórica y descriptiva* (New York: Syracuse Univ. Press, 1956).

102.   Subirá, "Le style," p. 72, discusses *villancico* variations of a musical nature as well.

103.   Otto Ursprung, " 'Celos usw.,' Text von Calderón, Musik von Hidalgo, die älteste erhaltene spanische Oper," in *Festschrift Arnold Schering zum sechzigsten Geburtstag,* ed. Helmuth Osthoff, Walter Serauky, and Adam Adrio (Berlin: A. Glas, 1937), pp. 223-40; Charles van den Borren, "Un opéra espagnol du XVIIe siècle, 'Celos aun del aire matan,' texte de Calderón, musique de Juan Hidalgo," *La Revue Musicale,* 16 (1935), 253-60; Chase, pp. 101-102; and Grout, p. 271.

104.   A history of the collection can be found in José Augusto Alegría, *Biblioteca Pública de Evora. Catálogo dos Fundos Musicais* (Lisboa: Fundação Calouste Gulbenkian, 1977).

105.   Subirá, *Celos,* pp. xi-xiii; Subirá, "Calderón," p. 67-70; Stevenson, *La púrpura,* p. 28; Sage, "La música," pp. 191-201; and Sage, "Nouvelles lumières sur la genèse de l'opéra et la zarzuela en Espagne," *Baroque,* 5 (1972), 107-10.

106.   Subirá, "Calderón," pp. 69-70.

107.   Sage, "La música," pp. 192-201, and "Nouvelles," p. 108. For a musical definition of *villancico,* see Isabel Pope, "The Musical Development and Form of the Spanish *Villancico,"* in *Papers of the American Musicological Society, 1940* (Washington: American Musicological Society, 1946), pp. 11-17.

108.   Sage, "La música," pp. 198-99, and "Nouvelles," p. 109.

109.   For information on the publication of these *Partes,* see Everett W. Hesse, "The Publication of Calderón's Plays in the Seventeenth Century," *PQ,* 27 (1948), 37-51.

110.   "The Text of Calderón's *La púrpura de la rosa,"* in *Critical Studies of Calderón's Comedias,* ed. J. E. Varey (London: Gregg International, 1973), p. 181.

111.   Angel Valbuena Briones, *Perspectiva crítica de los dramas de Calderón* (Madrid: Ediciones Rialp, 1965), p. 360.

112.   Subirá, "Calderón," p. 61, dates the P version at about 1672; Cotarelo, *Historia,* p. 56n., estimates the date at 1676.

113.   For a discussion of the unauthorized textual changes typical of Vera Tassis editions, see Hesse, "The Publication," pp. 46-51; and N. D. Shergold, "Calderón and Vera Tassis," *HR,* 23 (1955), 212-18.

114.   Mildred Boyer, *The Texas Collection of* Comedias Sueltas: *A Descrip-*

tive Bibliography (Boston: G. K. Hall, 1978), p. 594, indicates that the indication, "A costas de la Compañía," that appears at the end of this version implies that it dates from 1765-78 when there was in fact a Real Compañía de Impresores y Libreros in Madrid.

115.   Edwin Honig, "En torno a las traducciones de Calderón," *Arbor*, 80 (1971), 21-30; trans. and rpt. as "On Translating Calderon," *Michigan Quarterly Review*, 11 (1972), 264-71.

CELOS AUN DEL AIRE MATAN

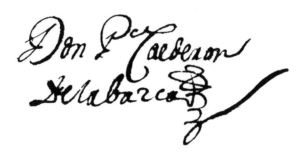

Jornada 1ª   [1ʳ(1)]

[La escena es en Lidia.]

[Jardín del templo de DIANA.]

[Sale por una parte un coro de ninfas, y POCRIS, trayendo en
medio de todas a AURA, cubierto el rostro; y por otra parte
DIANA, con venablo, y otras ninfas con flechas.]

[POCRIS]	Esta, hermosa Diana,	
	(a)cuia incauta velleza	
	baldón es de tus montes,	
	oprobrio de tus selvas,	
	es Aura, a q*uie*n tus ninfas,	5
	al sacro culto atentas	
	del puro amor q*ue* ensalzas,	
	del torpe que desprecias,	
	presentan ante ti . . .	
A 4	. . . y en forma de querella,	10
	de su amante delito	
	te piden la sentencia.	
[AURA]	¡Ay, infeliz de aquella	[1ᵛ]
	que hizo verdad aber q*uie*n de amor muera!	
[POCRIS]	Eróstrato, un pastor	15
	a quien por su soberbia	
	todos los [moradores	
	destos confines] tiemblan	
	de noche tras sus ansias,	
	de día tras sus fieras,	20
	por ella de tus cotos	
	la línea sale y entra,	
	[disfamando de todas . . .]	
A 4	. . . la botada pureza	[2ʳ]
	con que tu templo siruen,	25
	tus aras reverencian.	
[AURA]	¡Ay, infeliz de aquella	
	que hizo verdad aver [quien de amor] muera!	
[POCRIS]	[Ano]che quando en sombras	
	la luz (la luz) del sol enbuelta	30
	dejó la de la(s) [luna]	

---

1 Ac. E: missing   2 *cuya,* E: a cuia/*incauta,* G H S: incasta   4 *oprobrio,* A B C G H J
M P S T V: y oprobio   10 Ac. A B C G H J M P T V: Coro; S: Coro de Ninfas
11 *su,* L S: tu   13 Ac. E: missing   13 *infeliz,* T: infelice   14 *aber,* S:
a ver   15 Ac. E: missing   15-16 L: missing   17 *todos los moradores,* E: todos
los; L: missing   18 *de estos confines, E L: missing   21 ella,* A: ellas/*tus,* A C J P S: sus

Act One

[The scene is in Lydia.]

[Garden of the Temple of DIANA.]

[Enter from one side a chorus of nymphs and POCRIS, bringing
AURA in their midst, her face covered; from the other
direction DIANA, with a spear, and other nymphs with arrows.]

POCRIS	This one, lovely Diana,	
	whose heedless beauty	
	is an affront to your mountains,	
	a defamation of your forests,	
	is Aura, whom your nymphs,	5
	intent on the holy cult	
	of pure love that you extol,	
	of base love that you disdain,	
	present before you. . .	
CHORUS	. . . and in the form of a dispute	10
	ask of you the sentence	
	for her lover's crime.	
AURA	"Oh, unhappy is she	
	who proved that one could truly die of love!"	
POCRIS	Erostrato, a shepherd	15
	whom for his arrogance	
	all the residents	
	of these regions fear,	
	by night in pursuit of his anxieties,	
	by day in pursuit of his animals,	20
	for her comes and goes across	
	the boundary of your lands,	
	discrediting for everyone . . .	
CHORUS	. . . the devoted purity	
	with which they serve your temple,	25
	revere your altars.	
AURA	"Oh, unhappy is she	
	who proved that one could truly die of love!"	
POCRIS	Last night, when the light	
	of the sun, wrapped in shadows,	30
	left that of the moon	

---

22 *entra,* L: missing   23 E L: missing   24-26 L: missing   24 Ac. A B C H J
M P T V: Coro; S: Coro de Ninfas   27 Ac. E: missing   28 *aver,* S: a ver/*quien de
amor,* E: de quien   29 Ac. E: missing; J: Coro   29-35 L: missing   29 *Anoche,*
E: che   30 *la luz,* E: la luz la luz   31 *la luna,* E: las nubes

bañada en nubes [densas   [2ᵛ]
– porque también tuviese
Prometeo su es]fera
q*ue* tus raios robas[e] –   35
entre esas flores vellas
vrtos de amor lograua.

A 4   Y como a él no puedan
                     seguirle nuestras plantas,
                     prendimos sólo a ella.   40

AURA   ¡Ay, infeliz de aquella   [3ʳ]
                     que hizo verdad aver [quien de amor] muera!

[DIANA]   Descubri[d]la la cara,
                     q*ue* quiero q*ue* me vea,
                     porq*ue* antes q*ue* mi hira,   45
                     la mate su bergüenza.
                     Sacrílega hermosura,
                     que torpemente ciega,
                     de mi deidad no sólo
                     el sacro onor desdeñas,   50
                     pero de mi enemiga
                     Benus el triumfo aumentas,
                     pues quieres q*ue* mis aras
                     sirban a tus ofrendas.
                     ¿Cómo atrebida intentas   55   [3ᵛ]
                     q*ue* reine amor donde el olvido reina?

[AURA]   Yo . . . si . . . quando . . .

DIANA   Suspende
                     la voz, el labio sella;
                     que ay delitos que crezen
                     la culpa con la enmienda.   60
                     A ese tronco la atad
                     las manos atrás bueltas,
                     y pues es de mis ritos
                     establezida pena,
                     quien flechas de su amor   65
                     indignamente sienta,
                     sienta no indignamente (ente)   [4ʳ]
                     de mi(s) rencor las flechas,
                     examine las vuestras,
                     y al mismo impulso de q*ue* biue muer[a].   70

32 *densas*, E: missing   33 E: missing   34 *Prometeo su esfera*, E: fera
35 *tus*, A B C H J M P S T V: sus/*robase*, E: robas   36 *entre esas flores*, L: missing/*esas*, A B C
H J M P S T V: sus   37 *vrtos*, J L P: huertos   38 Ac. A B C H J M P T V: Coro; S: Coro
de Ninfas   39 *seguirle*, J P: segarle   42 *aver*, S: a ver/*quien de amor*, E: de amor quien
43 Ac. E: missing   43 *Descubridla*, E: descubrirla   53 *pues quieres*, B C H J M P S T V: haciendo

                     bathed in dense clouds
                     (so that Prometheus might
                     also wield his power
                     to steal your rays)   35
                     among those beautiful flowers
                     she achieved thefts of love.
CHORUS   And since our feet
                     could not follow him,
                     we seized only her.   40
AURA   "Oh, unhappy is she
                     who proved that one could truly die of love!"
DIANA   Uncover her face,
                     for I want her to see me
                     so that her shame might kill her   45
                     before my anger does.
                     Sacrilegious beauty,
                     you who, ineptly blind,
                     not only disdain
                     the holy honor of my divinity   50
                     but increase the triumph
                     of my enemy Venus,
                     since you want my altars
                     to serve your offerings,
                     how dare you try   55
                     to make love reign where oblivion reigns?
AURA   I. . . if . . . when . . .
DIANA   Cease
                     your voice, seal your lips,
                     for there are crimes that increase
                     the guilt with emendation.   60
                     Tie her to that tree trunk
                     with her hands behind her,
                     and, since it is the established
                     penalty of my rites
                     that the one who feels the arrows   65
                     of love unworthily
                     should feel not unworthily
                     the arrows of my rancor,
                     examine your own,
                     and, by the same impulse by which you live, die.   70

---

54 *ofrendas,* A B C H J L M P S T V: ofensas   57 Ac. E: missing   57 *Yo . . . si,*
L: y así   59 *crecen,* G: acrecen   61 *A ese,* L S: De este; V: A este   65 *quien,*
G: que quien/*flechas,* J L P S: flecha/*de su,* A B H M T V: del; G: de   67 *indignamente,*
E: indignamente ente   68 *mi,* E: mis   70 *mismo impulso,* B H M T V: impulso/*de,*
B H J L M P S T V: missing/*muera,* E: muere; B H J L M P S T V: al mismo muera

POCRIS	Ven, fiera.	
A 4	Ven, tirana.	
AURA	Tú, Pocris, que antes eras	
	mi más amiga, ¿más	
	contraria te [me] muestras?	
POCRIS	Sí, y por más amiga,	75
	me toca más tu ofensa.	
AURA	¡O pliegue [a] Amor, o pliegue	
	a Venus, que padezcas	
	lo que padezco, en ti	[4ᵛ]
	vengadas las ofensas,	80
	la primera de todas!	
POCRIS	Yo le doi la licencia	
	de ser, como me vea	
	Amor amar, su indignación primera.	
DIANA	Atadla, ¿qué esperáis?	85

[Atan a AURA al tronco.]

AURA	Soberanas esferas,	
	poderosas deidades,	
	cielo, sol, luna, estrellas,	
	fuentes, arroyos, mares,	
	montañas, cumbres, peñas,	90
	árboles, flores, plantas,	
	aves, pezes y fieras,	
	compadezeos de mí,	[5ʳ(2)]
	tened de mí clemenzia,	
	no permitáis que digan	95
	ayre, agua, fuego y tierra,	
	"¡Ay, infeliz de aquella	
	que hizo verdad aver quien de amor muera!"	
ZÉFALO	[Dentro.]	
	Jemido es de muger	
	que aflijida lamenta.	100
CLARÍN	[Dentro.]	
	Si ella obró noramala,	
	quédese norabuena,	[5ᵛ]
	y sigue tu camino.	
ZÉFALO	[Dentro.]	
	¿Cómo, [oyendo su] queja,	
	podrá el balor de un hombre	105
	no ir a faborezerla?	

71 Pocris. Ven, fiera., L S: missing   72 Ac. A B C G H J M P T V: Coro; S: Coro de Ninfas
74 me, E: missing   75 y, A B C G H J L M P S T V: que/más, J L: missing
77 a, E J L P S: missing   80 las, A B C H J L M P S T V: sus   98 aver, S: a ver
100 lamenta, V: se lamenta   102 quédese, A B C G H J L M P S T V: quéjese

POCRIS	Come, barbarian.
CHORUS	Come, tyrant.
AURA	You, Pocris, who used to be
	my best friend, now show yourself
	to be the most hostile to me?
POCRIS	Yes, and because I am your best friend,
	your offense touches me more.
AURA	Oh, may it please Cupid, may it please
	Venus, that you suffer
	what I suffer, with
	my offenses avenged,
	on you first of all!
POCRIS	I give permission to Venus
	to take revenge on me first
	whenever Cupid may find me in love.
DIANA	Tie her. What are you waiting for?

75

80

85

[They tie AURA to the tree trunk.]

AURA	Sovereign spheres,
	powerful divinities,
	heaven, sun, moon, stars,
	fountains, streams, seas,
	mountains, peaks, rocks,
	trees, flowers, plants,
	birds, fish, and beasts,
	have pity on me,
	have clemency for me,
	do not permit air, water,
	fire, and land to say,
	"Oh, unhappy is she
	who proved that one could truly die of love!"
CÉFALO	[Offstage.]
	It is the cry of a woman
	who, afflicted, laments.
CLARÍN	[Offstage.]
	If she labored in danger,
	let her now remain in safety,
	and continue your journey.
CÉFALO	[Offstage.]
	How, hearing her complaint,
	can the valor of a man possibly
	not go to her aid?

90

95

100

105

104 *oyendo su queja,* E: siendo tu; A B C G H J M P T V: oyendo sus quejas
105 *hombre,* A B C H J M P T V: noble

CLARÍN   [Dentro.]
           Yendo por otra parte.
ZÉFALO   [Dentro.]
           Conmigo Clarín llega.
DIANA   Pues fue de todas sombra,
           blanco de todas sea.   110

[Salen CÉFALO y CLARÍN.]

ZÉFALO   ¿Qué tirana biolencia
           se atreue a hazer [a] vna muger ofensa?   [6r]
           Pero ¿qué es lo que miro?
CLARÍN   A una banda de vellas
           señoras cupidillas,   115
           q*ue* están en armas puestas
           contra vna a un tronco atada.
ZÉFALO   [Aparte.]
           No [sé] cómo obre cuerda
           acción, q*ue* ofende a muchos
           en una que defienda.   120
DIANA   ¡O tú, estrangero jóben   [6v]
           −que quiero crêr las señas
           de el traje, por no acer
           tu culpa más grosera
           en aberte atrebido   125
           a penetrar la senda
           que este sagrado guarda,
           que este sitio reserba,
           tanto que nadie a él llega,
           que no escriba su muerte con su güella−   130
           sin que más examines
           ni sin que más entiendas   [7r]
           del duelo en que nos allas,
           tranze en que nos encuentras,
           buelbe atrás, y agradeze   135
           a la deidad suprema
           q*ue* estos montes abita,
           que quiere que se sepan
           sus yras, y por eso,
           sin que cómplize seas   140
           de errores que castiga,
           permite que te buelbas.
           Bete, pues, si no esperas   [7v]
           que la voz del indulto se arrepienta.

---

109 *todas sombra*, J P: todas sombras; V: todos sombra   110 B H J M P T V: missing
111 *tirana*, A B C G H J L M P S T V: villana   112 *a vna*, E: vna/*ofensa*, J L P: missing
114 *A una*, A B C G H J M P T V: Una   116 *armas*, A B H J L M S T V: bandas; C P: vanda

CLARÍN	[Offstage.]
	By going in another direction.
CÉFALO	[Offstage.]
	Come with me, Clarín.
DIANA	Since she was the blot on all,
	let her be the target of all.

110

[Enter CÉFALO and CLARÍN.]

CÉFALO	What tyrannical violence
	dares to offend a woman?
	But, what is this I see?
CLARÍN	A band of beautiful
	little cupids
	who have taken up arms
	against one tied to a tree trunk.
CÉFALO	[Aside.]
	I do not know how prudent action
	may work, for it offends many
	in order to defend one.
DIANA	Oh you, young stranger
	(for I want to believe the signs
	of your attire, in order not to make
	your crime more gross
	for having dared
	to penetrate the path
	that guards, that preserves,
	this sacred site,
	so much that no one reaches it
	who does not write his death with his footprints),
	without investigating more,
	nor understanding
	the ordeal in which you find us,
	the crisis in which you discover us,
	return, and thank
	the supreme divinity
	that inhabits these mountains,
	who wants her ire
	to be known, and, therefore,
	without your being an accomplice
	to errors that she punishes,
	permits you to return.
	Go, then, if you do not wish
	that my voice repent of this pardon.

115

120

125

130

135

140

---

118 *sé*, E: missing   119 *ofende*, A B C G H J M P S T V: ofendo/*muchos*, A B C G H J L M
P S T V: muchas   121 *estrangero joben*, L S: joven estranjero   122 *quiero*, J L P: quieres
132 *ni*, A B C H J L M P S T V: y   137 *abita*, J L P: habitan   138 *quiere*, V: quieren
139 *eso*, A B H M S T V: esto   140 *cómplize*, M: cómplices

ZÉFALO   E[n] quanto a [que], estrangero,   145
             no sé qué estancia es ésta,
             lo que el traje te dijo,
             no desdirá la lengua;
             pero [en] quanto a que oý
             míseras vozes tiernas   150
             de mujer, cuio azento
             a discurrir me enseña
             lo inculto de estos montes,   [8ʳ]
             ¿cómo, llegando a berla,
             della llamado, [puedo]   155
             dejar de socorrerla?
DIANA   Biendo que más a[rr]iesga
             ser que me enoje yo que en morir ella.
ZÉFALO   Reconozco el peligro
             de tu ceño; mas piensa   160
             que nobles culpas hazen
             amigas las ofensas;
             pues aunq*ue* aora te [e]nojes,
             podrá ser q*ue* agradezcas   [8ᵛ]
             tú mesma mi despecho   165
             después contra ti mesma,
             q*ue* hidalgos procederes
             tienen tal encomienda
             en lo ylustre de un alma,
             q*ue* obligan aunq*ue* ofendan.   170
DIANA   Según eso, ¿aún intentas
             contra mí proseguir en su defensa?
ZÉFALO   En su defensa, sí,   [9ʳ(3)]
             contra ti, no.
DIANA   ¿No echas
             de ver que es imposible   175
             mantener la propuesta?
             Porque ¿cómo, si a darla
             la muerte estoi resuelta,
             y tú a darla la vida,
             quieres que te combengan   180
             dos acciones que están
             [tan] cara a cara opuestas?
ZÉFALO   No sé, si no me bale
             vna industria.
DIANA   ¿*Qué* es?   [9ᵛ]

---

145 *En cuanto a que,* E: es quanto a   148 *desdirá,* L: se desdirá
149 *en,* E V: missing   152 *enseña,* A B C H M S T V: empeña; J P L: empeñan
155 *puedo,* E: missing   157 *arriesga,* E: ariesga; A B C G H J L M P S T V: arriesgas

CÉFALO	Since as a stranger 145
	I do not know what situation this is,
	that which the attire told you,
	the tongue will not recant.
	But since I heard
	miserable, tender cries 150
	of a woman, whose voice
	shows me how to traverse
	the wilds of these mountains,
	how, arriving to see her,
	called by her, can I 155
	keep from helping her?
DIANA	By seeing that you risk more in
	my being angry than in her dying.
CÉFALO	I recognize the danger
	of your displeasure, but keep in mind 160
	that noble responsibilities make
	friends of offenses;
	for although now you are angry,
	it may be that you yourself
	will reward my defiance 165
	of you afterwards,
	for noble actions
	have such support
	in the honor of a soul
	that they oblige even though they offend. 170
DIANA	So, do you still intend
	to continue in her defense against me?
CÉFALO	In her defense, yes;
	against you, no.
DIANA	Do you not
	see that it is impossible 175
	to maintain this course of action?
	Because, how, if I am resolved
	to give her death
	and you to give her life,
	do you intend that two actions 180
	so diametrically opposed
	might be compatible?
CÉFALO	I do not know, unless some plan
	works for me.
DIANA	What is it?

158 *ser,* A B C G H J L M P S T V: en/*en,* M: es 163 *enojes,* E: nojes 177, 179 *la,* G: le
180 *te,* A B C G H J L M P S T V: se 182 *tan,* E: missing 183 *me vale,* P: me le

ZÉFALO   Esta.
                    [Pónese delante de AURA.]
                La templada cuchilla   185
                que, blandida en tu diestra,
                a tus ojos les pide
                para matar lizencia,
                contra mí arbola(n); y todas
                bosotras, nimfas vellas,   190
                tremolad contra mí
                las embebidas cuerdas;
                que de su vida escudo,
                mi vida, a sus pies, puesta,
                muriendo yo primero,   195
                que [a] ella morir la vea.
                Cumpliré entrambas deudas,   [10ʳ]
                pues ni me opongo a ti, ni falto a ella.
DIANA   Por más que generoso
                facilitar pretendas   200
                ni rendido mi saña,
                ni altiba tu soberbia,
                no as de poder. Aparta.
ZÉFALO   Advierte, considera
                que no es querer que viva   205
                pedirte que yo muera.
[AURA]   ¡Ay, infeliz de aquella
                que hizo verdad aber [quien de amor] muera!   [10ᵛ]
CLARÍN   Apártate, señor,
                y que la tiren deja: 210
                tendrás vn lindo rato.
ZÉFALO   ¿Eso, bil, me aconsejas?
CLARÍN   Pues, dime, ¿vbiera fiesta
                como ver asaetear todas la embras,
                quánto más vna?
DIANA   Aparta,   215
                di[g]o otra vez.
ZÉFALO   Espera.   [11ʳ]
[POCRIS Y   [¿Qué hay que esperar?]
  EL CORO]
AURA   ¡Los dioses
                mi vida faborezcan!

---

185 *templada,* P J: templança   189 *arbola; y,* E: arbolan   193 *escudo,* J L: escusado
194 *sus,* B C H J M P T V: esos   196 *a,* E: missing   197 Ac. E: despacio
197 *deudas,* C J P: vidas; L: dudas   200 *pretendas,* B C H J M P T V: intentas
201 *ni,* A B H L M S T V: o/*rendido,* A C J L P S T: rendida/ *mi,* G: a mí.   202 *ni,* A B H L M
S T V: o/*altiba,* B C H J M P T V: altivo   207 Ac. E: missing   207 A B H J M T V: missing

CÉFALO   This one.
                              [He places himself in front of AURA.]
                     Raise against me   185
                     the tempered blade
                     that, brandished in your right hand,
                     asks your eyes
                     for permission to kill; all of
                     you, beautiful nymphs,   190
                     flount your wizened
                     ropes against me
                     so that, with my life as a shield
                     for her life, placed at her feet,
                     I might die before   195
                     I see her die.
                     I shall fulfill both obligations,
                     as I neither oppose you nor fail her.
DIANA   However generously
                     you may try to dispatch   200
                     either my betrayed rage
                     or your haughty pride,
                     you shall not succeed.
CÉFALO   Observe: consider
                     that wanting her to live   205
                     is not asking that I die.
AURA   "Oh, unhappy is she
                     who proved that one could truly die of love!"
CLARÍN   Depart, sir,
                     and let them shoot her: 210
                     you will have a good time.
CÉFALO   That, wretch, you advise me?
CLARÍN   Well, tell me, what could be more amusing
                     than seeing all these women shot with arrows,
                     much less this one?
DIANA   Go away,   215
                     I say again.
CÉFALO   Wait.
POCRIS and   What is there to wait for?
  CHORUS
AURA   May the Gods
                     favor my life!

208 A B H J M T V: missing/*quien de amor,* E: de quien   209 *Apártate,* J M P: Aparta
210 *la,* G: le   211 *rato,* V: retrato   212 *me,* A G L S: missing   216 *digo,* E: dio
217 E L: missing

DIANA   ¿Quál podrá contra mi?
AURA   El que [al] ver mi trajedia,   220
             porque tú no blasones
             q*ue* contra amor ay quej(j)as,
             no bastando la humana
             que trujo a socorrerla,
             vse de la divina   225
[A 4]   como desta manera.
                    [Vuela el tronco con AURA.]
AURA   [Dentro.]
             No ya infeliz [de aquella
             que hizo verdad aber quien de amor muera.]   [11ᵛ]
A 4   En aire combertida,
             desbanezida buela   230
             las diáfanas esferas.
DIANA   ¿Quién duda que las ciegas?
             fantasías de amor,   [12ʳ]
             quando más se [defiendan],
             en vmos se consuman,   235
             en ayre se combiertan.
POCRIS   Como Venus del agua
             nazió para que sea
             fuego el amor, y el ayre
             de agua y fuego se mezcla,   240
             los imperios de Venus,
             que ambos estremos median,
             el ayre son; y así
             la traslada a su esfera   [12ᵛ]
             para que, sin que tú   245
             la mates, viua eterna
             ninfa del ayre Aura,
             diziendo lisongera . . .
AURA   [Dentro.]
             No ya [infeliz de aquella
             que hizo verdad aber quien de amor muera.]   250
DIANA   Este aleue estranjero,
             q*ue* a tan mal tiempo llega
             a embaraza[r] mis yras,
             que da aliento a q*ue* puedan
             volar a ella sus vozes   255 [13ʳ(4)]

220 *al*, E: el; C J P: a   222 *quejas*, E: quejjas; A B C G H J M P S T V: fuerza   225 *vse*,
C J P: usé; B M T V: usó   226 Ac. E: missing; S: Coro/For the word "¿Cómo?", A B C H J M P
T V: Coro; G: Coro (1)/For the words "De esta manera," B C J M P T V: Coro 2 dentro; A H:
La voz de Venus dentro; G: Coro (2)   227-228 E: Too few notes in music for corresponding text
227 *No ya*, A B H J L M P S T V: Ay/*infeliz de aquella*, E: infeliz; L: missing   228 É L: missing/
aber, S: a ver   229-231 L: missing   229 Ac. A B C G H J M P S T V: Coro
231 Ac. C J P: Diana   231 *las diáfanas esferas*, A B C G H J L M P S T V: los diáfanos espacios

DIANA   Which one of them can possibly do anything against me?
AURA   The one who, upon seeing my tragedy,   220
             so that you cannot boast
             that there are accusations against love,
             with the human force that he brought
             to help her not sufficing,
             may use divine force,   225
CHORUS   as in this manner.
                              [The tree trunk flies with AURA.]
AURA   [Offstage.]
             No longer unhappy is she
             who proved that one could truly die of love.
CHORUS   Transformed into air,
             haughtily she flies   230
             through the diaphanous spheres.
DIANA   Who doubts that the blind
             fantasies of love,
             whenever they defend themselves
             are consumed in smoke,   235
             and transformed into air?
POCRIS   Since Venus was born
             of water so that love
             might be fire, and the air
             is a mixture of water and fire,   240
             the realms of Venus,
             which lie between both extremes,
             are air; and thus
             she carries her off to her sphere
             so that, without your   245
             killing her, Aura may live,
             an eternal nymph of the air,
             saying as flattery . . .
AURA   [Offstage.]
             No longer unhappy is she
             who proved that one could truly die of love.   250
DIANA   This perfidious stranger,
             who arrives at such a bad time
             to interfere with my wrath,
             who gives breath so that his shouts
             may cause her to fly,   255

232 Ac. C J P: missing   232 ciegas, E: sigas   234 quando, L S: cuanto/defiendan, E: detienen
235 vmos, G: humo; B: el ayre; A C H J L M P S T V: aire   236 en ayre, G: y en aire;
A B C H M P S T V: y en humo; J L: y en buen humo   240 de, A H P S: es de/se, A B H J M
P S T V: missing   242 estremos, J L S: estrechos   243 el ayre, G: los aires   244 traslada,
A B C G H J L M P S T V: trasladó   249 infeliz de aquella, E L S: missing   250 E L: missing/
aber, S: a ver   252 tiempo, A B C H J L M P S T V: punto   253 embarazar, E: embarazas

	de mi cólera fiera, será despojo.
CÉFALO	En bano temor ponerme intentas, q*ue* eroicos pechos no matan sin resistencia.
DIANA	No es matar bentajosa el castigar sebera, y así, de mi biolenta saña tu vida el desempeño sea.

                                        260

                              [Cáesele el venablo de
                              la mano al ejecutar el golpe.]

        Pero ¿qué es esto? El dardo   265
        q*ue* azerado cometa   [13ᵛ]
        tan siempre [fue] del bosque,
        que despedido apenas
        de mi mano salió,
        cuando [a] mi[s] planta[s] puestas   270
        bio tantas brutas ruinas
        si[n] que sañuda fiera
        o ya la garra armada
        o ya armada la testa
        por veloz se re[d]i[m]a,   275
        por feroz se defienda,   [14ʳ]
        me falta. ¡Qué tristeza!
        ¡Qué asombro! ¡Qué temor! ¡Qué ansia! ¡Qué pena!

                              [Vanse DIANA, y las ninfas,
                              dejándose el venablo.]

ZÉFALO	De tanto misteriosso pasmo testigo sea en el templo de Marte este benablo. [Cógele.]

                                        280

POCRIS	Suelta, que prenda de Diana es tan sagrada prenda que [a]un dejada no ay amor que la merezca.

                                        285
                                                                    [14ᵛ]

CÉFALO	¡Diana!
POCRIS	Sí.
ZÉFALO	Aunq*ue* a oír su nombre me estremezca para llebarle, más q*ue* me inpides me alientas.

                                        290

---

257 *despojo,* L: despejo   264 *tu,* C J P: su   265 *El,* A C J P: missing   267 *fue,*
E: missing   270 *a mis plantas,* E: mi planta   271 *ruinas,* A H S: vidas; L: deudas
272 *sin,* E: si   274 *armada la,* A B H M T V: la armada   275 *redima,* E: remida

	will be a victim of my	
	wild anger.	
CÉFALO	In vain	

CÉFALO   In vain
do you try to instill fear in me,
for heroic hearts do not
kill without resistance.   260

DIANA   Punishing severely is not
killing unjustly,
and so, let your life
be the fulfillment of my fury.

                [The spear falls from her
                hand upon executing the blow.]

But, what is this? The lance   265
that has always been a sharp
comet of the forest,
that left my hand,
barely discharged,
when it saw so many brutish ruins   270
placed at my feet,
without a fierce beast,
either its claw armed
or its head readied,
redeeming itself by speed,   275
or defending itself by ferocity,
fails me. What sadness!
What horror! What fear! What anxiety! What pain!

                [Exeunt DIANA, and the nymphs,
                leaving the spear.]

CÉFALO   Of such a mysterious
wonder let this spear   280
be a witness in the temple
of Mars.   [He takes it.]

POCRIS   Let go,
for this article of Diana's
is such a sacred article
that even left behind there is no   285
love that deserves it.

CÉFALO   Diana's!

POCRIS   Yes.

CÉFALO   Even though I tremble
upon hearing her name,
more than it impedes me,
it encourages me to take it.   290

---

278 *temor,* B C H J M P T V: terror   285 *aun,* E: un   286 *amor,* A B C G H J L M P T V: mortal
287 Ac. *Pocris,* S: Diana   287 *a,* A B C G H J L M P S T V: missing
288 *nombre,* L: monb^e.   289 *llebarle,* G: llevarlo/*más,* V: no más

                     ¿A quién, beldad divina,
                     despojos de tan nueba
                     lid tocan, sino a q*uie*n
                     con la campaña pueda?
POCRIS   A quien deue cobrarlos   295
                     por su d[u]eño.
ZÉFALO   Deja,
                     ya que buelbo dichoso   [15ʳ]
                     q*ue* onrrado tanbién buelba.
POCRIS   No en bano lo pretendas.
ZÉFALO   No en bano tú quitarme este onor quieras.   300
POCRIS   No as de llebarle.
ZÉFALO   No agas
                     que tan alta empresa
                     aventure el respeto
                     ajando de la fuerza.
POCRIS   ¿Qué es ajado? Primero   305
                     que por tuio le tengas,
                     con él as de quitarme
                     la vida.   [15�v]
ZÉFALO   Advierte . . . .
POCRIS   Suelta.
                     [Quiere quitarle el venablo, luchan, y
                       hiérese POCRIS con él.]
                     Mas ¡ay de mí infelize!
ZÉFALO   ¿Qué a sido?
POCRIS   Con la ciega   310
                     cólera, no advertí
                     que en la cuchilla puesta
                     tenía(s) [l]a mano, y tanto
                     al herirme con ella
                     la púrpura del rojo   315
                     cristal q*ue* ensangrienta,
                     me estremeze, me iela,
                     me desmaia, me aflige, me atormenta,   [16ʳ]
                     que ni al[i]ento ni viuo,
                     y en ofuscada ydea   320
                     de sombras q*ue* me asaltan,
                     de errores que me zercan,
                     no sé, no sé de mí.
                     Detente, aguarda, espera;
                     no, no me mates.

292 *despojos,* A B G H J L M S T V: despojo; P: despejos   293 *tocan,* A B G H L M S T: toca
294 *con,* L: missing/*pueda,* A B C G H J L M P S T V: queda   295 *cobrarlos,*
A H S: cobrarlo   296 *por,* A B C H J M P T V: por de/*dueño,* E: deño
300 *quitarme este onor,* A B C G H M P S T V: quitarme el honor; L: quitar mi honor;
J: quitarme onor   301 *llebarle,* L S: llevarla; G: llevarlo

	To whom, divine beauty,	
	do the spoils of such a novel	
	battle belong, except to the one	
	who wins the campaign?	
POCRIS	To the one who must recover them	295
	for their owner.	
CÉFALO	Stop,	
	now that I return with joy,	
	let me also return with honor.	
POCRIS	Attempt it not in vain.	
CÉFALO	Desire not in vain to take this honor from me.	300
POCRIS	You are not to take it.	
CÉFALO	Do not cause	
	this lofty enterprise	
	to risk respect	
	by abusing force.	
POCRIS	What is abused? Before	305
	you hold it as your own,	
	you must first take my life	
	with it.	
CÉFALO	Consider	
POCRIS	Let go.	

[She tries to take the spear from him,
they struggle, and POCRIS wounds herself with it.]

	But, oh, unhappy me!	
CÉFALO	What has happened?	
POCRIS	With blind	310
	rage, I did not notice	
	that I had my hand	
	placed upon the knife, and upon	
	wounding myself with it,	
	the purple of the red	315
	stream that bloodies,	
	frightens me, chills me,	
	disheartens me, afflicts me, torments me,	
	so much that I neither breathe nor live,	
	and, in a cloudy idea	320
	of shadows that assault me,	
	of errors that approach me,	
	I do not know, I do not know about myself.	
	Stop, hold, wait;	
	no, do not kill me.	

302 *empresa,* A B C G H J L M P S T V: presea   304 *ajando,* A B C G H J L
M P S T V: ajado   306 *le,* G: lo   310 *a sido* A B C H J L M P S T V: has hecho
312 *puesta,* L: opuesta   313 *tenía la mano,* E: tenías a mano; B H L M T V: la mano tenía
316 *cristal,* A B C G H J L M P S T V: coral   318 *me atormenta,* A B H M T V:
y me atormenta   319 *aliento,* E: alento   322 *errores,* A B C G H M S T V: horrores

ZÉFALO   Yo . . .   325
             quando . . . si . . . .
POCRIS   Cessa, cesa.
             Pero ¿qué es lo que digo?
             ¿Yo a un acaso sujeta?
             ¿Yo a un delirio postrada?
             ¿Yo a un frenesí suspensa?   330   [16ᵛ]
             ¡Qué fantasía tan nezia!
             ¡Qué ylusión! ¡Qué delirio! ¡Qué quimera!   [Vase.]
ZÉFALO   Vello prodigio, aguarda;
             hermoso asombro, espera.
CLARÍN   ¡Pues ba mui bien servida   335
             para que se detenga!
ZÉFALO   No quiero más, ¡ay triste!,
             sino sólo que sepa
             que el nácar que purpúreo(s)   [17ʳ(5)]
             manchó la niebe tersa,   340
             al ver que los jazmines
             en claveles se bueluan,
             herido el corazón
             en el pecho me deja,
             como diciendo muestras   345
             de mi dolor.
TODOS   [Dentro.]
                     Al monte, a la ribera.
CLARÍN   Ruido de cazadores
             a estotra parte suena;
             y pues no as de seguirlos,
             busquemos por la(s) selva   350   [17ᵛ]
             los caballos [que sueltos]
             se quedaron en ella,
             y bamos dónde bamos.
ZÉFALO   Dices bien. ¡Quién pudiera
             siguiendo yr(e) su velleza!   [Vanse.]   355
A 4   [Dentro.]
                     Al monte, [al prado, al valle, a la ribera.]

[Soto que linda con el jardín del templo de DIANA.]

[Sale ERÓSTRATO.]

ERÓSTRATO Ya que dexo esparzida
           por toda la campaña la batida,
           cuias confussas vozes,

---

339 *el*, L S: al/ *purpúreo*, E: purpúreos; L: por pureo   345 *muestras*, A B C G H J L M P S T V:
en muestras   349 *seguirlos*, A B C G H J M P T V: seguirla   350 *la selva*, E: las selva

CÉFALO	I . . .	325
	when . . . if	
POCRIS	Stop, cease.	
	But, what is it that I am saying?	
	I, subject to an accident?	
	I, prostrate before a madness?	
	I, bewildered by an insanity?	330
	What a foolish fantasy!	
	What an illusion! What madness! What delusion! [Exit.]	
CÉFALO	Beautiful prodigy, stay;	
	lovely marvel, wait.	
CLARÍN	Well! She goes very well disposed	335
	to stop!	
CÉFALO	I want no more (oh miserable me!)	
	than that she might only know	
	that the mother-of-pearl that stained	
	purple the smooth snow,	340
	upon seeing that the jasmines	
	turn into carnations,	
	leaves me with my heart	
	wounded in my chest,	
	as though giving signs	345
	of my pain.	
ALL	[Offstage.]	
	To the mountain, to the stream.	
CLARÍN	The noise of hunters	
	sounds in this other direction,	
	and since you are not to follow them,	
	let us look through the forest	350
	for the horses that remained	
	unbridled in it,	
	and let us go where we go.	
CÉFALO	You speak well. Oh, to be able	
	to go after her beauty! [Exeunt.]	355
CHORUS	[Offstage.]	
	To the mountain, to the meadow, to the valley, to the stream.	

[Grove that borders on the garden of the Temple of DIANA.]

[Enter ERÓSTRATO.]

ERÓSTRATO Now that I leave the bushes beaten
and all the animals dispersed,
whose confused, quick voices,

351 *que sueltos*, E: missing   355 *yr*, E: yre   356 *al prado, al valle, a la ribera*, E L: missing
356 Ac. H S: Eróstrato   357 *dexo*, P J: dexó

que son mis señas, es fuerza q*ue* belozes   360
ayan la soberana   [18ʳ]
esfera penetrad[o] de Diana,
en el inculto soto,
q*ue* de esta línea a [s]u bedado coto
dibide el [l]inde, quiero   365
recatado esperar al jardinero,
de quien mi amor fiado
sus términos rompió; con que el cuidado
de q*ue* anoche sentido
fuesse de alguna gente, cuyo ruido   370   [18ᵛ]
me obligó a que saliese
veloz, porque con Aura no me biese,
me tiene [con recelo]
de si fu[i] bisto o no.

[Sale RÚSTICO.]

RÚSTICO   ¡Válgame el cielo!
                   ¡En qué cossas se mete   375
                   él que se mete consonante! Bete,
                   pues nombre es más pulido
                   ajente de negozios de Cupido.   [19ʳ]
                   Dígalo yo, testigo
                   de tantos sustos, pues.
ERÓSTRATO   Rústico, amigo,   380
                   mui bien benido seas.
RÚSTICO   Y tú mui mal allado.
ERÓSTRATO   Si deseas
                   sacarme de un cuidado,
                   dime de anoche acá lo que a pasado.   [19ᵛ]
RÚSTICO   Aunq*ue* la istoria es mucha,   385
                   toda la e de decir.
ERÓSTRATO   Empieza.
RÚSTICO   Escucha.
                   Persiguiendo fieras
                   dicen q*ue* un día
                   con un coro topaste
                   de hermosas nimfas.   390
                   Viste entre ella[s a] Aura,
                   y el que te incline
                   es razón, que la estrella
                   ni da ni pide.

360 *mis señas,* A B C G H J L M P S T V: mi seña   362 *penetrado,*
E: penetrada   364 *su,* E: tu   365 *el linde,* E L: el inde
366 *esperar,* V: esperado/*al,* L S: el   368 *con que,* A B C G H J L M
P S T V: porque   373 *con recelo,* E: el corazón rezeloso

that are my signs, have   360
necessarily penetrated
the sovereign sphere of Diana
in the untilled grove
that divides the border of her
forbidden land by this line, I want,   365
concealed, to wait for the gardener
who, trusted with my love,
broke her barriers; and so this worry
that I might have been perceived
by some people last night, whose noise   370
obliged me to leave
quickly, so that I would not be seen with Aura,
has me fearing
whether I was seen or not.

[Enter RÚSTICO.]

RÚSTICO   Heaven help me!
In what things does he get involved   375
who gets involved willingly! Go on,
for "Agent of Cupid's Affairs"
is a more polite name.
Let me say it, then, as a
witness to such frights.
ERÓSTRATO   Rústico, friend,   380
you came at a good time.
RÚSTICO   And you at a bad one.
ERÓSTRATO   If you desire
to extract me from a care,
tell me what has happened since last night.
RÚSTICO   Although the story is a long one,   385
I shall tell it all.
ERÓSTRATO   Begin.
RÚSTICO   Listen.
Pursuing beasts,
they say that one day
you ran into a chorus
of lovely nymphs.   390
You saw among them Aura,
and that which directs you
is reason, for the stars
neither give nor request.

---

374 *fui,* E: fue   374 Ac. H S: Rústico; A C G P: Sale Rústico, villano   376 *se mete,*
A G H L S: se mete a   387 *fieras,* A H S: las fieras   389 *topaste,* A B H M T V: encontraste
391 *ellas a,* E: ella; J L: ellas   393 *que,* A B H M S T V: pues

De explicarte buscastes   395   [20r]
medios, y fuimos,
si ella la paraninfa,
yo paranimfo.
Dejo aquí villetes,
jardines, coches,   400
ingredientes comunes
de otros amores;
y boi solo a que todas
sus compañeras
la azecharon, quejosas   405   [20v]
de sus finezas.
Biéronte, y aun*que* fueron
acciones tales
siempre mui zibiles
oy criminales,   410
pues que la acussaron
de cuyo enojo,
resultó *que* Doña Ana
la atasse a un tronco,
Pocris, su más amiga,   415
fue la primera   [21r(6)]
que la diera la muerte,
si no acudiera
[n]o sé *quién* [a] ampararla,
mas sin efecto,   420
pues quien sólo pudo
diz que fue Venus
que, mostrando *que* aun*que* éstas
son cosas graues
en Doña Ana, en ella   425
son cosas de ayre,
conbertida en ayre   [21v]
se lleuó a Aura
donde . . .
ERÓSTRATO   No prosigas,
villano, calla.   430
Calla, que no quiero oír
que con piadosas [crueldades]
a mí me conbierta en estragos de fuego
quien a ella combierta en alagos de ayre.

---

395 *buscastes*, A B C H J L M P S T V: buscamos   398 *paranimfo*, A B C H J L M P S T V:
el paraninfo   399 *aquí*, A B H M T V: aparte   400 *coches*, A B C H J L M P S T V: noches
405 *azecharon*, A B C H J L M P S T V: acusaron   406 *sus finezas*, B H M T V: no ser ella;
A C G J L P S: no ser ellas   407 *y aunque*, A G H S: con que   408 *acciones*, C J L P:
no acciones; A B H M S T V: razones   409 *siempre*, A B C G H J L M P S T V: si siempre
411 *pues que la*, C J P: porque la; A B G H L M S T V: porque a Aura   416 *la*, C J L P: la más

You sought ways to explain   395
yourself, and we went,
if she the bride,
then I the best man.
I leave here love letters,
gardens, coaches,   400
common ingredients
of other loves;
and I go alone because all
her companions
spied on her, resentful   405
of her favors.
They saw you, and although
such actions
were always very civil,
today they are criminal,   410
for they accused her,
from whose anger
it results that Doña Ana
tied her to a tree trunk.
Pocris, her best friend,   415
was the first one
who would have given her death
if someone, I know not who,
had not come to help her,
but without effect,   420
since the only one who could,
they say, was Venus
who, showing that, although these
are grave matters
for Doña Ana, for her   425
they are matters of the air,
carried off Aura,
transformed into air,
where . . .

ERÓSTRATO   Do not continue,
peasant, be quiet.   430
Be quiet, for I do not want to hear
that with pious cruelty
whoever transforms her into puffs of air
should transform me into ruins of fire.

---

417 *la diera*, G: le diera   418 *acudiera*, A B C H J L M P S T V: viniera
419 *no*, E: yo/a, E: missing   421 *pues quien sólo*, B H M T V: porque sólo quien;
A G: pues que sólo quien   423 aunque *éstas*, A B C H J L M P S T V: aquestas
425 *en ella*, A B H M T V: y en ella; J: en ellas   427 A H: en aire convertida;
C J P: convertido en ayre   428 *Aura*, P: Aurora   429 *donde*, A B G H M T V: adonde
432 *crueldades*, E: palabras   434 *combierta*, A B C H J M P T V: convierte

RÚSTICO   Pues ¿tengo la culpa yo   435   [22ʳ]
               para que yo te lo pague?
ERÓSTRATO   Tanpoco la tengo yo, y pago la pena.
RÚSTICO   ¡Ajentes de amor, beis aquí buestros gajes!
ERÓSTRATO   Desbanezida hermosura,
               que bagamente constante,   440
               dejando de ser lisonja a las flores,
               a ser te trasladas lisonja a las aves:
               a llorarte boy perdida,   [22ᵛ]
               y no me atrebo a llorarte,
               porque a la tierra las lágrimas corren,   445
               y no está en la tierra aun caduca tu ymagen.
               Y así en suspiros presumo
               que mejor mi fe te halle,
               pues el ayre mereze tu sombra,   [23ʳ]
               y son los suspiros alajas del ayre.   450
               Mas ¿cómo en lástimas, cielos,
               se combierten mis pesares?
               ¿Desde quándo en Eróstrato a sido
               v dócil la queja, o lágrima fácil?
               Abiendo rencores y hiras,   455
               ¿apelan a las piedades   [23ᵛ]
               mis sañas, mis penas, mis ansias, mis furias?
               ¡Malaya dolor que me hizo cobarde!
               ¡viven los cielos, villano . . .
RÚSTICO   ¡Viuan, sin que a mí me maten!   460
[ERÓSTRATO] . . . que an de ver mi vengan[za] no sólo
               (a) los troncos, los riscos, [los montes,] lo[s] mares,
               pero Diana y sus ninfas,   [24ʳ]
               padeciendo los vltrajes
               del abrasado despecho de un hombre,   465
               pues ya para serlo, bastó ser amante!
               Essa Pocris, esa fiera,
               que más amiga mostrarse
               debiera, [verá] que si (a) un elemento   [24ᵛ]
               de aquella hermosura la pompa desaze,   470
               otro elemento la venga.
               ¡A, Eróstrato!, si grande
               tu fama no puede hacerte oy eterno,
               beamos si eterno tu infamia te haze.   [Vase.]

436 *para que yo,* A B H M T V: di, para que   437 *pago,* A B C H J L M P S T V: tengo
449 *pues,* L: pues que; A B H M S T V: puesto que   451 *lástimas,* B H J M P T V:
lástima   454 *lágrima,* A B C H J M P S T V: la lágrima   455 *rencores y hiras,* A C J P:
rigores e iras; B H M T V: iras y rigores   458 *dolor,* A B C G H J L M P S T V: el dolor
460 *maten,* C J P: mate; B H M T V: mates   461 Ac. E: missing
461 *an,* A B G H M S T V: hoy han/*venganza,* E: vengan   462 E: a los troncos, los riscos, lo mares;
C J P: los mares, los troncos, los riscos, los montes   465 *hombre,* A B C H J M P S T V: loco
466 *pues,* B C H J L P S T V; que/*ser,* A B C H J M P S T V: el ser

RÚSTICO	Well, do I have the blame	435
	so that I should pay for it?	
ERÓSTRATO	I do not have it either, and I pay the penalty.	
RÚSTICO	Agents of love, you see here your wages!	
ERÓSTRATO	Vanished loveliness,	
	who, vaguely constant,	440
	ceasing to be a delight to the flowers	
	has come to be a delight to the birds:	
	I am going, lost, to weep for you,	
	yet I do not dare to weep for you	
	because tears run over the earth	445
	and now not even your fallen image remains on earth.	
	And so, in sighs, I assume	
	that my faith may find you better,	
	for the air deserves your shadow,	
	and sighs are jewels of the air.	450
	But how, heavens, are my troubles	
	transformed into complaints?	
	Since when in Eróstrato has either	
	the complaint been docile or the tear easy?	
	Having rancor and ire,	455
	do my rages, pains, anxieties, furies	
	call on the pieties?	
	Damn the pain that made me a coward!	
	By the heavens, wretch . . .	
RÚSTICO	By the heavens, without their killing me!	460
ERÓSTRATO	. . . they shall see my vengeance: not only	
	the trees, the cliffs, the mountains, the seas,	
	but Diana and her nymphs,	
	suffering the outrages	
	of the inflamed despair of a man,	465
	since in order to be thus, it was enough to be a lover!	
	That Pocris, that beast,	
	who should have shown herself to be	
	friendlier, will see that, if one element	
	destroys the grandeur of that beauty	470
	another element will avenge it.	
	Oh, Eróstrato! If your	
	fame cannot make you eternal today,	
	let us see if your infamy makes you eternal. [Exit.]	

467 *Essa,* A B C H J L M P S T V: Y esa   469 *verá,* E L: missing/*un*, E: a un
471ff. A B C H J M P T V: Y pues tan presto se abren
                               las puertas del templo, y en su sacrificio
                               a todos es dado tocar sus altares,
                               yo . . . Mas el tiempo lo diga.
G: ¡Yo . . .! Mas el tiempo lo diga.; E L S: missing
472 *A,* A B C G H J L M P S T V: Ea   473 *no puede,* L S: nos pueden
474 *tu infamia;* L S: tu fama; A B C H J M P T V: hoy tu infamia

RÚSTICO	Furioso ba, y no sé cierto	475
	por qué, que muchos galanes,	
	aún no combertida en ayre su dama,	[25ʳ(7)]
	por sólo adorar, adoran al ayre.	
	Mas, como viuo me deje,	
	¿qué tengo de qué quejarme?	480
	Y así, la desecha haciendo de que	
	en quanto a pasado estoy ignorante,	
	me bolberé al jardín. Pero	
	mi muger con Diana sale.	[25ᵛ]
	De aquí e de escuchar el intento que lleva	485
	el ver quán a solas al monte la trae.	
	[Retírase entre unas matas.]	

[Salen DIANA, FLORETA.]

DIANA	Tú, Floreta, has de decirme	
	la verdad, pues tú la sabes.	
RÚSTICO	[Aparte.]	
	Será la primera que a dicho en su vida.	
FLORETA	Sí aré, que soy boca de todas verdades.	490
DIANA	¿Quién es quien estos jardines	[26ʳ]
	a desoras cierra y abre?	
RÚSTICO	[Aparte.]	
	Seguro estoi que lo sepa, si es fuerza	
	que porque no diga verdad, se lo calle.	
DIANA	¿No respondes?	
FLORETA	[Aparte.] ¿Qué diré?	495
[RÚSTICO]	[Aparte.]	
	¿Mas que echa la culpa [a] alguien?	
DIANA	¿Qué esperas, pues? Prosigue.	
RÚSTICO	[Aparte.] Ella está	[26ᵛ]
	pensando vn inbuste con que disculparme.	
FLORETA	Yo, señora . . . quando . . . si . . .	
DIANA	¿Qué te turbas?	
FLORETA	No te espante[s],	500
	porque decirte que Rústico a sido	
	el bil, el traidor, el pícaro infame	
	que por interés o miedo	
	a Eróstrato espaldas haze,	
	no lo e de hazer, porque es mi marido,	505
	y no as de saberlo de mí, aunque me mates.	[27ʳ]

476 *que*, A B H M S T V: pues   478 *sólo*, A: sola/*adorar*, A B H M S T V: adorarla/*al*,
A B H M S T V: el   479 *deje*, B H: deja   480 A: qué tengo de quejarme; B H M T V:
por aquí pienso quedarme; C J P: missing   482 *estoy*, L S: estoy yo
484 *con*, L S: como   486 *el*, A B G H M S T V: y; C J P: al; L: que al/*quán*, A B G H M S T V:
lo que/*monte*, A B C G H J L M P S T V: campo/*la*, L S: le; G: las   490 *todas*, A B G H M S T V:

RÚSTICO   He goes in a rage, and I do not know for sure   475
               why, for many gallants,
               even with their ladies not transformed into air,
               only for the sake of adoring, adore the air.
               But, since he leaves me alive,
               of what do I have to complain?   480
               And so, assuming the pretense that
               I am ignorant of what has happened,
               I shall return to the garden. But
               my wife comes out with Diana.
               From here shall I listen to the intent that is conveyed, 485
               seeing how all alone she brings her to the mountain.
                           [He withdraws behind some bushes.]

[Enter DIANA, FLORETA.]

DIANA   You, Floreta, will tell me
               the truth, since you know it.
RÚSTICO   [Aside.]
               It will be the first that she has told in her life.
FLORETA   Yes, I shall, for I am the teller of all truths.   490
DIANA   Who is it that opens and closes
               these gardens at all hours?
RÚSTICO   [Aside.]
               I am sure that she knows, if it is necessary
               for her to say nothing in order not to tell the truth.
DIANA   Do you not answer?
FLORETA   [Aside.]   What shall I say?   495
RÚSTICO   [Aside.]
               Well, is she going to blame someone?
DIANA   What are you waiting for, then? Go on.
RÚSTICO   [Aside.]   She is
               thinking of a trick with which to pardon me.
FLORETA   I, madame . . . when . . . if . . .
DIANA   What is bothering you?
FLORETA   Do not worry,   500
               because to tell you that Rústico has been
               the wretch, the traitor, the infamous rogue
               who, for money or fear,
               looks the other way for Eróstrato,
               I shall not do, because he is my husband,   505
               and you will not find it out from me even though you kill me.

muchas; J L: missing   491 *quien estos,* C J P: quien en estos; B H M T V: el que en los
492 *desoras,* A B C G H J L M P S T V: deshora   496 Ac. E: missing
496 *a,* C E J L P: missing   500 *turbas,* L S: burlas/*espantes,* E: espante
505 *lo,* L S: le/*hazer,* A B H M T V: decir

RÚSTICO   [Aparte.]
               ¡A, muger mía! Mintió
               contigo la más constante
               con el balor q*ue* ressiste el decirlo.   [Vase.]
DIANA   No, no me lo digas.
               [Aparte.]   Oy e de vengarme   510
               de un villano con su muerte,   [27ᵛ]
               mas dar la muerte es desaire,
               que no me mereze castigo tan noble
               el rústico objeto de un pecho cobarde.
               A Anteón mudé la forma   515
               en venganza de otro [ul]traje,
               y aqu(e)este a de ser que nadie le bea   [28ʳ]
               que en forma distinta de bruto no le halle.
               Parézca lo q*ue* es, pues es
               ocasión que Venus cause   520
               en mí este rencor que entre muertas zenizas
               pareze que yela, y no es sino q*ue* arde.   [Vase.]
FLORETA   Ella pensó que era boba,
               y que abía de sacarme   [28ᵛ]
               que Rústico fue él que tubo la culpa,   525
               Pues no, que no soy de engañar yo mui fácil.

[RÚSTICO, que sale con una cabeza de cuatro caras
diferentes, y vestido de pieles.]

RÚSTICO   Ya que Diana se fue,
               hermosa Floreta, dame
               los brazos.
FLORETA   ¡Ay triste! ¿Qué [es] esto que miro?
RÚSTICO   ¿Por qué te retiras?
FLORETA   Cruel león, no me mates,   530   [29ʳ(8)]
RÚSTICO   ¡Yo león! ¿Estás borracha,
               muger? ¡Quando a que te pague
               mi amor la fineza de no aver contado
               que fu[i] el agresor de culpa tan graue,
               bengo como un corderito,   535
               león te parezco!
FLORETA   ¡Amparadme,
               cielos!
RÚSTICO   Espera.   [29ᵛ]
FLORETA   ¡Ay qué garras y dientes!
RÚSTICO   Pues ¿q*ué* ay q*ue* io muerda, ni q*ué* ay q*ue* yo agarre?

507 *A*, A B C G H J L M P S T V: Oh   509 G: con qué valor se resiste a decirlo
510 *No, no,* A B C H J M P T V: No/*Oy,* B H M T V: Que hoy   512 *dar la,* A B C G H J L M P
S T V: darle   513 *me,* G: se; A B C H J M P T V: missing   515 *Anteón* J L: Anteó; A B
G H M S T V: Acteón/*forma,* J L: fortuna   516 *ultraje,* E L: traje   517 *y,* A B C G H J
M P S T V: y a/*aqueste,* E: a que este/*a de ser,* A B C G H J M P S T V: he de hacer/*le,* G: lo

RÚSTICO   [Aside.]
           Oh, wife of mine! She tried to trick
           you, the most constant of women,
           with an audacity that defies words.   [Exit.]
DIANA   No, do not tell me.
           [Aside.]   Today I shall avenge myself   510
           on a villain with his death,
           but giving him death is foolishness,
           for the rustic object of a cowardly heart
           does not deserve such a noble punishment.
           I changed the form of Acteon   515
           in revenge for another outrage,
           and this one is to be such that no one may see him
           who does not find him in a different animal form.
           Let it appear to be what it is, since it is
           Venus' doing that   520
           my rancor seems to lie cold
           in dead embers, but still burns.   [Exit.]
FLORETA   She thought that I was a fool,
           and that she was going to get out of me
           that Rústico was the one who had the blame.   525
           But no, for I am not so easy to deceive.

[RÚSTICO, who enters with a head of four different animals, and
dressed in skins.]

RÚSTICO   Now that Diana has gone,
           lovely Floreta, give me
           your arms.
FLORETA   Miserable me! What is this that I see?
RÚSTICO   Why do you withdraw?
FLORETA   Cruel lion, do not kill me!   530
RÚSTICO   I, a lion! Are you drunk,
           woman? When, so my love
           can repay you the kindness of not having told
           that I was the perpetrator of such a grave crime,
           I come as a little lamb,   535
           I seem to you a lion!
FLORETA   Help me,
           heavens!
RÚSTICO   Wait.
FLORETA   Oh, what claws and teeth!
RÚSTICO   But what is there that I should bite nor what that I should claw?

---

518 *le,* J P: la; G: lo   519 *Parezca,* A B C H J M P T V: Padezca/*pues es,* L: pues es, pues es
520 *que,* E G L: de   521 *en mí,* A B H M T V: missing   525 *él que,* A B G H M T V: quien
526 *mui,* B H M T V: tan   529 *es,* E: missing   530 *león,* L S: missing
534 *fui,* E L S: fue/*graue,* A B C H J M P T V: grande   537 *y,* A B G H M T V: qué

[Sale POCRIS.]

POCRIS   ¿De qué, Floreta, das vozes?
            Mas, ¿qué mucho que te espantes,   540
            mirando, ¡ai de mí!, vn osso tan fiero?
RÚSTICO   ¿Qué llama vsted osso? Así Dios la guarde.
FLORETA y   ¿No ay quien de tan bruta fiera   [30r]
  POCRIS   nos faborezca y ampare?

[Sale CÉFALO con el venablo, y CLARÍN.]

ZÉFALO   Sí, pues mi destino a sólo seguir,   545
            oy voz de muger perdido me trae.
CLARÍN   Tente, señor.
ZÉFALO   Suelta. No
            temáis, que para este tranze
            no en bano perdió su benablo Diana,
            y tú le dejaste en mi mano no en balde.   550   [30v]
CLARÍN   ¿Que quieras con tan ambriento
            lobo meterte en combate?
RÚSTICO   Aún más lisonjero el delirio es de aqueste,
            pues lobo, animal de su especie, me hace.
ZÉFALO   Manchado tigre, conmigo   555
            embiste; puesto delante
            me allarás de esta dama por quien
            ya importa bruñir con tu sangre otra sangre.   [31r]
RÚSTICO   ¡Viue Dios, que ba de beras!
            Y si se le antoja darme   560
            con el benablo, lo ará; mientras pasa
            su frenesí, mejor es que io escape.   [Vase.]
ZÉFALO   Sin el trofeo de aber
            logrado aquesta ocasión
            no as de irte.   [31v]
POCRIS   ¡No le sigas   565
            pues buelue huiendo [veloz].
ZÉFALO   Aunque vengarte del susto
            fuera mi aplauso mayor,
            me para tu vista, más
            inperios[a] que tu voz;   570
            entre a la parte el cuidado
            de aquel pasado dolor.

538 *ni qué ay,* L S: ni/*agarre,* B H M S T V: arañe   538 Ac. H S: Pocris; y después
Céfalo y Clarín   542 B H M T V: pues ella por león me tenía de antes;
C J P: missing   543 Ac. A B C G H J M P T V: Las dos   545 *Sí,* L: crossed out
547 *Suelta. No,* A B H M T V: No temáis   548 *temáis que,* A B H M T V: que solo
550 *le,* G: lo   551 *tan,* B H M T V: un   556 *puesto,* L: pues todo
557 *esta,* A B C H J M P S T V: la   558 B H M T V: ya intento este acero bañar con tu sangre;
J: ya importa bruñir con tu sangre la otra sangre   560 *si,* L: missing   562 *io,* M: missing

[Enter POCRIS.]

POCRIS	Why, Floreta, are you shouting?
	But, why not be afraid, 540
	seeing (oh me!) such a fierce bear?
RÚSTICO	Whom are you calling a bear? May God keep you thus.
FLORETA	Is there no one who may favor us
AND POCRIS	and save us from such a brute beast?

[Enter CÉFALO with the spear, and CLARÍN.]

CÉFALO	Yes, since, while only following my destiny 545
	today, the voice of a woman leads me here, lost.
CLARÍN	Hold, sir.
CÉFALO	Let go. Be not
	afraid, for Diana did not lose
	her spear in vain for this crisis,
	and you left it in my hand not in vain. 550
CLARÍN	You want to place yourself in combat
	with such a hungry wolf?
RÚSTICO	The madness of this one is even more flattering,
	since he makes me a wolf—an animal of his own kind.
CÉFALO	Spotted tiger, attack 555
	me, you will find me
	in front of this woman for whom
	it is now important to burnish another blood with your blood.
RÚSTICO	By God, he means it!
	And if it pleases him to strike me 560
	with the spear, he will do it; until
	his rage passes, it is better for me to escape. [Exit.]
CÉFALO	Without the triumph of having
	won on this occasion,
	you are not to leave.
POCRIS	Do not follow him 565
	since, fleeing quickly, he returns!
CÉFALO	Although to avenge you of your fright
	would be my greatest praise,
	the sight of you, more imperious
	than your voice, stops me; 570
	let care enter at the site
	of that past pain.

564 *logrado,* A: logrado a; B H M T V: llegado a; C J P: llegado   565 *le,* C G H L P S: lo
566 *buelue,* J P: vuelvo; L: buebo/*veloz,* E: tu voz   569 *me,* J L: que
570 *inperiosa,* E: inperioso   571 *entre a la parte,* A B H T V: a que entre a parte;
S M: a que entre aparte; J: entre a parte; L: entre la parte

POCRIS   No le tengas, y dejando   [32ʳ]
            el acaso y la ilusión,
            no el averte detenido   575
            atribuias a fabor;
            q*ue* es bien, si tú un riesgo inpid[e]s
            q*ue* inpida otro riesgo yo.
            Por esto que no siguiesses,
            dije, a esa fiera.

[CÉFALO]   Aunque son   580
            piedades y no carizias,
            p[e]rdóneme tu rigor,   [32ᵛ]
            que io me e de persuadir
            a lo que me está mejor,
            y ya que no soi dichoso,   585
            darme a entender que [lo] soy.

POCRIS   Persuadirte a lo imposible
            es banagloriosa acción.

[CÉFALO]   Dar[s]e por venzido antes
            del riesgo, poco balor.   590

POCRIS   El que su bien anticipa,   [33ʳ(9)]
            peligr[a] en la persuasión.

ZÉFALO   ¿Q*ué* importa que él no lo sea
            para que lo piense yo?

CLARÍN   ¿Y usted en aqueste alcázar,   595
            no me dirá quién es?

FLORETA   Soi
            nimfa de escalera abajo.

CLARÍN   La norabuena me doi.

FLORETA   ¿La norabuena? ¿De qué?

CLARÍN   De que, por lo menos, no   600   [33ᵛ]
            llegará a sus [ac]cesorias
            desalentado mi ardor.

FLORETA   Antes sí, que en las sirbientes
            corre contraria razón;
            pues las de escalera abajo   605
            de desbán arriba son.

[Sale AURA, en el aire sobre un águila, invisible para CÉFALO,
POCRIS, FLORETA y CLARÍN.]

AURA   [Para sí.]
            Ya que a la merzed de Venus,
            dejando en nueba mansión

---

576 *atribuias,* L S: atribuyes   577 *es,* L S: en/*inpides,* E: inpidas   579 *esto,* A B C H J L
M P S T V: eso/*siguiesses,* L S: siguieres   581 L S: caricias y no piedades
582 *perdóneme,* E: pordaneme; J P: perdóname   586 *darme,* A L S: dadme/*lo,* E: missing
588 *banagloriosa,* B J M P T V: una gloriosa 589 Ac. E: missing   589 *Darse,* E L: darte
591 *anticipa,* A J L S: anticipe   592 *peligra,* E: peligro/*persuasión,*

POCRIS	Have no care, and, leaving	
	the accident and the illusion,	
	do not attribute my having	575
	stopped you as a favor,	
	for it is well, if you stop one risk,	
	that I stop another.	
	For this reason I told you	
	not to follow that beast.	
CÉFALO	Even though they are	580
	pieties and not caresses,	
	may your rigor pardon me,	
	for I must persuade myself	
	as to what is best,	
	and, since I am not happy,	585
	to make myself understand that I am.	
POCRIS	To persuade yourself of the impossible	
	is vainglorious action.	
CÉFALO	To give oneself up for defeated before	
	the risk, little valor.	590
POCRIS	He who anticipates his well-being	
	risks danger in the conviction.	
CÉFALO	What difference does it make that it is not so	
	in order for me to think it?	
CLARÍN	And you, in this castle,	595
	will you not tell me who you are?	
FLORETA	I am	
	the downstairs nymph.	
CLARÍN	I congratulate myself.	
FLORETA	Congratulate? Why?	
CLARÍN	Because, at least, my ardor	600
	will not arrive at its destination	
	out of breath.	
FLORETA	Rather it will, for in servants	
	reason runs contrary;	
	for those of the downstairs	
	are loftier than the garrets.	605

[Enter AURA, in the air, on an eagle, invisible to CÉFALO,
POCRIS, FLORETA, and CLARÍN.]

AURA	[To herself.]
	Now that, at the mercy of Venus,
	ceasing, in a new house,

A B C H J M P S T V: presunción   593 *él,* B C H J M P T V: missing   595 *aqueste,*
A H: aquese   598, 599 *norabuena,* L S: enhorabuena   601 *accesorias,* E: cesorias
602 *desalentado,* M T: desalentando/*ardor,* A B C H J L M P S T V: amor
605 *pues,* A B C G H J M P T V: que   606 Ac. *Sale,* H: missing/*el aire,* A B C H J
L M P S T V: lo alto/*un,* B: una   608 *nueba,* A B C H J M P T V: nuestra

	de ser de los bosques nimfa,	[34^r]

de ser de los bosques nimfa,   [34ʳ]
nimfa de los vientos soy,   610
a cuio suabe aliento
an de benir desde oy,
de Aura inspirados, la planta,
la abe, el cristal y la flor,
en flor, cristal, ave y planta,   615
no aia o música o berdor
que amor no publique; y pues   [34ᵛ]
deví a Zéfalo [el favor],
y el rencor le deuo a Pocris,
y se allan juntos los dos,   620
a lograr los dos asuntos
del fabor y del rencor,
inspire suave el aura de amor.

POCRIS   [Aparte.]
           ¿Qué muerta voz, ¡ay de mí!,. . .
[CÉFALO]   [Aparte.]
           ¡Ay de mí!, ¿qué viua boz . . .   625
LOS DOS   [Aparte.]
           . . .así a la parte del alma   [35ʳ]
           ablando está el corazón?
POCRIS   [Aparte.]
           Mas con çerrar al encanto
           el oído, libre estoy.
ZÉFALO   [Aparte.]
           Mas con morir al echizo,   630
           cunpliré mi obligación.
POCRIS   ¿Dónde vas?
ZÉFALO   Asegurando   [35ᵛ]
           el pasado riesgo boy.
POCRIS   No, no as de pasar de aquí.
ZÉFALO   Perdone esta vez tu voz,   635
           que no la e de obedezer
           como antes.
POCRIS   ¿Por qué no?
ZÉFALO   Porque mandarme quedar
           en la pesada ocasión,
           quando a no mirarte iba   640
           tras aquel bruto terror,
           no es lo mismo que mandarme   [36ʳ]
           quedar quando a verte voy.

---

612 *benir*, A B C G H J M P S T V: vivir   616 *o*, A B C H J L M P S T V: missing
617 *no*, L S: les   618 *el favor;* E: ber; P: es fauor   619 *rencor*, G: rigor/*deuo*,
A B C G H J M P S T V: debí   621 *asuntos*, L S: asientos   622 *fabor*, L S: rencor/
rencor, A B C G H J M T V: rigor   626 *así a*, A B C G H J L M P S T V: hacia

	to be a nymph of the forests,	

to be a nymph of the forests,
I am a nymph of the winds,   610
to whose soft breath,
inspired by Aura, the plant,
the bird, the brook, and the flower
must conform so that in
flower, brook, bird, and plant   615
there may be no music or greenery
that does not publicize love; and since
I owed favor to Céfalo,
and I owe rancor to Pocris,
and they find themselves together,   620
to achieve the two tasks
of favor and rancor,
inspire softly the breath of love.

POCRIS   [Aside.]
What a dead voice, oh my!,. . .

CÉFALO   [Aside.]
Oh me! What a live voice . . .   625

BOTH OF   [Aside.]
THEM   . . .is speaking thus to the
part of the soul, the heart?

POCRIS   [Aside.]
But by closing my ear to the
enchantment, I am free.

CÉFALO   [Aside.]
But by dying enchanted   630
I shall fulfill my obligation.

POCRIS   Where are you going?

CÉFALO   I go,
insuring the past risk.

POCRIS   No, you are not to leave here.

CÉFALO   May your voice forgive me this time,   635
for I shall not obey
as before.

POCRIS   Why not?

CÉFALO   Because ordering me to remain
on that painful occasion
when, not to see you, I was going   640
after that brutal terror
is not the same as ordering me
to remain when I go to see you.

627 *el*, B G H M S T: al   628 *al*, L: el   630 *morir*, B H J M V: mirar
639 *pesada*, A B C H J L M P S T V: pasada   640 *iba*, L: ibas   641 *terror*, A B C H J M
P S T V: feroz   644 *gusto*, A B C H J M P T V: riesgo

POCRIS   Quien sólo al gusto obedeze,
poco deue a su pasión;   645
que obedezer contra el gusto
es la fineza maior.

ZÉFALO   Porque beas que no es
[interés] sino atención,
bete en paz.

POCRIS   En paz te queda.   650

                          [Hace que se va.]

AURA   [Para sí.]
Aunque se aparten los dos,   [36ᵛ]
inspire [suave el aura de amor.]

POCRIS   [Aparte.]
¡Porque digo que se quede
no más, se queda! ¿Quién vio
tan mal mandada obediencia?   655

ZÉFALO   [Aparte.]
¡Porque me diga que no
la siga, temo! ¿Quién, cielos,
bio en la ciega confusión
del temor y la ossadía   [37ʳ(10)]
tam bién mandado al temor.   660

AURA   [Para sí.]
Ynspire [suave el aura de amor.]

POCRIS   [Aparte.]
Pero si se fue, veré.

ZÉFALO   [Aparte.]
Mas beré si se ausentó.

POCRIS   ¿A qué buelues?
ZÉFALO   ¿Y[o] qué sé?
¿A qué buelues?

POCRIS   ¿Qué sé yo?   665
AURA   [Para sí.]
Inspire [suave el aura de amor.]   [37ᵛ]

POCRIS   Yo a decirte que si quedas
en toda aquesta región,
supuesto que de estranjero   670
el indulto se acabó,
corre peligro tu vida.

ZÉFALO   Yo a decir que le corrió
ya, pues le tengo dos luzes,
si me quedo y si me boy.

---

649 *interés,* E: entereza   652 E: inspire; L: ins   660 *al,* L S: el
661 E: ynspire, L: ins   664 *Yo,* E: y   665 *A,* A B C G H J L M P S T V: Tú a
666 E: inspire; L: ins   670 *el,* A B C G H J L M P S T V: ya el   672 *decir que le,*

POCRIS   He who obeys only his pleasure
                 owes little to his passion;   645
                 for to obey against pleasure
                 is the greatest refinement.

CÉFALO   So that you may see that it is not
                 presumption but attention,
                 go in peace.

POCRIS   Remain in peace.   650

                                         [She begins to go.]

AURA   [To herself.]
                 Although the two of them part,
                 inspire softly the breath of love.

POCRIS   [Aside.]
                 Only because I say that he should
                 stay, he stays! Who has seen
                 such ill-mannered obedience?   655

CÉFALO   [Aside.]
                 Because she may tell me not
                 to follow her, I am afraid! Who, heavens,
                 has seen in the blind confusion
                 of fear and daring
                 one so well ordered to fear?   660

AURA   [To herself.]
                 Inspire softly the breath of love.

POCRIS   [Aside.]
                 But I shall see if he has gone away.

CÉFALO   [Aside.]
                 But I shall see if she has left.

POCRIS   Why are your returning?

CÉFALO   What do I know?
                 Why are you returning?

POCRIS   What know I?   665

AURA   [To herself.]
                 Inspire softly the breath of love.

POCRIS   I, to tell you that if you remain
                 in this entire region,
                 supposing that the pardon   670
                 of a stranger has ended,
                 your life is in danger.

CÉFALO   I, to say that it already is,
                 since I am in a quandary
                 whether I stay or whether I go.

A B C H J M P T V: decirte que; G: decir que lo/*corrió,* C J P: corro
673 *le tengo dos,* A B H M T V: le tengo a dos; C J P: te tengo a dos; G: la tengo a dos

POCRIS	Pues si te dan a escoger,	675	[38r]
	au(n)sentarte es el menor.		
ZÉFALO	Si el menor es ausentarme,		
	¡ay Dios!, ¿quál será el maior?		
POCRIS	A mí, él que fuere sea.		
	Bete, pues; no buelua yo	680	
	a allarte aquí quando buelva.		
ZÉFALO	Eso es decirme que no		
	me baia, si as de bolver.		
POCRIS	Y ésa, locura.		
ZÉFALO	Doi		
	que sea locura, pero	685	[38v]
	locura puesta en razón.		
POCRIS	¿No te bas?		
ZÉFALO	Si tú te bas.		
POCRIS	[Aparte.]		
	¡Qué pena!		
ZÉFALO	[Aparte.] ¡Qué confusión!		
POCRIS	[Aparte.]		
	Pero yo sabré vencer[la].		
ZÉFALO	[Aparte.]		
	Mas sabré seguirla yo.	690	
POCRIS	Por más que ignorado acento . . .		
ZÉFALO	Por más que ignora[da voz] . . .		
POCRIS	. . . en mi oprobio . . .		
ZÉFALO	. . . en mi desdicha . . .		[39r]
POCRIS	. . . en mi imjuria . . .		
ZÉFALO	. . . en mi temor . . .		
POCRIS	. . . en mi ofenssa . . .		
[CÉFALO]	. . . en mi fortuna . . .	695	
POCRIS	. . . en mi agravio . . .		
ZÉFALO	. . . en mi favor . . .		
POCRIS	. . . esté diciendo al oído . . .		
[CÉFALO]	. . . diciendo esté al corazón . . .		
A 4	. . . inspire [suave el aura de amor.]		

676 *ausentarte*, E: aunsentarte/*menor*, A B C H J L M P S T V: mejor
677 *menor*, A B C H J L M P S T V: mejor   678 *maior*, A B H M S T V: peor
679 *él que*, A B C H J M P T: que él que; L S: cual que; V: que él   681 *a allarte*, M: allarte
682 *eso*, A B H J M P T V: esto/*decirme*, C: decir   684 *Y ésa, locura*, B C H J M P T V:
Esa es locura; L S: Eso es locura; A: Esta es locura/*Doi*, A B C G H J L M P S T V: Yo doy
689 *vencerla*, E: vencer   690 *seguirla*, L S: vencerla   691 *ignorado*, L: ignorando
692 *Por más*, G: Porque/*ignorada voz*, E: ignorando voy; L S: ignorado voy; G: una
ignorada voz   695 Ac. E L: missing   697 *esté*, A B C G H J M P T V: me esté
699 Ac. A B H M T V: Vanse los dos; C J P: Vanse; S: missing   699ff. B C J M P T V follow with:
CLARÍN   ¿Y los dos en qué quedamos?
FLORETA   En que los dos a otros dos.
CLARÍN   Con que diremos cantando
              de nuestros amos al son.
LOS DOS   Inspire suave el aura de amor.

POCRIS	For if they are given to take you,	675
	to leave is the least danger.	
CÉFALO	If the least is to leave,	
	(oh God!) what is the greatest?	
POCRIS	To me, it makes no difference.	
	Go then, let me not again	680
	find you when I return.	
CÉFALO	That is telling me not	
	to go, if you are to return.	
POCRIS	And that is madness.	
CÉFALO	I grant	
	that it may be madness, but	685
	madness set in reason.	
POCRIS	Are you not going?	
CÉFALO	If you go.	
POCRIS	[Aside.]	
	What pain!	
CÉFALO	[Aside.] What confusion!	
POCRIS	[Aside.]	
	But I shall know how to overcome.	
CÉFALO	[Aside.]	
	But I shall know how to pursue her.	690
POCRIS	For as much as an unknown accent . . .	
CÉFALO	For as much as an unknown voice . . .	
POCRIS	. . . in my malice . . .	
CÉFALO	. . . in my unhappiness . . .	
POCRIS	. . . in my insult . . .	
CÉFALO	. . . in my fear . . .	
POCRIS	. . . in my offense . . .	
CÉFALO	. . . in my good luck . . .	695
POCRIS	. . . in my affront . . .	
CÉFALO	. . . in my favor . . .	
POCRIS	. . . may say to my ear . . .	
CÉFALO	. . . may say to my heart . . .	
BOTH OF THEM	. . . inspire softly the breath of love.	699

A G H have the same verses with the following exception:
FLORETA   En lo que los otros dos.
L S have the same verses with the following exceptions:
FLORETA   ¿En qué quedamos los dos?
CLARÍN   Con que diremos bailando
Following these verses G and S add:
I CORO   Ven tirana, ¿qué hay que esperar?
            ¿Cómo?
II CORO   De esta manera.
I CORO   En aire convertida desvanecida vuela
            los diáfanos espacios.
            Al monte, a la ribera.
TODOS   Inspire suave el aire de amor.
G indicates the final six verses only as Coro (Dentro)

Jornada 2   [1r]

[Entrada a una huerta vecina al templo de DIANA.]

[Dentro grita, y sale cantando el Coro 1° compuesto
de pastores y pastoras, y detrás de ellos CÉFALO, ERÓSTRATO y
CLARÍN, de villanos, con dones en las manos, excepto CLARÍN, que
no le trae.]

CORO	Venid, moradores de Lidia, venid;	700
	Venid, que oy de marzo la luna se cumple	
	en que, partidos el día y la noche,	
	yguala Díana las sombras y luzes.	[1v]
SOLO	Venid, y trayendo de rosas y flores,	
	de fieras y aves los dones comunes,	705
	las unas sus rizos coronen guirnaldas,	
	las otras sus aras adornen perfumes.	[2r]
[A 4]	Venid, [que oy de marzo la luna se cumple	
	en que, partidos el día y la noche,	
	yguala Diana las sombras y luzes.]	710
ERÓSTRATO	[Aparte.]	
	Pues ya el día amaneció,	
	en que estos montes saluden	
	de Diana el templo, a cuyo	
	fin tantas gentes concurren,	
	bien entre ellos mi rencor	715
	disfrazado se introduze,	
	aziendo que este villano	
	traje (se) encubra y disimule	[2v]
	persona [e] yntento, pues	
	como entre todos me oculte,	720
	verán Venus y Amor y Aura	
	que si ay quien su pompa injurie,	
	ay quien sus agravios vengue;	
	y assí, con todos procure	
	mezclarme, diziendo, a fin	725
	de que mi erro[r] se oculte:	
	venid, y tejiendo con blancos azâres	[3r]
	los rojos claveles, violetas azules,	
	l[a]s un[a]s sus rizos coronen guirnaldas,	
	l[a]s otr[a]s sus aras adornen perfumes.	730
AL 4	[Venid, que oy de marzo la luna se cumple	
	en que, partidos el día y la noche,	
	yguala Diana las sombras y luzes.]	

700 Ac. A B M T V: Coro de hombres; C J P: Coro de hombres segundo; H: Coro de pastores; G: Coros
704 Ac. A B C H J M P T V: missing   704 *rosas,* G: hojas   708 Ac. A B C H J M P T V:
Todos; G: Coros   708 E: Venid & a los ʃ del 4; G: Venid, moradores de Lidia, venid . . .
709-710 A B C G H J M P T V: missing   715 *ellos,* G: ellas   716 *se,* A B C G H J M P T V: me

Act Two

[Entrance to a garden next to the temple of DIANA.]

[Offstage, Chorus I, composed of shepherds and shepherdesses, shouts, and enters singing, and after them CÉFALO, ERÓSTRATO, and CLARÍN, and peasants, with offerings in their hands, except for CLARÍN, who does not have one.]

CHORUS	Come, residents of Lydia, come;	700
	come, for today the March moon is full	
	and Diana divides the light and the dark	
	equally into the day and the night.	
SOLO	Come, and bearing the common gifts	
VOICE	of roses and flowers, of beasts and birds,	705
	let some crown their locks with garlands,	
	let others adorn their altars with perfumes.	
CHORUS	Come, for today the March moon is full	
	and Diana divides the light and the dark	
	equally into the day and the night.	710
ERÓSTRATO	[Aside.]	
	Since now the day has dawned,	
	on which these mountains will salute	
	the temple of Diana, to which	
	end so many people come together,	
	disguised, my rancor mingles	715
	well among them,	
	causing this peasant	
	attire to cover and hide	
	both my identity and my purpose, for	
	since I hide among everyone,	720
	Venus, Cupid, and Aura will see	
	that if there is someone whom their ritual affronts,	
	there is also someone who avenges their abuse;	
	and thus, so that my	
	error may be hidden, I	725
	shall manage to blend in by saying:	
	come, and weaving with white orange blossoms	
	red carnations and blue violets,	
	let some crown their locks with garlands,	
	let others adorn their altars with perfumes.	730
CHORUS	Come, for today the March moon is full	
	and Diana divides the light and the dark	
	equally into the day and the night.	

718 *encubra,* E: se encubra   719 *e intento,* E: yntento; A G: e intentos   721 *y Amor,* A B C G
H J M P T V: Amor   726 *error,* E: erro, G: yerro/*se oculte,* A B H J M T V: ejecute; C P: se ejecute
729, 730 *las,* E: los   731 Ac. A B C H J M P T V: Todos; G: Coros
731-733 E: repite al 4

[Vanse todos, y quedan
Céfalo y Clarín.]

CÉFALO   Sigue, Clarín, essa tropa.

CLARÍN   El juicio que no tube,   735
           tus cosas quitarme intentan.

CÉFALO   Pue[s] ¿qué a[y hoy] que en ellas culp[e]s?

CLARÍN   Noble en Trinachia naciste,   [3ᵛ]
           y como nunca se (a)unen
           de la fortuna y la sangre   740
           las varias solicitudes,
           ca[n]sando al mundo vivías,
           por lo mal q*ue* en él se sufre[n],
           sobre escasezes de pobre,
           las vanidades de ylustre.   745
           Quiso dios y su ventura
           q*ue* en este estado te acude   [4ʳ]
           la erencia de un tío q*ue* en Lidia
           mataron sus senectudes,
           con cuyas nuebas alegre   750
           −por esta[r] puesto en costumbre
           q*ue* se regozige el vivo
           de lo q*ue* el muerto se pudre−,
           a tomar la posesión
           venías, quando en la cumbre   755
           [de] aquesse monte, los cielos
           quisieron q*ue* el eco escuches   [4ᵛ]
           de una de[s]mayada voz,
           y q*ue* de oírla resulte
           q*ue* una ninfa pague en sangre   760
           lo q*ue* otr[a] en ayre consume.
           Volvimos −porq*ue* no sea
           la relación pesadumbre−
           a buscar nuestros caballos
           que por essos zerros huyen,   765
           quando otra vez nos allamos,   [5ʳ]
           sin saber para q*ué* use
           de vozes contigo amor;
           pues en lo tierno y lo dulce
           de tu condición, no dudé   770
           cuán[t]o [es] diligencia inútil,
           quien siempre tubo buen pleyto,
           ver q*ue* a voze[s] lo reduze.

734 *essa*, G H T V: esta   735 *no*, A B H M T V: nunca   737 E: pue q aras q en ellas culpas
739 *unen:* E R: aúnen   741 varias: A B C H J M P T V: vanas   742 *cansando,*
E: causando   743 *sufren*, E: sufre   746 *su*, A B C G H J M P T V: tu   749 *sus*, G: las
751 *estar*, E: esta   756 *de aquesse*, E: aquesse; A G: de aquesta

| | [Exeunt all; Céfalo and |
| | Clarín remain.] |

CÉFALO   Follow, Clarín, that group.

CLARÍN   Your affairs are intent on taking away   735
          the judgment that I never had.

CÉFALO   Now, what do you have against them today?

CLARÍN   You were born a noble in Sicily,
          and since the various demands
          of fortune and lineage   740
          never come together well,
          you have lived, tiring everyone
          because of the grievous way in which one suffers
          the vanities of nobility
          over and above the deprivations of poverty.   745
          God and your fortune willed
          that in this state the inheritance
          of an uncle, who succumbed in Lydia
          to old age, should come to you,
          with which good news   750
          (for it is the custom that
          the living rejoice as much
          as the dead rot)
          you came to take
          possession, when on the summit   755
          of that mountain, the heavens
          wanted you to hear the echo
          of a faint voice,
          and the result of hearing it
          is that one nymph pays in blood   760
          for that which consumes another in air.
          We returned (in order to
          go on with the story)
          to look for our horses
          that were running through these hills,   765
          when here we are again,
          without knowing why love
          uses voices against you,
          since in the tenderness and sweetness
          of your condition, I did not doubt   770
          the uselessness of diligence,
          seeing that he who always put up a good
          fight stoops to shouting.

758 *desmayada*, E: demayada   761 *otra*, E: otro   762 Ac. E: aprisa
766 Ac. E: despacio   766 *vez*, A C H J M P T: vos/*allamos*,
A B C H J M P T V: llamó   770 *dudé*, A B C G H J M P T V: dudo
771 *quánto es*, E: qdo   773 *vozes*, E: voze/*lo*, A B G H M T V: le; C J P: se

Segunda vez la tal ninfa
viste; y en vez de q*ue* busque[s]   775   [5ᵛ]
los caballos, y te vayas
donde acomodado triunfes,
veo q*ue* en una alquería
te alvergas, y en ella, el lustre
de tu explendor disfrazado   780
en tosco sayal encubres.
¿Qué es esto, señor?

CÉFALO   Clarín,
es un destino q*ue* induce,
es u[n] hado q*ue* domina,
es una estrella, q*ue* influye,   785   [6ʳ]
en busca de los caballos,
para q*ue* seguir procure
mi viaje, llegue a este
pobre alberg[u]e, donde supe
que la Luna, en q*ue* Diana   790
la rústica muchedumbre
destas comarcas celebra,
en este día se cumple,
y q*ue* en su solemnidad   [6ʳ]
eran a todos comunes   795
los umbrales de su templo,
para q*ue* (a) todos tributen
a sus ninfas las ofrendas,
q*ue* en tibia trémula lumbre
sacrifican, para q*ue*   800
quando sus aras aúmen,
suban al cielo en pavesas:
cuyas condensadas nubes,
como el himno dice, la hazen   [7ʳ]
deydad de sombras y luzes.   805
Y siendo assí, q*ue* por pocos
días más o menos, pu[de]
de tanta celebridad
lograr e[l] día, no acuses
quedarme en aqueste traje   810
en q*ue* mis (des)dichas dispuse.
Pues si la verdad te digo
−bien q*ue* tú te la presumes−,   [7ᵛ]
no sólo curiosidad
me muebe; pues no es bien dudes   815

774 Ac. E: aprisa   774 *la tal,* A B H J M P T V: a esta; C: fatal   775 *busques,* E: busque
784 *un,* E: u   785 *es,* A B C G H J M P T V: y es   788 *este,* A B C G H J M P T V: ese
789 *albergue,* E R: alberge   790 *que,* A B C G H J M P T: que a; V: a que

A second time you saw the
nymph; and instead of your looking for   775
the horses, and going
where you might triumph comfortably,
I see that you are lodged
in a farmhouse, and in it, you cover
the luster of your splendor   780
disguised in coarse burlap.
What is this, sir?

CÉFALO   Clarín,
it is a destiny that leads,
it is a fate that dominates,
it is a star that impels,   785
so that I, in search of the horses,
in order to carry out
my journey, should arrive at this
poor inn, where I discovered
that the moon, in which form   790
the peasant population
of these regions worships Diana,
becomes full today,
and that, in its solemnity,
the doors of the temple   795
are open to all together
so that everyone might pay homage
to the nymphs with their offerings
that in warm, flickering light
they sacrifice, so that   800
when the altars begin to smoke
they might rise to heaven in cinders:
whose condensed clouds,
as the hymn says, make her
the deity of shadow and light.   805
And, since, with it this way
a few days more or less, I was able
to take advantage of this day
of such celebration, do not chide
me for remaining in this outfit   810
in which I have prepared my happiness.
For if I tell you the truth
(since you already presume to know it),
not only curiosity
moves me; for it is not well that you should doubt   815

---

797 *todos,* E: a todos   804 *el himno,* A B H J M P T V: Elcino; C: Eligno   807 *pude,*
E: puedo   809 *el,* E: e   811 *dichas,* E: desdichas

que con aquesta ocasión
logren mis solicitudes
el volver a ver a aquella
que con divinas vislumbres
luciendo a par de Diana,   820
a par de los cielos luce.
Y assí, ven tras esta tropa,   [8r]
que ya del templo descubre
el dorado capitel,
almenas y balaustres,   825
mas no vengas sin ofrenda.
De esas vellas flores pule
siquiera algún ramillete
y tras mí con todos sube;
pues yo, para disfrazar   830   [8v]
el alto intento que truje,
yré diciendo con todos,
para que su aplauso ayude:
venid, y mezclando de flores y aves
matices que alaguen, lisonjas que adulen,   835
las unas sus rizos coronen guirnaldas,
las otras sus aras adornen perfumes.   [Vase.]

[CORO]   [Dentro.]
           [Venid, que oy de marzo la luna se cumple
           en que, partidos el día y la noche,
           yguala Diana las sombras y luzes.]   840
CLARÍN   Ya que, aviendo de seguir   [9r]
           la tropa es fuerza procure
           llebar ofrend[a], de aquesta
           güerta algunas frutas urte.

[Sale RÚSTICO con máscara de lebrel y collar y pieles.]

RÚSTICO   [Aparte.]
           —¿Si se abrán cansado ya   845
           todos del pasado enbuste
           de acerme creer que soy
           monstruo? En aqueste lo apure.—
           ¡A pastor!
CLARÍN   ¡Ay infelize!
           ¡Qué perro tan fiero acude   850   [9v]
           a guardarlas!
RÚSTICO   ¡A pastor!

818 *a aquella,* A B C H J M P T V: aquella   822 *esta,* A B C G H J M P T V: esa
823 *templo,* A: tiempo   834 *flores,* A B C G H J M P T V: fieras   836 *las,* G: los
838 Ac. E: Coro, from page 1r; A B C H J M P T V: Coro 2; G: Coros

	that with this opportunity	
	my solicitudes will manage	
	to see again that one	
	who, with divine radiance	
	shining on a par with Diana,	820
	shines on a par with the heavens.	
	And so, go follow that group,	
	that now discovers the golden	
	spire of the temple,	
	the merlons and the banisters,	825
	but do not go without an offering.	
	Pick perhaps some bouquet	
	of these beautiful flowers	
	and ascend behind me with everyone;	
	for I, in order to disguise	830
	the great purpose that I have brought,	
	shall go singing in unison	
	so that I might add to their praise:	
	come, and mingling of flowers and birds,	
	hues that flatter, flatteries that praise,	835
	let some crown their locks with garlands,	
	let others adorn their altars with perfumes. [Exit.]	

CHORUS   [Offstage.]
          Come, for today the March moon is full
          and Diana divides the light and the dark
          equally into the day and the night.   840

CLARÍN   Now that it is necessary
          to take an offering as I
          follow the group, let me steal
          some fruit from that orchard.

[Enter RÚSTICO with a mask of a whippet and collar and skins.]

RÚSTICO   [Aside.]
          (I wonder if perhaps those who   845
          made me believe that I was
          a monster have tired yet
          of their joke. Let's try it on this one.)
          Oh, shepherd!

CLARÍN   Unhappy me!
          What a fierce dog comes   850
          to guard them!

RÚSTICO   Oh, shepherd!

838 E: a los ſ repᵒⁿ/*marzo,* H: mayo   840-841 A B C H J M P T V: missing
843 *ofrenda,* E: ofrende   844 Ac. *Sale Rústico,* H: Rústico
850 *perro,* C J P: pero   851 *¡A pastor!,* G: missing

CLARÍN   No, señor mastín, aguze
            contra mí las pre[s]as; que
            no he tocado una legumbre
            tan sola en toda su güerta.   855
RÚSTICO   Oye, aguarda. ¿De quién huyes?
CLARÍN   ¡Ay cómo ladra rabioso!
RÚSTICO   No ya el cordelejo dure.
            Basta, pastor, y di, ¿quién   [10r]
            a aquesta burla te induce?   860
CLARÍN   Fiestas me aze, y no me muerde;
            y si es que el discurso arguye
            que [a] una deydad cazadora
            un perro es don de gran fuste,
            se le he de llebar. Tus, tus,   865
            cito.
RÚSTICO   Por más que me atufe,
            nada enmienda; y pues no ay
            perro que con am[o] ayune,   [10v]
            dejarme llebar de aqueste
            quiero.
CLARÍN   Tus, tus. ¡Quál acude!   870
            ¡Y luego dirán que no ay
            a perro viejo tustuses!
            Traílla he de azer de la onda.
            Yr conmigo no reúses.
RÚSTICO   No aré, si a comer me llebas.   875
CLARÍN   Con todos ahora pronuncie:
EL 4°   Venid, moradores de Lidia, venid,   [11r]
            venid, que oy de marzo [la luna se cumple
            en que, partidos el día y la noche,
            yguala Diana las sombras y luzes.]   [Vanse.]   880

[Templo de DIANA.]

[Por una puerta el Coro de pastores y FLORETA, y por otra el Coro 2°, que es de
ninfas. DIANA, en un trono; después ERÓSTRATO, CÉFALO, CLARÍN y RÚSTICO.]

[CORO 1°]   Venid, y trayendo [de rosas y flores
            de fieras y aves los dones comunes,
            las unas sus rizos coronen guirnaldas,
            las otras sus aras adornen perfumes.]
DIANA   Rústicos moradores   885   [11v]
            de essos montes de Lidia,

853 *presas,* E: prezas   861 *me,* A B H M T V: missing   863 *a,* E: missing   865 *le,* G: lo
867 *enmienda;* A B C H J M P T V: enmiendo   868 *amo,* E: ama   872 *a,* J P:
en/*perro viejo,* A B C G H J M P T V: perros viejos   877 Ac. E: sigue el 4, el 4°; G: Coros y Clarín;
A B C H J M P T V: missing   877 C J P: Venid, moradores de Lidia &c; B H M T V: Venid,
moradores, etc.   878 E: Venid, que oy de marzo y luego sigue este otro; B C H J M P T V: missing

CLARÍN   Sir dog, please do not sharpen
              your teeth on me, for
              I have not touched even one lone
              vegetable in all your garden.   855
RÚSTICO   Listen, wait. Why are you running?
CLARÍN   Oh, how furiously he barks!
RÚSTICO   Let this bantering cease.
              Enough, shepherd, tell me, who
              put you up to this jest?   860
CLARÍN   He plays with me, and he does not bite me;
              and if it is true that the discourse argues
              that to a hunting goddess
              a dog is a gift of great importance,
              I shall take him to her. Here, boy!   865
              Here!
RÚSTICO   However much I get angry,
              it changes nothing; and since there is no
              dog who starves with a master,
              I believe I shall let myself be taken
              by this one.
CLARÍN   Here, boy! How he comes!   870
              Later they will say that there are no
              ways to make an old dog come!
              I shall make a leash of this sling.
              Do not refuse me.
RÚSTICO   I shall not, if you take me to eat.   875
CLARÍN   Now let me say with everyone:
CHORUS   Come, residents of Lydia, come,
              come, for today the March moon is full
              and Diana divides the light and the dark
              equally into the day and the night.   [Exeunt.]   880

[Temple of DIANA.]

[Through one door enter the Chorus of shepherds and FLORETA, and through
another Chorus II, which is of nymphs, and DIANA, on a throne; afterwards,
ERÓSTRATO, CÉFALO, CLARÍN, and RÚSTICO.]

CHORUS   Come, and bearing the common gifts
              of roses and flowers, of beasts and birds,
              let some crown their locks with garlands,
              let others adorn their altars with perfumes.

DIANA   Rustic residents   885
              of these mountains of Lydia,

879-880 B C E H J M P T V: missing   880ff. A B C H J M P T V: repeat lines 879-880,
indicated as "Todos"   881-882 G: missing   881 Ac. E: Coro, from above;
A B C H J M P T V: Coro 1°   881-884 E: Venid, y trayendo &   884ff. C J P: Venid, que hoy de
marzo la luna se cumple; A B H M T V have the same line indicated as "Todos"   886 *essos montes,*
G: estos montes; R: estos campos (essos montes); A B C H J M P T V: estos campos

para que más la embidia
de vuestros sacros loores
ofenda a la deydad de los amores
−pues para mí no ha avido   890
ni dádiva ni ofrenda,
sino la que pretenda
publicar que ést[e] ha sido   [12ʳ⁻ᵛ]
contra el amor el templo del olvido−,
y buestros altos dones   895
dando a ninfas bellas,
y alternando con ellas
las músicas canziones,
dezid para blasón de mis blasones:

CORO DE   Pues la victoria mayor   900   [13ʳ]
NINFAS   vencerse a sí mismo a sido,
              ¡muera el amor y viva el o[l]vido!
              ¡Viva el olvido y muera el amor!

ERÓSTRATO   [Aparte.]   [13ᵛ]
              −Mi sobervia el primero
              a la ofrenda me lleba: 905
              la voz el lavio muev[a],
              no el corazón, si espero
              lograr postrado lo que altibo muero.−

                        [Llega a una ninfa con el
                        arco y flecha.]

              Si el arco de amor −¡[oh] bella
              deidad!−el mayor trofeo   910
              para Venus es, bien creo
              que este vengue a Diana de ella,   [14ʳ]
              pues su estrella
              verá que a [e]sta media luna
              no ay ninguna   915
              fuerza que no sea inferior,
              y más quando su explendor
              diga de su flecha erido:
              ¡muera el amor y viva el olvido!

[CORO DE   [¡Viva el olvido y muera el amor!]   920
NINFAS]

                        [Llega CÉFALO a POCRIS con
                        un ramillete o guirnalda.]

---

893 *éste*, E: esta; V: missing   893 Ac. E page 12ʳ is blank except for the indication, "A la
buelta sigue presto"   894 *el templo*, A B C H J M P T V: empleo
895 *y*, A B C G H J M T V: Id   896 *a*, A B C G H J M P R T V: a mis
899 Ac. E: sigue el Coro de ninfas   900 Ac. A B C H J M P T V: Coro 1   901 *vencerse*,
B: vencerla   902 *olvido*, E: ovido   906 *el*, A: al/*mueva*, E: mueve   908 *muero*,

so that the envy of
your sacred praises may
offend more the goddess of love
(since for me there has been   890
no present nor offering
except that which intends
to publicize that this has been
the temple of oblivion against love),
and giving to the beautiful nymphs
your great offerings,
and alternating with them
the musical songs,
say as a boast of my glories:

CHORUS OF   Since the greatest victory   900
NYMPHS   has been to conquer oneself,
             let love die and oblivion live!
             Let oblivion live and love die!

ERÓSTRATO   [Aside.]
             (My pride leads me to be
             the first to the offering: 905
             let the voice move the lips
             but not the heart, if I hope
             to achieve prostrate that for which I die nobly.)
                              [He approaches a nymph with a
                              bow and arrow.]

             If the bow of love (beautiful
             goddess) is the greatest trophy   910
             for Venus, I believe indeed
             that this one will avenge Diana on her,
             for her star
             will see that there is no force
             that is not inferior   915
             to this half moon,
             and more, when her splendor,
             wounded by its arrow, may say:
             let love die and oblivion live!

CHORUS OF   Let oblivion live and love die!   920
NYMPHS

                              [CÉFALO approaches POCRIS
                              with a bouquet or garland.]

A G H: quiero   909 *oh*, E G: missing   912 *de ella*, A B C H J M P R T V: bella
914 *a esta*, E: asta; R: hasta (a esta)   916 *fuerza*, A B C H M T V: fiera; J P: figura
920 Ac. E G: Coro de ninfas, taken from E page 13ʳ; A B C H J M P T V: missing
920 E: repite el coro de la señal)(

CÉFALO   [Aparte.]   [14ᵛ]
            Cobarde [a] ablarla llego.
            ¿Cómo podré, divino
            amor, si a tu destino
            los inpulsos [no] niego,
            de yelo ablar y padecer el fuego?   925
POCRIS   [Aparte.]
            ¡Cielos! ¿Qué es lo que miro?
            ¿No es éste el estranjero?
CÉFALO   [Aparte.]
            Turbado al verla muero.
POCRIS   [Aparte.]
            Muerta al verl[e] respiro.
CÉFALO   [Aparte.]
            −¡O si ablara sin vozes el suspiro!−   930   [15ʳ]
            De azuzena y rosa [v]es
            [u]n yris, cuya velleza
            símbolo es de la pureza,
            y sangre de Venus es;
            y assí [a] tus pies,   935
            rosa y azuzena, infiero
            lisonjero
            don, pues una es del candor
            ymagen, y otra en verdor,   [15ᵛ]
            de una púrpura teñido.   940
            ¡Muera el amor y viva el olvido!
[CORO DE   (y) ¡Viva el olvido [y muera el amor!]
 NINFAS]
POCRIS   De azuzena y rosa fuera,
            acepto el don que me das,
            si la pureza no más   945
            sin la púrpura viniera.
CÉFALO   Mal pudiera,
            si la vi en sangre teñida.
POCRIS   [Aparte.]
            ¡Ay de mi vida,
            si se acuerda del dolor!   950   [16ʳ]
CÉFALO   [Aparte.]
            −¡Ay de la mía!, al rigor
            de aver de decir rendido,−
            ¡muera el amor y viva el olvido!
TODOS   [¡Viva el olvido y muera el amor!]

___

921 *a*, E: missing/*ablarla*, G: hablarle   924 *inpulsos*, A B C H J M P T V: influjos/*no*, E: missing
925 *y*, T: missing   928 *muero*, C J P: llego   929 *verle*, E V: verla; G: verlo
931 *De*, B C J M P T V: missing/*rosa ves*, E: rosales   932 *un*, B C E J M P T V: en
935 *a*, E: missing   939 *en*, A B C G H J M P T V: el   940 *de una*, A B C G H J M P T V:

CÉFALO	[Aside.]
	As a coward I come to speak to her.
	How can I, divine
	love, if I do not deny
	the impulses of your destiny,
	speak of ice and suffer fire? 925
POCRIS	[Aside.]
	Heavens! What is this I see?
	Is not this one the stranger?
CÉFALO	[Aside.]
	Tormented by seeing her, I die.
POCRIS	[Aside.]
	Dead upon seeing him, I breathe.
CÉFALO	[Aside.]
	(Oh, if the sigh could speak without words!) 930
	You see an iris, of lily
	and rose, whose beauty
	is the symbol of purity,
	and is the blood of Venus;
	and so, with rose and lily 935
	at your feet, I offer
	a flattering
	gift, for one is the image of
	whiteness, the other of greenness,
	colored in crimson. 940
	Let love die and oblivion live!
CHORUS OF NYMPHS	Let oblivion live and love die!
POCRIS	I accept the gift that you give me,
	as it were, of lily and rose,
	if only the purity 945
	would come without the stain.
CÉFALO	It could not very well,
	if I saw it tinged in blood.
POCRIS	[Aside.]
	Upon my life,
	he remembers the conflict! 950
CÉFALO	[Aside.]
	(And upon mine, having to say,
	conquered, under duress,)
	let love die and oblivion live!
ALL	Let oblivion live and love die!

dice, en   942 Ac. A B C H J M P T V: Todos   942 E: y viva el olvido repe[on] desde la
señal ⟨   945 *pureza,* A B G H M T V: blancura; C J P: púrpura   951 *Ay,* A B C H J
M P T V: Y ay   954 Ac. G: coro de ninfas   954 E: repet[on] todos ⟨

CLARÍN	Estrafalaria beldad,	955
	q*ue* ni turba ni enbaraza,	
	este lebrel para caza	
	en nombre mío tomad.	
RÚSTICO	[Aparte.]	
	¡Qué maldad!	
	¿Yo lebrel de mi muger?	960
FLORETA	Agradecer	
	devo el don por el mejor.	[16ᵛ]
CLARÍN	Es famoso c[a]zador.	
RÚSTICO	[Aparte.]	
	¿De q*ué* lo avéis vos savido?	
CLARÍN	¡Muera el amor y viva el olvido!	965
TODOS	[¡Viva el olvido y muera el amor!]	
CORO DE	Todos de n*uest*ro exercicio	
HOMBRES	las primicias dedicamos.	
CORO DE	Y todas l[a]s aceptamos	[17ʳ]
MUGERES	de Diana en sacrificio.	970
DIANA	Ya, propicio	
	a vuestro gusto, desvelo,	
	culto y celo,	
	os [ofrezco] mi favor;	
	q*ue* no es el oro el favor,	975
	sino el aver repetido:	[17ᵛ]
AURA	[Dentro.]	
	¡Viva el amor y muera el olvido!	
DIANA	¿Muera el olvido y viva el amor?	
	Esperad. ¿Qué nueva voz,	
	sacrílegamente infiel,	980
	en los coros de Diana	
	cláusula de Venus es?	
A 4 Y	A nadie vemos, y sólo	[18ʳ]
TODOS	sentimos, al parecer,	
	un viento q*ue* blando inspira.	985
DIANA	Pues te oyes y no te bes,	[18ᵛ]
	¿quién eres, o tú del ayre	
	boreal vaticinio?	

[Aparece AURA en el aire en un carro tirado de dos camaleones,
y cantando baja al tablado, atravesándole por delante
de todos sin que la vean, y vuelve a subir por la otra parte,
con el último verso.]

---

963 *cazador,* E: cozador   966 E: todos ʆ   967 Ac. A B C H J M P T V: Coro 2°
969 Ac. A B C H J M P T V: Coro 1°; G R: Coro de ninfas   969 *las,* E: los
971 *Ya,* A C H J M P T V: Yo   972 *gusto,* A B C H J M P T V: justo
974 *ofrezco,* E: ofende   975 *el oro el favor,* B C J M P T V: el oro el valor; A G H: del don el valor

CLARÍN	Outlandish beauty,
	who neither confuses nor embarrasses,
	take this hunting whippet
	in my name.
RÚSTICO	[Aside.]
	How evil!
	I, a dog to my wife?
FLORETA	I must
	appreciate this gift as the best.
CLARÍN	He is a famous hunter.
RÚSTICO	[Aside.]
	How have you found out about that?
CLARÍN	Let love die and oblivion live!
ALL	Let oblivion live and love die!
CHORUS OF MEN	We all dedicate the first fruits of our labors.
CHORUS OF WOMEN	And we all accept them as a sacrifice to Diana.
DIANA	Now, favorable
	to your pleasure, vigilance,
	worship, and zeal,
	I offer you my favor;
	for the favor is not gold
	but having repeated:
AURA	[Offstage.]
	Let love live and oblivion die!
DIANA	Let oblivion die and love live?
	Wait. What new voice,
	sacrilegiously unfaithful,
	speaks for Venus
	in the chorus of Diana?
ALL	We see no one, and we only
	perceive, as it seems,
	a breeze that softly sighs.
DIANA	Since you are heard and are not seen,
	who are you, oh boreal prophecy
	of the air?

955

960

965

970

975

980

985

[Aura appears in the air in a cart drawn by two chameleons,
and, singing, she descends to the stage, passing in front of everyone
without their seeing her, and she ascends again on the other side
with the last line.]

978 Ac. A B C G H M P T V: missing   979 Ac. A B C G H M P T V: Diana
983 Ac. E: sigue a 4 y todos; A B C H J M P T V: Todos   986 *oyes,* A B C H J M P T V:
oyen/*ves,* A B C H J M P T V: ven   988 *boreal,* B H M T V: veloz; A C J P: voraz

AURA   Quien,
                    perturbando en tus aplausos
                    la ingratitud [de tu] fe,   990
                    sin que le inpidas la entrada,
                    penetrar puede y romper
                    claraboyas al templo   [19ʳ]
                    y las cercas al vergel,
                    entre amo[r] y olvido,   995
                    publicando que
                    no enmienda al amar
                    el aborrecer.
                    No, pues, de ingrata blasones;
                    que bien puede una muger   1000
                    mantener un ser contan[te],
                    sin pasar(se) a ser cruel;
                    y es darle templo al estremo,
                    querer no aya medio, pues   [19ᵛ]
                    entre el favor de su agrado   1005
                    y el odio de su desdén,
                    puede partirse el camino,
                    a cuya causa a[y] quien fiel,
                    penetrando tus umbrales,
                    repita una y otra vez,   1010
                    y contra el olvido
                    amor viva, pues   [20ʳ]
                    no enmienda [al] amar
                    [el] aborrecer.   [Vase.]
DIANA   ¡Trayción [en] el templo ay   1015
                    de algún amante por quien
                    quiere Júpiter que el viento
                    estas noticias me dé!
ERÓSTRATO   [Aparte.]
                    ¡Ay de mí, si me conoce!
                    Pues ha llegado a saber   1020
                    el intento con que vine,   [20ᵛ]
                    ¿qué disculpa [he] de tener?
CÉFALO   [Aparte.]
                    ¡Ay de mí, si en mí repara,
                    pue[s] es fuerza conocer
                    que la intención que me trujo   1025
                    del amor afecto fue!

990 de tu, E: missing   991 le, A B H M T V: la   993 claraboyas, A B C H J M T V:
las claraboyas   995 amor, E: amo   1001 mantener un: A B C G H J M P T V:
mantenerse en/constante, E: constan   1002 pasar, E: pasarse   1003 templo, B C J M P
T R V: tiempo; A G H: rienda   1008 ay, E: a   1013 al, E: el   1014 el, E: al

AURA   She who,
                    in your celebration upsetting
                    the ingratitude of your faith,   990
                    without your forbidding her entry,
                    can penetrate and break
                    the transoms of the temple
                    and the fences of the garden,
                    making public that,   995
                    between love and oblivion,
                    hate has no effect
                    if one loves.
                    Do not, indeed, boast as an ingrate;
                    for a woman may well   1000
                    maintain her constancy
                    without becoming cruel;
                    and to desire there to be no moderation
                    is to give a temple to the extreme, for
                    between the favor of its pleasure   1005
                    and the hatred of its disdain,
                    the road may divide,
                    for which cause let someone faithful,
                    entering your doorways,
                    repeat again and again: 1010
                    and let love live
                    against oblivion, for
                    hate has no effect
                    if one loves.   [Exit.]
DIANA   In the temple there is treason   1015
                    by some lover through whom
                    Jupiter wants the wind
                    to give me this news.
ERÓSTRATO [Aside.]
                    Woe to me, if she recognizes me!
                    Since she has managed to discover   1020
                    the purpose with which I came,
                    what excuse can I have?
CÉFALO   [Aside.]
                    Woe to me, if she notices me,
                    since she is bound to discover
                    that the intention that brought me   1025
                    was a whim of love!

1015 *en,* E: missing   1020 *ha llegado,* A B C H J M P T V: en llegando; G: si ha llegado
1021 *vine,* J M P T V: viene   1022 *he,* E: ha   1024 *pues,* E: pue
1026 *del amor afecto,* A B H M T V: afecto del amor

CLARÍN   [Aparte.]
              ¡Ay de mí, si ve que quiero
              a esta maldita muger!
RÚSTICO   [Aparte.]
              ¡Ay de mí, si se le antoja
              que el perro el que rabia es!   1030
DIANA   A todos miro, y en nadie   [21ʳ]
              el alma penetro. ¿Qué
              poder soberano ay
              que se oponga a mi poder?
              Yo de Júpiter, ¿segunda   1035
              hija no soy? [¿No soy] quien
              en mayorazgo de luz
              part[e] al sol [el] rosicler?
              ¿No soy la que con tres rostros,
              siendo mis inperios tres,   1040
              Diana en la verde selba,   [21ᵛ]
              Luna en el azul dosel,
              y Proserpina en el negro
              centro, los mortales ven
              tal vez presidir opuesta,   1045
              y favorable tal vez?
              Y dejando la deydad
              aparte, ¿no soy la que
              de los montes de la luna
              predomina la altibez,   1050   [22ʳ]
              cuyas venenosas plantas,
              inficionadas [hacer]
              prodigios se miran, quantos
              al hombre mudan el ser,
              pues madre de orror y miedo,   1055
              [le] trueco el semblante, bien
              empañando al sol la faz,
              y a todo el día la tez?
              Pues ¿cómo, deydad humana,   [22ᵛ]
              no alcanzo, ¡ay de mí, a saber   1060
              quién me ofende, quién me injuria,
              ni quién me ultraja, ni quién
              la luz de mi penetrar,
              la fuerza de mi entender,
              impide? Mas, ¡ay de mí!,   1065
              buelbo a decir otra vez,

1030 *el que,* A B H M R T V: que   1032 *penetro,* A: penetra   1036 *No soy,* E: missing
1037 *mayorazgo,* A B C H J M P T: mayorazgos   1038 *parte,* E: parto/*el,* E: en
1052 *hacer,* E: aser   1056 *le,* E: las; B C J M R T V: les   1057 *empañando al sol,*

CLARÍN	[Aside.]
	Woe to me, if she sees that I love
	this damned woman!
RÚSTICO	[Aside.]
	Woe to me, if she happens to think
	that it is the dog who raves!

1030

DIANA   I look at everyone, and I penetrate
the soul of no one. What
sovereign power is there
who opposes my power?
Am I not the second daughter   1035
of Jupiter? Am I not the one who
gives the pinkness of dawn
to the sun by birthright?
Am I not the one whom, with three faces,
since I have three kingdoms,   1040
Diana in the green forest,
Luna in the blue canopy,
and Proserpina in the black
underworld, the mortals see
rule sometimes adversely   1045
and sometimes favorably?
And leaving the divinity
aside, am I not the one who
dominates the heights
of the mountains of the moon,   1050
whose venomous plants,
infected, are seen
to cause such prodigious acts
as changing the form of a man,
for, as the mother of horror and fear,   1055
I change his appearance, indeed,
by dimming the face of the sun
and the complexion of the entire day?
But how, as a human deity,
do I not manage (unhappy me!) to find out   1060
who offends me, who affronts me,
nor who outrages me, nor who
prevents my force from
understanding, my light from
penetrating? But (miserable me!)   1065
I come to say again

que si contra yras de amor
[hizo b]ando mi esquivez,   [23ʳ]
¿qué mucho, cielos, qué mucho
que todos contra mi estén   1070
banderizados los dioses,
pues perturbando la ley,
quando de mí recusados,
están sobornados de él?
¡Mal ubie[s]en una lluvia   1075
de oro, una adúltera red(uciendo),
[y en] los caístros de un cisne   [23ᵛ]
los verdores de un laurel!
Essos profanados dones
dejad, arrojad, romped;   1080
que con sospechas de algun[o],
ninguno he de agradecer.
Salid, pues, salid, villanos,
del templo, y todas después
cerrad sus puertas que más   1085   [24ʳ⁻ᵛ]
no se han de abrir asta que
de este oprovio, este baldón,
el fin sepa. ¡Y assí de aquél
por quien el ayre me avisa,
tras cuyos ecos yré,   1090
pues aunque todos los dioses
favor a algún traydor den
contra mí, no contra mí   [25ʳ]
han de mantenerle, al ver
que penetrando el supremo   1095
solio, suba a proponer
a Júpiter mi querella;
aunque recele y aunque
tema que, de su delito
siendo reo, le aga juez,   1100
que en Júpiter aun no es fácil
obrar mal y juzgar bien,   [25ᵛ]
y más quando voy
a alegar contra él
que enmienda [al] amar   1105
el aborrecer.   [Desaparece DIANA.]

1068 *hizo bando,* E: y cobrando   1072 *perturbando,* A B C H J M P T V: perturbada
1075 *ubiesen,* E: u bien en; C J P: o viessen   1076 *red,* E: reduciendo
1077 *y en,* E: missing   1081 *alguno,* E: alguna   1084 *y,* A H T: missing
1085 E page 24ᵛ is blank except for "A la vuelta presto."   1088 *assí,* A B C G H J M P T V: ay
1094 *mantenerle,* J P: matarle   1096 *suba,* A B C H J M P T V: subo   1105 *al,* E: el
1106ff. B C J M P T:
POCRIS   Sube al sacro solio, sube,
            sube al supremo dosel,

that if my disdain made a
decree against the ires of love,
why should it surprise me, heavens,
that all the gods are banded   1070
together against me
since, confusing the law,
having rejected me,
they are corrupted by it?
May they suffer badly a shower   1075
of gold, an adulterous net,
and in the songs of a swan,
the greenery of a laurel!
Abandon, throw away, destroy
those profaned offerings;   1080
for, when one is suspect,
I can appreciate none.
Leave, then, leave the temple,
peasants, and all of you afterwards
close the doors, for they are   1085
not to be opened again until
I discover the end of this insult,
this affront. And so it shall be for the one
through whom the air warns me,
after whose echoes I shall go,   1090
for although all the gods give
their favor to some traitor
against me, not against me
shall they sustain it, upon seeing
that, entering the highest   1095
ground, I ascend to propose
my argument to Jupiter;
even though he distrusts and even though
he fears that, being a prisoner
of his crime, I should make him a judge;   1100
even for Jupiter it is not easy
to do ill and to judge well,
and even more when I go
to complain against him
that hate has no effect   1105
if one loves.   [DIANA disappears.]

               y pues a todas nos toca,
               de parte de todas ve.
TODAS   Y sepa que vas
               a alegar contra él,
               que enmienda al amar
               el aborrecer.
A H V have the same lines with these exceptions: *Todas,* A H: Ninfas/*vas,* V: va

A 4	Viamos todos.			
	[Huyen los pastores y pastoras.]			
RÚSTICO	Viamos.			
CLARÍN	Esso no, señor lebrel, que pues nos buelben los dones, ha de ir conmigo vsted.	[Vanse RÚSTICO y CLARÍN.]	1110	[26ʳ]
ERÓSTRATO	[Aparte.] Aunque su enojo me dio en qué dudar y qué temer, perdido en su ausencia el miedo, detrás de aqueste laurel me he de quedar escondido; que no tengo de perder la ocasión de mi venganza, por si no la allo otra vez.	[Vase.]	1115	
CORO A 4	Pues hemos quedado solas, el templo a ce[rr]ar bolbed: no en ausencia de Diana esté abierto.		1120	[26ᵛ]
POCRIS	Decís bien.	[Vanse las ninfas.]		[27ʳ]
CÉFALO	No dicen, si no le cierran al ayre, que dijo . . .			
[POCRIS]	[¿Qué?]			
[CÉFALO]	. . . que puede una ser constante sin pasar a ser cruel.		1125	
POCRIS	¿Qué importa esso?			
CÉFALO	Mucho.			
POCRIS	¿Por qué, di?			
CÉFALO	Porque no enmienda [al] amar [el] aborrecer.		1130	
POCRIS	Sí, mas vos, ¿Cómo aquí solo os quedáis?			
CÉFALO	Como no sé la senda que me desvía de vos.			[27ᵛ]
POCRIS	¿Aquesa no es?			
CÉFALO	Sí deve de ser.			
POCRIS	Pues ¿cómo, viéndola, no la sabéis?		1135	

1107 Ac. A B C H J M P T V: Coro 2; G: Coro de pastores   1112 *en,* A B C G H J M P T V: missing   1114 *laurel,* A B C H J M P T V: cancel   1119 Ac. E: sigue el coro, coro a 4; A B H M T V: Coro; J P: Coros; C: Coro 1; G: Coro de ninfas

CHORUS   Let us all flee.
                                [The shepherds and
                                shepherdesses flee.]
RÚSTICO   Let us flee.
CLARÍN   No you don't, sir whippet,
            for since they are returning our offerings,
            you are to come with me. [Exeunt RÚSTICO and CLARÍN.] 1110
ERÓSTRATO [Aside.]
            Even though her anger gave me
            reason to doubt and to fear,
            the fear having been lost with her absence,
            I shall wait, hidden,
            behind this laurel;   1115
            for I must not lose
            this opportunity for my vengeance,
            in case I do not find another.   [Exit.]
CHORUS   Since we have remained alone,
            close the temple again: 1120
            Let it not be open in
            Diana's absence.
POCRIS   You speak well.   [Exeunt nymphs.]
CÉFALO   No they do not, if they close it not
            to the air, who said . . .
POCRIS   What?
CÉFALO   . . . that a woman can maintain her constancy   1125
            without becoming cruel.
POCRIS   What difference does that make?
CÉFALO   A lot.
POCRIS   Why, tell me?
CÉFALO   Because
            hate has no effect
            if one loves.   1130
POCRIS   Yes, but you, how do you remain
            here alone?
CÉFALO   Because I do not know
            the path that takes me away
            from you.
POCRIS   Is it not this one?
CÉFALO   Yes, it must be.
POCRIS   Then how,   1135
            seeing it, do you not know it?

1120 *a cerrar,* E: a cerar; R: acerar   1123 *le,* G: lo   1124 Ac. E: missing; G: Aura
1124 *Qué,* E G: quien   1125 Ac. E: missing   1129 *al,* E: el   1130 *el,* E: al

CÉFALO   ¿Quién quita verla los ojos
          y no acertarla los pies?
POCRIS   Por esso la enseño yo.
          Ydos, forastero; bed   1140
          q*ue* el templo se ha de cerrar,
          y q*ue* empieza [a] anochecer.
CÉFALO   Sí aré; pero permitidme
          q*ue* estrañe q*ue* al tiempo q*ue*   [28ʳ]
          bos me mandáis q*ue* me vaya,   1145
          q*ue* me quede me mand[é]is.
POCRIS   ¿Yo q*ue* os quedéis? ¿Quándo?
CÉFALO   Qua*n*do
          decís que me vaya.
POCRIS   Pues
          el advertir que os bais,
          ¿es deciros q*ue* os quedéis?   1150
CÉFALO   Sí, q*ue* el oír es criado
          tan mal mandado del ver,
          q*ue* todo lo q*ue* le dice
          siempre lo entiende al revés.
          Y así, entre veros y oýros,   1155   [28ᵛ]
          perdonad si descortés
          abandona el corazón
          lo q*ue* oye por lo q*ue* ve.
POCRIS   Perdonadme vos a mí
          q*ue* no me atrevo a [e]ntender   1160
          plática q*ue* a mis oýdos
          llega la primera vez.
CÉFALO   ¿No viste[i]s estrellas?
POCRIS   Sí.
CÉFALO   ¿No viste[i]s flores?
POCRIS   También.
CÉFALO   ¿No oíste[i]s aves?
POCRIS   Sí, (ho) ohí.   1165   [29ʳ]
[CÉFALO] ¿Cristales no escuchasteis?
POCRIS   Sí escuché,
          mas con la plática, estrellas y flores,
          cristales y aves, ¿qu*é* tienen que ver?
CÉFALO   Preguntádselo al ardor
          de aquella primera estrella,   1170
          veréis q*ue* al blando rumor
          del ayre q*ue* inspira, responde por ella . . .

1139 *la,* A B C H J M P T V: os la   1142 *y,* A B H T V: ya/a, E: missing   1146 *mandéis,*
E J: mandáis   1149 *el advertir,* A B C H J M P T V: advertiros   1153 *dice,* A B C H J M
P T V: dicen   1160 *entender,* E: ntender   1163 *visteis,* E: vistes   1164 *visteis,* E: vistes

CÉFALO	Who keeps my eyes from seeing it
	and my feet from not knowing it?
POCRIS	For that reason I show it to you.
	Go, stranger; see 1140
	that the temple is to be closed,
	and that night is beginning to fall.
CÉFALO	Indeed I shall; but permit me
	to find it strange that at the same time that
	you command me to go, 1145
	you command me to stay.
POCRIS	I? That you should stay? When?
CÉFALO	When
	you tell me to go.
POCRIS	But,
	advising you to go
	is telling you to stay? 1150
CÉFALO	Yes, for hearing is such a
	bad servant of seeing,
	that everything one tells it,
	it always understands the reverse.
	And so, between seeing you and hearing you, 1155
	forgive me if my heart
	discourteously abandons
	what it hears for what it sees.
POCRIS	May you forgive me
	if I do not dare to understand 1160
	this discourse that comes to my
	ears for the first time.
CÉFALO	Have you not seen stars?
POCRIS	Yes.
CÉFALO	Have you not seen flowers?
POCRIS	As well.
CÉFALO	Have you not heard birds?
POCRIS	Yes, I have. 1165
CÉFALO	Have you not listened to streams?
POCRIS	Yes, I have listened,
	but what do stars, flowers, streams,
	and birds have to do with the discourse?
CÉFALO	Ask the warmth
	of that first star, 1170
	you will see that the soft rumor
	of the air that stirs answers for it . . .

1165 *oísteis,* B E: oístes; A: oíste/*aves,* A: ayes/*ohí,* E: hoohí   1166 Ac. E: missing
1166 B: ¿No oístes cristales? POCRIS Bien.   1167, 1168 *y,* A B C G H J M P T V: o
1169 *al,* R: missing   1171 *al,* A B C G H J M P T V: en

[Atraviesa AURA en un carro por el tablado. CÉFALO y POCRIS sin verla.]

AURA	¿Qué estrella no influye afectos de amor?	[29ᵛ]
CÉFALO	Al verde botón q*ue* esconde	
	de aquella flor el matiz,	1175
	lo preguntad, veréis dónde,	
	dudando si nazca, el ayre responde . . .	
AURA	¿Qué flor no es de amor un concepto feliz?	
CÉFALO	Al tierno dulce clamor	
	lo preguntad de aquella ave,	1180·
	veréis cómo a su dolor	
	el ayre responde, diciendo suave . . .	[30ʳ]
AURA	¿Qué cláusula no es gemido de amor? [Vase.]	
POCRIS	¿Qué importa [que ame la bella	
	luz, ni que amen – ¡ay de mí! –	1185
	matiz, rumor y querella,	
	si nunca han de ser ejemplar para mí	
	el ave, el cristal, ni la flor, ni la estrella?]	
	Ydos, [pues, que siento ruido.]	[30ᵛ]
CÉFALO	Yo, ¡ai [infelice!, me iré,	1190
	mas con una condición.]	
POCRIS	¿Que os adivino [cuál es?]	
CÉFALO	No aréis mucho, [que es muy fácil.]	
POCRIS	[Pues decidla.]	
CÉFALO	No diré,	
	[hasta que vos la digáis,	1195
	por ver si el alma me veis.]	
POCRIS	Esto es querer [cortesano	[31ʳ]
	decir que es ella después.]	
CÉFALO	Pues digámoslo [a la par.]	
POCRIS	Es q*ue* avirtáis . . .	
CÉFALO	E[s] q*ue* notéis . . .	1200
POCRIS	. . . q*ue* siendo constante . . .	
CÉFALO	. . . y no siendo cruel . . .	
LOS DOS	. . . no enmienda [al] amar	
	el abo[rr]ecer.	
POCRIS	Es verdad . . .	
CÉFALO	Verdad es . . .	1205
POCRIS	. . . q*ue* todo mi mal . . .	
CÉFALO	. . . que todo mi bien . . .	
POCRIS	. . . está en q*ue* entendáis . . .	[31ᵛ]
CÉFALO	. . . está en q*ue* penséis . . .	

1177 *nazca,* A B C H J M P T V: nace   1180 *aquella,* A B C G H J M P T V: aquel
1183 *gemido,* A B G H M T V: un gemido   1183ff. A B C H J M P T:
CÉFALO   Preguntádselo al sonido
                      de aquese cristal, que herido
                      baja del monte al verjel,
                      veréis que responde el aire por él . . .
AURA   Aquí está el amor pues aquí se hace el ruido.

[AURA crosses the stage in a cart. CÉFALO and POCRIS do not see her.]

AURA	What star does not influence the whims of love?	
CÉFALO	Ask the green bud that hides	
	the color of that flower,	1175
	you will see where,	
	doubting if it is born, the air answers . . .	
AURA	What flower is not a happy conceit of love?	
CÉFALO	Ask the tender, sweet cry	
	of that bird,	1180
	you will see how the air	
	answers its pain, saying softly . . .	
AURA	What statement is not a lament of love? [Exit.]	
POCRIS	What does it matter that the beautiful light	
	loves, or that (unhappy me!) the	1185
	color, noise, and cry love,	
	if the bird, the stream, the flower, and the star	
	are never to be an example to me?	
	Go, for I hear noise.	
CÉFALO	I shall go (unhappy me!),	1190
	but on one condition.	
POCRIS	Shall I guess what it is?	
CÉFALO	It will not take much, for it is very easy.	
POCRIS	Then say it.	
CÉFALO	I shall not,	
	until you say it,	1195
	to see if you see my soul.	
POCRIS	That would be what a courtesan does,	
	agreeing afterwards with whatever I say.	
CÉFALO	Then let us say it at the same time.	
POCRIS	It is that you should consider . . .	
CÉFALO	It is that you should notice . . .	1200
POCRIS	. . . that being constant . . .	
CÉFALO	. . . and not being cruel . . .	
BOTH OF	. . . hate has no effect	
THEM	if one loves.	
POCRIS	It is true . . .	
CÉFALO	True it is . . .	1205
POCRIS	. . . that all my misfortune . . .	
CÉFALO	. . . and all my good luck . . .	
POCRIS	. . . depends on your understanding . . .	
CÉFALO	. . . depends on your thinking . . .	

M is the same except for "aquel" instead of "aquese"
1184-1188 E: qué importa/*amen*, J: aman   1189 E: ydos
1190-1191 E: yo ai/*mas*, T: missing   1192 E: que os adivino   1193 E: no aréis mucho
1194 E: no diré   1195-1196 E: missing   1197 E: esto es querer/*Esto*, C P: Esso
1198 E: missing/*es*, J: missing   1199 E: pues digámoslo   1200 *Es*, E: e
1203 *al*, E: el   1208 entendáis, C J P: conozca

A DUO   . . . q*ue* siendo constante,   1210
             [y no siendo cruel,
             no enmienda al amar
             el aborrecer.]   [Vanse.]

[Campo inmediato al templo.]

[Sale FLORETA.]

FLORETA   El templo cierra[n], y yo,
             como no soy ninfa de él,   1215   [32^r]
             fuera he qu[e]dado, y no acaso;
             si para discurrir es,
             ¿q*ué* se abrá Rústico hecho,
             q*ue* en día de tal plazer
             no ha parecido? Hacia dónde   1220
             vaya a buscarle no sé.

[Salen CLARÍN y RÚSTICO.]

(CLAR)   [Por] donde mi amo echaría
   CLARÍN   conmigo a buscarle ven,
             cito, cito, pue[s] ya tu amo   [32^v]
             soy.
RÚSTICO   [Aparte.]   Y se le echa de ver   1225
             q*ue* es amo, pues s[ó]lo cuyda
             del mal dar y no comer.
             Mas sígole, porq*ue* otro
             en otra tema no dé.
CLARÍN   Mas ¡q*ué* miro!
FLORETA   Mas, ¡q*ué* veo!   1230
CLARÍN   ¿No es aquella . . .
FLORETA   ¿No es aquél . . .
CLARÍN   . . . la ninfa de mala mano?   [33^r]
FLORETA   . . . el escudero de a pie?
CLARÍN   Dígame, usted, mi reyna,
             si sabe por dónde fue   1235
             un amo q*ue* Dios me dio.
FLORETA   Dígame si sabe usted
             de un maridillo q*ue*
             me dio el diablo.
RÚSTICO   [Ladrando.]   Yo sé de él,
             por señas de q*ue* a estas oras,   1240
             sin saber cómo o por q*ué,*
             me dicen q*ue* está echo un perro.   [33^v]

1210 Ac. A B C G H J M P T V: Los dos   1211-1213 E: &   1213 Ac. *Sale,* H: missing
1214 *cierran,* E: cierra   1216 *quedado,* E: qudado   1219 *en,* A B C H J M P T V: missing
1221 *buscarle,* A: buscarte   1222 Ac. E: clar clarín   1222 *Por,* E: missing
1224 E: cito, cito, pue; A B C H J M P T V: cito, to, pues   1226 *sólo,* E: se lo

BOTH OF	. . . that being constant,	1210
THEM	and not being cruel,	
	hate has no effect	
	if one loves. [Exeunt.]	

[Field next to the temple.]

[Enter FLORETA.]

FLORETA   She closes the temple, and I,
as I am not a nymph in it,   1215
have remained outside, and not by chance;
if one might conjecture,
what can have become of Rústico,
who has not appeared on a day
of such pleasure? I do not know   1220
where to go look for him.

[Enter CLARÍN and RÚSTICO.]

CLARÍN   Come with me to find out
where my master could have gone;
here, boy, for now I am your
master.

RÚSTICO   [Aside.]   He boasts of appearing   1225
to be a master, for he takes care
to give little and not to eat.
But I follow him, so that another
might not insist on something else.

CLARÍN   But, what do I behold!

FLORETA   But what do I see!   1230

CLARÍN   Is that one not . . .

FLORETA   Is not that one . . .

CLARÍN   . . . the nymph with the bad hand?

FLORETA   . . . the squire on foot?

CLARÍN   Tell me, you, my queen,
if you know where a master   1235
that God gave to me went.

FLORETA   Tell me if you know
about a husband
that the devil gave me.

RÚSTICO   [Barking.]   I know about him,
by means of signs that lately   1240
tell me, without knowing how
or why, that he has become a dog.

1227 A B C H J M P T V: del mandar y no el comer; G: del mandar, no del comer
1233 *escudero,* A B C H J M P T V: lacayuelo   1234 *mi reyna,* A B H M T V: reina mía
1238 *que,* A B C G H J M P T V: que a mí   1239 Ac. *Ladrando,* H: Labrando, B C G J M P T V:
missing   1242 *dicen,* A B H J M T V: dice

FLORETA   Sal aquí.   [Ahuyentan a RÚSTICO.]

CLARÍN   No le peguéis,
que para los jabalíes
es una pieza de rey.   1245
Y pues marido y amos
no son prendas de perder,
de nuestras cosas ablemos,
y busquémoslos después.
Y así, Floreta, sabrás   1250
q*ue* él se ha quedado por ver   [34^r]
una ninfa de retorno;
y yo he quedado con él
tan solo por verte a ti.

FLORETA   Y diga, amante nobel,   1255
¿cómo es esso de retorno?
¿Soy yo ninfa de alquiler?

CLARÍN   Azte tú de propiedad,
y si he ablado descortés,
enmiénde[n]lo . . .

FLORETA   ¿Quién?   [34^v]

CLARÍN   . . . los brazos.   1260

FLORETA   ¿Cómo?

CLARÍN   Assí.   [Abrázala.]

[Vuelve RÚSTICO con cabeza de
jabalí.]

RÚSTICO   [Gruñendo.]
                ¡Qué llego a ver!
No ha de pasar ante mí
de tal abrazo la fe.

LOS 2   ¿*Qué* es esto?

RÚSTICO   El perro que rabia.

FLORETA   ¡Qué javalí tan cruel!   1265

CLARÍN   Jamás mayor puerco vi.

RÚSTICO   Esso es onrrarme vsted.
Jabalí me han hecho; pero   [35^r]
¿de q*ué* me enojo? ¿De qué,
si en no averme hecho venado,   1270
me han echo mucha merced?
Mas vengaré [en los dos
mi furia, empezando en él.]
                 [Le embiste.]

1246 *marido,* A B C G H J M P T V: maridos   1250 *Floreta,* T: y Floreta   1252 *una,*
A B C G H J M P T V: a una/*de,* A C G J P: y de   1253 *y yo,* A B C G H J M P T V: yo me
1257 *ninfa,* A B C H J M P T V: mula   1260 *enmiéndenlo,* E: enmiendelo

FLORETA   Get out of here.   [They chase away RÚSTICO.]
CLARÍN   Do not hit him,
               because for chasing wild boars
               he is a dog fit for a king.   1245
               And since husband and master
               are not things to lose,
               let us speak of our things,
               and let us look for them afterwards.
               And so, Floreta, you will know   1250
               that he has remained to see
               a nymph in return;
               and I have remained with him
               only to see you.
FLORETA   And tell me, novel lover,   1255
               what is this about a return?
               Am I nymph for hire?
CLARÍN   Put on your airs of propriety,
               and if I have spoken discourteously,
               let them remedy it . . .
FLORETA   Who?
CLARÍN   . . . my arms   1260
FLORETA   How?
CLARÍN   Like this.   [He hugs her.]

[RÚSTICO returns with the head
of a wild boar.]

RÚSTICO   [Growling.]
                               What do I come to see!
               The faith of such an embrace
               must not take place before me.
BOTH OF THEM What is this?
RÚSTICO   The dog that rages.
FLORETA   What a cruel boar!   1265
CLARÍN   I have never seen a bigger pig!
RÚSTICO   That is an honor you give me.
               He has made me a boar; but
               why am I angry? Why,
               if in not having hunted me,   1270
               they have done me a great service?
               But I shall avenge my fury on
               both of them, beginning with him.
               [He attacks him.]

1267 *Esso,* M: Esto/*onrrarme,* A B G H M T V: por honrarme
1269 *enojo,* A B G H M T V: quejo   1272 *vengaré,* A B C G H J M P T V: vengaráse/
en los dos, E: missing   1273 E: missing

[CLARÍN]	[¡Ay, que, A]donis del trapillo,		
	sin por q*ué* ni para qué	1275	
	me da muerte un jabalí!		[35^v]

[CLARÍN]   [¡Ay, que, A]donis del trapillo,
            sin por q*ué* ni para qué   1275
            me da muerte un jabalí!   [35ᵛ]
FLORETA   Tu perro te ayude, pues
            él para los jabalíes
            es una pieza de rey.
CLARÍN   Cito, to ¿cómo te llamas?   1280
RÚSTICO   Aora tras ella iré. [Vanse FLORETA y RÚSTICO.]

[Sale CÉFALO.]

CLARÍN   Perro mío de oy acá,
            a darme la vida ven.   [36ʳ]
CÉFALO   Clarín, ¿de qué das vozes?
CLARÍN   Aý es un puerco que me a mue[r]to a coces.   1285
CÉFALO   ¿Estás borracho o loco?
CLARÍN   Lo uno no merecí, lo otro tanpoco.
CÉFALO   Cobra aliento y sentido.
CLARÍN   ¡Cozes a mí, q*ue* lacayuelo he sido!
CÉFALO   ¿Quién? Aquí no ay persona.   1290
CLARÍN   ¡Coces a mí, galán de una fregona!   [36ᵛ]
CÉFALO   ¿De q*ué* (na) nace esse yerro?
CLARÍN   De q*ue* un perro me a dado pan de perro,
            pues mi amo se aleja
            de un jabalí, y en su poder me deja.   1295
CÉFALO   Deja aquesas locuras.
CLARÍN   Sí aré, en dejando tú tus aventuras,
            pues mientras estuvieres   [37ʳ]
            aquí es fuerza durarme.
CÉFALO   ¿Cómo quieres
            q*ue* me ausente de aquella   1300
            q*ue*, imperioso destino de mi estrella,
            no s[o]lamente el día
            en estos montes, más la noche fría,
            qual ve[s] me tiene en calma,
            rémora de la vida, ymán del alma,   1305   [37ᵛ]
            y con mortal despecho,
            un Etna el corazón, bolcán el pecho,
            siempre q*ue* a verla llego,
            todo es decir a mis sentidos . . .

1274 Ac. E: missing   1274 *Ay, que, Adonis*, E: donis/*del*, G: de   1276 *da*, J P: dé
1277 *perro*, P: cerro   1280 A B C H J M P T V: missing/*to*, G: tus
1281 A B H J M T V: missing   1281 Ac. *Sale*, H: missing   1285 *muerto*, E: mueto
1290-1291 A B C H J M P T V place these lines after 1295   1290 *Aquí*, A B H J
M P T V: que aquí   1292 *nace*, E: na nace   1294 *mi amo*, A B C G H J M P T V: huyendo

CLARÍN	Oh, that a boar, without why or	
	wherefore, gives death to	1275
	me, an Adonis in peasant clothes!	
FLORETA	Let your dog help you, because	
	for chasing wild boars	
	he is a dog fit for a king.	
CLARÍN	Here, boy, what is your name?	1280
RÚSTICO	Now I shall go after her. [Exeunt FLORETA and RÚSTICO.]	

[Enter CÉFALO.]

CLARÍN	My dog, here, today,	
	come to give me life.	
CÉFALO	Clarín, why are you shouting?	
CLARÍN	There is a pig that has kicked me to death.	1285
CÉFALO	Are you drunk or crazy?	
CLARÍN	I deserved neither your first insult nor your second.	
CÉFALO	Catch your breath and your senses.	
CLARÍN	Kicking me, who has been a lackey!	
CÉFALO	Who? There is no one here.	1290
CLARÍN	Kicking me, the gallant of a kitchenmaid!	
CÉFALO	How was that error conceived?	
CLARÍN	Because a dog has made a monkey out of me,	
	since my master keeps his distance	
	from a boar, and leaves me in its power.	1295
CÉFALO	Stop those insanities.	
CLARÍN	Yes, I shall, when you stop your adventures,	
	for as long as you are	
	here, I have to continue.	
CÉFALO	How do you want	
	me to leave that one	1300
	who, imperious destiny of my star,	
	not only the day	
	in these mountains, but the cold night,	
	has me, as you see, in tranquility,	
	an obstruction to life, a magnet to the soul,	1305
	and with mortal despair,	
	with my heart an Aetna, my breast a volcano,	
	every time that I come to see her	
	everything seems to say to my senses . . .	

1298 A B H M T V: con que en las selvas eres; C J P: missing   1299 *aquí es fuerza durarme,*
A B H M T V: *amante de novela;* C J P: missing   1302 *solamente,* E: se lamente
1304 *ves,* E: vez; C J P: voz   1308 *que,* M: missing   1309 *todo,* T: todas/
decir a mis sentidos, A B C H J M P T V: decirme (¡ay triste!) . . ./
Fuego, A B C H J M P T V: Fuego, fuego

[GENTE]   [Dentro.]   ¡Fuego!
CÉFALO   Pero ¿qué confusas vozes   1310
             son éstas que de los vientos
             adivinadas, las hurta,   [38r]
             antes de decirlas el eco?
CLARÍN   No sé; pero [a] aquella parte
             se ve un pavoroso incendio,   1315
             q*ue* de la noche desmiente
             la obscuridad.
CÉFALO   Hacia el templo
             es de Diana.
CLARÍN   Y aun él
             q*ue* se abrasa, pues dentro
             es donde se oye el confuso   1320   [38v]
             clamor decir:
[GENTE]   [Dentro.] ¡Fuego, fuego!
CÉFALO   ¿Quié[n] nos dirá lo q*ue* ha sido?
CLARÍN   ¿Quién lo a de decir más cierto
             ni claro q*ue* el fuego mismo?

[Sale ERÓSTRATO.]

ERÓSTRATO [Aparte.]
             Logróse mi atrevimiento;   1325
             la llama q*ue* de sus aras
             en sagrado culto ardiendo,   [39r]
             era su mayor aplauso,
             será su mayor desprecio.
CÉFALO   ¿Quién ba? ¿Quié[n] es?
ERÓSTRATO   No lo sé,   1330
             q*ue* esse asombro, esse despecho,
             essa desesperación,
             esse escándalo, esse estruendo
             me an dejado tan sin mí,
             de mí, ¡ay de mí!, tan ajeno,   1335   [39v]
             q*ue* de quién soy olvidado,
             de lo q*ue* fui no me acuerdo.
             Pero esse estrago lo diga,
             quando de su saña huyendo,
             a los montes a ampararme   1340
             voy de mí contra mí mesmo.

1309 Ac. E: missing; B M T V: Dentro todos; C J P: Dentro; G: Coro (Dentro)
1312 *hurta,* J P: hurtas   1313 *decirlas,* A B C H J M P T V: oírlas   1314 *a,* E: missing
1315 *pavoroso,* V; vaporoso; G: missing   1319 *que,* A B C G H J M P T: el que
1321 Ac. B M T V: Dentro todos; C J P: Dentro; G: Coro (Dentro)   1322 *Quién,* E: quie

PEOPLE	[Offstage.]	Fire!
CÉFALO	But, what confused voices	1310
	are these that, carried	
	on the wind, the echo steals	
	before I hear them?	
CLARÍN	I do not know; but in that direction	
	is seen a frightful conflagration	1315
	that takes away the darkness	
	from the night.	
CÉFALO	It is in the direction	
	of the temple of Diana.	
CLARÍN	And even it	
	burns, for from within	
	one hears the confused	1320
	shouts saying:	
PEOPLE	[Offstage.] Fire! Fire!	
CÉFALO	Who will tell us what has happened?	
CLARÍN	Who needs to say it more certainly	
	or more clearly than the fire itself?	

[Enter ERÓSTRATO.]

ERÓSTRATO	[Aside.]	
	My daring has succeeded;	1325
	the flame that, from its altars	
	burning in sacred cult,	
	was its greatest praise,	
	will be its greatest scorn.	
CÉFALO	Who goes there? Who is it?	
ERÓSTRATO	I do not know,	1330
	for that surprise, that despair,	
	that desperation,	
	that scandal, that confusion	
	have left me so much beside myself,	
	such a stranger (unhappy me!) to myself,	1335
	that, having forgotten who I am,	
	I do not remember who I was.	
	But let that destruction say it	
	while, fleeing from its savagery,	
	I go to the mountains to	1340
	save me from myself.	

1324 Ac. *Sale,* H: missing   1330 *Quién,* E: quie   1331 *esse asombro,* A: es asombro
1334 *an,* A B C G H J M P R T V: ha   1341 *de mí,* M T: de

[Aparte.]
—Aura, pues q*ue* de los ayres
tienes el veloz imperio,   [40r]
aviva la llama tú,
pues yo encendida la dejo.—   [Vase.]   1345

[Sale AURA, en el aire, sobre una salamandra.]

AURA   Sí aré, q*ue* si de amor y yra
              partimos los dos estremos,
              es bien q*ue* de yra y amor
              partamos los elementos;
              y pues el fuego te toca   1350
              que encendió tu atrevimiento   [40v]
              y a mí el ayre q*ue* le avive,
              el templo arda.   [Vase.]
[GENTE]   [Dentro.]
                        ¡Fuego, [fuego!]
CÉFALO   El templo es él q*ue* se abrasa,
              q*ue* en humo y llamas enbuelto   1355
              de más cerca se divisa.
              Conmigo ven.
CLARÍN   ¿A qué efecto?
CÉFALO   De socorrer a quien pueda.
CLARÍN   Ve tú, q*ue* eres caballero
              pues los socorros jamás   1360   [41r]
              tocan a los lacayuelos
CÉFALO   Entra conmigo, cobarde.
CLARÍN   Por sola una cosa quiero
              entrar, y es por ver si allas
              quemadas quantas ay dentro.   [Vanse.]   1365

[Vista exterior del templo de DIANA incendiado.]

[Sale AURA, volando invisible sobre el fuego; ninfas, que pasan huyendo.]

A 8   Moradores de estos riscos,   [46r]
              pastores de [estos desiertos,]   [46v]
              cazadores de estas selbas,   [47r]
              acudid, acudid presto.

[Vanse, y sale gente.]

[UNO]   El gran templo de Diana,   1370   [47v]
              abrasado Monjibelo,
              arde en pavesas.

1342 *pues,* A B C G H J M P T V: ya   1344 *aviva,* A B G H J M P T V: anima
1344 Ac. *Sale,* H: missing   1352 *le,* G: lo   1353 *el templo arda,* A B C H J M P T V: arda todo
1353 Ac. B C J M P T V: Dentro; G: Coro (Dentro)   1353 *Fuego,* A B C G H J M P T V:
Fuego, fuego   1360 *pues,* A B C H J M P T V: que   1364 *allas,* A B C G H J M P T V: hallo
1365 Ac. *Sale,* H: missing/E: Síguese el ocho q. dize Moradores &

[Aside.]
(Aura, because you have the
swift command of the air,
keep the flame alive,
for I leave it lit.)   [Exit.]   1345

[Enter AURA, in the air, on a salamander.]

AURA   Yes, I shall, for if we part
            the two extremes of love and anger,
            it is well that we should also part
            the elements of anger and love;
            and since the fire, that your daring   1350
            started, was up to you,
            and to keep it alive is up to me, the air,
            let the temple burn.   [Exit.]
PEOPLE   [Offstage.]
                            Fire! Fire!
CÉFALO   The temple is what is burning,
            for it is seen from up close   1355
            to be enveloped in smoke and flames.
            Come with me.
CLARÍN   What for?
CÉFALO   To help whom I may.
CLARÍN   You go, for you are a gentleman,
            since rescues are never   1360
            the business of lackeys.
CÉFALO   Enter with me, coward.
CLARÍN   For only one reason do I want
            to enter, and that is to see if you find
            all the nymphs that are inside burned.   [Exeunt.]   1365

[Exterior view of the temple of DIANA, aflame.]

[Enter AURA, flying invisible over the fire; nymphs passing by, fleeing.]

CHORUS   Residents of these cliffs,
            shepherds of these fields,
            hunters of these forests.
            Go, go quickly.

[Exeunt, and enter people.]

ONE VOICE   The great temple of Diana,   1370
            a burning Hades,
            blazes in embers.

1366 Ac. A B G H M T V: Ninfa 1ª; C J P: Una ninfa   1367 Ac. A B G H M T V:
Ninfa 2ª; C J P: Otra 2   1367 *estos desiertos:* E: estas campañas   1368 Ac. A B G H M T V:
Ninfa 3ª; C J P: 3   1369 Ac. A C G H J T: Todas, B M P V: Todos   1370 Ac. E: missing

[OTRO]	Besuvio	[48r]
	su gran fáv[r]ica se a buelto.	
[A 8]	[Dentro.]	
	¡Fuego, que me abraso! ¡Fuego!	
	¡Que me aogo! ¡Piedad, cielos!	1375 [48v]
[UNO]	¡Al altar!	
[OTRO]	¡Al capitel!	
[OTRO]	¡A la torre!	
[OTRO]	¡Al claustro!	
[A 8]	¡Al templo!	
	¡Fuego, fuego! ¡Piedad, dioses!	[49r]
	¡Piedad, cielos! ¡Fuego, fuego! [Vase la gente.]	[49v]
AURA	Aunque más acudáis todos	1380 [41v]
	en vano será el intento,	
	si fénix de tanta oguera,	
	yo con mis alas la enciendo.	

[Salen CÉFALO, CLARÍN.]

CÉFALO	Entre las caducas ruyna[s]	
	que ya el voraz elemento	1385
	unas de su centro arranca	
	y otras reduce a su centro,	[42r]
	he de arrojarme.	
CLARÍN	Yo no. [Vase.]	
CÉFALO	Por si venturoso puedo,	
	aunque sobre mí se venga	1390
	toda su máquina al suelo,	
	socorrer alguna vida. (¡Fuego!)	
A 8	[Dentro.]	
	[¡Que me muero! ¡Fuego!	
	¡Que me aogo! ¡Fuego!	
	¡Que me abraso! ¡Fuego!	1395
	¡Que me quemo! ¡Fuego!]	

1372 Ac. E: missing   1373 *fávrica*, E: favica   1374 Ac. E: Two lines of the 8-part
partitura are indicated "tiple 2° del 2° coro" and "tenor del 1° coro"   1374 A B H M T V:
      ¡Fuego!
Voz 1ª   ¡Que me abraso! ¡Fuego!
C J P have the same indications except "Voz 1ª" is "Vna"
G is the same except that the second "Fuego" is for "Coro"
1375 A B G H M T:
Voz 2ª   ¡Que me quemo!
UNAS   ¡Piedad, dioses!
V is the same except that "Voz 2ª" is "Voz 1"; J has only the second half of the line;
C P: OTRA   ¡Que me quemo, fuego!
             OTRA   ¡Que me ahogo, fuego!
             VNAS   ¡Piedad, dioses!
             OTRAS   ¡Piedad, cielos!
1375ff. A B G H M T: AURA Arda todo.
                     OTRAS   ¡Piedad, cielos!
V is the same except that "Otras" is "Otro"

ANOTHER	Its great
	structure has become a Vesuvius.
CHORUS	[Offstage.]
	Fire, I am burning! Fire!
	I am suffocating! Have pity, heavens! 1375
ONE VOICE	To the altar!
ANOTHER	To the spire!
ANOTHER	To the tower!
ANOTHER	To the cloister!
CHORUS	To the temple.
	Fire, Fire! Have pity, gods!
	Have pity, heavens! Fire, Fire! [Exeunt people.]
AURA	However much all of you run, 1380
	the attempt will be in vain,
	if, as a phoenix of such a fire,
	I fan it with my wings.

[Enter CÉFALO, CLARÍN.]

CÉFALO	Among the fallen ruins
	of which the voracious element 1385
	tears some from their midst
	and reduces other to their essence,
	I must rush in.
CLARÍN	Not I. [Exit.]
CÉFALO	To see if I may, with luck,
	save some life 1390
	even though the entire machinery
	might fall in on top of me.
CHORUS	[Offstage.]
	I am dying! Fire!
	I am suffocating! Fire!
	I am burning! Fire! 1395
	I am aflame! Fire!

1376 Ac. E: missing/*Uno,* C P: Unos; T V: Una; J: Otros/*Otro,* C J P: Otros; T V: Otra
1377 Ac. E: missing/Otro, C J P: Otros/*A 8,* A B G H M T V: Otro; C J P: Otros
1378-1379 A B C G H J M P T V: missing   1379 Ac. E: y fin   1383 *la,* B C J M P T V: le
1383 Ac. *Salen,* H: missing; C J: Sale   1384 *ruynas,* E: ruyna
1393 Ac. A B H M T V: Voz 1ª; C J P: Vna; G: Coro de ninfas (Dentro)
1393 *Que me muero,* A B C H J M P T V: Que me abraso; G: missing
1394 Ac. A B M T V: Voz 2ª; C J P: 2   1394 *Que me aogo,* A B H M T V: Que me muero;
C J P: Que me quemo; G: missing   1395 Ac. A B H M T V: Voz 3ª; C J P: 3
1395 *Que me abraso,* A B H M T V: Que me quemo; C J P: Que me muero; G: missing
1396 Ac. A B H M T V: Voz 4ª; C J P: 4   1396 *Que me quemo,* A B C H J M P T V:
Que me ahogo; G: missing   1396ff. A B C H J M P T: UNAS ¡Piedad, dioses!
OTRAS ¡Piedad, cielos! V is the same except that "Unas" is "Unos"

AURA   A pesar de sus clamores,
              arda todo.
A 8   [Dentro.] ¡Fuego, [fuego!]
POCRIS   [Dentro.]   [42ᵛ]
              ¡Ay infelice de mí!
CÉFALO   [Dentro.]
              Azia aquí se oye el acento.   1400
              Si fuera el báratro, entrara
              en su abismo.   [Saca CÉFALO a POCRIS.]
POCRIS   ¡Bálgame el cielo!
              ¿Cómo, donde todo es llamas,
              en sólo sombras tropiezo?
              ¿De qué me sirben sus luzes,   1405
              si a ver, ¡ay de mí!, no acierto?   [43ʳ]
CÉFALO   No temas, que yo por ti
              fénix soy de amor. No temas
              su estrago, por más que activo
              qui[e]ra abrasarme.
POCRIS   ¿Quién?, pero   1410
              ni el aliento ni la voz,
              la vida ni el alma puedo
              usar. Pero ¿qué mucho si faltan   [43ᵛ]
              alma, vida, voz y aliento?
                           [Cae desmayada.]
CÉFALO   En mis brazos ha caído.   1415
              Pues ¿qué aguardo? Pues, ¿qué espero?
              Y si sólo en esta vida
              logradas mis dichas veo,
              arda el templo de Diana.   [44ʳ]
                     [Vase, llévandola en los brazos.]
AURA   Sí arderá, mas no por eso   1420
              Pocris dejará de arder,
              pues va de uno en otro incendio,
              donde su lamento diga,
              zifrados estos lamentos . . .   [44ᵛ]
A 8   [Dentro.]   [45ʳ]
              ¡Que me muero! ¡Fuego!   1425
              ¡Que me aogo! ¡Fuego!
              ¡Que me abraso! ¡Fuego!   [45ᵛ]
              ¡Que me quemo! [¡Fuego!]

1398 Ac. A B C H J M P T V: Todos; G: Coro (Dentro)   1398 *Fuego, fuego,* E: fuego &
1400 *aquí se oye,* A B C H J M P T V: allí se oyó; G: aquí se oyó   1402 *en,* A B C G H
J M P T V: missing   1403 *llamas,* A B G H M T V: llama   1405 *sus,* A B C H J M P T V: las
1407 A B C H J M P T V: No temas, pues mariposa   1408 A B C H J M P T V:
yo por ti de Amor, no temo   1409 *su estrago,* A B C H J M P T V: la llama

AURA	In spite of their shouts,
	let everything burn.
CHORUS	[Offstage.] Fire, fire!
POCRIS	[Offstage.]
	Oh, unhappy me!
CÉFALO	[Offstage.]

CÉFALO   From over here the voice is heard.   1400
          Even if it were hell, I would enter
          its abyss.   [CÉFALO brings out POCRIS.]

POCRIS   May heaven help me!
          How, where all is flames,
          do I stumble only upon shadows?
          What good are their lights,   1405
          if I am not (oh my!) able to see?

CÉFALO   Do not fear, because I for you
          am a phoenix of love. Do not fear
          its destruction, however much it may actively
          want to burn me.

POCRIS   Who? But   1410
          I can use neither my breath
          nor my voice nor my
          soul. But, why I am surprised that I lack
          soul, life, voice, and breath?
                              [She faints.]

CÉFALO   She has fallen in my arms.   1415
          But for what do I wait? Why do I stay?
          And if only in this life
          I see my happiness realized,
          let the temple of Diana burn.
                        [Exit, carrying her in his arms.]

AURA   Indeed it will burn, but not for that   1420
          will Pocris cease to blaze,
          for she goes from one fire to another,
          where her lament may say
          these coded laments . . .

CHORUS   [Offstage.]
          I am dying! Fire!   1425
          I am suffocating! Fire!
          I am burning! Fire!
          I am aflame! Fire!

1410 *quiera,* E: quira   1413 *Pero,* A B C H J M P T V: missing   1418 *veo,*
A B C H J M P T V: llevo   1420 *Sí,* G: missing   1424 A B C H J M P T V:
cifrando esotros lamentos   1425-1428 See notes to 1393-1396 above.
The only change this time is that C J P indicate all as "Todos."

	¡Al altar! ¡Al capitel!	[39ᵛ]
	¡A la torre! ¡Al claustro! ¡Al templo! 1430
[AURA]	[Todo acabe.]
[TODOS]	¡Piedad, dioses!	[40ʳ]
[AURA]	Arda todo.
[TODOS]	¡Piedad! ¡Fuego!

1429 A B C H J M P T V: missing/E: pages found in Jornada 1   1430 Ac. A B H M T V: Todos.
1431 Ac. E: missing   1431 A C H J M P T V:
AURA   Arda todo.
TODOS   ¡Piedad, dioses!
G: ¡Piedad, dioses!
AURA   Todo acabe.
B: Same as A above except "Todos" is "Todas"; E: piedad dioses; 1432 Ac. E: missing

To the altar! To the spire!

To the tower! To the cloister! To the temple!   1430

AURA   [Let everything end.]

ALL   Have pity, gods!

AURA   Let everything burn.

ALL   Have pity! Fire!

1432 A H M T V:

AURA   Todo acabe.

TODOS   ¡Piedad, cielos!

B: Same as A above except "Todos" is "Todas"; C J P:

AURA   Todo acabe.

TODOS   ¡Piedad, cielos, fuego, fuego!

G:

COROS   ¡Piedad!

AURA   ¡Arda todo!

COROS   ¡Fuego!

3ª Jornada   [1r(1)]

[Estando puesto el teatro del bosque, que fue con el que se cubrió
el incendio, sube un peñasco con cuatro personas: DIANA en
lugar eminente; MEGERA en un lado, TESIFONE en otro, y ALECTO a
los pies, vestidas de velillo negro, el de DIANA con estrellas de
oro, y el de las tres con algunas llamas de oro.]

DIANA   Ya que aqueste peñasco,
               cuia esmeralda bruta,
               pedazo desasido   1435
               del venenoso monte de la luna,
               es mi trono, despés
               que ni pompa más suma
               ni do(e)sel más excelso
               a de tener mi magestad augusta,   1440
               hasta que a su explendor
               el templo restituia,
               que sacrílego fuego   [1v]
               en pardas ruinas combirtió caducas;
               desde él de mi benganza   1445
               las leyes distribuia;
               que tribunal es digno
               un risco a quien brutos delitos juzga.
               Y pues, como [a] deidad
               de la esfera nocturna,   1450
               bino a mi inbocación
               en [alas] el terror [de] las tres furias;
               supuesto que de Au(ro)ra,
               a quien Venus ayuda,   [2r]
               los dioses no me vengan   1455
               más que en berla bolar golfo de pluma;
               en Eróstrato el zeño
               empieza. Tú le busca
               en los montes adonde
               le rretiró el asombro de su culpa,   1460
               ¡o Mejera!, y, humana
               fiera, le obliga a que huia
               de las gentes, sintiendo
               ansias, fatigas, cóleras i angustias.   [2v]
               Tú, (a) Electo, pues que Pocris   1465
               con Zéfalo me injuria,
               pues apóstata mía,

1439 *ni dosel,* E: nido es el   1448 *brutos delitos,* A B H M T V: delitos brutos   1449 *a,* E: missing
1452 *alas,* E: las tres/*terror,* A G H T: furor/*de,* E: da   1453 *Aura,* E: Aurora
1456 *golfo,* A B C G H J M P T V: golfos/*pluma,* C J P: plumas   1458 *empieza,*

Act Three

[Still in place the forest scene, which was covered by the fire scene;
a boulder rises up with four people: DIANA, in top position;
MEGERA on one side, TESIFONE on another, and ALECTO
at the bottom, all dressed in black gauze, Diana's adorned with
gold stars, and the others' with some gold flames.]

DIANA   Since this boulder,
whose wild emerald,
a piece snatched   1435
from the venomous mountain of the moon,
is my throne, because
neither greater pomp
nor loftier altar
is available to my august majesty   1440
until it restores to its
splendor the temple
that sacrilegious fire
turned into fallen ruins,
from it let me distribute   1445
the laws of my vengeance;
for a cliff is a worthy court
for the one who judges brutal crimes.
And since, as goddess
of the nocturnal sphere,   1450
the terror of the three
Furies came on wings at my invocation,
since the gods do not
avenge me against Aura,
whom Venus aids,   1455
more than in seeing her fly, a multitude of feathers,
the threat begins with
Eróstrato. You, look for him
in the mountains where
shock of his guilt made him retire,   1460
oh Megera, and, a human beast,
oblige him to flee
from people, feeling
anxiety, fatigue, anger, and anguish.
You, Alecto, since Pocris   1465
insults me with Céfalo,
for, as an apostate of mine,

con él de amor en las delicias triumfa,
en su rendido pecho
harás q*ue* se introduzga   1470
de los celos el áspid,
q*ue* entre las flores del amor se oculta.
Tú, Tesífone, a él   [3ʳ]
los sentidos perturba,
para q*ue* mi venablo,   1475
de quien aora tan hufano vsa,
le aga yo el instrumento
de sus tragedias, cuya
lástima sea el blandón
de deidad q*ue* a ser llama nació espuma.   1480
Y porq*ue* un bil castigo
no piense[n] q*ue* en mí dura
a vista de estos, cobre   [3ᵛ]
Rústico la primera forma suya.

MEJERA	. . . Tú berás q*ue* obedientes . . .	1485
TESÍFONE	. . . a las órdenes tuias . . .	
ELECTRO	. . . hacemos que l[o]s tres . . .	
LAS 3	. . . padezcan, penen, jiman, lloren, sufran.	
DIANA	Pues antes que del día,	
	que a mi pesar madruga,	1490 [4ʳ]
	del monte y del alcázar	
	corone el capitel, dore la punta,	
	cada vna por su parte	
	a su exercicio acuda.	
[MEGERA]	Pues a l[o]s riscos, donde	1495
	a las gente[s] Eróstrato se urta.	
TESÍFONE	A los bosques en [que]	
	a Aura Céfalo adula.	
ELECTRO	A los palacios, donde	
	Pocris de amor la vanidad ylustra.	1500
DIANA	A la sagrada esfera,	
	desde donde yo influia	
	rigores, que l[o]s tres . . .	[4ᵛ]
LAS 3	. . . padezcan, penen, jiman, lloren, sufran.	
[ALECTO]	Y pues soi la primera	1505
	que de Pocris [va] en busca,	
	desde [e]sta parte haga	
	q*ue* el palacio en que vibe se descubra.	

1470 *introduzga,* C J P V: introduzgan   1477 *le,* G: lo/*el,* A B G H J M P T V: missing
1479 *el blandón,* A B C H J M P T V: baldón   1480 *a,* C J P: missing
1482 *piensen,* E: pienses   1485 Ac. A B H M T V: Las tres; C J P: Coro de las tres
1486 Ac. A B C H J M P T V: missing   1487 Ac. A B C H J M P T V: missing
1487 *los,* C E J P V: las   1488 Ac. A B C H J M P T V: missing   1495 Ac. E: missing

she triumphs with him in the delights of love,
in her conquered heart
will you cause to be introduced   1470
the viper of jealousy
that is concealed among the flowers of love.
You, Tesífone, confuse
his senses
so that my spear,   1475
which he now uses so haughtily,
I may cause to be the instrument
of his tragedy, whose
pity may be the candle
of the goddess who was born of foam to be a flame.   1480
And so that you not think
that a vile punishment still persists in me
in view of these others, let
Rústico recover his original form.

MEJERA   . . . You will see that, obedient . . .   1485
TESÍFONE   . . . to your orders . . .
ELECTO   . . . we cause the three of them to . . .
ALL THREE . . . hurt, ache, mourn, weep, and suffer.
DIANA   Now, before the day
              which dawns in spite of me   1490
              crowns the spire of the castle
              and gilds the summit of the mountain,
              go each one of you in your own
              direction to your own exercise.
MEGERA   Then, to the cliffs, where   1495
              Eróstrato hides from people.
TESÍFONE   To the forests in which
              Céfalo worships Aura.
ELECTO   To the palace, where
              Pocris illustrates the vanity of love.   1500
DIANA   To the sacred sphere,
              from where I shall direct
              my inclemency, so that the three of them. . .
ALL THREE . . . hurt, ache, mourn, weep, and suffer.
ALECTO   And since I am the first,   1505
              who goes in search of Pocris,
              from this direction let be
              discovered the palace in which she lives.

1495 *los,* E: las   1496 *gentes,* E: gente   1497 *que,* E: missing   1498 *a Aura,*
A B C H J M P T V: Aura a/*adula,* A B C H J M P T V: busca   1503 *los,* C E J P: las
1504 Ac. A B C G H J M P T V: Todas   1505 Ac. E: tesifone   1505 *soi,* A: yo
1506 *va,* E: missing   1507 *esta,* E: sta   1508 *vibe,* A B G H M T V: habita

[Divídese el peñasco en cuatro partes, desapareciéndose las
cuatro personas, y descúbrese a este tiempo el salón regio, con
los fondos de retretes y jardines, y salen CÉFALO con el venablo,
y POCRIS deteniéndole, y CLARÍN y FLORETA.]

POCRIS   Mi bien, mi señor, mi esposo, mi dueño,
              supuesto que amor supo vsar contra mí   1510   [5r(2)]
              tal [vez] de la sangre, del fuego tal vez,
              haciéndome a sangre y fuego la lid
              −de aqueste benablo el presagio lo diga,
              bien como de aquel incendio el ardid−,
              no, ya que feliz dos acasos me hizieron,   1515
              permitas que me haga un cuidado infeliz.
ZÉFALO   Pues, mi esposa, mi cielo, mi gloria,
              mi dueño, mi bien, ¡cuidado, tú!   [5v]
POCRIS   Sí.
ZÉFALO   Adviérteme dél, y berás quán atento
              procuro enmendarle.
POCRIS   Pues óyeme.
ZÉFALO   Di.   1520
POCRIS   Del desmaio, del susto, del miedo,
              a cuyo pabor el sentido perdí,
              de un fuego a otro fuego escapando mi vida,
              apenas cobrada en tus brazos me bi,
              quando deudora, ¡ay triste!, al amparo   1525
              y aún más que al amparo deudora −¡ay de mí!−
              a la blanda queja del llanto,
              si torpe en la voz, en los ojos sutil,   [6r]
              me dexé venzer de tu ruego,
              siguiéndote donde estoi tan feliz,   1530
              como en tu lustre publican las pompas
              desde este palacio asta este jardín;
              y más al cumplirme aquella palabra,
              que fue la disculpa con que me rendí;
              pues sin ajar sumisiones de amante   1535
              imperios de esposo, vno y otro, te bi.   [6v]
              Hasta aquí confiesso la dicha;
              pero prosiga el temor desde aquí,
              pues quando contigo me miro más vana,
              es quando más triste me miro sin ti.   1540
              De la caza el afán generoso
              tanto(s) estos días te lleua tras sí,
              que, enbidiosa del monte, trocara

1511 *tal vez de,* E: tal de   1517-1560 J: missing   1520 *enmendarle,*
G: enmendarlo/*óyeme,* A B C H M P T V: óyele; G: óyelo   1522 *sentido,* C P: gemido

[The rock divides in four parts, with the four people disappearing, and at this time is discovered the royal salon, with the background of gazebos and gardens, and enter CÉFALO with the spear, and POCRIS stopping him, and CLARÍN and FLORETA.]

POCRIS	My dearest, my lord, my husband, my master,	
	supposing that love knew how to use against me	1510
	blood, perhaps, and perhaps fire,	
	creating for me a battle of fire and blood	
	(let the omen of this spear say it	
	just as did the spark of that fire)	
	since the two accidents have made me happy	1515
	do not allow a worry to make me unhappy.	
CÉFALO	But, my wife, my Elysium, my glory,	
	my mistress, my darling: you, a worry!	
POCRIS	Yes.	
CÉFALO	Tell me about it, and you will see how attentively	
	I try to remedy it.	
POCRIS	Then hear me.	
CÉFALO	Speak.	1520
POCRIS	As a result of the swoon, of the fright, of the fear,	
	I lost my senses because of the terror,	
	escaping with my life from one fire into another,	
	barely did I find myself recovered in your arms,	
	when, owing (miserable me!) to the aid	1525
	and even more than to the aid, owing (oh my!)	
	to the soft complaint of the weeping,	
	if clumsy in the voice, subtle in the eyes,	
	I allowed myself to be conquered by your suit,	
	following you here where I am as happy	1530
	as fame makes known, in your magnificence,	
	from the palace to the garden;	
	and more so upon fulfilling that promise	
	which was the excuse with which I yielded	
	since without abusing a lover's submissions	1535
	I gave to you again and again a husband's powers.	
	Up to now, I confess my happiness;	
	but let fear continue from here,	
	for when I see myself more vain with you	
	is when I see myself more sad without you.	1540
	The noble cult of the hunt	
	entices you so much these days	
	that, envious of the mountain, I would trade	

1527 *queja*, A B H M T V: querella   1532 *este jardín*, A B H M T V: ese jardín
1535 *ajar*, B: alegar   1536 *bi*, A B H M T V: di   1542 *tanto*, E: tantos

el techo dorado al verde pensil.   [7r]
Apenas el alva corona risueña   1545
los rizos de rosa, clavel y jazmín,
quando por ella me dexas gustando
por verme llorar, de verla reír.
Del lecho mi amor apela a la messa,
y apenas el sol traciende al zenit,   1550
quando en bez que esta sombra te albergue,
te alverga el ardor de un pajizo país.   [7v]
La tarde declina, y passa[s] la tarde,
talando del bosque vno y otro confín;
y aun las noches, pues muchas me ferias,   1555
penachos de enero a catres de abril.
Con que las quatro edades del día
muriendo la[s] viuo pues son para mí
la aurora, la siesta, la tarde y la noche,
penar y temer, llorar y jemir.   1560   [8r]

[CÉFALO] Hermosa Pocris mía,
¡viue tu fe, tu alago, tu fineza,
que desde el primer día
que mi amor al crisol de tu velleza
se examinó tan ciego,   1565
que le sobró para azendrarse el fuego,
te adoro tan postrado,
tan fino, tan rendido y ta[n] gozosso,   [8v]
que sin haber surcado
los golfos que ay desde galán a esposo,   1570
con el amor primero
galán te amo que esposo te venero!
Lo mismo que me culpa,
me absuelbe de tu queja, Pocris vella;
pues ¿qué mayor disculpa   1575
que aver, siguiendo el rumbo de mi estrella,   [9r(3)]
buscando mis desbelos,
dibersión que no pueda darte celos?
Confiesso que estos días
la caza más que otros me divierte,   1580
y es que las ansias mías
lograr en brutos triunfos veo de suerte
que apenas (que) ago tiro,
quando no ay fiera que a mis pies no miro.   [9v]
Si cansado me siento,   1585

1546 *rizos*, A B C G H M P T V: riscos   1548 *por*, A B G H M T V: de/*de*, A B C G H M T V:
por; C P: el   1550 *al*, A B H M T V: el   1551 *sombra*, A B H M T V: alfombra
1553 *passas*, C E P: passa   1556 *penachos*, A B C G H M P T V: peñascos   1558 *las*, E: la

that gilded roof for the green garden.
Barely does dawn crown with a smile   1545
her locks of rose, carnation, and jasmine,
than you leave me for her, enjoying
seeing her laugh by seeing me cry.
From bed does my love call me to table,
and barely does the sun pass its zenith,   1550
than, instead of this shade here protecting you,
the ardor of a straw land protects you.
The afternoon declines, and you spend it
devastating one and another confine of the forest;
and even the nights (and you give me many),   1555
January's proud plumes crushed into April's featherbeds.
With which, the four stages of the day
I live dying, since they are for me
the dawn, the midday, the afternoon, and the night,
pain and fear, weeping and lamenting.   1560

CÉFALO   My beautiful Pocris,
your faith, your flattery, your refinement live;
for since that first day
when my love, in the crucible of your beauty,
examined itself so blindly   1565
that it was more than enough that the fire should purify,
I adore you so utterly,
so finely, so obediently, and so enjoyably,
that without having crossed
the gulfs that exist between suitor and husband,   1570
with the first love
as a suitor I love you, and as a husband I respect you!
The same thing for which you blame me
absolves me of your complaint, beautiful Pocris,
for what greater pardon is there   1575
than having, following the destiny of my stars,
looking out for my concerns,
a pastime that cannot give you jealousy?
I confess that these days
the hunt more than other things entertains me,   1580
and it is true that I see my worries
achieve brutal triumphs so luckily
that rarely do I hurl my spear
when there is not a beast that I see at my feet.
If I feel tired,   1585

1561 Ac. E: 1 Cop.   1562 *fineza*, A B C H J M P T V: belleza   1564 *velleza*,
A B H M T V: fineza   1568 *tan*, E: tal   1577 *buscando*, A B C H P V: buscado
1583 *apenas*, E: apenas que

feliz a la fatiga el hozio iguala,
pues un templado viento
me consuela, me alibia, y me regala
con delicias tan sumas,
que es vn ventall[e] de rizadas plumas.   1590
Las aves le acompañan
con tan sonoras cláusulas velozes,
que mil vezes me engañan   [10ʳ]
si son o no de alguna deida[d] vozes
que a grande fin me llaman,   1595
según tal vez recuerdan, tal inflaman.
Virtud quizá diuina
contiene este benablo de Diana;
y pues él me destina
sin duda alguna empresa en quien vfana   1600
mi fama se corone
hasta hallarla, tu quexa me perdone: [10ᵛ]
que he de seguir el monte,
en quien oy anda vna ignorada fiera,
que orror de este orizonte,   1605
escándalo es del monte y la rribera,
y e de ver si consigo
su trofeo. Clarín, vente conmigo.   [Vase.]

POCRIS   Escucha, Clarín, primero
                que a él le sigas.

CLARÍN   ¿Qué me mandas?   1610

POCRIS   Saber de ti lo que dél   [11ʳ]
                no deben sauer mis ansias,
                porque no es justo que en propia
                muger escrúpulos aya
                que aventuren el respecto   1615
                al ber mi desconfianza.
                Y si las disculpas suias,
                o bien ciertas o bien falsas,
                bastan para mi decoro,
                para mi temor no bastan.   1620   [11ᵛ]
                Y así tú me as de decir
                qué bientos, qué aves, qué cazas
                son éstas que días y noches
                tanto a Zéfalo le arrastran.

1588 *y*, A B C H J M P T V: missing   1590 que es vn ventalle de, E: que es vn ventallo de: J P: que
es un venablo de; C: que es un ventablo de; A B H M T V: moviendo suave   1594 *deidad*, E: deida

happily rest is equal to the fatigue,
for a moderate breeze
consoles me, relieves me, and regales me
with delights so great
that it is a little fan of curled feathers.   1590
The birds accompany it
with such sonorous, quick phrases,
that a thousand times they deceive me as to
whether or not they are voices of some divinity
that call me to a great purpose, and   1595
according to what they perhaps recall, they inflame.
Perhaps this spear
of Diana contains divine power;
and since it destines for me
without doubt some lofty enterprise in which   1600
my fame may be crowned,
until I find it, may your complaint forgive me:
for I must follow the mountain,
in which today there goes an unknown beast
that is the terror of this horizon,   1605
the scandal of the mountain and the stream,
and I must see if I may obtain
its trophy. Clarín, come with me.   [Exit.]

POCRIS   Listen, Clarín, before
                you follow him.

CLARÍN   What do you command?   1610

POCRIS   To know from you what about him
                my anxieties should not know,
                because it is not right that in a proper
                woman there should be misgivings
                that risk respect   1615
                upon seeing my distrust.
                And if his excuses,
                either certainly true or certainly false,
                are enough for my propriety,
                they are not enough for my fear.   1620
                And so you must tell me
                what breezes, what birds, what hunts
                are these that, night and day,
                lead Céfalo on so.

1596 *recuerdan,* A B C H J M P T V: recrean   1600 *alguna,* A B C G H J M P T V: a alguna
1615 *el,* A B C G H J M P T V: su

CLARÍN   Yo, señora, soi criad[o],   1625
            y si supiera la causa,
            por decirla la dijera;
            sólo sé que en la campaña
            se rretira de nosotros
            a la más inculta estancia   1630   [12ʳ]
            de el monte, donde a sus solas
            lo más de las [s]iestas passa
            en las músicas suspenso
            de unos páxaros que cantan
            como con humana voz: 1635
            cuia dulze consonancia,
            una vez q*ue* quise oírla,
            no pude, porque vna estraña
            fiera atrabesó la senda,   [12ᵛ]
            que es la que oy el valle espanta   1640
            como él dijo, y para mí
            algún sátiro es que anda
            en busca de alguna nimfa.
            Pienso q*ue* su nombre es Laura,
            porque a modo de bramido   1645
            oý que dijo en vozes altas:
            "Laura es mi pena, Laura es
            la q*ue* me hiela y me abrasa."
            Pero esto a ti, ¿q*ué* te importa?   [13ʳ(4)]
            Y puesto que poco o nada,   1650
            adiós, que Zéfalo espera.   [Vase.]
POCRIS   Espera tú, infame, aguarda.
FLORETA   Pues ¿por qué con él te enojas?
POCRIS   ¡Ay, Floreta, que no alcanza
            lo rústico de tu pecho   1655
            a lo sutil de mis ansias!
            Ya q*ue* de una fortuna
            cómplizes, en la passada
            ruina del templo q*ue*damos
            por viuas çenizas ambas,   1660   [13ᵛ]
            siendo Zéfalo y Clarín
            los que nos libraron, haga
            la nezesidad virtud,
            haziendo la confianza
            de ti, que no pu[e]do de otra,   1665

1625 *criado*, E: criada   1632 *siestas*, E: fiestas   1636 *cuia*, G: y con   1640 *oy el valle*,
A B C H J M P T V: dijo que   1641 *como él dijo*, A B C H J M P T V: hoy el valle; G: según tengo

CLARÍN	I, mistress, am a servant,	1625
	and if I knew the cause,	
	I would say it just to say it;	
	I only know that in the countryside	
	he withdraws from us	
	to the wildest place	1630
	of the mountain, where alone	
	he spends the greatest part of his afternoon	
	caught up in the music	
	of some birds that sing	
	as if with human voice:	1635
	whose sweet consonance,	
	once when I tried to hear it,	
	I could not, because a strange	
	beast crossed the path,	
	the beast that today terrorizes the valley	1640
	as he said, and that for me	
	is some satyr who goes	
	in search of some nymph.	
	I think that her name is Laura,	
	for in the manner of a shout	1645
	I heard him say aloud:	
	"Laura is my pain, Laura is	
	she who chills me and burns me."	
	But what does this matter to you?	
	And since little or nothing,	1650
	good-bye, for Céfalo is waiting. [Exit.]	
POCRIS	Wait, wretch, stay.	
FLORETA	Now, why are you angry at him?	
POCRIS	Oh, Floreta, the coarseness	
	of your breast cannot attain	1655
	the subtlety of my anxieties!	
	Since, as accomplices of	
	fortune we remained in the	
	past ruin of the temple,	
	both of us as living cinders,	1660
	being Céfalo and Clarín	
	those who freed us, let	
	necessity create virtue,	
	as I confide	
	in you because I can in no other	1665

1646 *vozes altas,* A B H J M P T V: voz alta   1653 *pues,* M: missing/*con él te enojas,*
A B C H J M P T V: te enojas con él   1657 *Ya,* A B C H J M P T V: Mas ya
1662 *nos,* R: no   1665 *puedo,* E: pudo

	¡ay infelize!, de quántas		
	de Zéfalo en los palacios		
	me asisten y me acompañan.		
FLORETA	Bien puedes fiar de mí,		
	porque a mí, di, ¿qué me falta,	1670	[14ʳ]
	sino sólo entendimiento,		
	para ser tu secretaria.		

[Sale ALECTO, invisible para POCRIS y FLORETA.]

ELECTO	[Aparte.]		
	Ya es tiempo que de los celos		
	la parte esparciendo baya		
	que le a tocado a mis furias.	1675	
	[Pone a POCRIS la mano en los		
	pechos.]		
FLORETA	¿Qué tienes, pues?		
POCRIS	Vna ansia,		
	vna pena, vna congoja,		
	que a ser güéspeda de alma		
	e[n]tra como que es terneza,		[14ᵛ]
	y sale como que es rabia.	1680	
	en fin, es un no sé qué,		
	que sobre mis miedos causan		
	aquestas noticias.		
FLORETA	¿Cómo?		
POCRIS	Como si boi a apurarlas		
	hallo . . .		
	[ALECTO le canta bajo al oído,		
	y ella repite con despecho lo		
	mismo, de modo que para la		
	Música son dos, y para la		
	representación no es más que		
	uno; porque lo uno ha de ser		
	repetición de lo otro.]		
ELECTRO	. . . que Zéfalo ya	1685	
	de [tus] finezas se cansa . . .		
POCRIS	. . . que Zéfalo ya	1685 bis	
	de mis finezas se cansa . . .		
ELECTRO	. . . pues por un monte te deja . . .		
POCRIS	. . . pues por un monte [me] deja . . .		
ELECTRO	. . . que a sus solas se recata		[15ʳ]
	en lo oculto dél . . .		

1672 Ac. *Sale,* H: missing   1675 *mis furias,* A B C H J M P T V:
mi furia   1676 *Vna,* G: Un   1678 *güéspeda,* J P: huésped   1679 *entra,* E: etra/
terneza, B J M P T V: eterna; A H: envidia   1686 *tus,* E V: mis   1687 bis *me,* E J: te

	(miserable me!) of all the women	
	in the palaces of Céfalo	
	who attend and accompany me.	
FLORETA	Well can you trust in me,	
	because what is lacking to me, tell me,	1670
	except only understanding,	
	for me to be your secretary?	

[Enter ALECTO, invisible to POCRIS and FLORETA.]

ALECTO	[Aside.]	
	Now it is time for me to cast forth	
	the part of the jealousy	
	that has fallen to my fury.	1675

                    [She places her hand on POCRIS'
                    breast.]

FLORETA	But, what is the matter?	
POCRIS	A worry,	
	a pain, an uneasiness,	
	that to be a guest of the soul	
	enters as though it were tenderness	
	and leaves as though it were rage.	1680
	In short, I know not what it is	
	that this news causes	
	above and beyond my fears.	
FLORETA	How?	
POCRIS	As if I am going to verify them,	
	I find . . .	

                    [ALECTO sings softly to her ear,
                    and she repeats with despair the
                    same thing, so that for the
                    music they are two parts, but
                    for the staging it is only one;
                    because one is to be the
                    repetition of the other.]

ALECTO	. . . that Céfalo now	1685
	is tired of your refinements . . .	
POCRIS	. . . that Céfalo now	1685 bis
	is tired of my refinements . . .	
ALECTO	. . . since he leaves you for a mountain . . .	
POCRIS	. . . since he leaves me for a mountain . . .	
ALECTO	. . . and alone he hides	
	in its recesses . . .	

POCRIS	. . . que a sus solas se rrecata	
	en lo oculto dél . . .	
ELETRO	. . . adonde . . .	
POCRIS	. . . adonde . . .	
ELECTRO	. . . blandos bientos le regalan. . .	1690
POCRIS	. . . blandos bientos le regalan . . .	1690 bis
ELECTRO	. . . tiernas vozes le divierten . . .	
POCRIS	. . . tiernas vozes le divierten . . .	
ELETRO	. . . dulces pájaros le cantan . . .	
POCRIS	. . . dulces pájaros le cantan . . .	
ELECTRO	. . . quando otro a vna Laura busca.	[15v]
POCRIS	. . . quando otro a una Laura busca.	
	¿Por quánto pudiera —¡o baga	
	fantasía del temor,	1695
	quánto (d)el discurso adela[n]tas!—	
	por quánto —bueluo a decir—	
	pudiera ser que el buscarla	
	fuera zelosso de que	
	con Zéfalo. . .? La voz falta	1700
	Pero ¿qué mucho, qué mucho,	[16r]
	si no ay decentes palabras,	
	que no decentes pasiones	
	se atreban a pronunciarlas?	
	Y puesto que es el decirlas	1705
	aún peor que ymajinarlas,	
	ven conmigo, que e de ver	
	—si otro traje me disfraza,	
	y sin ser dél conozida,	
	sigo de enbozo sus plantas—	1710 [16v]
	qué aves, qué vientos, qué vozes,	
	qué ylusiones, qué fantasmas,	
	qué delirios, qué quimeras	
	son éstas que le arrebatan	
	tanto el sentido, y en fin,	1715
	quién es esta Laura.	
ELECTRO	Aur[a].	
POCRIS	¿Aura, no dixeron?	
FLORETA	Sí;	
	mas ¿qué admiras?, mas ¿qué estrañas	
	el que el eco te rresponda	
	quando tú la voz lebantas?	1720 [17r(5)]

1696 *el*, E: del/*adelantas*, E: adelatas   1702 *si*, A B G H M T V: que
1703 *que*, A B H MTV: si/*no*, A B H J M P T V: no hay   1704 *se*, A B H M T V: que se/

POCRIS   . . . and alone he hides
            in its recesses . . .
ALECTO   . . . where . . .
POCRIS   . . . where . . .
ALECTO   . . . soft breezes regale him. . .   1690
POCRIS   . . . soft breezes regale him . . .   1690 bis
ALECTO   . . . tender voices entertain him . . .
POCRIS   . . . tender voices entertain him . . .
ALECTO   . . . sweet birds sing to him . . .
POCRIS   . . . sweet birds sing to him . . .
ALECTO   . . . while another looks for a Laura.
POCRIS   . . . while another looks for a Laura.
            How could it be (oh vague
            fantasy of love,   1695
            as much as you advance the argument!)
            how (I repeat)
            could it be that looking for her
            he might be jealous that
            with Céfalo. . .? My voice fails   1700
            But why should I be at all surprised,
            if there are no decent words,
            that indecent passions
            dare to pronounce them?
            And since saying them is   1705
            even worse than imagining them,
            come with me, for I must see
            (if another dress disguises me
            and, without being recognized by him
            I follow, concealed, his footprints)   1710
            what birds, what breezes, what voices,
            what illusions, what ghosts,
            what ravings, what chimeras
            are these that torment
            so much his senses, and, finally   1715
            who this Laura is.
ALECTO   Aura.
POCRIS   Aura, did they not say?
FLORETA   Yes,
            but at what do you marvel, why do you wonder
            that the echo answers you
            when you raise your voice?   1720

pronunciarlas, A B H M T V: explicarlas   1716 *Aura,* E: auros   1717 *Aura,* C J P: Laura
1719 *el que,* A B C H J M P T V: que/*te,* A B H M T V: a ti te

POCRIS Dices bien; mas ¡ay, que hace(r)
    sentido el eco a mis ansias!
    No sin razón me estremeze,
    me asusta y me sobresalta;
    y más si en Aura me acuerda   1725
    la prometida amenaza
    de que Venus y Amor tomen
    en mí de su error venganza,
    a cuyo fin (l)Aura es   [17ᵛ]
    la que a Zéfalo le encanta   1730
    en el monte.
FLORETA   No, señora,
    casso del acasso hagas.
    Aura, ¿ya no es ayre?
POCRIS   Sí,
    pero sepa tu ignorancia
    que si el ayre diere celos   1735
    celos aun del ayre matan.
    Sígueme, pues.
ELECTO   ¡Ay de ti . . .
POCRIS   ¡Ay de ti . . .
FLOR[ET]A   ¡Ay de ti . . .
ELECTO . . . Pocris, si a mirar alcanzas . . . [18ʳ]
L[A]S DOS . . . Pocris, si a(l) mirar alcanzas . . .
A 4 . . . que si el ayre diere celos,
    celos aun del aire matan. [Vanse.] 1740

[MONTE]

[Sale ERÓSTRATO, vestido de pieles, huyendo.]

ERÓSTRATO ¡Que si el ayre di[er]e celos, [18ᵛ]
    celos aun del ayre matan!
    Según lo que a mí me pasa,
    amante del ayre, pues
    (l)Aura es mi pena, (l)Aura es   1745
    la que me hiela y me abrasa,
    conmigo deue de ablar
    sin duda esta aleue voz,
    que discurriendo veloz,   1750
    no ay intrincado lugar   [19ʳ]
    que no me busque, ¡ay de mí!
    Por más que el centro me esconde
    de aquestos peñascos, donde

1721 hace, E: hacer; C J P: hazen 1729 Aura, E C J P: Laura 1737 bis Ac. Floreta, E: florra
1738 mirar, A B C H J M P T V: saber   1738 bis Ac. E: los dos; G: Pocris y Floreta
1738 bis a mirar, E: al mirar; A B C H J M P T V: a saber 1739 Ac. A B C G H M P T:

POCRIS   You speak well, but oh, the echo
                      makes sense to my anxieties!
                      Not without reason does it shake me,
                      frighten me, and startle me;
                      and more if I remember Aura's   1725
                      promised threat
                      that Venus and Cupid should
                      take revenge on me for her error,
                      to which end Aura is
                      the one who enchants Céfalo   1730
                      on the mountain.

FLORETA   Do not, madame,
                      pay attention to this accident.
                      Aura, is she not now air?

POCRIS   Yes,
                      but your ignorance should know
                      that if the air causes jealousy,   1735
                      jealousy, even of the air, kills.
                      Follow me, then.

ALECTO   Woe to you . . .
POCRIS   Woe to you . . .
FLORETA   Woe to you . . .
ALECTO   . . . Pocris, if you understand by seeing . . .
BOTH OF THEM . . . Pocris, if you understand by seeing . . .
CHORUS   . . . that if the air causes jealousy,
                      jealousy, even of the air, kills.   [Exeunt.]   1740

[MOUNTAIN]

[Enter ERÓSTRATO, dressed in skins, fleeing.]

ERÓSTRATO   "That if the air causes jealousy,
                      jealousy, even of the air, kills!"
                      According to what is happening to me,
                      the lover of the air, since
                      Aura is my pain, Aura is   1745
                      she who chills me and burns me,
                      without doubt this lofty voice
                      must speak to me,
                      for, travelling quickly,   1750
                      there is no tangled place
                      that it does not seek me, oh my!
                      For as much as the group of these
                      boulders hides me, where

Toda la música; H: Un Coro; V: Todos   1740 Ac. B M T V: Dentro y las tres. Todos;
C J P: Dentro y las tres; H: Ellas, y el coro dentro; A: Dentro, y ellas; G: Las tres, y Coros
1740 Ac. *Sale,* H: missing   1741 *diere,* E: dize   1745 *Aura,* E C J P: Laura

de la llama q*ue* enzendí
me deslumbra el resplandor   1755
tanto, que aun mi misma sonbra
me atemoriza y me asombra,
¿no me bastaba el terror
con que trascendiendo esferas
de unos a otros orizontes,   1760
ciudadano(s) de los montes,   [19ᵛ]
compañero de las fieras,
voy de las gentes huyendo,
sino el terror, ¡ay de mí!,
de que me siga hasta aquí,   1765
est[a] armonía, diciendo
por ver si más se dilata[n]
mis sacrílegos rezelos . . .

A 4   [Dentro.]
                          . . . que si el ayre diere celos,
                          celos aun del ayre matan.   1770

ERÓSTRATO ¿Quién duda −pues mal pudiera
                          en tanto mortal desdén
                          dar celos el ayre a quien   [20ʳ]
                          galán del ayre no fuera−
                          q*ue* habla conmigo? ¡O si más   1775
                          se declarara! ¿Es a mí,
                          Eco, la amenaza?

[Sale MEGERA, atravesando el tablado.]

MEJERA   Sí.
ERÓSTRATO ¿Cómo?
MEJERA   Presto lo sabrás . . .
ERÓSTRATO Nuebas furias me arrebatan.
MEJERA   . . . biendo [al] seguir mis ahnelos . . .   1780
AL 4°   . . . q*ue* [si el ayre diere celos,
               celos aun del ayre matan.]   [Vase.]
ERÓSTRATO Hacia allí la voz se oyó;
                          y aunq*ue* con nuebas injurias
                          de ansias, yras, rabias, furias,   1785   [20ᵛ]
                          ciego el eco me dejó,
                          seguirle tengo.
                                        [Anda a ciegas por la escena.]

[Sale RÚSTICO.]

1761 *ciudadano*, E: ciudadanos   1766 *esta*, E: estu   1767*dilatan*, E: dilata
1769 Ac. E: Al 4 de atrás; A B G H M T V: Coro; C J P: Músicos   1773 *el ayre a*,
A B H M T V: al aire   1777 Ac. *Sale*, H: missing   1780 *al*, E: missing/*mis*, G: tus

by the flame that I ignited
the brilliance dazzles me   1755
so much that even my own shadow
terrorizes and frightens me,
was there not enough terror
with which, crossing spheres
from one to another horizon,   1760
a citizen of the mountains,
a companion of the beasts,
I go, fleeing from people,
without the terror (oh, me!)
that this music follows me   1765
even here, saying,
to see if my sacrilegious
fears increase more . . .

CHORUS   [Offstage.]
             . . . for if the air causes jealousy,
             jealousy, even of the air, kills.   1770

ERÓSTRATO Who doubts (since hardly could
             the air cause jealousy
             in such mortal disdain to one
             who was not the lover of the air)
             that it speaks to me? Oh, if only   1775
             it would declare itself more. Is
             the threat, Echo, for me?

[Enter MEGERA, crossing the stage.]

MEGERA   Yes.
ERÓSTRATO How?
MEGERA   You will soon find out . . .
ERÓSTRATO New furies torment me.
MEGERA   . . . seeing as you follow my desires . . .   1780
CHORUS   . . . that if the air causes jealousy,
             jealousy, even of the air, kills.   [Exit.]
ERÓSTRATO The voice was heard from over there;
             and, although with new injuries
             of anxiety, anger, rage, and fury,   1785
             the echo left me blind,
             I have to follow it.
                          [He walks blindly around the stage.]

[Enter RÚSTICO.]

1781 Ac. B M T V: Ella, y música; A G H: Ella, y Coro (Dentro); C J P: Músicos   1781-1782 E: que
1785 *ansias, yras,* A B C H J M P T V: iras, ansias   1787 Ac. *Sale,* H: missing

RÚSTICO   En efecto,
                no me atrebo a parezer
                entre gentes, por no ser
                animal más inperfecto   1790
                del que me an echo asta aquí;
                y así a los montes me vengo.
                            [ERÓSTRATO a ciegas se abraza
                                con RÚSTICO.]
ERÓSTRATO Pues ya en mis brazos te tengo,
                sombra cuia voz seguí,
                e de saber qué me quieres   1795   [21ʳ(6)]
                y lo q*ue* tu voz me dize.
RÚSTICO   ¿Qué monstruo es, ¡ay infelize!,
                el que me acosa?
ERÓSTRATO   ¿Quié[n] eres?
RÚSTICO   Ymajine su me[rc]é
                —en quanta alimaña [hay] oy—   1800
                [la] que quiere; que ésa soi,
                ésa e sido, ésa seré,
                sin más dilación, pues tales
                son mis varios atributos,
                que echo pericón de brutos   1805   [21ᵛ]
                y pendanga de animales,
                del manjar que ba a buscar,
                al punto le serbiré;
                pero no me coma, aunque
                le dé a escojer el manjar.   1810
ERÓSTRATO ¡Rústico!
RÚSTICO   ¡Eso es bueno!
ERÓSTRATO   Espera.
RÚSTICO   ¿Rústico yo?
ERÓSTRATO   ¿Q*ué* ay que asombre?
RÚSTICO   Ser para las fieras hombre,
                y para los hombres fiera.   [22ʳ]
ERÓSTRATO ¿Qué quieres decir? Detente.   1815
RÚSTICO   Que ninguno ay que me vea
                que alimaña no me crea,
                no quitando lo presente,
                sino su merzed.

1788 *parecer,* G: aparecer   1793 *ya,* A B C H J M P T V: missing   1798 *acosa,* A B C G H
J M P T V: agarra/*Quien,* E: quier   1799 *mercé,* C E J P: mesté   1800 *hay,* E: missing
1801 la, E: lo   1805 *pericón de brutos,* J: petición de brutos; B: missing

RÚSTICO   In effect,
                     I do not dare to appear
                     among people, in order not to be
                     a more imperfect animal   1790
                     than that which they have made me so far;
                     and so I come to the mountains.
                                          [ERÓSTRATO, blind, hugs
                                             RÚSTICO.]
ERÓSTRATO Since now I have you in my arms,
                     shadow whose voice I followed,
                     I must know what you want of me,   1795
                     and what your voice tells me.
RÚSTICO   What monster is this (unhappy me!)
                     that pursues me?
ERÓSTRATO   Who are you?
RÚSTICO   Imagine, your grace,
                     what you will about which beast   1800
                     I seem today; for that I am,
                     that I have been, that shall I be,
                     without further delay, since such
                     are my various attributes
                     that, having been made the joker of brutes   1805
                     and the jack of animals,
                     I shall serve you at once
                     for the food you are going to seek,
                     but do not eat me, although
                     I let you choose the food.   1810
ERÓSTRATO Rústico!
RÚSTICO   That's a good one!
ERÓSTRATO   Wait.
RÚSTICO   I, Rústico?
ERÓSTRATO   Why be surprised?
RÚSTICO   Being a man for beasts
                     and a beast for men.
ERÓSTRATO What do you mean? Stop.   1815
RÚSTICO   That there is no one who sees me
                     who does not believe me to be a beast,
                     not excepting the present,
                     except your grace.

ERÓSTRATO   ¿*Que* aún no
                    me as conozido?
RÚSTICO   En q*uié*n es,   1820
                    a caer no me atrebo.
ERÓSTRATO   Pues
                    ¿no soy Eróstrato yo?
RÚSTICO   Agora le conozí,
                    y ya no me admira el traje;   [22ᵛ]
                    que no es mucho sea salbaje   1825
                    el que henamorado vi.
                    Mas [dime, ¿q*ué* es lo q*ue* passa?]
ERÓSTRATO   Desde q*ue* Aura el aura es
                    de Venus, es mi ansia, pues
                    (l)Aura me hiela y me abrasa.   1830
                    Dime tú si acasso oíste
                    vna voz, y adónde fue.
RÚSTICO   Ni yo la oý, ni la sé.   [23ʳ]
ERÓSTRATO   Pues yo e de seguirla, ¡ay triste!,
                    hasta ber en qué rematan,   1835
                    publicando mis desbelos . . .
A 4   . . . que si el ayre [diere celos,
                    celos aun del ayre matan.]   [Vase.]
RÚSTICO   Vaia norabuena,
                    que yo, abiendo oído   1840
                    gente a aquella parte,
                    aunq*ue* le aya visto
                    llamarme mi nombr[e],
                    pretendo escondido   [23ᵛ]
                    que q*uie*n son no buelban   1845
                    al primer delirio.   [Vase.]

[Salen CÉFALO, CLARÍN.]

ZÉFALO   Aquí, Clarín, qued[a],
                    pues al verde sitio
                    de este inculto seno
                    no as de entrar conmigo.   1850
CLARÍN   ¿Posible es q*ue* encubras
                    qué ai aquí escondido
                    de mí, conociendo
                    quán leal te sirbo?

1823 *le,* A B C G H J M P T V: lo   1825 *sea,* A B C G H J M P T V: vea   1826 *el,* A B C
G H J M P T V: al   1827 E G: mas qué es lo que passa, dime; C J P: Mas qué es lo que passa;
B: quien, que es lo que pasa   1830 *Aura,* C E J P: Laura   1832 *adónde,* A B C G H J M P T V:
dónde   1833 *la sé,* A B C G H J M P T V: lo sé   1836 *mis,* A B C H J M P T V: sus

ERÓSTRATO	Have you still	
	not recognized me?	
RÚSTICO	Who you are	1820
	I do not dare find out.	
ERÓSTRATO	Well,	
	am I not Eróstrato?	
RÚSTICO	Now I recognize you,	
	and no longer does the attire astonish me;	
	for it is no wonder that the one whom I saw	1825
	in love should be a savage.	
	But, tell me, what is happening?	
ERÓSTRATO	Ever since Aura became the breeze	
	of Venus, she is my anxiety, for	
	Aura chills me and burns me.	1830
	Tell me if by chance you heard	
	a voice, and where it went.	
RÚSTICO	Neither did I hear it, nor do I know.	
ERÓSTRATO	Well, I must follow it (unhappy me!)	
	until I see how it turns out,	1835
	publicizing my woes . . .	
CHORUS	. . . for if the air causes jealousy,	
	jealousy, even of the air, kills.	[Exit.]
RÚSTICO	Go in Godspeed,	
	for I, having heard	1840
	people in that direction,	
	although I have seen him	
	call me by my name, I shall	
	try to see, hidden,	
	that, whoever they are, they do not return	1845
	to their first madness.	[Exit.]

[Enter CÉFALO, CLARÍN.]

CÉFALO	Stay here, Clarín,	
	since you are not to enter	
	the green site	
	of this primitive hollow.	1850
CLARÍN	Is it possible that you are hiding	
	from me what might be hidden	
	here, knowing	
	how loyally I serve you?	

1837 Ac. E: a 4 ʃ; B C M T V: El, y la música; J P: El, y su música; A H: El, y Coro, dentro; G: Eróstrato y Coro (Dentro) 1837-1838 E: que si el ayre   1840 *oído,* A B G H M T V: visto 1842 *visto,* A B G H M T V: oído   1843 *nombre,* E: nombr   1845 *son,* G: soy 1846 Ac. *Salen,* H: missing   1847 *queda,* E: quedo   1852 *ai,* A: haya

CÉFALO   Porque no presumas   1855   [24r]
           que de ti no fío
           lo que a Pocris callo,
           berás que te digo.
           Aquella veldad,
           a quien todos vimos   1860
           combertida en ayre,
           conse[r]bando el mismo
           nombre de Aura, es quien
           en el cristalino
           imperio de Venus   1865   [24v]
           oy goza el dominio.
           Esta, agradecida
           a quando mi brío
           intentó librarla
           en aquel peligro,   1870
           viéndome vna siesta
           del ardiente estío
           postrado al cansancio,
           a la sed rendido,
           el sudor, que el rostro   1875
           partió con los rizos,   [25r(7)]
           ya que no a zendales,
           enjugó a suspiros.
           Mullidos a fuerza
           de rosas los riscos,   1880
           vi lechos en quien
           fue el sueño mi alibio,
           en que, o mal despierto
           o no bien dormido,
           en humana voz   1885
           su deydad me dixo:
AURA   [Dentro.]
           Siempre que ansioso el afán   [25v]
           de la caza te fatigue,
           llama a Au(ro)ra que le mitigue
           a cuyas vozes verán   1890
           tus congoxas quánto están
           en tu fabor los fabores
           de aquella que oy entre albores
           poner puede de su mano,
           en los hombros del verano,   1895
           el imperio de las flores.   [26r]

1858 *que te,* A B H M P T: que lo; V: lo que   1862 *conserbando,* E: consebando
1864 *en,* J P: missing   1874-1875 A B C H J M P T V: missing

CÉFALO	So that you do not assume	1855
	that I do not tell to you	
	what I do not tell to Pocris,	
	you will see what I have to say.	
	That beauty,	
	which we all saw	1860
	transformed into air,	
	keeping the same	
	name of Aura, is she who	
	today enjoys power	
	in the crystalline	1865
	realm of Venus.	
	She, appreciative	
	of the time my daring	
	tried to free her	
	from that danger,	1870
	seeing me one afternoon	
	stretched out from the fatigue	
	of the hot summer,	
	conquered by thirst,	
	with her sighs she wiped away	1875
	the perspiration that	
	my hair kept from my face	
	so that I should not be drenched.	
	The cliffs softened	
	by the force of roses,	1880
	I saw beds in which	
	sleep was my relief,	
	in which, either not fully awake	
	nor well asleep,	
	in a human voice,	1885
	her divinity said to me:	
AURA	[Offstage.]	
	Since the anxious desire for the	
	hunt always tires you,	
	call to soften it upon Aura,	
	at whose words your pains	1890
	will see how much	
	her favors are in your favor,	
	since today at dawn	
	she can place by her hand	
	the mantle of flowers	1895
	on the shoulders of summer.	

1878 *enjugó,* A B H M T V: el fuego; C J P: en fuego
1879 *a fuerza,* A B H M T V: a fuer; C J P: afuera   1889 *Aura,* E: Aurora/*le,* G: lo; M; él

CÉFALO   Aun aora pareze
           que suenan en mi oýdo,
           y pues de su agrado
           paso diuertido   1900
           las treguas que da
           el noble exercicio,
           logrando dichoso,
           sin que yerre tiro,
           los altos trofeos   1905
           de aqueste (e) divino   [26v]
           arpón de Diana,
           ¿qué mucho que altibo
           busque aquella fiera
           que tantos an bisto   1910
           y yo nunca encuentro;
           y más quando miro
           que en esto no agrabio
           el tierno cari[ñ]o
           con que a Pocris bella   1915
           adoro y estimo?
           Y así, pues no es
           la caza desbío,   [27r]
           bien ambos enpleos
           lograr solicito   1920
           de monte y reg[a]zo,
           siendo a un tiempo mismo,
           Pocris por quien muero,
           (l)Aura por quien vibo.   [Vanse.]

[Sale POCRIS, de villana, y FLORETA, escuchando, ambas rebozadas.]

POCRIS   "¡Pocris por quien muer[o],   1925
           (l)Aura por quien vibo!"
           ¡O nunca, Floreta,
           le vbiera seguido
           hasta donde, haciendo   [27v]
(FLORETA) canzel este risco,   1930
           llegara ocasión
           en que ubiera oído,
           "¡Pocris por quien muero,
           (l)Aura por quien vibo!"
           Espera, amante traidor,   1935
           mira que es mucho rigor,

1898 *suenan,* A B C G H J M P T V: suena   1906 *divino,* E: e divino   1914 cariño, E: carino
1921 *regazo,* E: regozo   1924 *Aura,* E: Laura   1924 Ac. *Sale,* H: missing

CÉFALO   Even now they seem
to sound in my ear,
and since, because of her pleasure,
I suffer happily   1900
the tribulations that
noble exercise causes,
achieving happily
the great victories
of this divine   1905
spear of Diana
without its ever missing the mark,
why should I not seek,
haughtily, that beast
that so many have seen   1910
and that I never find;
and, moreover, when I see
that in this I do no harm
to the tender affection
with which I adore and respect   1915
beautiful Pocris?
And so, since hunting
is no vice,
I try to carry out
well both enterprises   1920
of the mountain and the home, and
it is at the same time,
Pocris for whom I die,
Aura for whom I live.   [Exit.]

[Enter POCRIS, as a peasant, and FLORETA, listening, both covered.]

POCRIS   "Pocris for whom I die,   1925
Aura for whom I live!"
Oh, Floreta, would that I
had never followed him
here where, making
a screen of this cliff,   1930
the occasion might arise
in which I should have heard,
"Pocris for whom I die,
Aura for whom I live!"
Wait, treasonous lover,   1935
see that it is great severity,

1925 *muero,* E: muera   1926 *Aura,* E G H: Laura   1930 Ac. E: Floreta; A B C
G H J M P T V: missing   1930 *este,* A B G H M T V: de ese
1931 *ocasión,* A B C G H M T: a ocasión   1934 *Aura,* E G H: Laura

    doblándome los rezelos,
    que tú me mates de celos,   [28ʳ]
    y yo me muera de amor.
    Si mi bida te estorbó,   1940
    no tú quitármela trates,
    pues yo lo aré, pues no es, ¡no!,
    menester que tú me mates
    para q*ue* me muera yo.
    Déjame con los consuelos   1945
    de que yo te hize el fauor,
    pues no mejora el dolor
    que tú me mates de celos,   [28ᵛ]
    y yo me muera de amor.
    Mas ¿q*ué* es lo q*ue* hago?   1950
    Mas ¿q*ué* es lo q*ue* digo?
    Las lágrimas cesen,
    cesen los suspiros,
    y ya echo el empeño,
    veuer solizito   1955
    l[a] ponzoña al vasso
    y al ayre el [he]chizo.
    Y así, tú, Floreta,   [29ʳ(8)]
    porque menos ruido
    haga vna en su azecho,   1960
    en aqueste sitio
    te queda, entre tanto
    que sola le sigo
    hasta que mis penas
    vean si aberiguo   1965
    qué (l)Aura es aquesta
    por q*uie*n [el] a dicho:
    "¡Pocris por quien muero,   [29ᵛ]
    (l)Aura por q*uie*n viuo!"
    Que aunq*ue* cobarde el temor,   1970
    flores pise y sienta hielos,
    nada abenturo en rigor,
    en q*ue* él me mate de celos,
    si yo me muero de amor.   [Vase.]

[Salen CLARÍN; RÚSTICO, que se queda entre unas ramas.]

1941 *tú,* G: de   1942 *pues yo,* A B C G H J M P T V: que yo/*no es, ¡no!,* A B H M T V: que no;
G J: no es; P: no   1943 *menester que tú,* A B H M T V: es menester que   1947 *mejora,*
A B C H J M P T V: me deja   1948 *mates,* T: matas   1949 *y,* A B C G H J M P T V: si;
muera, A B C G H J M P T V: muero   1956 *la,* E V: lo   1957 *hechizo,* E: chizo

doubling for me my woes,
that you kill me with jealousy,
and I die with love.
If my life has encumbered you,   1940
do not try to take it from me,
because I shall do it, for it is not, no,
necessary that you kill me
for me to die.
Leave me with the consolation   1945
that I did you the favor,
for it is no relief for the pain
that you kill me with jealousy
and I die for love.
But, what is this I am doing?   1950
But, what is this I am saying?
Stop the tears,
let the sighs cease,
and now, with the pledge made,
I ask to drink   1955
the glass of poison
and the air of enchantment.
And, you, Floreta,
so that one woman may make less
noise in her spying,   1960
stay in this
place while
I alone follow him
until my suffering
sees that I determine   1965
what Aura is this
for whom he has said,
"Pocris for whom I die,
Aura for whom I live!"
For although fear intimidates me, and   1970
I walk on flowers yet feel ice,
I risk nothing in harshness
in that he kills me with jealousy
if I die for love.   [Exit.]

[Enter CLARÍN; RÚSTICO, who remains among some branches.]

1963 *le,* J P: la   1966 *Aura,* B C E G H M P T: Laura   1967 *él,* E: seña; C J P: será
1969 *Aura,* E G H: Laura   1971 *hielos,* A B C H J M P T V: celos
1974 Ac. *Salen,* H: missing; C J P: quedan; B M T V: quédanse

CLARÍN   [Aparte.]
            Dos zagalas venían,   1975
            y a la espesura
            como apuesta se [ha entrado]
            de dos la vna.   [30r]
FLORETA   [Aparte.]
            Yo y Clarín bien mostramos
            que los sirbientes,   1980
            como malas espadas,
            se queda[n] siempre.
RÚSTICO   [Aparte.]
            Ya no ay ruido: yo salgo . . .
            pero aún no es tiempo,
            que el azar de estos días   1985
            está al encuentro.   [Retírase.]
CLARÍN   Pues busté, reina, espera
            quando yo espero,
            la es[pe]ranza hagamos   [30v]
            divertimiento.   1990
FLORETA   ¿Quién será tan grosero,
            tan bano, que haga
            su divertimiento
            de su esperanza?
RÚSTICO   [Aparte.]
            Si es discreto y requiebra,   1995
            tendré buen rato;
            y mejor si requiebra
            y es mentecato.
CLARÍN   Primorcitos fueran
            en gente baja   2000
            guarnezer alcorcones
            con filigrana.   [31r]
            Y así, solo a mi modo
            decirla intento . . .
FLORETA   ¿Qué?
Y CLARÍN   . . . que nos queramos   2005
            por pasatiempo.
FLORETA   Si Floreta lo oyera,
            saltara aora.
CLARÍN   De floretas se hazen
            las cabriolas.   2010
            Pero tú, ¿de qué sabes
            que yo la quiero?

1975 zagalas, J M P R T: zagales   1977 ha entrado, E: entraron   1982 quedan, E: queda;
A B C H J M P T V: vuelven   1984 aún, A B C H J M P T V: missing   1985 de estos,
A B H M T V: estos   1989 E: la esranza hagamos; A B H M T V: hagamos la esperanza

CLARÍN	[Aside.]	
	Two maidens were coming,	1975
	and, as though appointed,	
	one of them has	
	entered the thicket.	
FLORETA	[Aside.]	
	Clarín and I demonstrate well	
	that servants,	1980
	like bad swords,	
	stay around forever.	
RÚSTICO	[Aside.]	
	No longer is there noise: I shall come out . . .	
	but it is not time yet,	
	for opportunity these days	1985
	is in the finding. [He withdraws.]	
CLARÍN	Since you, queen, wait	
	while I wait,	
	let us make of the expectation	
	an entertainment.	1990
FLORETA	Who is possibly so gross,	
	so vain, that he might	
	make an entertainment	
	of his expectations?	
RÚSTICO	[Aside.]	
	If he is discreet and flatters her,	1995
	I shall have a good time;	
	and a better one if he flatters her	
	and is a liar.	
CLARÍN	To adorn acorns	
	with filigree	2000
	would be great refinement	
	in lowly people.	
	And so, in my own way,	
	I only try to say . . .	
FLORETA	What?	
CLARÍN	. . . that we should love each other	2005
	as a pastime.	
FLORETA	If Floreta heard you,	
	she would jump on you.	
CLARÍN	Great leaps are made	
	for Floretas.	2010
	But how do you know	
	that I love her?	

1999 *Primorcitos*, A B C H J M P T V: Primoritos   2001 *alcorcones*, A B H: alcornoques
2012ff. A B C H J M P T V: RÚSTICO De saber lo que había/de no saberlo.
A C H P have the same lines indicated "Aparte."

FLORETA	Ella me lo a dicho.		
CLARÍN	¡Ve aquí, señores,		[31^v]
	cómo su remedio	2015	
	pierden los hombres!		
	Andaráse alabando		
	porque vna tarde,		
	ninfa del baratillo,		
	la amé de balde.	2020	
FLORETA	Pues infame, picaño,		
	loco, atrebido, [Descubriéndose.]		
	esta cara, ¿es cara		
	de baratillo?		
CLARÍN	Conociéndote, había	2025	[32^r]
	Tente, Floreta.		
FLORETA	Ya eso [es] biejo.		
RÚSTICO	[Aparte.] – Por Baco,		
	que ella es por ella.		
	Y, animal más o menos,		
	hacerles tengo	2030	
	que me tiemble[n]. – Ya basta. [Sale.]		
FLORETA	¡Qué es lo que veo!		
	Mi marido, ¿no es éste?		
CLARÍN	Billano, aparta.		
RÚSTICO	¡Oyga! ¿Qué hace[n] bustedes	2035	
	que no se espantan?		
CLARÍN	Pues ¿por qué [ha] de espantarme		[32^v]
	ber un villano?		
FLORETA	¿Ni a mí, quando te busco,		
	ver que te hallo?	2040	
RÚSTICO	¿Luego yo soy yo mismo?		
FLORETA	¿De qué lo dudas?		
RÚSTICO	Que animal soy sepamos;		
	baste la burla.		
	Denme el nombre y huian	2045	
	que es gran contento		
	ver al enemigo		
	quando ba huiendo.		
FLORETA	¿Qué locura es ésta,		[33^r(9)]
	Rústico, amigo?	2050	
CLARÍN	Diga el tonto.		
RÚSTICO	Aora beo		
	que soi yo mismo.		

2018 *vna tarde,* A B H M T V: de balde   2020 *la,* J: missing/*de balde,* A B H M T V: una tarde
2023 A B C G H J M P T V: ¿es esta cara cara   2025 *Conociéndote,* A B C H J M P T V:
conocido te   2027 Ac. *Floreta,* A B C H J M P T V: Rústico   2027 *es,* E: missing/
A B C H J M P T V: RÚSTICO Ya eso es viejo. Por Baco,   2031 *tiemblen,* E: tiemble

FLORETA	She told me so.
CLARÍN	You see here, gentlemen,
	how men lose 2015
	their redress!
	She is probably going around boasting
	that one afternoon,
	idle, I loved her,
	a second-rate nymph. 2020
FLORETA	Well, wretch, rogue,
	madman, scoundrel, [Uncovering her face.]
	this face, is it
	a second-rate face?
CLARÍN	Recognizing you, I was only 2025
	Stop, Floreta.
FLORETA	This is becoming tiresome.
RÚSTICO	[Aside.] (By Bacchus,
	she is her own woman.
	And, as an animal, more or less,
	I have to make 2030
	them fear me.) Enough.
FLORETA	What is this that I see?
	Is this not my husband?
CLARÍN	Begone, villain.
RÚSTICO	Listen! Why are you two 2035
	not afraid of me?
CLARÍN	Well, why is seeing a rustic
	supposed to frighten me?
FLORETA	Nor me, when I look for you,
	seeing that I find you? 2040
RÚSTICO	Then I am myself?
FLORETA	Why do you doubt it?
RÚSTICO	Let us all know that I am an animal;
	enough of the joke.
	Call me a name and run away, 2045
	for it is a great pleasure
	to see the enemy
	when he runs away.
FLORETA	What madness is this,
	Rústico, my friend? 2050
CLARÍN	Let the fool speak.
RÚSTICO	Now I see
	that I am myself.

2035 *hacen,* E: hace   2037 *ha,* E: missing   2047 *ver,* A B H M T V: el ver
2049 *ésta,* A B G H M T V: aquesta   2050 *amigo,* A B C G H J M P T V: Mío

CLARÍN	¿Qué es lo que aquí quiere?		
RÚSTICO (RUS)	Que me conozca por meno[r] marido de esta señora.	2055	
FLORETA	Pues ¿por qué te(e)nblando decirlo estrañas?		
RÚSTICO	Por si león me hacías, traigo cuartana.	2060	
FLORETA	¿Qué torpeza es ésta?		[33ᵛ]
RÚSTICO	Por si soi osso.		
CLARÍN	Mas que biene borracho.		
RÚSTICO	Por si soi lobo.		
FLORETA	¿Cómo tan asquerosso, tan sucio, andas?	2065	
RÚSTICO	Desde que fui tigre todo soy manchas.		
FLORETA	Dime, ¿qué te has echo? ¿Dónde as estado?	2070	
RÚSTICO	El señor lo diga, que bendió el galgo.		
FLORETA	No te entiendo; abla claro.		[34ʳ]
RÚSTICO	Pues oye atenta. Oyga busted. Yo yendo . . .	2075	
TODOS A 4	[Dentro.] Guarda la fiera.		
RÚSTICO	Pero de essas vozes la gritería, pues por mí lo dicen, por mí lo diga.	2080	
FLORETA	¿Cómo por ti? Espera, que aque(e)sta[s] vozes, acosando una fiera, bajan del Monte.		
RÚSTICO	Yo me entiendo.	2085	[34ᵛ]
CLARÍN	[Yéndose.] A esta parte biene furiosa.		
FLORETA	¿Qué hazes?		
CLARÍN	Huio.		
FLORETA	Pues ¿quieres dexarme sola?		
RÚSTICO	¿Esa es cortesía?		

2055 Ac. E: Rústico Rus   2055 *menor,* E: meno; A B C H J M P T V: el menor
2057 *tenblando,* E; te en blando   2060 *cuartana,* A B C H J M P T V: cuartanas
2061 *ésta,* A B H M T V: aquesta; C: essa   2063-2064 A B H M T V:
FLORETA   Pues, ¿por qué a mí me riñes?
RÚSTICO   Ya estoy muy otro.   C J P: missing

CLARÍN	What is it that he wants here?	
RÚSTICO	Let me be known	
	as the humble husband	2055
	of this lady.	
FLORETA	Well, why, trembling, do you	
	find it strange to say it?	
RÚSTICO	If you made me a lion,	
	I have quartans.	2060
FLORETA	What indelicacy is this?	
RÚSTICO	Or if I am a bear.	
CLARÍN	But he comes quite drunk.	
RÚSTICO	Or if I am a wolf.	
FLORETA	Why do you go about	2065
	so disgusting, so dirty?	
RÚSTICO	Since I was a tiger,	
	I am nothing but spots.	
FLORETA	Tell me, what has become of you?	
	Where have you been?	2070
RÚSTICO	Let the master speak,	
	the one who sold the greyhound.	
FLORETA	I do not understand; speak clearly.	
RÚSTICO	Then listen attentively.	
	Listen. I was going . . .	2075
ALL	[Offstage.]	
	Beware of the beast.	
RÚSTICO	Let the shouting of	
	these voices	
	talk for me since	
	they talk about me.	2080
FLORETA	About you? How? Wait,	
	for these voices	
	in pursuit of a beast	
	are coming down the mountain.	
RÚSTICO	I know what I am doing.	2085
CLARÍN	[Leaving.] It is	
	coming wildly in this direction.	
FLORETA	What are you doing?	
CLARÍN	Fleeing.	
FLORETA	Well, do you want	
	to leave me alone?	
RÚSTICO	Is that chivalrous?	

2066 *tan,* A B H J M T V: y tan   2071 *lo,* A B H M T V: te lo   2073 *te,* B H M T: missing   2075 A G: RÚSTICO Pues oye atenta. (A Clarín) Oiga usted. Yo he sido . . . . B H M T V: CLARÍN Yo de Floreta . . . . Sepa que siempre he sido . . . .   2075 C J P: Oye vsted, yo he sido.   2076 Ac. A G H: Gente; B M T V: Dentro; C J P: Dizen dentro 2077 *essas,* A B H J M P T V: aquestas; C: estas/*vozes,* M: vezes   2079 *lo,* A B H M T: no lo 2080 *diga,* B C J M T V: digan   2082 *aquestas,* E: a que esta; C V: aquessa

[CLARÍN]	Sí, que hasta hallar[t]e	2090
	sólo tube ausencias	
	y enfermedades.	[Vase.]
RÚSTICO	Pues por mí no es justo	
	—yo me iré, y buelua—	
	que a busté enfermedades	2095
	falten y ausencias.	[Vase.]	[35ʳ]
FLORETA	Oye, espera, que sola	
	quedo en el riesgo.	
	¿Qué haré?	
TODOS A 4	[Dentro.]	
	Guarda la fiera.	
FLORETA	¡Lindo consuelo!	2100
	Mas el ser libiana	
	no es ser lijera,	
	según boi tropezando.	[Vase.]
TODOS A 4	[Dentro.]	
	Guarda la fiera.	

[Sale CÉFALO.]

CÉFALO	Pues por gozar tu fabor,	2105	[35ᵛ]
	no boi tras aquellas vozes	
	que, discurriendo belozes,		[36ʳ]
	apellidan mi balor.	
	A templar de el resplandor	
	del sol el vello desdén,	2110
	ven, Aura, ven.	

[Sale a una parte POCRIS, oyéndole]

POCRIS	[Aparte.]	
	¿Ven, Aura, ven, dijo? Sí;	
	ya el equíboco acabó.	
	Aura es a quien llam[ó].	
	No en bano dudé y temí	2115
	que Aura venga[da] de mí,	
	quiera perturbar mi bien.		[36ᵛ]
CÉFALO	Ven, Aura, ven,	
	ven y en cromáticos tales	
	den al[i]bio a mis congoxas	2120
	los pasajes de las ojas,	
	las pausas de los cristales,	

2090 Ac. E: missing   2090 *hallarte,* E: hallarle   2091 *tube,* A B H M T V: tuve yo
2094 *y,* A B C H J M P T V: missing   2097 *que sola,* A B H M T V: me dejas;
C J P: sola   2098 *quedo,* A B H M T V: sola; C J P: he quedado   2099 Ac. A G H: Gente
2100 *consuelo,* A B C H J M T V: consejo

CLARÍN	Yes, for until I found you,	2090
	I only knew absence	
	and illness.	[Exit.]
RÚSTICO	Well, it is not fair on my account	
	(I shall leave, come back)	
	that you lack	2095
	illness and absence.	[Exit.]
FLORETA	Listen, wait, for I am left	
	alone in danger.	
	What shall I do?	
ALL	[Offstage.]	
	Beware of the beast.	
FLORETA	Splendid advice!	2100
	But to be light	
	is not to be nimble,	
	since I go stumbling about.	[Exit.]
ALL	[Offstage.]	
	Beware of the beast.	

[Enter CÉFALO.]

CÉFALO	Since, in order to enjoy your favor	2105
	I do not follow those voices	
	that, travelling quickly,	
	call on my valor,	
	to soften the beautiful disdain	
	of the brightness of the sun,	2110
	come, Aura, come.	

[Enter on one side POCRIS, hearing him.]

POCRIS	[Aside.]	
	"Come, Aura, come," did he say? Yes;	
	now the misunderstanding is resolved.	
	Aura is the one he called.	
	Not in vain did I doubt and fear	2115
	that Aura might take revenge on me,	
	might want to disturb my well-being.	
CÉFALO	Come, Aura, come,	
	come, and let the passages	
	of the leaves, the rests	2120
	of the brooks, give relief	
	to my cares in such chromatics	

2104 Ac. A G H: Gente (Dentro); B M T V: Dentro; C J P: Vozes   2104 Ac. E: todo lo q
se sigue sobra (3 lines of music)/Sale, H: missing   2109 de, A B C H J M
P T V: missing   2114 llamó, E: llama   2115 No, C J P: missing   2116 vengada,
E: venga   2119 cromáticos, C J P: drogmáticos; V: crocmáticos   2120 alibio, E: albio

que, sustenidos mis males,
haziendo fugas estén.
Ven, Aura, ven.   2125   [37ʳ(10)]

[Sale AURA, en el aire, invisible para CÉFALO y POCRIS.]

AURA   [Aparte.]
              ¿Ven, Aura, ven? Aunque oý
              su voz, no rrespondo a ella;
              que oyéndola Pocris vella,
              sorda e de estar, porque así,
              al ver que me llama a mí,   2130
              más penas sus penas den.
CÉFALO   Ven, Aura, ven,
              ven y con cláusulas sumas
              mueban trinados primores   [37ᵛ]
              inquietos golfos de flores,   2135
              blandos embates de plumas.
              Tus penachos las espumas
              sean, y el ámbar también.
              Ven, Aura, ven.
POCRIS   [Aparte.]
              Ven, Aura, ven, vna y mil   2140
              vezes repite; y aunque
              de zelos murien[do] esté,
              hasta aberiguar su vil
              traición, ea, varonil   [38ʳ]
              dolor, paciencia, prevén.   2145
CÉFALO   Ven, Aura, ven,
              ven, y porque el armonía
              con que esta mansión desierta
              oye que el día despierta,
              oyga que se duerme el día;   2150
              vna y otra fantasía
              falsas con la aurora estén.
              Ven, Aura, ven.
AURA   [Aparte.]
              Ven, Aura, ven, repitió;   [38ᵛ]
              mas sufra Pocris y pene.   2155
POCRIS   ¿Ven, Aura, ven, y no viene?
              No soi a quien llama yo.
AURA   [Aparte.]
              ¿Quién el fabor dilató?
POCRIS   [Aparte.]
              ¿A quién tardó el mal, a quién?

that, carrying away my woes,
they might make a rapid chase.
Come, Aura, come.   2125

[Enter AURA, in the air, invisible to CÉFALO and POCRIS.]

AURA   [Aside.]
            "Come, Aura, come"? Although I heard
            his voice, I shall not respond to it;
            for, with beautiful Pocris hearing it,
            I am to be deaf, so,
            upon seeing that he calls me,   2130
            her troubles may give her more troubles.

CÉFALO   Come, Aura, come,
            come, and let trilled elegance
            move restless multitudes of flowers,
            soft rushings of feathers,   2135
            with supreme declamations.
            Let your haughtiness be the
            froth, and the amber as well.
            Come, Aura, come.

POCRIS   [Aside.]
            "Come, Aura, come," a thousand and one   2140
            times he repeats it; and although
            I am dying of jealousy,
            overcome, patience, until I
            verify his vile treason, indeed,
            his manly sorrow.   2145

CÉFALO   Come, Aura, come,
            come, and so the harmony,
            with which this deserted mansion
            hears that the day is awakening,
            may hear that the day is falling asleep,   2150
            let one and another fantasy
            prove false with the dawn.
            Come, Aura, come.

AURA   [Aside.]
            "Come, Aura, come," he repeated;
            but let Pocris suffer and ache.   2155

POCRIS   "Come, Aura, come," and she does not come?
            It is not I whom he calls.

AURA   [Aside.]
            Who extended the favor?

POCRIS   [Aside.]
            For whom did misfortune come late, for whom?

CÉFALO   Ven, Aura, ven,   2160
              ven y jurando en tu esfera
              al mayo rosas y mieses
              por rey de los doze meses   [39ʳ]
              por dios de la primabera,
              diga el sol . . . .
A 4   [Dentro.] Guarda la fiera.   2165
[LOS TRES]   Ya que no prosiga, [e]s vien:
              ven, Aura, ven.
[A 4]   [Dentro.]
              De lo fraguoso de monte   [39ᵛ]
              se faboreze y ampara.
              En bano a de ser su fuga;   2170
              seguidle todos.

[Sale ERÓSTRATO.]

ERÓSTRATO [Aparte.]   [¡Qué ansia!]
              Aun hasta aquí donde más
              se texen y se enmarañan   [40ʳ]
              con lo arisco de las breñas,
              lo escabroso de las plantas,   2175
              siguiéndome bienen. ¡Cielos!
              Si son yras de Diana,
              bien podrán lograr castigos;
              pero no tomar venganzas.
              Pues quando mi lijereza   2180
              o su zentro no me balga,
              me sabré desesperar   [40ᵛ]
              desde la peña más alta
              al piélago más profundo,
              muerto a manos de mi rabia,   2185
              antes que a la[s] de sus yras.
CÉFALO   Bruto horror de estas montañas,
              pues que de tantos el cielo
              para mi triumfo te guarda,
              y solo, de este sagrado   2190   [41ʳ(11)]
              benablo blandida el asta,
              en fe de su dueño puedo
              proseguir enpresa tanta,
              muere a su inpulso.

2165 Ac. A G H: Gente (Dentro); B C H M P T V: Voces   2166 Ac. E: missing
2166 *prosiga, es,* E: prosigas   2168 Ac. E: missing; A G H: Gente (Dentro); B M T V:
Vnos dentro; C J P: Vnos vozes   2168 *de monte,* A B G H J M P T V: del monte
2170 Ac. A B C G H J M P T V: Otros   2171 *sequidle,* R: sequide   2171 Ac. *Sale,* H: missing

CÉFALO	Come, Aura, come,	2160
	come, and promising in your sphere	
	roses and grains to May,	
	as king of the twelve months,	
	as god of the springtime,	
	let the sun say	
CHORUS	[Offstage.] Beware of the beast.	2165
THE THREE	It is well that he not continue to say:	
OF THEM	"Come, Aura, come."	
CHORUS	[Offstage.]	
	He is helped and favored	
	by the dense part of the mountain.	
	In vain must his flight be;	2170
	follow him, all.	

[Enter ERÓSTRATO.]

ERÓSTRATO	[Aside.] What anxiety!	
	Even here where	
	the roughness of the plants	
	is woven and entangled	
	with the harshness of the brambles,	2175
	they come following me. Heavens!	
	If this is Diana's anger,	
	clearly her punishment will come to pass,	
	but not her revenge.	
	For when my agility	2180
	or its center is to no avail,	
	I shall know how to give up hope,	
	from the highest rock	
	to the lowest sea,	
	dead at the hands of my madness	2185
	rather than at those of her anger.	
CÉFALO	Savage horror of these mountains,	
	since heaven keeps you from so many	
	to be my triumph,	
	I alone, brandishing the shaft	2190
	of this sacred spear,	
	faithful to its owner,	
	can carry out such an endeavor.	
	Die by its thrust.	

2171 *¡Qué ansia!*, E: missing   2180 *Pues*, A B C H J M P T: Que; V: missing/*lijereza*,
A B C H J M P T V: diligencia   2185 *manos*, H T: mano   2186 *las*, C E P T: la/*sus yras*,
A B C H J M V: su ira   2190 *y*, A B C G H J M P T V: yo
2192 *puedo*, A B H J M P T: pude; C V: puede   2193 *proseguir*, A B C H J M P T V: conseguir

ERÓSTRATO   Detente,
            gallardo joben; no hagas,   2195
            fiera haciendo a un hombre, que
            enbilezida azaña
            con humana sangre borre
            tus aplausos.
CÉFALO   Si me daua   [41ᵛ]
            en lo(s) o[rror]oso, en lo fiero   2200
            del aspecto, [antes] del abla,
            por [ver] tu bista, tu voz,
            más que a pabor le adelanta.
AURA   [Aparte.]
            ¿Quién creerá que siendo el dueño
            de mi amor y mi benganza   2205
            Eróstrato, no sea él
            quien mis fabores a[rr]astra   [42ʳ]
            sino Zéfalo? Mas ¿quién
            no lo creerá, si repara
            que él que n[o] está en sí, no está   2210
            capaz de fabores de Aura?
ZÉFALO   ¿Hombre humano eres?
[ERÓSTRATO]   Sí.

[Sale TESÍFONE, invisible para CÉFALO y POCRIS.]

[TESÍFONE] [Aparte.]   Agora
            lo que a mi furia se encarga
            es perturbar sus sentidos.
ZÉFALO   Mientes, [mientes,] o me engañan   2215   [42ᵛ]
            o tu semblante o tu voz,
            pues a tan poca distancia
            ni te percibo las señas,
            ni te aberiguo las ansias;
            y pues lo que me aseguras   2220
            desdice lo que me espantas,
            muere otra bez a este arpón
            digo.
ERÓSTRATO   Si el ser no me salba
            hombre, sálbeme el se[r] fiera,   [43ʳ]
            apelando a las entrañas   2225
            de los montes, tan sañuda,
            ta[n] ciega y desesperada,

2195 *joben,* C J P: oso, ven   2197 *azaña,* A B C H J M P T V: la hazaña   2200 *lo orroroso,*
E: los onrroso   2201 *antes,* E: en la   2202 *por ver,* E: por; A G H: pavor
2203 *le,* A B C H J M P T V: se; G: lo   2207 *arrastra,* E: arastra
2210 *no está en sí,* E: ne está en sí; A B C H J M P T V: está sin sí   2212 Ac. E: missing

ERÓSTRATO   Stop,
    gallant youth; do not cause,   2195
    as a beast pretending to be a man,
    this mean act
    to erase your accolades
    with human blood.

CÉFALO   If I gave in
    to the horror, to the wildness   2200
    of your appearance by seeing you,
    your voice, even more your manner of speech,
    takes it beyond fright.

AURA   [Aside.]
    Who will believe that, Eróstrato being
    the master of my love and my   2205
    vengeance, it is not he
    who carries off my favors,
    but Céfalo? But who
    will not believe it, if he notices
    that he who is beside himself is not   2210
    capable of receiving the favors of Aura?

CÉFALO   Are you a human being?
ERÓSTRATO   Yes.

[Enter TESÍFONE, invisible to CÉFALO and POCRIS.]

TESÍFONE   [Aside.]   Now,
    that which is entrusted to my fury
    is to confuse his senses.

CÉFALO   You lie, you lie, and either   2215
    your appearance or your voice deceives me,
    since from such a short distance
    I can neither make out your features
    nor verify your worries;
    and since that of which you assure me   2220
    destroys my fear of you,
    die by this harpoon, I say
    again.

ERÓSTRATO   If being a man does not
    save me, let being a beast save me,
    calling on the inner recesses   2225
    of the mountains, so that,
    not being able to do otherwise,

2212 Ac. *Sale,* H G: missing Tesífone, E: eróstrato   2215 *Mientes, mientes,* E J P:
Mientes/*o,* A B C G H J M P T V: y/*engañan,* A B C G H J M T V: engaña 2222 *lo,* A B H̄ M T V: a lo
2222 A B H M T: muere a este arpón otra vez; V: muere a esse harpón otra vez
2224 *ser,* E: se   2227 *tan,* E: ta

	que a más no [poder, de] aquella	
	roca despeñado, caiga	
	al mar.	[Vase.]
AURA	[Aparte.] Lo más que yo puedo	2230
	es ofrezerte mis alas.	
ZÉFALO	Mal huirás, si este de fresno	

que a más no [poder, de] aquella
roca despeñado, caiga
al mar.   [Vase.]

AURA   [Aparte.] Lo más que yo puedo   2230
            es ofrezerte mis alas.

ZÉFALO   Mal huirás, si este de fresno
            áspid, bíbora de plata,   [43ᵛ]
            relámpago sin rumor,
            y rayo sin luz, te alcanza.   2235

TESÍFONE   [Aparte.]
            Sí alcanzará; pero a quien
            le destina soberana
            deidad, que de sus sentidos
            priuar el aura me manda.

POCRIS   [Aparte.]
            Porque tan horrible monstro   2240
            no siga, al paso le salga.   [44ʳ]

                    [Va a dirigirse hacia CÉFALO.]

ZÉFALO   De vista le perdí; pero
            allí se mueben las ramas.

                    [Dispara el venablo hacia POCRIS.]

POCRIS   ¡Ay infelize de mí!
ZÉFALO   Logré la empressa más alta,   2245
            pero ¿quándo a errado el tiro
            el venablo de Diana?

AURA   [Aparte.]
            Presto lo verás; y pues
            cómplice de tu desgracia
            en el todo de ser tuya,   2250
            a mí la parte me alcanza,   [44ᵛ]
            buelta en lástima la yra,
            muestro, intentando enmendarla,
            que más allá de la muerte
            no llegan nobles venganzas.   [Vase.]   2255

ZÉFALO   Agora, pues ya la fiera
            cayó erida, a rematarla
            de aqueste puñal el filo
            acuda.

[Sale POCRIS, herida, cayendo sobre un peñasco.]

POCRIS   ¡El cielo me balga!   [45ʳ(12)]
ZÉFALO   Pero ¿qué miro?, ¡ay de mí!   2260
            ¡Qué transformación tan rara

2228 *poder, de,* E: puede   2229 A B H M T V: alta roca despeñada; C J P: de aquella roca despeñada
2230 *al,* A B C H J M P T V: caiga al/*yo,* A B H M T V: missing   2237 *le,* G: lo
2238 *sus,* A B C G H J M P T V: tus   2239 *aura,* A B C G H J M P T V: uso/*me manda,*

	so enraged, so blind and desperate,	
	I may fall into the sea, having slipped	
	from that rock.	[Exit.]
AURA	[Aside.] The most that I can do	2230
	is offer you my wings.	
CÉFALO	In vain will you flee, if this asp	
	of ash-wood, snake of silver,	
	lightning without sound,	
	and ray without light, reaches you.	2235
TESÍFONE	[Aside.]	
	Indeed it will, but it will reach the one for whom	
	the sovereign deity	
	destines it, for she orders me to deprive	
	the breeze of its senses.	
POCRIS	[Aside.]	
	So that he may not follow such a horrible	2240
	monster, let me stand in his way.	

[She begins to go toward CÉFALO.]

CÉFALO	I lost him from sight; but	
	the branches are moving there.	

[He hurls the spear toward POCRIS.]

POCRIS	Oh, unhappy me!	
CÉFALO	I succeeded in the greatest endeavor;	2245
	but, when has Diana's spear	
	ever missed its mark?	
AURA	[Aside.]	
	You will soon see; and since,	
	as an accomplice in your disgrace,	
	part of everything that is yours	2250
	belongs also to me,	
	with anger having turned into pity,	
	I shall show, trying to make amends,	
	that noble revenge does not	
	go beyond death.	[Exit.] 2255
CÉFALO	Now, since the beast	
	fell wounded, let me go	
	to finish it off with the edge of this	
	dagger.	

[Enter POCRIS, wounded, falling on a rock.]

POCRIS	May heaven help me!	
CÉFALO	But, what do I see? Oh, me!	2260
	What bizarre transformation	

A H: demanda   2242 *le,* G: lo   2246 *pero,* J P: porque/*el,* A B C H J M P T V: missing
2253 *muestro,* A B C G H J M P T V: muestre   2259 Ac. *Sale,* A G H P: missing

        es la que hiriendo a la noche,
        en púrpura tiñe al alua?
        Si monstruo de hombre y de fiera
        fue [e]l que de estas verdes ramas   2265
        se amparó, ¿cómo muger,
        la que con mortales bascas,
        destiñendo los berdores   [45ᵛ]
        a estas brutas esmeraldas,
        lechos que la admiten niebe,   2270
        la ba[n] conbirtiendo en nácar,
        si ylusión, si debaneo,
        si delirio, si fantasma
        [es] de los ojos . . ., mas ¡ay!   [Mírala al rostro.]
        no es sino de toda el alma.   2275
        No sé si otra vez me atreba   [46ʳ]
        a berla, por si otra guarda
        aparentes señas, que
        en tupidas sombras pardas
        de la ydea, como objeto   2280
        que en mí viue, me retrata
        la ymagen de . . .— Pero berla
        me atrebo, y no a pronunciarla. —
        de . . .
POCRIS   . . . de Pocris. ¿Qué rezelas,
        qué dudas ni qué recatas,   2285   [46ᵛ]
        si en mi muerte no el efecto
        alteras, sino la causa?
        Pues no mudando la esencia
        mi muerte, la circunstancia
        muda sólo en que tu azero   2290
        mate a quien tus celos matan.
        Y así, mi esposso, mi dueño
        del ser, del onor, del alma,   [47ʳ]
        y si no digo la vida
        es porque no digo nada,   2295
        no sientas, no de este influxo
        la constelación tirana;
        pues es dicha, ya que muero,
        morir a mejores armas.
ZÉFALO Pocris vella, Pocris mía,   2300
        dulce dueño, esposa amada,   [47ᵛ]
        que a fuerza de tu hermosura
        debió de ser tu desgracia . . . .

2262 *a,* V: missing   2263 *al,* A B C G H J M P T V: el
2265 *él,* E: al   2271 *ban,* E: ba   2274 *es,* E: missing   2279 *sombras,* C J P: sendas
2284 *de. . . de Pocris,* A B G H J M P T V: De Pocris/*rezelas,* B C G H J M P T:

is it that, wounding the night,
colors the dawn red?
If he who was aided by these green
branches was a monster of man and   2265
beast, how do they,
beds that admit the snow,
transform a woman, who with
mortal vileness discolors
the green of these wild   2270
emeralds, into mother-of-pearl,
if it is an illusion, a raving,
a madness, a specter
to the eyes . . ., but oh! [He sees her face.]
It is nothing less than my entire soul.   2275
I do not know if again I dare
to see her, in case another woman has
similar features, that
in dense olive shadows
of the idea, as an object   2280
that lives within me, paints me
the image of . . . But I dare only
to see her, and not to say her name,
of . . .

POCRIS   . . . of Pocris. Why are you suspicious,
why are you doubting, or why are you afraid to speak,   2285
if you change not the effect of my
death, but the cause?
Since, my death not changing
its essence, circumstance
changes only the fact that your sword   2290
kills whom your jealousy kills.
And so, my husband, the master
of my body, of my honor, of my soul,
and if I do not say of my life
it is because I do not say anything,   2295
do not resent the tyrannical constellation
of this occurrence;
for it is said, now that I am dying,
that I die in better arms.

CÉFALO   Beautiful Pocris, my Pocris,   2300
sweet mistress, beloved wife,
that your beauty had to
bring on your disgrace . . . .

---

te recelas; A: te recatas   2286 *efecto,* B M T V: defecto   2293 A B C H J M P T:
mi bien, mi señor, mi alma; V: mi bien, señor, mi alma   2294 *la,* A B C H J M P T V: mi

¿Tuya dije? Digo, y mía.
¿Tú zelossa? ¿De quién?

POCRIS   De Aura,   2305
a quien buscas, a quien sigues,
a quien quieres, a quien llamas.

ZÉFALO   Aura, ¿no es vn ayre?

POCRIS   Pero
¿qué enmienda — el aliento falta —   [48ʳ]
ser — el pecho se estremeze —   2310
Aura — el corazón se arranca —
ayre — la voz titubea —
si — el espíritu desmaia —
en quien — la bista se turba —
quiere — el ánimo se pasma —   2315
como — la razón delira —   [48ᵛ]
quiero, es consequencia clara,
que si el ayre diere celos,
celos aun del ayre matan.   [Muere sobre el peñasco.]

ZÉFALO   Espiró la luz pura   2320
del sol, sin espirar la de su esfera,
en cuia peña dura
la hermo(mo)sura naciera,   [49ʳ(13)]
si naciera sembrada la hermosura.
¿Cómo en el desconsuelo   2325
de todos, más por buestro que por mío,
del día el azul belo
a este cadáuer frío
no hacen exequias que. . .? ¡Válgame el cielo!   [49ᵛ]
                           [Cae desmayado.]

VNO SOLO   [Dentro.]
Deydad de nubes y estrellas.   2330

OTRO SOLO   [Dentro.]
Diossa de seluas y bosques.

OTRO SOLO   [Dentro.]
Reina de sombras y abismos.

DIANA   [Dentro.]
Aquesos son mis tres nombres.

[Salen las cuatro.]

¿Qué me queréis?
¡Nimfas, que de aquella ruina   2335
perdonaron los horrores,

2304 _y,_ A B C G H J M P T V: missing   2307 _quieres, a,_ A B C G H J M P T V: quieres y a
2308 _vn,_ A B C H J M P T V: missing/_Pero,_ A B C H J M T V: Sí; pero   2314 _la bista se turba,_
A B H M T V: la vida se rinde; C J P: el ánimo se pasma   2315 C J P: missing
2317 _es consequencia,_ A B H M T V: consecuencia es   2323 _hermosura,_ E: hermomosura

	Did I say yours? And mine, I say.	
	You, jealous? Of whom?	
POCRIS	Of Aura,	2305
	whom you seek, whom you follow,	
	whom you love, whom you call.	
CÉFALO	Aura? Is she not a breeze?	
POCRIS	But	
	what does it help (my breath is failing)	
	if (my bosom trembles)	2310
	Aura (my heart is uprooted)	
	is air (my voice wavers),	
	if (my spirit swoons)	
	for the one (my sight is confused)	
	she loves (my soul is chilled)	2315
	as I (my reason reels)	
	love, it is a clear consequence	
	that if the air causes jealousy,	
	jealousy, even of the air, kills. [She dies on the rock.]	
CÉFALO	She breathed the pure light	2320
	of the sun, without breathing that of her own sphere,	
	on whose hard rock	
	beauty would have been born,	
	if beauty had been born of seed.	
	Why, in the desolation	2325
	of everyone, more yours than mine,	
	do they not make funeral rites	
	for this cold cadaver	
	of the blue veil of the day that. . .? Heaven help me!	
	[He faints and falls.]	
A VOICE.	[Within.]	
	Deity of clouds and stars.	2330
ANOTHER	[Within.]	
	Goddess of forests and woods.	
ANOTHER	[Within.]	
	Queen of shadows and depths.	
DIANA	[Within.]	
	Those are my three names.	

[Enter DIANA and the furies, all four of them.]

	What do you want of me?	
	Nymphs, who forgave	2335
	the horrors of that ruin,	

2328 *a este,* A B C H J M P T V: de este   2329 *hacen,* A B G H M T V: hace en
2330 Ac. A B C G H J M P T V: Tesífone   2331 Ac. A B C G H J M P T V: Alecto
2332 Ac. A B C G H J M P T V: Megera   2334 A B H M T V: Ya sé lo que me queréis;
                                                     y así, atended a mis voces;

C J P: ¿Qué es lo que me queréis?; G: missing

zagalas de estas montañas,   [50r]
de estas seluas moradores!
[Salen ninfas y pastores, CLARÍN, RÚSTICO.]

[NINFAS Y PASTORES]	¿Qué nos mandas? ¿Qué nos quieres?	
RÚSTICO	¿Qué es lo que miro, señores?	2340 [50v]
[CLARÍN]	Cumplido el refrán que dice,	
	quien escucha su mal oye.	
DIANA	Que de tres venganzas mías	
	publiquéis los tres blasones	
	vna y mil vezes conmigo,	2345
	diciendo en so[no]ras vozes:	
	¡Viua la deidad . . .	[51r]
[CORO]	¡Viua la deidad . . .	
[DIANA]	. . . que a los corazones . . .	
[CORO]	. . . que a los corazones . . .	[51v]
[DIANA]	. . . que prende el amor . . .	
[CORO]	. . . que prende el amor . . .	
[DIANA]	. . . los grillos les rompe!	2350 [52r-v]
[CORO]	. . . los grillos les rompe!	2350 bis
	[Repiten.]	

[Sale AURA, apareciendo en lo alto.]

AURA	Suspended, suspended los azentos,	
	los ecos parad, parad las canciones;	[53r(14)]
	que aunque son nobles tal vez las venganzas,	
	tal bez blasonadas desdicen de nobles.	
	Y pues que nimfa del aire	2355 [53v]
	puedo hacer que se transforme	
	la [e]scena en nubes y estrellas	
	que me ylustre[n] y me adoren,	
	sabed que, a Zéfalo atenta,	
	quise, ofendida de Pocris,	2360
	que ella me pagase en celos	
	lo que él me deuió en fauores.	[54r]
	Pero a lástima p[a]sando	
	lo infeliz de sus amores,	
	solicito que sus hierros	2365
	el aura de amor los dore,	
	que aunque son nobles tal bez las venganzas,	[54v]

2339 A B G H M T V: NINFAS ¿Qué nos mandas? ZAGALES ¿Qué nos quieres?; C J P: ¿Qué nos mandas?
2341 Ac. E: missing   2346 *sonoras vozes,* E: soras vozes; A B H M T V: ecos acordes
2347-2350 A B C G H J M P T V indicate that these lines alternate between
"Todos" and "Diana"   2350ff. A E G: repeat lines 2347-2350 without echo response; C J P:
TODOS. Viua la deidad &c.   2350 bis Ac. *Sale Aura apareciendo,* H: Aura apareciendo; A B C

shepherdesses of these mountains,
residents of these forests!

[Enter nymphs and shepherds, CLARÍN, RÚSTICO.]

NYMPHS AND SHEPHERDS	What do you command us? What do you want of us?
RÚSTICO	What is this I see, gentlemen? 2340
CLARÍN	The realization of the proverb that says:
	he who listens for slander, hears it.
DIANA	Of these three vengeances of mine,
	make known the three announcements,
	saying with me, in sonorous 2345
	voices, a thousand and one times:
	Long live the deity . . .
CHORUS	Long live the deity . . .
DIANA	. . . who breaks the bonds . . .
CHORUS	. . . who breaks the bonds . . .
DIANA	. . . of the hearts . . .
CHORUS	. . . of the hearts . . .
DIANA	. . . that love captures! 2350
CHORUS	. . . that love captures! 2350 bis
	[Repeat.]

[Enter AURA, appearing on high.]

AURA	Stop, stop your voices,
	stop the echoes, cease the songs;
	for although vengeance is perhaps noble,
	perhaps, heralded, it forfeits nobility.
	And since, as a nymph of the air, 2355
	I can make the scene be
	transformed into clouds and stars
	that illuminate and adorn me,
	know that, attentive to Céfalo,
	offended by Pocris, I wanted 2360
	her to pay me in jealousy
	what she owed me in favors.
	But, because the unhappiness
	of their love has become pitiable,
	I ask that the air of love 2365
	gild their mistakes,
	for although vengeance is perhaps noble,

G H M P T V: Aparécese Aura   2353 *tal vez,* A B C H J M P T V: también
2357 *escena,* C E M T V: scena; J P: cena   2358 *ylustren,* E: ylustre/*adoren,*
A B C G H J M P T V: adornen   2359 *atenta,* B C J M P T V: atento   2363 *lástima,*
J: la lástima/pasando, E: pensando   2366 *los,* C J P: les
2367 *tal bez,* A B C H M P T V: también; J: missing

          tal bez blasonadas desdicen de nobles.
          Y así Venus a mi ruego,
          y a ruego de Venus, Jobe   2370
          manda[n] q*ue* de un fino amor
          la trajedia se mejore
          sin el orror de trajedia,
          con q*ue* Pocris se coloque   [55ʳ]
          sobre el orbe de la luna,   2375
          de los astros en el orbe;
          y Zéfalo, conserbando
          la cláusula de su nombre,
          quando por Zéfalo el ayre
          nombre de Zéfiro tome,   2380
          estrella y alientos ambos,   [55ᵛ]
          ya en suplos, ia en resplandores,
          como prodijios de amor,
          inspiren castos amores.
          Subid, pues, restituidos   2385
          a mejor ser, donde dioses,
          astros, planetas y signos,
          sol, luna y estrellas noten   [56ʳ]
          que aunq*ue* son nobles tal bez las benganzas,
          tal bez blasonadas desdicen de nobles.   2390
                               [Van subiendo Céfalo y
                               Pocris, hasta juntarse con
                               Aura, y suben todos tres.]

Zéfalo   ¡Feliz yo, Pocris, p*ue*s quiere
          Júpiter que a berte torne!
Pocris   ¡Feliz yo, Zéfalo, pues
          quiere Aura que este bien logre!   [56ᵛ]
Aura   Subid conmigo los dos   2395
          al supremo solio, donde
          a Júpiter deis las gracias,
          diciendo en ecos belozes . . . (çes)
[Los tres] Que aunq*ue* son nobles tal bez las venganzas,   [57ʳ(15)]
          tal bez blasonadas desdicen de nobles.   2400
Diana   Vna vez vengada yo,   [57ᵛ]
          poco importa q*ue* blasonen
          de estrella y ayre.

2371 *mandan,* E: manda/*de un,* B J M T V: de; A H: del   2379 *el,* B J M P T V: missing
2381 *alientos,* A B C G H J M P T V: aliento   2383 *como,* B C J M P T V: como en
2389 *son,* B: tan/*tal bez,* A B C H J M P T V: también   2391 *Pocris,* B C J M P T V: feliz
2397 *las,* T: los   2398 *ecos,* C J P: vozes/*belozes,* E: belozes çes
2399 Ac. E: missing; C J P V: Las tres   2399 *tal bez,* A B H M T V: también

perhaps, heralded, it forfeits nobility.
And so, Venus at my request,
and Jupiter at the request of Venus,   2370
order that the tragedy of a
good love be made better
without the horror of tragedy,
with which Pocris may be placed
above the orbit of the moon,   2375
in the sphere of the stars;
and Céfalo, conserving
the sound of his name,
when instead of Céfalo the wind
takes the name of Zephyr,   2380
both of them, star and wind,
now in gusts, now in light,
as prodigies of love,
let them inspire chaste loves.
Rise, then, restored   2385
to a better being, where gods,
orbs, planets, and signs,
sun, moon, and stars may notice
that although vengeance is perhaps noble,
perhaps, heralded, it forfeits nobility.   2390

[Exeunt rising CÉFALO and
POCRIS, until they join with
AURA, and all three rise.]

CÉFALO   Happy am I, Pocris, because Jupiter
         desires that I see you again!

POCRIS   Happy am I, Céfalo, because
         Aura wants me to have this blessing!

AURA   Rise with me, both of you,   2395
         to the highest place, where
         you may give thanks to Jupiter,
         saying in quick echoes . . .

THE THREE that although vengeance is perhaps noble,
  OF THEM perhaps, heralded, it forfeits nobility.   2400

DIANA   Once I am avenged,
         it matters little that you boast
         of stars and air.

2402 *blasonen*, A B C H J M P T V: blasones   2403 Ac. A B C H J M P T V: Todos;
G: Los cuatro   2403-2405 E G R: repeat "Con que diremos" and "todos conformes" once each;
G alone indicates that statement and response alternate between "Los 4" and "Los demás"

A 4   Con q*ue*
              diremos todos conformes: [58ʳ]
              si celos del ayre matan,   2405
              tanbién del ayre fabores
              dan vida, porque se bea
              en Aura, en Zéfalo y Pocris,   [58ᵛ]
              que aunq*ue* son nobles tal bez las venganzas,
              tal vez blasonadas desdicen de nobles.   2410   [59ʳ]

2409 *tal bez*, A B H M T: también

CHORUS   With which
                 we shall all say together:
                 if jealousy of the air kills,   2405
                 favors of the air also
                 give life, so that it may be seen
                 in Aura, in Céfalo and in Pocris,
                 that although vengeance is perhaps noble,
                 perhaps, heralded, it forfeits nobility.   2410

Notes

1 Ac. Lydia was a territory in western Asia Minor and from time to time included the important coastal cities of Smyrna and Ephesus. Ephesus itself was founded near the holy place of the Anatolian goddess whom the Greeks called Artemis, and it had a grand Temple of Artemis toward the construction of which the famous King Croesus contributed. The temple was burned on the night that Alexander the Great was born in 356 B.C. The alleged culprit was Herostratus. As a result, we may assume that the Temple of Diana in this play is that of Ephesus. (William Moir Calder, "Ephesus" and "Lydia," in *Oxford Classical Dictionary,* ed. M. Cary *et al.* [Oxford: Clarendon Press, 1949; rpt. 1961], pp. 318, 522.)

5. Nymphs were female spirits that inhabited woods, waters, mountains, and the like, and represented deities. They were not immortal although they tended toward longevity. They liked singing and dancing and generally were benevolent to mankind. They brought flowers to gardens, watched over flocks, etc. It was thought that a man who saw a nymph became possessed by her and that they took with them any mortals whom they loved. (George M. A. Hanfmann, "Nymphs," in *OCD,* p. 615.)

24 Ac. The stage direction to indicate a change of character is placed over an incorrect note in the music. Such misplacement occurs additionally in lines 174, 183, 301, 429, 489, 580, 635, 690, 1134, 1135, 1166, 1194, 1200, 1201, 1203, 1206, 1363, 2054, and 2064.

34. Prometheus stole fire from Zeus and brought it to men. In punishment, Zeus gave man woman, Pandora, who married Epimetheus, the brother of Prometheus, and she let loose all the world's evils. In another tale, Prometheus is chained to a rock. Zeus punished him by sending an eagle every day to eat his liver. His liver was as immortal as he was and grew at night as fast as the eagle could devour it by day. Prometheus, a master craftsman, made man from clay or clay plus bits from other animals. (Herbert Jennings Rose, "Prometheus," in *OCD,* p. 734.) The reference in this line is to the fact that Prometheus stole the sun's rays and he steals those of Diana's moon on cloudy nights.

43. As a mythological figure, Diana, associated with the Greek Artemis, was the goddess of the hunt and of woods and wild places. Her hunting instruments were arrows. It is very likely that she also had a fertility function, although for historical Greeks she was a virgin goddess who nevertheless aided women in childbirth. She is commonly confused with Silene or Luna, goddess of the moon, and Hecate or Proserpina, goddess of the underworld, thus giving her the status of the goddess with three faces (cf. ll. 1041-43). Her greatest cult developed in Ephesus where there was a famous temple to her. She was largely a goddess of women, and processions of women in her honor were not uncommon. (H. J. Rose, "Artemis" and "Diana," in *OCD,* pp. 104-5, 274-75; W. M. Calder, "Ephesus," in *OCD,* p. 318; Edith Hamilton, *Mythology* [New York: New American Lib., 1969], pp. 31-32.)

52. Venus, associated with the Greek Aphrodite, was the goddess of love, beauty, and fertility. Hesiod *(Theogony,* 188-206) gives the version that she was born of the sea *(aphros* means "foam"), and she was as a result the goddess of the sea and seafarers as well. That Venus and Diana should be considered enemies is not surprising considering the strong erotic associations of Venus and the idea that Diana was a virgin who scrupulously guarded over her nymphs. The Diana of Ephesus was Asian and quite different from the Greek and Roman versions, having only the name in common. (Francis Redding Walton, "Aphrodite," in *OCD,* p. 67; Hamilton, pp. 32-33; "Diana," in *Enciclopedia universal ilustrada europeo-americana* [Madrid: Espasa-Calpe, 1908-33], XVIII, 843-50).

56. Time was a great healer of past love because eventually one forgot the delights or the torments of love. Only memory could bring love back, thus the opposition of love and forgetfulness, developed more fully in Act Two, ll. 900-78. Cf. Jorge de Montemayor, *Los siete libros de la Diana,* ed. Francisco López Estrada, 4th ed. (Zaragoza: Ebro, 1968), p. 26: "¡Ay, memoria mía, enemiga de mi descanso! ¿No os ocupáredes mejor en hazerme olvidar desgustos presentes, que en ponerme delante los ojos contentos passados?"

65-68. Two different associations of "arrows" are compared. On the one hand, Cupid's arrows induce love; on the other, the arrows associated with Diana as goddess of the hunt punish those who fall prey to the arrows of love. In a sense, Aura is twice the victim of arrows which, in yet another association, were the weapons of preference of the Santa Hermandad, whose duty it was to maintain order and punish offenders in rural and wilderness areas. (Sebastián de Covarrubias y Horozco, *Tesoro del idioma castellano o español,* ed. Martín de Riquer [Barcelona: Horta, 1943], pp. 919-20.)

71. Pocris here addresses Aura, as "fiera," and then the chorus calls to Diana, as "tirana."

77. Cupid, or Eros, was the god of love as violent, physical desire. Because he brings danger and destruction, he is often pictured as cunning, unmanageable, and cruel. He is at times playful. His weapons are arrows. (G. M. A. Hanfmann, "Eros," in *OCD,* pp. 338-39.)

86-95. These great lists of Calderón are known in Spanish as *plurimembraciones.* Whether they serve to illuminate the plot, tie together various philosophical strands, or add suspense to the action, they always present a pure, Baroque version of the use of poetry in their elegance, their wit, and their ornamentation. At times they serve correlative functions, as here they relate various entities to their appropriate elements and to Aura's plight. For more on this type of correlative poetry, see Dámaso Alonso, "La correlación en el teatro calderoniano," in *Seis calas en la expresión literaria española,* by Dámaso Alonso and Carlos Bousoño, 3d ed. (Madrid: Gredos, 1963), pp. 109-75.

96. The four elements, air, water, fire, and earth, were the basis of all matter and existed in fixed proportions. Each had certain attributes (for example, fire was warm and dry), and the tensions created by their opposing natures caused

instability on earth. Mankind was subject to their forces which also had equivalents in the humors of the human body and in the levels of heaven. Calderón utilized the four elements to enhance his imagery and include all of nature at the same time, as is implied here with respect to Aura's pitiful situation. Additional references to the elements are in ll. 240-43, 1163-66, 1345. See E. M. Wilson, "The Four Elements in the Imagery of Calderón," in *Critical Studies of Calderón's Comedias,* ed. J. E. Varey (London: Gregg, 1973), pp. 191-207; and Otis Green, *Spain and the Western Tradition* (Madison: Univ. of Wisconsin Press, 1968), II, 34-35 and 55-57.

101-2. "Noramala" and "norabuena" actually have to do with Fortune. To bid someone to remain "enhorabuena" was to wish them to go in peace or with good luck. On the other hand, to have labored "noramala" was to have labored unluckily. The pun is untranslatable as a pun.

109-10. The Spanish text included a play on words that does not translate into English. "Blanco" is not only whiteness and purity, the opposite of "sombra," or shadow, it is also the center of a target, a bull's-eye.

154. Sight was not only the principal sensory organ, but also the portal through which love entered the body. See Frank G. Halstead, "The Optics of Love: Notes on a Concept of Atomistic Philosophy in the Theatre of Tirso de Molina," *PMLA,* 58 (1943), 108-21.

189. "Arbolar," a derivative of "árbol": "Arbolar, 'enarbolar, levantar en alto,' propiamente 'poner derecho como el árbol de un navío.' " (J. Corominas, *Diccionario crítico etimológico de la lengua castellana* [Bern: Francke, 1954], I, 249.)

209-15. Clarín here displays not only the passivity of the *gracioso* in the comedia, an attribute more often than not based on cowardice, but also a strong tendency toward misogyny that went hand in hand with the idolatry of women. Cf. H. R. Hays, *The Dangerous Sex: The Myth of Feminine Evil* (New York: Pocket Books, 1965), especially pp. 86-167, in which Hays traces literary and cultural misogyny from Ovid through Milton. In addition, see Ruth Kelso, *Doctrine for the Lady of the Renaissance* (Urbana: Univ. of Illinois Press, 1956), pp. 5-13. For an overview of the qualities of *graciosos* in general, see José María Díez Borque, *Sociología de la comedia española del siglo XVII* (Madrid: Cátedra, 1976), pp. 239-53.

240-43. Another reference to the four elements. According to Hesiod, Venus was born of water, yet her effects, and those of Cupid, take the form of fire (passion). Since the mixture of fire (warm and dry) and water (cool and moist) was air (warm and moist), the air is now the realm of Venus, and, therefore, Aura is now a nymph of the air. See notes to ll. 52 and 96.

260. Calderón's sense of morality is reflected in the idea that, although noblemen have on occasion reason to kill (war, self-defense, etc.), it is still a heinous crime against nature and must not be undertaken lightly. Cf. Green, *Spain,* I, 16-21.

261-62. Diana draws a standard distinction between punishment and murder. To punish a wrongdoer was the rightful duty of authority and was part of God's plan. To murder and, frequently, to kill in revenge, were grave sins. Dramatic characters, especially in honor plays, often address this distinction before they kill their wives. See Thomas Aquinas, QQ.58a12-61a4 in *Summa Theologica,* trans. English Dominican Fathers (New York: Benzinger Bros., 1947), II, 1443-55.

281. Mars was the chief Italian God next to Jupiter and was associated with the Greek Ares, but with additional agricultural functions. He was the deification of the warlike spirit, an instigator of violence or tempestuous love, and a helper of foreigners. He is often said to be either the husband or the lover of Venus. As a god, he had no moral functions and was unpopular. (H. J. Rose, "Ares" and "Mars," in *OCD,* pp. 85-86, 541.)

358. "Batida, 'acción de batir el monte para que salga la caza.' " (Corominas, I, 427.)

376. "Se mete consonante": to be in agreement, comply. Cf. "Consonar. Ser de acuerdo con otro, y su contrario disonar. Consonancia, disonancia. Consonante, asonante." (Covarrubias, p. 350.)

394. The effect of the stars on human lives and its relationship to Catholic doctrine were favorite topics of Calderón. His solution to the problematic mixture was to indicate that the stars and planets do not determine any particular action, but they do influence the problems that one must face. As a result, many of Calderón's protagonists are faced with an astrological prediction, such as Segismundo in *La vida es sueño* and Herodes in *El mayor monstruo del mundo.* The prophecies frequently come true, often in an ironic way, but the characters must never give up the ideal of self-control and self-determination. The process of individuation in the face of Fate or celestial adversity is one that ennobles the Christian soul. See Green, *Spain,* II, 212-78.

397-98. A play on words. "Paraninfo" is "el que anuncia una buena nueva" as well as a "padrino de bodas." (Corominas, III, 100-101.) The meaning of "paraninfo" as the bearer of good news is lost in the English translation.

400. "Coches": The alternate reading of "noches" is perhaps superficially more appropriate, but the role of the coach as a meeting place for seventeenth-century lovers is well documented. See Melveena McKendrick, *Woman and Society in the Spanish Drama of the Golden Age: A Study of the* Mujer Varonil (Cambridge: Cambridge Univ. Press, 1974), p. 33.

413. Doña Ana is an alternate name for the goddess Diana.

428. Aurora was the third party in the Ovidian version, not Aura. The use of "Aurora" for "Aura" occurs again in the manuscript in ll. 1453 and 1889.

432. "Piadosas crueldades": Clearly an oxymoron to express the ironic position of the courtly lover. Cf. "Muerte cruel, la que se da con impiedad, haziendo padecer al que muere con mucho dolor y sentimiento o haziendo en él gran estrago y carnicería." (Covarrubias, p. 373.)

454. That "e" and "i" should rhyme is a slightly nonstandard, although not irregular, occurrence here and in ll. 771, 2360, and 2408. Such usage is based on the Castilian principle of vowel relaxation in an unaccentuated syllable

following a stress. See Tomás Navarro Tomás, *Manual de pronunciación española,* 11th ed. (Madrid: C.S.I.C., 1963), pp. 44-46, and Rafael de Balbín, *Sistema de rítmica castellana* (Madrid: Gredos, 1962), pp. 237-38.

469-71. Cf. note to line 96. The idea is that one element, fire, will avenge the transformation of Aura into another element, air.

485-86. The syntax of this reading is perhaps more difficult than that of the alternate versions, but it is nevertheless intelligible. The subject of "lleva" is "el ver."

513. "Me" here is a dative of interest. See Vicente García de Diego, *Gramática histórica española* (Madrid: Gredos, 1961), p. 344.

515. Actaeon, son of Aristaeus and Autonoe, was a famous hunter. One day, by chance, he happened to come upon Diana as she was bathing. She, embarrassed and angry, threw water in his face, and he began to sprout antlers and change into a stag. His own hounds then attacked and killed him. (Ovid, *Metamorphoses,* III, 138-252, cited in H. J. Rose, "Actaeon," in *OCD,* p. 6; Hamilton, pp. 255-56; and Thomas Bulfinch, *Bulfinch's Mythology of Greece and Rome with Eastern and Norse Legends* [New York: Collier Books, 1971], pp. 42-44.)

526 Ac. Hartzenbusch adds a footnote to this stage direction: "Supone el autor que mientras conserva Rústico la figura irracional, nadie le oye o nadie entiende lo que habla," that is, "The author assumes that as long as Rústico appears in an irrational form, no one hears him, or no one understands what he says." In *BAE,* XII, p. 476.

534. "Fue" would indicate that the subject is "mi amor," in this case, for Floreta. Such usage would be inappropriate with respect to his dealings with Eróstrato.

571-72. "Entrar a": ". . . en la Edad Media y en los clásicos era *entrar en* o *entrar a* indiferentemente." (Corominas, II, 303.)

626. "Así a la parte" is appropriate to the context. The alternate version, "hacia," is a possible reading of the Evora manuscript, as "asia." There are other instances of confusion between "z" and "s," but not in this act. Cf. ll. 853, 1052, and 1304.

672-78. The pronoun "le" as well as the substantivized adjectives "mayor" and "menor" refer to "peligro."

673. "Le tengo dos luzes": "I have two indications of it (danger)." Cf. "Luz . . . fig. s. XVI al XX. Conocimiento, aviso de una cosa." (Martín Alonso, *Enciclopedia del idioma* [Madrid: Aguilar, 1958], II, 2617.)

692. "Ignorada voz" was preferable to "ignorando voy" not on the basis of syntax or semantics, but in consideration of the inherent parallel construction of ll. 691-92.

699 ff. The dialogue between Clarín and Floreta is missing in the manuscript. Moreover, additional lines for Act One are found only in the Liria manuscript and repeated in the versions by Subirá and García Valdecasas.

746. Otis Green (*Spain,* II, 279-316) has identified two variations of the concept of Fortune, that *de tejas arriba,* which concerns God, the cosmos, the soul, etc., and that *de tejas abajo,* or the vicissitudes of daily life, represented frequently by a blind diety who spins a wheel. It is part of Céfalo's blasphemy that he mistakes human chance as God's will. Such idolatry and blasphemy were commonplace in the courtly and Neo-Platonic love traditions. See also Green, *Spain,* I, 72-160.

783-85. Fate was indeed a force to be dealt with, but again Céfalo is blindly mistaking the impulse of erotic passion for cosmic Fate. Cf. the notes to ll. 394 and 746. In addition, see Green, *Spain,* II, 316-337.

804. The hymn to which Céfalo refers is that of the processional at the opening of Act Two. The alternate "Elcino" has no historical or etymological significance.

853. The copier of Act Two confuses "z" and "s" three times: here, at 1052, and at 1304.

858. A play on words between "cordelejo" as a leash and symbol of Rústico's condition, and also as aggravation, as in "dar cordel, agravar la contrariedad de uno insistiendo en aquello mismo que la causa." (M. Alonso, I, 1222.)

865. Common ways of calling a dog were "tus" (ll. 865, 870, and 872) and "cito" (ll. 866, 1224, and 1280). See M. Alonso, I, 1082, and III, 4075.

873. "Traílla": "La cuerda con que va asido el perro, el hurón, el pájaro. Atraillar, echarles la traílla, *a trahendo."* (Covarrubias, p. 972.)

875. In addition to passivity and general cowardice, *graciosos* were also noted for their interest in creature comforts, especially food. Cf. note to ll. 209-15.

880ff. The alternate repetition of the choral section is possible within the Evora text, but not explicit. The version here represents a strict and literal reading of the *dal segno* sections and in all cases omits repetitions that serve only musical, and not dramatic, functions.

901. Again the idea of self-control and self-determination. Cf. the note to line 394. In this case, the self-control is over internal instincts (love and sex) rather than external predestination.

909. "Oh" was added strictly on the basis of the correspondence between syllables and musical notes.

909-16. A double image involving bows and arrows, similar to that in ll. 65-68. This time Eróstrato offers a bow (associated with Venus and Cupid) to one of Diana's nymphs with the promise that the bow, in the shape of a half moon (and therefore associated with Diana as goddess of the moon), can overcome any other force. It is ironic that Eróstrato offers the bow as a gift because he is the one who brings ruin to Diana's temple because of the force of love.

931-46. While the beauty of the iris may be symbolic of Venus because of its red and white colors, the myrtle, not the iris, was sacred to Venus. Nevertheless, by carrying the visual image one step farther to include the concept of the red color of blood, the reference repeats the idea of blood associated with Pocris from Act One (cf. ll. 309-23) and foreshadows her bloody death in Act

Three (cf. ll. 2261-74).

978 Ac. The Evora manuscript assigns this line to Diana; all the others give it to Aura. As the repetition of Aura's statement, this time in the form of a question in disbelief, the line makes sense in the context of Diana's subsequent speech.

1051. Primitive cultures such as those of the early Greeks and Romans tend to ascribe evil influence to the changeability of the moon. Diana, as its goddess, has access to all its malevolent features. Cf. "Luna," in *Enciclopedia universal ilustrada europeo-americana,* XXXI, 787-95.

1059. Diana was not part human in mythology and, for that reason, some editions prefer "u maga" to "humana." Nevertheless, in the context of Calderón's anthropomorphic vision of the classical deities, and in light of Diana's human emotions in this play, "humana" seems an appropriate reading.

1076-78. The references in these lines are to various incarnations of Zeus, the great sky-god, *pater familias,* and protector of laws, morals, and political freedom. Danae was the mother of Perseus by Zeus, who visited her in a shower of gold after her father, fearing a prophecy that his grandson would kill him, locked her in a bronze room. Leda was the mother of Helen and Polydeuces after Zeus came to her in the form of a swan. A "caístro" is a song, in this case, a swan song, a song of death. Daphne was the daughter of a river god and loved by Apollo. She refused his advances, ran from him, prayed for help, and was turned into a tree bearing her name (Greek *daphne,* laurel). Diana is complaining that other gods are successful in their endeavors but she is not because of divine treason. (H. J. Rose, "Daphne," "Jupiter," "Leda," and "Perseus," in *OCD,* pp. 254, 472, 492, 667; Nils Martin Persson Nilsson, "Zeus," in *OCD,* p. 966; M. Alonso, I, 842.)

1105ff. The various repetitions of this refrain have been regularized and made parallel.

1107. "Viamos" is archaic spelling for "huyamos."

1163-66. Céfalo mentions one representative of each of the four elements: stars-fire; flowers-earth; birds-air; and brooks-water. Cf. the note to line 96.

1177. The present subjunctive was possible after "si" in the seventeenth century when modern usage takes the present subjunctive after "que," as in "dudando que nazca." (Federico Hanssen, *Gramática histórica de la lengua castellana* [Halle: Max Niemeyer, 1913], p. 239.)

1183ff. Six lines are missing in the manuscript and their lack is noticed in the reading of the text. Nevertheless, the music does not include the lines nor is there any abnormality of the musical line without the text.

1197-98. A courtier would wish to please, of course, and might well wait until the other person spoke in order to agree after the fact with whatever was said.

1252-57. Floreta takes Rústico's words "de retorno," "again" or "in return" adjectivally rather than adverbially, inferring that Rústico thinks of nymphs as something to be rented and later returned.

1270. "Venado" here is not so much a stag as any hunted animal (from Latin *venor, venari,* to hunt). Rústico is happy that they have not tried to kill him.

1274. Adonis was the beautiful youth with whom Aphrodite fell in love. While hunting, he was killed by a boar or, as some say, by either Hephaestus or Ares disguised as a boar. (F. R. Walton, "Adonis," in *OCD,* pp. 6-7.) That Clarín should call himself an Adonis in common clothes is a comic reference to the general role of the *gracioso* as a poor reflection of the protagonist.

1293. "Pan de perro": figuratively, "daño y castigo que se hace o da a uno. Dícese por alusión al pan con zarzas que suele darse a los perros para matarlos." (M. Alonso, III, 3117.) Because "dog's bread" has no meaning in English, an alternate expression meaning that a trick was played on Rústico has been employed.

1307. Etna (Aetna) is a volcano in Céfalo's native Sicily.

1345 Ac. The salamander had the fame of being the only animal to inhabit the element of fire. ("Salamandra," in *Enciclopedia universal ilustrada europeo-americana,* LIII, 138.) That Aura (air) should appear on a salamander (fire) is a metaphorical representation of the action on stage, because fire cannot exist without air.

1365. More of Clarín's misogyny. Cf. the note to lines 209-15.

1366-69. In the manuscript, this section comes at the end of Volume Two, accounting for the discrepancy in foliation.

1367. Although "campanas" is more appropriate to the setting than "desiertos," the image is not important enough to override considerations of rhyme (assonance in e-o).

1371. "Monjibelo": "Infierno." (M. Alonso, II, 2876.)

1372. Besuvio: The famous Italian volcano alleged by Virgil to be near entrance to the underworld. (Bulfinch, p. 155.)

1393-96. The manuscript refers to folio 45^{r-v} for these lines. The alternate lines that follow l. 1396 have no corresponding music in the manuscript.

1401. "Báratro": " 'infierno,' tomado del latín *barathrum,* 'abismo.' " (Corominas, I, 395.)

1407. The Evora version as it appears in the text is clearly incorrect for the rhyme. The alternate text, however, which probably reflects later changes, does not include the important image of the phoenix as a symbol of secular love. Cf. Sebastian Neumeister, "La fiesta mitológica de Calderón en su contexto histórico *(Fieras afemina amor)*," in *Hacia Calderón. Tercer coloquio anglo-germano,* ed. Hans Flasche (Berlin: Walter de Gruyter, 1976), p. 164.

1429-32. The text for these lines can be found at the end of the first volume of the manuscript (Act One) rather than with the rest of Act Two, a fact that explains the differences in foliation.

1452. The Furies in Rome were associated with the Erinyes in Greece (Latin *furere* = Greek *erinyein*). They were spirits of punishment and regularly worked by disturbing the mind. Named Tisiphone, Megaera, and Alecto, their heads were wreathed with serpents. In later classical literature they were often confused with the Eumenides, or benign spirits. (H. J. Rose, "Erinyes" and "Furiae," in *OCD*, pp. 338, 373; Hamilton, p. 40; Bulfinch, p. 20.)

1456. "Golfo": figuratively, "multitud, abundancia." (M. Alonso, II, 2153.)

1461-62. "Humana fiera" refers to Eróstrato's condition after Mejera casts her spell, not to Mejera herself.

1465 Ac. Clearly the copier confused the Fury Alecto and the tragic character Electra. The proper spelling never occurs in the manuscript.

1471. "Aspide. Una especie de bívora cuyo veneno es tan eficaz y tan prompto que si no es cortado al momento el miembro que ha mordido, para que no passe al coraçón, no tiene remedio." (Covarrubias, p. 159.)

1479. "Blandón": a taper or torch. Although "baldón" might seem more appropriate to the idea of offense, "blandón" fits quite well with the concept of flame in l. 1480, as though Diana wished to fight fire with fire.

1508 Ac. "Retrete": "s. XVI al XX. Cuarto pequeño en la casa o habitación destinado para retirarse . . . . Aposento pequeño en la parte más secreta de la casa." (M. Alonso, III, 3616.)

1546. There is nothing inappropriate in the image of Aurora's crowning her locks with flowers. Therefore, the manuscript "rizos" remains in the text instead of the alternate "riscos." Concerning Aurora herself, cf. Covarrubias, p. 170: "Fingen los poetas aver sido la Aurora una diosa hija de Titán y de la Tierra, madre del lucero y de los vientos . . . . Danle los poetas varios epítetos, llamándola clara, fúlgida, áurea, blanca, roscida, purpúrea, aljofarada, húmida, luzífera, práevia, flava, rubicunda, hermosa y otros muchos . . . ."

1556. "Penachos" are plumed crests or arrogance; "catres" are cots or beds. The image is that the proud crests of January are now put to common use in April because of Céfalo's absence.

1564. Céfalo's love for Pocris is a direct result of his having seen her beauty (see note to l. 154). Because of the fiery nature of his love, her beauty becomes a crucible to test his amorous resolve.

1630. "Estancia": "s. XVI y XVII. Lugar espacioso y cubierto por el follaje." (M. Alonso, II, 1878.)

1642. Satyrs, often confused with Sileni, were spirits of wildlife in woods and hills. They were usually young and had the traits of a goat. They were mischievous and, in some sense, were the male counterparts of nymphs. (G. M. A. Hanfmann, "Satyrs," in *OCD*, p. 797.)

1716. The confusion begun in l. 1647 between the names "Aura" and "Laura" is part of the Ovidian myth. The confusion in the texts of this play after the current line are most likely due to insecurity about the function of the misunderstanding. Because Alecto corrects the name to "Aura," all the subsequent misreadings have been corrected as well.

1736. In the tradition of courtly love, jealousy could easily destroy love and, figuratively, life. In the *comedia,* jealousy very often leads to a realization of the metaphorical death at the hands of the aggrieved party, exemplified most notably in Calderón's honor plays.

1805-6. A pun with reference to the card game *quínolas.* "Pericón" has two meanings: "aplicado al que suple por todas, y más comunmente hablando del caballo o mula que en el tiro hace a todos los puestos," and "en el juego de quínolas, caballo de bastos, porque se puede hacer que valga lo que cualquiera otra carta y del palo que se quiere." "Pendanga" is "la sota de oros." (M. Alonso, III, 3227.) The jack of coins was the second highest card behind the horse of coins. The game of *quínolas* had as its object collecting four cards of the same suit. If more than one player had a *quínola,* the player with the cards of highest value won the hand. ("Quínola," in *Enciclopedia universal ilustrada europeo-americana,* XLVIII, 1355.) Rústico is a "pericón" because he plays so many animal roles in this play and acts as a "joker" because each one sees him in a different way.

1827. The transposition of word order was necessary to preserve the rhyme scheme (abba).

1833. The usage of "la" rather than the alternate "lo" can be attributed to the phenomenon in which the feminine form refers to unknown entities, as in "Me la pagarán." See García de Diego, p. 347.

1898. "Suenan" refers to "cuyas vozes" (l. 1890) not to "humana voz" (l. 1885).

1925-26. The connection among life, death, and love in the courtly tradition was commonplace. Pocris misunderstands the reference, however, believing that Céfalo speaks of death in unpleasant terms, not as a manifestation of his love for her.

1987-90. The Spanish pun on "espera" and "esperanza" is not easy to translate. While "expect" and "expectation" carry both of the Spanish meanings of "to wait" and "to hope," the repeated use of the English word in this passage would be forced and unnatural. The pun was sacrificed for readability.

1999. The use of "-cito" as the suffix rather than the alternate "-ito" represents a standard Latin to Castilian transition, although in this case its nonstandard usage makes Clarín sound more comical. See Ramón Menéndez Pidal, *Manual de gramática histórica española,* 11th ed. (Madrid: Espasa-Calpe, 1962), pp. 229-30.

2001. "Alcorcones," while a possible Castilian word for cork trees, is nonstandard. Because of the comic nature of Clarín's role, however, the manuscript version was preferred over the standard "alcornoques."

2009-10. Another pun. "Saltar" is not only "to jump" but also "to resent visibly," "picarse o resentirse, dándolo a entender exteriormente." "Floreta," besides being the name of the woman, is a dance movement, "movimiento que se hacía con ambos pies." A "cabriola" is a leap, "brinco que dan los que danzan, cruzando varias vezes los pies en el aire." (M. Alonso, I, 822; II, 2022; III, 3695.) Clarín is jesting with the disguised Floreta, turning her reference to herself into an opportunity to demonstrate his wit.

2012ff. The missing lines complete the *copla,* but there is no music to accompany them, nor is there any indication of a lapse in the music.

2019. "Baratillo": "Conjunto de cosas usadas o de poco precio, que están de venta en paraje público." (M. Alonso, I, 639.) Clarín is casting doubts on Floreta's chastity.

2025. The alternate version "conocido te había" presents a complete thought, but considering the attack by Floreta, it is understandable that Clarín might have trouble creating a complete and logical statement, thus allowing for the Evora version given here.

2055. "Menor": humble; "s. XVI y XVII. Fórmula de humildad." (M. Alonso, II, 2789.)

2060. "Quartana": a fever that came every four days. Rústico compares the changeable nature of his affliction to such a fever. Cf. Covarrubias, p. 890: "Calentura que responde al quarto día, latine *quartana,* que suele causarse del humor melancólico."

2092. The absence of a lover might well produce melancholy. Clarín uses the courtly love image for comic effect, meaning literally that this entire affair has kept him from home and caused him considerable bother.

2111. "Ven, Aura, ven" is a repetition of the same locution by Céfalo in both Latin and Greek sources. In Latin, Céfalo called for an *aura,* or breeze; in Greek, he called for a *nephele,* or cloud, and also the name of a nymph. (H. J. Rose, "Cephalus," in *OCD,* pp. 180-81.)

2119-24. This passage is unified by references to music: chromatics, passages, pauses, and chases, or fugues. A chase was a piece in which one voice imitated the melody of another but not at the same time, coming in one after the other.

2133-38. Céfalo here compares a bird image with a sea image. "Trinados primores" are the trilled songs of the bird, and the bird in its flight over the meadow moves gulfs of flowers. "Embates" are the beating of the sea on the shore caused by the action of the wind. "Ambar" is not only the amber familiar today, but a kind of shimmering liquid that was said to rise from the depths of the ocean to the surface where it solidified and was washed to shore. (Covarrubias, pp. 111, 504.)

2162-64. May, as the month in which flowers bloomed and plants sprouted, was considered the principal month of spring. Mythologically, Maia, also called Fauna or Bona Dea, was the Roman goddess of the fields. The shift from feminine to masculine can be attributed to the additional god Faunus, grandson of Saturn and god of fields and shepherds. (Hamilton, pp. 327, 330; Bulfinch, p. 20.)

2178-79. Concerning the difference between punishment and revenge, see the note to ll. 261-62.

2199-2203. The Evora version is incomprehensible although the manuscript does not show any evidence of confusion on the part of the copier. Read the Spanish, "Si me daba en lo horroroso, en lo fiero del aspecto, por ver tu vista antes (de oír el) habla, tu voz le adelanta más que a pavor."

2215. A compound subject joined with "o . . . o" could take either a singular or a plural verb. See García de Diego, p. 304.

2239. The image of depriving Céfalo of Aura's cooling, calming effects is much more vivid than the alternate image of depriving him of the use of his senses.

2267. "Vascas. Las congoxas y alteraciones del pecho, quando uno está muy apassionado o de mal de coraçón o de enojo o de otro accidente . . . ." (Covarrubias, p. 995.)

2297. See note to line 394 concerning the power of the stars.

2335ff. The missing line and a half are essential to the meter and the rhyme, but once again there is no music in the manuscript to accompany the extra text, nor is there any indication of missing music.

2353-54. The humility implied by the refrain is again a moralistic touch that Calderón has added to the honor theme. Humility is not generally considered to be a common trait of honor, and, in fact, one's honor depended upon what others thought. For a discussion of honor, see Américo Castro, "Algunas observaciones acerca del concepto del honor en los siglos XVI y XVII," *RFE,* 3 (1916) 1-50, 357-86.

2376. In the Ptolemaic system, Pocris has been assigned to one of the spheres above that of the moon, thus taking precedence over Diana. See Green, *Spain,* II, 31-48.

Bibliography

Alegría, José Augusto. *Biblioteca Pública de Evora. Catálogo dos Fundos Musicais.* Lisboa: Fundação Calouste Gulbenkian, 1977.

Alonso, Dámaso and Carlos Bousoño. *Seis calas en la expresión literaria española.* 3d ed. Madrid: Gredos, 1963.

Alonso, Martín. *Enciclopedia del idioma.* 3 vols. Madrid: Aguilar, 1958.

Aubrun, Charles V. "Les débuts du drame lyrique en Espagne." In *Le Lieu théâtral à la Renaissance.* Ed. J. Jacquot. Paris: Editions du Centre National de la Recherche Scientifique, 1964, pp. 423-44.

————. "Estructura y significación de las comedias mitológicas de Calderón." In *Hacia Calderón. Tercer coloquio anglogermano.* Ed. Hans Flasche. Berlin: Walter de Gruyter, 1976, pp. 148-55.

Baehr, Rudolf. *Manual de versificación española.* Trans. and adapt. K. Wagner and F. López Estrada. Madrid: Gredos, 1973.

Balbín, Rafael de. *Sistema de rítmica castellana.* Madrid: Gredos, 1962.

Barrionuevo, Jerónimo de. *Avisos (1654-1658).* Ed. A. Paz y Melia. 4 vols. Madrid: M. Tello, 1892-4.

Boyer, Mildred. *The Texas Collection of* Comedias Sueltas: *A Descriptive Bibliography.* Boston: G. K. Hall, 1978.

Bulfinch, Thomas. *Bulfinch's Mythology of Greece and Rome with Eastern and Norse Legends.* New York: Collier Books, 1971.

Calder, William Moir. "Ephesus" and "Lydia." In *Oxford Classical Dictionary.* Ed. M. Cary *et al.* Oxford: Clarendon Press, 1949. Rpt. 1961.

Calderón de la Barca, Pedro. *Céfalo y Pocris.* Ed. Alberto Navarro González. Salamanca: Almar, 1979.

————. "Celos aun del aire matan, Fiesta cantada." In vol. III of *Comedias de don Pedro Calderón de la Barca.* In vol. XII of *Biblioteca de Autores Españoles.* Ed. Juan Eugenio Hartzenbusch. Madrid: Impresores de M. Rivadeneyra, 1850-52. Rpt. Madrid: Atlas, 1945, pp. 473-88.

————. "Deposición en favor de los profesores de la pintura, en el pleito con el Procurador General de esta Corte, sobre pretender éste se le hiciese repartimiento de soldados." In *Caxón de sastre.* By Francisco Mariano Nipho. Madrid: Gabriel Ramírez, 1781, p. 33.

————. "La fiera, el rayo y la piedra." With *loa* by Francisco Figueroa, 1690. Biblioteca Nacional, Madrid. MS.14614.

————. "La gran comedia, Zelos aun del ayre matan. Fiesta cantada, que se hizo á sus Magestades en el Coliseo del Buen-Retiro. De don Pedro Calderón de la Barca." In vol. X of *Comedias del célebre poeta español don Pedro Calderón de la Barca, que saca a luz don Juan Fernández de Apontes, y las dedica al mismo don Pedro Calderón de la Barca.* Madrid: Viuda de M. Fernández, 1763.

————. "La gran comedia, Zelos avn del ayre matan. Fiesta cantada que se hizo á sus Magestades en el Coliseo del Buen-Retiro. De don Pedro Calderón de la Barca." In *Séptima parte de Comedias del celebre poeta español D. Pedro Calderón de la Barca . . . Que nvevamente corregidas,* *publicó Don Jvan de Vera Tassis y Villarroel su mayor amigo.* Madrid: Juan Sanz, 1715.

_____. "La gran comedia, Zelos avn del aire matan. Fiesta que se representó á sus Magestades en el Buen Retiro. Cantada. De don Pedro Calderón." In *Parte qvarenta y vna, de famosas comedias de diversos avtores.* Pamplona: Ioseph del Espíritu Santo, n.d.

_____. "La gran comedia, Zelos avn del ayre matan. Fiesta que se representó á sus Magestades en el Buen Retiro. Cantada. De don Pedro Calderón." In vol. XIX of *Comedias nuevas escogidas de los mejores ingenios de España.* Por Domingo García y Morras. Madrid: Imprenta Real (Melchor Sánchez), 1663.

_____. "El laurel de Apolo." In vol. II of *Comedias de Don Pedro Calderón de la Barca.* In vol. IX of *Biblioteca de Autores Españoles.* Ed. Juan Eugenio Hartzenbusch. Madrid: Impresores de M. Rivadeneyra. 1850-52. Rpt. Madrid: Atlas, 1944, pp. 655-71.

_____. "No. 307. La gran comedia, Zelos aun del ayre matan. Fiesta cantada, que se hizo á sus Magestades en el Coliseo de Buen Retiro. De don Pedro Calderón." In vol. VII of *Comedias verdaderas del célebre poeta español don Pedro Calderón de la Barca . . . Nueuamente corr., publicó don Juan de Vera Tassis y Villarroel.* Madrid: Viuda de Blas de Villanueva, 1683.

_____. "No. 307. La gran comedia, Zelos avn del ayre matan. Fiesta que se representó á sus Magestades en el Buen Retiro. Cantada. De don Pedro Calderón de la Barca." In Parte XXVI of *Jardín ameno, de varias y hermosas flores, cuyos matices son doze Comedias, escogidas de los mejores Ingenios de Espana. Y las ofrece a los curiosos, vn aficionado.* Madrid: n.p., 1704.

_____. "Num. 78. Comedia famosa. Zelos aun del ayre matan. Fiesta cantada que se hizo á SS. MM. en el Coliseo de Buen-Retiro. De don Pedro Calderón de la Barca." Barcelona: Francisco Suria y Burgada, n.d.

_____. *Obras completas.* 3 vols. Ed. Angel Valbuena Briones. Madrid: Aguilar, 1959.

_____ and Juan Hidalgo. "Zelos aun del Ayre matan. Comedia de D. Pedro Calderón. Múzica de Juan Hidalgo." 3 vols. Biblioteca Pública, Evora. MS. CL 1/2-1.

"Calderón de la Barca." In vol. X of *Enciclopedia universal ilustrada europeoamericana.* Madrid: Espasa-Calpe, 1908-33.

Camargo, Ignacio de. *Discurso theológico sobre los theatros, y comedias de este siglo.* Salamanca: Lucas Pérez, 1689.

Castro, Américo. "Algunas observaciones acerca del concepto del honor en los siglos XVI y XVII." *Revista de Filología Española,* 3 (1916), 1-50, 357-86.

Chapman, W. G. "Las comedias mitológicas de Calderón." *Revista de Literatura,* 5 (1954), 35-67.

Chase, Gilbert. *The Music of Spain.* 2d ed. rev. New York: Dover, 1959.

Corominas, Joan. *Diccionario crítico etimólogico de la lengua castellana.* 4 vols. Bern: Francke, 1954.

Cossío, José María de. *Fábulas mitológicas en España.* Madrid: Espasa-Calpe, 1952.

Cotarelo y Mori, Emilio. "Actores famosos del siglo XVII: Sebastián de Prado y su mujer Bernarda Ramírez," *Boletín de la Real Academia Española,* 2 (1915), 251-93, 425-57, 583-621; 3 (1916), 3-38, 151-85. Rpt. Madrid: Artes Gráficas Municipales, 1933.

————. *Bibliografía de las controversias sobre la licitud del teatro en España.* Madrid: Tipografía de la "Revista de Archivos, Bibliotecas y Museos," 1904.

————. *Ensayo sobre la vida y obras de Calderón.* Madrid: Tipografía de la "Revista de Archivos, Bibliotecas y Museos," 1924.

————. *Historia de la zarzuela, o sea el drama lírico en España, desde su origen a fines del siglo XIX.* Madrid: Tipografía de Archivos, 1934.

————. *Orígenes y establecimiento de la ópera en España hasta 1800.* Madrid: Tipografía de la "Revista de Archivos, Bibliotecas y Museos," 1917.

Covarrubias y Horozco, Sebastián de. *Tesoro del idioma castellano o español.* Ed. Martín de Riquer. Barcelona: Horta, 1943.

Curtius, Ernst Robert. *European Literature and the Latin Middle Ages.* Trans. Willard R. Trask. New York: Pantheon Books, 1953.

"Diana." In vol. XVIII of *Enciclopedia universal ilustrada europeo-americana.* Madrid: Espasa-Calpe, 1908-33.

Díez Borque, José María. *Sociología de la comedia española del siglo XVII.* Madrid: Cátedra, 1976.

"Eróstrato." In vol. XX of *Enciclopedia universal ilustrada europeo-americana.* Madrid: Espasa-Calpe, 1908-33.

Frye, Northrop. *Anatomy of Criticism: Four Essays.* Princeton: Princeton Univ. Press, 1957. Rpt. 1973.

García de Diego, Vicente. *Gramática histórica española.* Madrid: Gredos, 1961.

García Valdecasas, José Guillermo, and Andrada Vanderwilde, trans. and adapt. "Celos, aun del aire, matan: (Céfalo y Pocris) de Pedro Calderón de la Barca," 1977. Biblioteca Nacional, Madrid. Unpublished typescript M32[13].

Gerard, Albert. "The Loving Killers: The Rationale of Righteousness in Baroque Tragedy." *Comparative Literature Studies,* 2 (1965), 209-32.

Green, Otis. *The Literary Mind of Medieval and Renaissance Spain.* Lexington: Univ. of Kentucky Press, 1970.

————. *Spain and the Western Tradition.* 4 vols. Madison: Univ. of Wisconsin Press, 1968.

Grout, Donald Jay. *A Short History of Opera.* New York: Columbia Univ. Press, 1947.

Halstead, Frank G. "The Optics of Love: Notes on a Concept of Atomistic Philosophy in the Theatre of Tirso de Molina." *Publications of the Modern Language Association,* 58 (1943), 108-21.

Hamilton, Edith. *Mythology.* New York: New American Library, 1969.

Hanfmann, George M. A. "Eros," "Nymphs," and "Satyrs." In *Oxford Classical Dictionary.* Ed. M. Cary *et al.* Oxford: Clarendon Press, 1949. Rpt. 1961.

Hanssen, Federico. *Gramática histórica de la lengua castellana.* Halle: Max Niemeyer, 1913.

Hartzenbusch, Juan Eugenio. "Catálogo cronológico de las comedias de don Pedro Calderón de la Barca." In vol. IV of *Comedias de Don Pedro Calderón de la Barca.* In vol. XIV of the *Biblioteca de Autores Espanoles.* Madrid: Impresores de M. Rivadeneyra, 1850-52. Rpt. Madrid: Atlas, 1945, pp. 661-82.

Hatzfeld, Helmut. *Estudios sobre el barroco.* 3d ed. Madrid: Gredos, 1972.

Hays, H. R. *The Dangerous Sex: The Myth of Feminine Evil.* New York: Pocket Books, 1965.

Henríquez Ureña, Pedro. *Estudios de versificación española.* Buenos Aires: Univ. of Buenos Aires, 1961.

Hesse, Everett W. *Calderón de la Barca.* New York: Twayne, 1967.

————. "Calderón's Popularity in the Spanish Indies." *Hispanic Review,* 23 (1955), 12-27.

————. "Courtly Allusions in the Plays of Calderón." *Publications of the Modern Language Association,* 65 (1950), 531-49.

————. "The Publication of Calderón's Plays in the Seventeenth Century." *Philological Quarterly,* 27 (1948), 37-51.

————. "The Two Versions of Calderón's 'El laurel de Apolo.' " *Hispanic Review,* 14 (1946), 213-34.

Hewitt, Barnard, ed. *The Renaissance Stage: Documents of Serlio, Sabbattini, and Furttenbach.* Trans. Allardyce Nicoll, John H. McDowell, and George R. Kernodle. Coral Gables: Univ. of Miami Press, 1958.

Hidalgo, Juan, and Pedro Calderón de la Barca. "Música de la Comedia Zelos aun del Ayre matan. Primera jornada." Palacio de Liria, Madrid. MS. Caja 174, no. 21.

Honig, Edwin. "En torno a las traducciones de Calderón." *Arbor,* 80 (1971), 21-30.

————. "On Translating Calderón." *Michigan Quarterly Review,* 11 (1972), 264-71.

Hume, Martin. *The Court of Philip IV.* London: Eveleigh Nash, 1907.

José Prades, Juana de. *Teoría sobre los personajes de la comedia nueva.* Madrid: Consejo Superior de Investigaciones Científicas, 1963.

Kelso, Ruth. *Doctrine for the Lady of the Renaissance.* Urbana: Univ. of Illinois Press, 1956.

Knights, L. C. "King Lear as Metaphor." In *Myth and Symbol: Critical Approaches and Applications.* Ed. Bernice Slote. Lincoln: Univ. of Nebraska Press, 1963, pp. 21-38.

"Luna." In vol. XXXI of *Enciclopedia universal ilustrada europeo-americana.* Madrid: Espasa-Calpe, 1908-33.

McKendrick, Melveena. *Woman and Society in the Spanish Drama of the Golden Age: A Study of the* Mujer Varonil. Cambridge: Cambridge Univ. Press, 1974.

Martin, Henry M. "Notes on the Cephalus and Procris Myth as Dramatized by Lope de Vega and Calderón." *MLN,* 66 (1951), 238-41.

Mazur, Oleh. "The Wild Man in Spanish Golden Age Drama." Diss. Univ. of Pennsylvania 1966.

Menéndez Pidal, Ramón. *Manual de gramática histórica española.* 11th ed. Madrid: Espasa-Calpe, 1962.

Menéndez y Pelayo, M. *Calderón y su teatro.* Madrid: Tipografía de la Revista de Archivos, 1910.

Montemayor, Jorge de. *Los siete libros de la Diana.* Ed. Francisco López Estrada. 4th ed. Zaragoza: Ebro, 1968.

Navarro Tomás, Tomás. *Arte del verso.* 4th ed. México: Colección Málaga, 1968.

————. *Manual de pronunciación española.* 11th ed. Madrid: Consejo Superior de Investigaciones Científicas, 1963.

————. *Métrica española: Reseña histórica y descriptiva.* New York: Syracuse Univ. Press, 1956.

Neumeister, Sebastian. "La fiesta mitológica de Calderón en su contexto histórico (*Fieras afemina amor*)." In *Hacia Calderón. Tercer coloquio anglogermano.* Ed. Hans Flasche. Berlin: Walter de Gruyter, 1976, pp. 156-70.

————. *Mythos und Repräsentation: Die mythologischen Festspiele Calderóns.* Munich: Fink, 1978.

Nilsson, Nils Martin Persson. "Zeus." In *Oxford Classical Dictionary.* Ed. M. Cary *et al.* Oxford: Clarendon Press, 1949. Rpt. 1961.

Orgel, Stephen. *The Jonsonian Masque.* Cambridge: Harvard Univ. Press, 1965.

————— and Roy Strong. *Iñigo Jones: The Theatre of the Stuart Court.* 2 vols. Berkeley: Univ. of Calif. Press, 1973.

Ovid. *The Art of Love.* Trans. J. H. Mozley. Cambridge: Harvard Univ. Press, 1962.

————. *Metamorphoses.* Trans. Frank Justus Miller. Cambridge: Harvard Univ. Press, 1951.

Parker, Alexander A. "Metáfora y símbolo en la interpretación de Calderón." In *Actas del Primer Congreso Internacional de Hispanistas.* Ed. Frank Pierce and Cyril A. Jones. Oxford: Dolphin Book Co., 1964, pp. 141-60.

_____. "The Spanish Drama of the Golden Age: A Method of Analysis and Interpretation." In *The Great Playwrights*. Ed. Eric Bentley. Garden City, N.Y.: Doubleday, 1970, I, 679-707.

Pedrell, Felipe. "L'Eclogue *La Forêt sans amour*," *Sammelbände der Internationalen Musik-Gesellschaft,* 11 (1909), 55-104.

_____. "La Musique indigène dans le théâtre espagnol du XVIIe siècle." *Sammelbände der Internationalen Musik-Gesellschaft,* 11 (1903), 46-90.

Pellicer y Tobar, Juan Antonio de. *Avisos históricos, que comprenden las noticias y sucesos mas particulares, ocurridos en nuestra monarquía desde el año de 1639.* In vols. XXXI-XXXIII of *Semanario erudito.* Ed. A. Valladares de Sotomayor. Madrid: Don Blas Román, 1788.

Pérez de Moya, Juan. *La philosophia secreta.* Madrid: Imprenta Real, 1585.

Pérez Pastor, C. *Documentos para la biografía de D. Pedro Calderón de la Barca.* Madrid: Fortanet, 1905.

Pitts, Ruth E. L. "Don Juan Hidalgo, Seventeenth-Century Spanish Composer." Diss. George Peabody College for Teachers 1968.

Pollin, Alice M. "Calderón de la Barca and Music: Theory and Examples in the *Autos* (1675-1680)." *Hispanic Review,* 41 (1963), 362-70.

Pope, Isabel. "The Musical Development and Form of the Spanish Villancico." In *Papers of the American Musicological Society, 1940.* Washington: American Musicological Society, 1946, pp. 11-17.

"Quínola." In vol. XLVIII of *Enciclopedia universal ilustrada europeo-americana.* Madrid: Espasa-Calpe, 1908-33.

Reichenberger, A. G. "Klassische Mythen im spanischen Goldenen Zeitalter." In *Studia iberica. Festschrift für Hans Flasche.* Ed. Karl-Hermann Körner and Klaus Rühl. Bern: Francke, 1973, pp. 495-510.

Rennert, Hugo A. "Spanish Actors and Actresses between 1560 and 1680." *Revue Hispanique,* 16 (1907), 334-538.

_____. *The Spanish Stage in the Time of Lope de Vega.* New York: Hispanic Society of America, 1909. Rpt. New York: Dover, 1963.

Rose, Herbert Jennings. "Actaeon," "Ares," "Artemis," "Cephalus," "Daphne," "Diana," "Erinyes," "Furiae," "Jupiter," "Leda," "Mars," "Perseus," and "Prometheus." In *Oxford Classical Dictionary.* Ed. M. Cary *et al.* Oxford: Clarendon Press, 1949. Rpt. 1961.

Rouanet, Léo. "Un autographe inédit de Calderón." *Revue Hispanique,* 6 (1899), 197-98.

Sage, Jack. "Calderón de la Barca." In *Die Musik in Geschichte und Gegenwart.* Ed. F. Blume. Kassel: Bärenreiter, 1973.

_____. "Calderón y la musica teatral," *Bulletin Hispanique,* 58 (1956), 275-300. Rpt. as "The Function of Music in the Theatre of Calderón." In *Critical Studies of Calderón's Comedias.* Ed. J. E. Varey. London: Gregg International, 1973, pp. 209-30.

_____. "La música de Juan Hidalgo." In *Los celos hacen estrellas.* By Juan Vélez de Guevara. Ed. and intro. J. E. Varey and N. D. Shergold. London: Tamesis, 1970, pp. 169-223.

————. "Nouvelles lumières sur la genèse de l'opéra et la zarzuela en Espagne." *Baroque,* 5 (1972), 107-14.

————. "Texto y realización de *La estatua de Prometeo* y otros dramas musicales de Calderón." In *Hacia Calderón. Coloquio anglogermano.* Ed. Hans Flasche. Berlin: Walter de Gruyter, 1970, pp. 37-52.

"Salamandra." In vol. LIII of *Enciclopedia universal ilustrada europeo-americana.* Madrid: Espasa-Calpe, 1908-33.

Schevill, R. *Ovid and the Renascence in Spain.* Univ. of Calif. Publications in Modern Philology, No. 4. Berkeley: Univ. of Calif. Press, 1913, pp. 1-268.

Seznec, Jean. *The Survival of the Pagan Gods.* Trans. Barbara F. Sessions. Princeton: Princeton Univ. Press, 1972.

Shergold, N. D. "Calderón and Vera Tassis." *Hispanic Review,* 23 (1955), 212-18.

————. "The First Performance of Calderón's *El mayor encanto amor."* *Bulletin of Hispanic Studies,* 35 (1958), 24-27.

————. *A History of the Spanish Stage from Medieval Times until the End of the Seventeenth Century.* Oxford: Clarendon Press, 1967.

———— and J. E. Varey. "Some Palace Performances of Seventeenth Century Plays." *Bulletin of Hispanic Studies,* 40 (1963), 212-44.

———— and J. E. Varey. *Representaciones palaciegas: 1630-99.* London: Tamesis, 1977.

Simpson, Percy and C. F. Bell. *Designs by Iñigo Jones for Masques and Plays at Court.* New York: Russell and Russell, 1924. Rpt. 1966.

Sobremonte, Gaspar de. "Información por decreto de Felipe IV referente al intento de incendio del Coliseo del Buen Retiro." In "Papeles del Buen Retiro," 1662. Biblioteca Nacional, Madrid. MS. 2280.

Stevenson, Robert. "The First New World Opera." *Americas,* 16 (1964), 33-35.

————, ed. and intro. *La púrpura de la rosa.* Lima: Instituto Nacional de Cultura, Biblioteca Nacional, 1976.

Subirá, José. "Calderón de la Barca, libretista de ópera: Consideraciones literario-musicales." *Anuario Musical,* 20 (1965), 59-73.

————, ed. *Celos aun del aire matan: Opera del siglo XVII. Texto de Calderón y música de Juan Hidalgo.* Barcelona: Institut d'Estudis Catalans, Biblioteca de Catalunya, 1933.

————. *La música en la casa de Alba.* Madrid: Sucesores de Rivadeneyra, 1927.

————. "Músicos al servicio de Calderón y de Comella." *Anuario Musical,* 22 (1967), 197-208.

————. "La ópera 'castellana' en los siglos XVII y XVIII." *Segismundo,* 1 (1965), 23-42.

————. "El operista español D. Juan Hidalgo: Nuevas noticias biográficas." *Revista de las Ciencias,* 1-2 (1934), 1-9.

————. *La participación musical en el antiguo teatro español.* Barcelona: Publicaciones del Instituto del Teatro Nacional, No. 6, 1930.

_____. "Le style dans la musique théâtrale espagnole." *Acta Musicologica,* vol. 4, fasc. II (1932), 67-75.

_____. *La tonadilla escénica.* 3 vols. Madrid: Tipografía de Archivos, 1928-1930.

Thomas Aquinas. Vol. II of *Summa theologica.* Trans. English Dominican Fathers. New York: Benzinger Bros., 1947.

Ursprung, Otto. " 'Celos usw.': Text von Calderón, Musik von Hidalgo, die älteste erhaltene spanische Oper." In *Festschrift Arnold Schering zum sechzigsten Geburtstag.* Ed. Helmuth Osthoff, Walter Serauky, and Adam Adrio. Berlin: A. Glas, 1937, pp. 223-40.

Valbuena Briones, Angel. *Perspectiva crítica de los dramas de Calderón.* Madrid: Ediciones Rialp, 1965.

Valbuena Prat, Angel. "La escenografía de una comedia de Calderón." *Archivo Español de Arte y Arqueología,* 6 (1930), 1-16.

_____. *Calderón: Su personalidad, su arte dramático, su estilo y sus obras.* Barcelona: Juventud, 1941.

Van den Borren, Charles. "Un opéra espagnol du XVIIe siècle, 'Celos aun del aire matan,' texte de Calderón, musique de Juan Hidalgo." *La Revue Musicale,* 16 (1935), 253-60.

Varey, John E., and N. D. Shergold, ed. and intro. *Los celos hacen estrellas.* By Juan Vélez de Guevara. London: Tamesis, 1970.

Vega Carpio, Lope Félix de. Vol. III of *Obras escogidas.* Ed. Federico Sainz de Robles. Madrid: Aguilar, 1967.

Vitoria, Baltasar de. *Del teatro de los dioses de la gentilidad.* 3 vols. Madrid: Imprenta Real, 1620-1623.

Wade, Gerald E. "A Note on a Seventeenth-Century *Comedia* Performance." *Bulletin of the Comediantes,* 10 (1958), 10-12.

Walton, Francis Redding. "Adonis" and "Aphrodite." In *Oxford Classical Dictionary.* Ed. M. Cary *et al.* Oxford: Clarendon Press, 1949. Rpt. 1961.

Watts, Harold. "Myth and Drama." In *Myth and Literature: Contemporary Theory and Practice.* Ed. John B. Vickery. Lincoln: Univ. of Nebraska Press, 1966, pp. 75-85.

Welsford, Enid. *The Court Masque: A Study in the Relationship between Poetry and the Revels.* New York: Russell and Russell, 1962.

Wilson, Edward M. "The text of Calderón's 'La púrpura de la rosa.' " *Modern Language Review,* 54 (1959), 29-44. Rpt. in *Critical Studies of Calderón's Comedias.* Ed. J. E. Varey. London: Gregg International, 1973, pp. 161-82.

_____. "The Four Elements in the Imagery of Calderón." *Modern Language Review,* 31 (1936), 34-47. Rpt. in *Critical Studies of Calderón's Comedias.* Ed. J. E. Varey. London: Gregg International, 1973, pp. 191-207.

Matthew D. Stroud is Assistant Professor of Foreign Languages at Trinity University. Since receiving his Ph.D. degree from the University of Southern California in 1977, he has actively pursued his research in the area of the Spanish Golden Age and has given papers at national and international conferences in both the United States and in Spain. Focusing on the works of Lope de Vega and Calderón de la Barca, his research reflects his particular interests in dramatic theory, women and honor in the *comedia,* and musical participation in Golden Age theater.

In addition to his responsibilities as editor of *Celos aun del aire matan,* he is the producer and Spanish coach for Trinity University's production of the opera in February 1981. Currently, he is also working on a book-length monograph on the Golden Age wife-murder plays.